THE REVELATIONS

THE REVELATIONS

A NOVEL

THE REVELATIONS

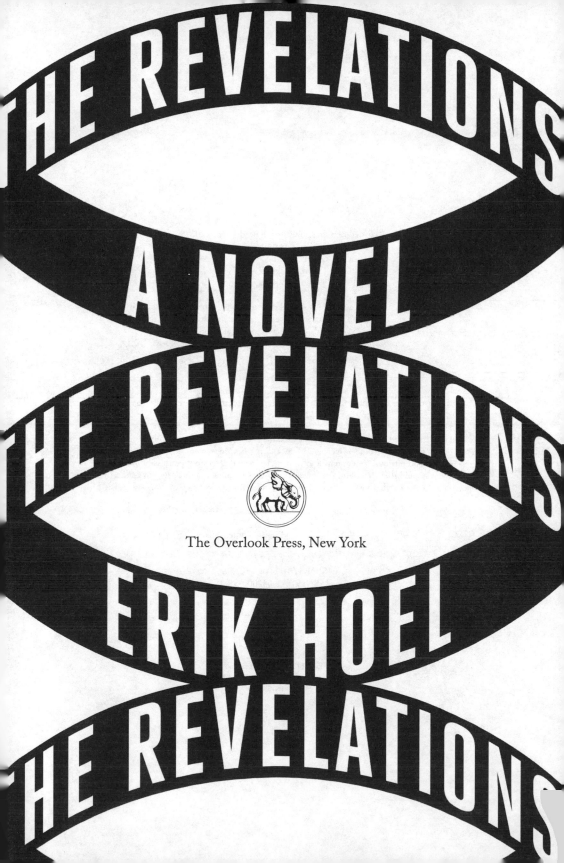

The Overlook Press, New York

ERIK HOEL

THE REVELATIONS

This edition first published in hardcover in 2021 by
The Overlook Press, an imprint of ABRAMS
195 Broadway, 9th floor
New York, NY 10007
www.overlookpress.com

Abrams books are available at special discounts when purchased in quantity
for premiums and promotions as well as fundraising or educational use.
Special editions can also be created to specification. For details,
contact specialsales@abramsbooks.com or the address above.

Library of Congress Control Number: 978-1-4197-5022-9

Printed and bound in the United States

1 3 5 7 9 10 8 6 4 2
ISBN: 978-1-4197-5022-9
eISBN: 978-1-647000-98-1

ABRAMS The Art of Books
195 Broadway, New York, NY 10007
abramsbooks.com

"Let us now return to our main problem. This is to locate the 'awareness' neurons and to discover what it is that makes their firing symbolize what we see. This is like trying to solve a murder mystery. We know something about the victim (the nature of awareness) and we know various miscellaneous facts that may be related to the crime."

—Francis Crick, *The Astonishing Hypothesis*

"Silly fish learn nothing in a thousand years."

—James Joyce, *Ulysses*

MONDAY

KIERK WAKES UP IN the back seat of his car, brought into being by a knocking on the window so loud and forceful the whole car shakes. Silhouetted by the dawn light coming through the back seat window the knocker is opaque and strangely shaped. Kierk's movement in the sleeping bag stirs books aside as he struggles to extricate himself, then, expecting another policeman come to hassle him about sleeping in his parked car, he unlocks the door. Quickly it swings open and then more than one set of arms pull him out, his shirt riding up, his form dragged and his palms skinned against the pavement until he's up, standing, pushing away, and then everyone retreats for a moment to look at one another and consider the scene. Beyond there is the expanse of a high school parking lot made wide and empty by morning. There are three of them. One has a nose ring, the other a shaved head, and the third is heavyset and shaggy. All are acned, teenagers or recent high school graduates. The shaggy one is lounging against the car and smoking a cigarette. The shaved head is now digging through Kierk's back seat, tumbling books out, angrily kicking aside the sleeping bag with a boot. He hands a plastic bag from the back seat to the one with the nose ring and he empties it, pages spilling.

"Your phone. Give us your phone."

"Cash, man. Where's your cash?"

Kierk fingers the small wad of cash inside his pocket. This money is supposed to be for gas, coffee, some trail mix to munch on, and, most importantly, a new notebook. Today Kierk had planned on using those

supplies to—not for the first time—give his writing one last try. He's
supposed to be out here in California devoting himself solely to his work,
living on what little he had stashed away. Back as a graduate student in the
wintery folds of Madison, Wisconsin, when he had found time to write in
the stolen midnight hours after leaving the lab, there had been a rich river
of prose waiting for him. Fiction, poetry, nonfiction, everything. But with
the hours of the day now empty, that torrential river had instead become
a stream, then a creek, then dried up altogether, running itself out in ink.
His previous attempts, all that writing, all those words failing to take hold,
are now being scattered on the ground . . .

Nose ring holds out his hand and Kierk sighs, warily giving over
the money, which is snatched away immediately and handed over to the
shaggy smoker.

"So who are you, anyways? We've seen you out here before, you know."

"Can I have a cigarette?" Kierk asks, scratching at his beard, watching
his pages stir in the wind. "And I don't have a phone, so that's it."

Ignoring him, nose ring holds up a book with a brain on the cover titled
The Neural Correlates of Consciousness: Vol 2.

"Who the fuck doesn't have a cell phone? You're some kind of college
student, right?"

"I left graduate school ABD . . . all but dissertation. Like T. S. Eliot."

"So you dropped out. Or got kicked out?" When Kierk only shifts
mutely, nose ring gestures to the books. "What's all this stuff about, anyway,
brain surgery?"

"Neuroscience. In fact, I ah, coauthored a paper with the writer of that
very book."

"No shit, a genuine scientist. I haven't met a homeless scientist before."

"Give us your fucking phone man."

Kierk looks at each of them in turn, then says sadly—"You're all just kids
who don't know what you're doing."

The closest, nose ring, first scoffs at him, then pretends to turn to the
others before whipping back around and punching Kierk squarely in the jaw.
Everything speeds up and they are all around Kierk, who's curled up in a
ball, both arms covering his head as they kick him. After a dull pause, after
the parking lot has emptied itself of all motion and the kid with the shaved
head has gone back to digging around in the car, Kierk realizes that he isn't

actually seriously injured. Next his feet are digging underneath him searching for traction and he takes off running to shouts and for a while there is
only the sound of eight pounding pairs of sneakers over pavement and then
grass and then pavement again and then Kierk hops a curb and has gotten
his speed and the kids fall behind halfheartedly. Kierk crashes through the
crowns of thickets and brambles and scrambles up the jungle of a chain-link
fence and then circles around to the other side of the parking lot to watch
the kid with a shaved head put a rock through his windshield like a punk.
After some fiddling around the kid pulls out the intestines of the car radio
and carries it under his arm out of the lot, the other two following. Kierk is
pretty sure they destroyed the radio in the process of extracting it.

He sits down in the tall beach grass and watches from afar as the morning fills up with sky and the car hemorrhages his meager belongings into
the windy lot. In the dry scrubs Kierk takes stock of his wounds. He notices
with interest that when there's a lot of blood in your mouth it doesn't hurt,
but rather it's like your mouth is overflowing with water, your tongue moving about in a pool. He thinks—my cup runneth over. Something keeps
leaking into his vision, and he wipes at the arch of his eyebrow, which a
stray sneaker had cut a significant gash into. His lungs are still ragged from
the mad sprint and as some sort of aftereffect of the violence his mind is so
crystalline bright it aches.

After about half an hour Kierk stalks his way back to his car, spinning
when he hears a noise to see the three of them just a couple hundred feet
away, running toward him now, and Kierk sprints the rest of the way, starts
his car, and in his haste throws it in drive instead of reverse and goes straight
into the lamppost in front of him, the hood giving a small cave and Kierk
bouncing forward in his seat. Then Kierk reverses and burns out of the lot.

After a couple miles, smoke starts billowing up in gulping gouts from
the hood, each plume swallowing the last, and Kierk pulls over to the side
of the road and starts yelling—"FUCK FUCK FUCK you little shits you're
going to die in a gutter little goddamn FUCK YOU and fuck ME stupid
stupid fuck me what the FUCK am I doing here"—and beats violently his
steering wheel and then in a frantic search finds an old bottled water under
a seat and pours it over his head to calm down and wash the blood from
the cut over his eye, leaving a damp spot on his jeans. By the side of the
road he uses a dirty T-shirt to beat at the smoking parts under the hood

until they subside. Panting and praying it hadn't been lost, he digs around the back seat for a letter that had arrived in his PO box last week. Finding it smudged and folded he lets out a small half sob, double-checking that it contains the number to call.

> *Dear Kierk Suren,*
>   *We are extremely pleased to accept you to the Francis Crick Scholarship program at New York University . . .*

With the letter folded in his back pocket he quickly stuffs what little is worth salvaging from the back seat into an old backpack of his, from journals to unwashed clothing to loose change to books with their bindings long broken. Leaving the rest behind, he starts hitching. No one picks him up. Cars blow past, children pressing their faces against the glass.

The arrival of the letter from the director of the program had been a shock given how tenuous his connection to the world was. Kierk has been living in his car for almost six months. Car insurance, his next meal, and a place to park overnight have been the daily concerns. Every week he's driven to the San Diego Public Library to grab a new pile of books and use the computers and revisit the bank to extract cash from his minimal savings, less and less each time, approaching the limit of being flat broke. The sunsets here have been like falling bundles of white wood, and standing amid the birch forests of light he had thought he might never return to civilization, that his brief life was over at twenty-seven. It's been months of dry California nights sleeping in his car somewhere on the coastline with his legs hanging out the window, his toes feeling out the slow seas of air. In all this Kierk has known that he was slowly receding from the world, that his depression was rising like an internal tide. He had sifted through the dog-eared copies of his favorite novels until they did nothing for him. In the halving and letting sunsets he would patrol the beach to write on the windy, scattering bugs of pages. Of the several books he had started writing (a monograph on measuring consciousness using information theory, a poetry collection, and an autobiographical bildungsroman), all had failed to take form, and he had been left in a cyclical pattern of self-reference, delving deeper and deeper into his own paths and roads and words.

Only a few reminders from his old academic life remain. Occasionally he would drive up to Caltech to hang out with a PhD student and have long arguments about twentieth-century philosophy, always returning in the end to the same question: who was the greater philosopher, Russell or Wittgenstein? The master or the student? But mostly he's spent a lot of time at a cafe on the outskirts of San Diego, until the older woman owner had started bringing him Tupperware filled with food, then inviting him over to her house if he needed a place to stay. It took a few visits to realize he was just one of a group of street people she let sleep in the basement. Kierk saw them as shaggy and smelly shamblemen nodding blearily, or drowsing like a dusking heap on the couch, making their awkward conversation and pauses, their tics. He knew that even if he wasn't there yet he would be soon. No one would have guessed that less than a year ago he had stood in a beautiful mansion, clean-shaven, wearing a blazer and with a glass of Chardonnay in hand, participating in toast after toast with famous scientists, each toast getting more and more extravagant—"To science!"—"To the next generation!"—"To the beautiful mystery of consciousness!"

Eventually his dusty and sweating form reels into the parking lot of a CVS. Inside Kierk grabs a bottle of hydrogen peroxide off the shelf which he uses to douse his bleeding forehead and then stands bent over swearing in the aisle when some of it gets in his eye. A young clerk is paused a bit away, one hand out, eyebrows raised.

"Wait, you're gonna need to buy that first." Then he sees the blood. "Whoa, are you okay, man?"

Kierk, standing in the aisle, stinking of smoke, blinded, holding his hands to his face while the hydrogen peroxide leaks between his fingers and makes small fizzling bubbles on the white tile, smiles, and responds—"As well as Saint Paul on the road to Damascus."

"What?"

"Do you know the Caravaggio? The second one of course. He didn't really get cooking until the second one. Next time you're in Rome, please, treat yourself and go see it. Paul's revelation is reified in the viewer. It's in the basilica off the Piazza del Popolo. Ack! This stings."

"Listen, if you don't leave I'm going to have to call the cops."

"I'm, um, being forced to reconsider my life choices here, so of course you will. But before you do: where is the nearest payphone?"

The clerk, after directing him to a payphone down the street, watches mutely as Kierk leaves clutching the brown bottle and a package of bandages without paying. Kierk walks up the street listening to the babbles and fizzes above his eye, trying to wipe away some of the blood on his cheek and spitting black globules on the sidewalk.

He had called the number on the letter last week, unsure if it was a lifeline or a temptation back into a world that had almost destroyed him. A professional voice had introduced itself as the director of a new scholarship program that was being assembled at New York University, the first of its kind. Eight positions in a research program on the neuroscientific basis of consciousness. Kierk had applied for the so-called Francis Crick Scholarship over a year ago for a potential postdoctoral position, before he knew he'd be abandoning his PhD, his research career, everything. But apparently the obscure workings of the government funders had kept the schedule and viability of the program in doubt until the last minute, and everyone was now rushing to put the program together. The director had said that Kierk was one of their top choices, even despite having never technically finished his PhD, and had offered Kierk a seventy-thousand-dollar stipend, dropped the names of the famous researchers who would be leading the program, and told Kierk that this, right here, was the opportunity of a lifetime. And most importantly, it was a chance to pursue consciousness again. Kierk had said no. Last time the pursuit had all but broken him, and the only solution had been to cut himself off from it completely.

Now, standing on that stretch of road outside of San Diego, his car with its crumpled hood a few miles away, everything worth anything in this ragged backpack, his clothes spotted with blood, listening to the operator's voice, hating himself for his stubbornness and pride, Kierk is praying that same voice will pick up and be his deliverance. When it does, he can barely croak his hello. But soon he's yelling into the receiver as cars whizz by. "I said: you told me last week you didn't have a replacement, right?"

"Oh, well, yes, that's right. We're working on—"

"I accept."

"What?"

"I accept the position. I officially accept. I'm coming to New York. There's an apartment, right, you said so last week?"

"The program starts in two days!"

Kierk says that he'll be there and hangs up before there can be any argument and he's left alone with just his ears buzzing and the fizzing of his eye. Eventually, after wrapping his head with comically misshapen and bloody bandages, he's able to call a local garage and offer to sell them his broken-down car for a few hundred bucks if they tow it. The rest of the day is a blur of activity and logistics. Later in the San Diego Public Library frantic emails between him and the scholarship program make everything official and get an emergency stipend transferred into his account. The only overnight flight with an available seat to the East Coast is to Boston, and that plane, that deep rumble when it finally reaches liftoff, is to Kierk like the sound of an angelic steed breaking atmosphere.

TUESDAY

KIERK WAKES UP FROM the first sleep he's been able to catch in the odyssey of cross-continental travel. Roused by the shudder of the bus over a pothole, shaken from his sleeping slouch against the window, Kierk's eyes blink open and the scene outside resolves into perception. Beyond the smudged glass is a busy sidewalk where people are fanning themselves with magazines, waiting for the walk signal, shielding their eyes as they exit the glare of glass doors, moving quickly carrying suitcases and purses and airs of motion. Dogs explore on leashes like searching filopodia as baseball caps are adjusted under lances of sun. There are vendors with coolers full of bottled water. People emerge from and disappear into the stark shadows the buildings cast like great sundials. The bus trundles along Manhattan's capillary-like streets, heading for the city's heart.

Kierk wipes at his mouth, sitting up straight. The woman next to him goes back to reading her magazine after eyeing the young man with the wild scraggly beard who had just woken from fitful, small-noised dreams. In his startled waking his arm had hit her thigh. There is another lurch and Kierk drops the notebook which had sat cupped in his lap, forcing him to grope around the rooted feet, the dark underbellies of smells. There is the tang of talcum powder and McDonald's from the seat behind him. Flipping to the folded page of his notebook, Kierk exhales slowly and blearily crosses out a sentence, pauses, and then expunges an entire diagram he had drawn right before he had drifted off from the buzzing of the bus engines. The pages in the notebook are overflowing with his distinctive byzantine scrawl, along with spidery drawings of neural networks, vector fields, probability spaces, attractor dynamics, but also unfinished portraits, the delicate treelike branching of dendrites under a microscope, while all throughout, between the drawings and equations and along the margins, words run in thick torrents. All the content is from months ago. Nothing is recent.

On entering a tunnel and facing his reflection in the window, Kierk realizes he cannot remember the last time he shaved—has it been three months, four? He reaches down in the darkness and fiddles with the zipper of his bulging backpack, then forces the notebook between a tangle of boxers, socks, books, and crumpled paper. Everything he owns is either in this backpack or a member of the flock of books en route to New York in heavy cardboard boxes that he had packed early yesterday evening back on the cold concrete floor of the storage unit he had been renting in San Diego.

The bus shakes and something, some arrangement of perception—the familiar angles of looking out a window beyond the frame of a seat—had unlocked something inside him, a shuddering click that is felt as déjà vu. What about? His earlier dream? No. A memory. Another bus ride in New England, also in the summer heat, and then he is suddenly on the way to see the body, the corpse left when the grandmother on his father's side had died. He had been eleven and Kierk's mother, all hands bundled up in urgency, had rushed about stern-faced trying not to let Kierk see exactly how much of an inconvenience this all was. Then the two clamored, all in silent black and under the eyes of the other riders, into another hot and sticky seat, and then the shaking and grinding bus headed northward to Maine.

In his memory the body was a monolith at the front of a carpeted room, a wooden grin with horns of flowers. Kierk had trailed behind the dark figure of his mother, who with her hair up looked like a bust of Hypatia, sad and regal, moving among plebeians. Approaching the coffin the first thing that struck him, as only an eleven-year-old just coming to realize himself can be struck, was that they had put makeup on her. Kierk had often watched his own mother stand in the brightly lit bathroom and, as she called it, "get dolled up." Kierk associated makeup with the unpleasant meeting of a towering and obtrusive figure—men who were always unnerved by this child, this child who was disturbingly articulate in his sarcasm, his barbed comments launched from behind the unassailable parapets his mother's unconditional love provided. The men, white-collar workers pudgy from middle management, but good men in the end, couldn't believe their luck to have met a single woman this vivacious and intelligently charming, and still beautiful (kept thin by mania: cleaning, working two jobs, taking care of three dogs, four cats, and responsible for providing Kierk with an intellectually stimulating environment and thus always taking it upon herself to learn a great deal about the Library of Alexandria, or read aloud every book in The Chronicles of Narnia series, or watch Carl Sagan's *Cosmos* with TV dinners on their laps). Under Kierk's assault they began to dread those family dinners and the learned helplessness induced by Kierk's subtle verbal dissection. But the biggest issue came from his mother and Kierk combined, because even when she purposefully dumbed herself down for the men in private she couldn't maintain it when Kierk was around—she wouldn't limit herself in his presence. So during those dinners Kierk and she would end up discussing some esoteric subject that Kierk at that age was interested in—Greek myths, proper Latin names for dinosaurs, Project Orion—and it would become apparent to the men that she would leave them because she was too good for them (she wouldn't have, not a single one), so they would decide, inevitably, to leave her first. Or perhaps the men could sense that it wasn't them in particular that she wanted, just someone, and although it is something to be sufficient, it is another thing entirely to be necessary. At the time of the funeral she was between such suitors, and when she stared down at this woman who had given birth to the man she had born a son to she felt something that to Kierk at that age would have been so complex and unknowable it may as well have been a sentence picked at random from the *Principia Mathematica*.

Standing there at the lower end of the coffin, his small hand on the smooth wood, the body before him seemed a fallen giant, and Kierk had begun to comprehend the personal momentousness that this should hold for him. Every decision, from moving to America when she was sixteen by taking a leap of faith away from Scotland (lost to history is that she was nearly gang-raped while waiting in a crowd at Ellis Island), to getting a job as a nurse during the war, where she had met Kierk's grandfather at a hospital-sanctioned dance. He had been a patient at the ward where she had worked with returning veterans, but she had not been his nurse, indeed had never seen him, but he had seen her, watched her from his bed pass across the doorway in the corridor, just a glimpse really, and he had shown up to the dance with a bandage over his left eye and wrapped around the back of his head, which he suspected made him look dashing. So when he saw her again, smiling vaguely out at the dancing crowd, beyond herself, looking brokenheartedly apart as only the world-weary but still innocent can, he had crossed that dance floor—the longest in his life (the music and the dark forms moving, him brushing past them, eyes on his target, he had crossed the sands of Iwo Jima and the tight ambushing forests of Guadalcanal to cross this dance floor)—to ask this girl, this one girl out of all the girls, to dance. Each minor choice seemed to Kierk to multiply and expand, reverberating, sprouting branches and offshoots diachronically, until Kierk had been dumbstruck by the specificity of this woman whom he barely knew, this denser knot of choices to which he owed his existence. It was then that Kierk had begun, in his manners and childish convictions, to confront the problem of choice.

As THE BUS PULLS to a stop and begins disembarking passengers, Kierk steps down onto the pocked underground of the city, breathes it, and is enchanted and disoriented at the same time. He makes his way through the bustle of Port Authority, down the long hot tunnels and veins of motions, advertisements, the clicks of polished business shoes. The boxed tunnels of the subway are haunted by jazz, the trembling notes of a saxophone clear, constant, real. He spends some awkward time standing in front of the big subway map, checking the address that's written on his hand.

Eventually Kierk exits in hot breaths of steam up the steps to the surface of Union Square Park. It had turned dark while he was underground. Smoking a cigarette and feeling that bone-deep tiredness that comes from a day of travel, he realizes that the program starts tomorrow morning and he still needs to buy new clothes. He picks at his falling-apart jeans and fingers the rips in his T-shirt, knowing this had been poor planning. Standing he mutters aloud—"New life. Don't fuck it up"—and then looks around the dark walkway to see if anyone heard. He's been talking to himself too much lately.

Eventually he locates an upscale clothing store on Broadway that's still open. Into the affair of wooden floors, brick walls, well-lit displays, and quiet indie music, slips a bearded and disheveled Kierk. A staff member spots him and comes up, looking wary with hands clasped.

"I'm sorry, sir, but we're actually getting ready to close."

Kierk can see a number of customers still browsing. There's a two-second pause and then Kierk's face transforms in emotive animation.

"Excuse me, but I've been backpacking around Europe and only just arrived at JFK and goddamn Air France lost all my bags, bags which contained not only irreplaceable souvenirs such as a Burgundy rosé I'd been anticipating for days but also my sartorial good side. *La vie est une chienne*, if you know what I mean. I simply look a mess but I have to breakfast with my fiancée's family, the Forbes, on the Upper East Side first thing tomorrow, and I'm going to need your help."

THE PROGRAM HAD SET him up in NYU's grad-student housing, in which he finds a spartan apartment where the lights flicker on in pulses. He notes that the windows are suicide-proof.

After setting down his backpack he strips and enters the bathroom to run a bath, rubbing at his beard. In the light the geometric designs tattooed across his pale white back form stark black lines, geometric wheels and circles that move as he moves. Across his inner left forearm there is tattooed writing spelling out three questions.

Kierk stands nude, quickly making a tangled nest of hair in the sink. There is still the yellow bruise on the side of his mouth, matching the fist that had recently caused it. Shaving away the last of the hair around the discoloration, Kierk is struck by this younger face in the mirror, a face with eyes expansive and a clear deep green, his nose more hawkish, his mouth wider, his cheekbones higher than he remembers. The top of his hair has begun thinning. But still, this is a face he had thought left behind, resembling for the first time in a long time his driver's license. Standing back and looking at his naked body he can tell he's lost a lot of muscle mass but still has those long legs and broad shoulders. His eyes are again acute and discerning, young and viridian, and Kierk can feel himself returning, catching fire just like he used to, ready to fall in love with something.

He wants this to work, wants this more than he's wanted anything in a long time. In this new apartment, among these new streets and new sounds he wants to create something, and knows he is so lucky, unbelievably lucky, to be given a second chance. He will not make the same mistakes as before, he will not go chasing what is impossible to catch. Instead he will focus on his career, become one of those ordained academics who get tenure young and line their shelves with their own books published by Harvard University Press. He thinks—I will become fully what it is my destiny to become, and everything prior to this will have been just events, spatiotemporal instances, and they are vanishing because the universe is merely one state transitioning to another with no memory of the past, whereas my destiny, to be an intellectual, a great scientist, is teleology pulling me toward it from the future.

He says to the mirror—"I choose this." Then wet and sopping over the tiles he gets down and does as many push-ups as he can. He takes a minute wheezing on the tiles, and then does another rep to exhaustion. And then again.

Later he lies on the bare mattress lolling about. Dim recollection causes him to root around for a long unworn watch and set an alarm. The city is a strange surf crashing in the distance, and slowly, but then all at once, Kierk dissolves . . .

MUCH LATER, OUT OF a void passing over itself in silence, there is quietly and surprisingly something small, right there, a little light in the black that soon balloons into a new, weaker cosmos. It is here that Kierk finds himself alone in a strange labyrinth. From a floating aerial viewpoint he watches himself investigate the corridors. How odd that he looks like an animal moving about down there scrounging and foraging for something. Then time passes in jerks and Kierk is suddenly underneath a heavy moving weight, a form. He wrestles it in the dark, something big and horned and bull-faced and huffing as it uses its muscular human body to pin Kierk down as he bats his hands against its wet snout and wide mouth. It breathes onto his face its hot breaths and he feels its human hands searching for his eyes, it wants to jelly his eyes so he cannot see, and then he is running in terror from that center of a labyrinth, running until he emerges into the woods of the city, and there is night coming down now like a great charioteer, whooping as it descends so loudly and then. Kierk can't find his way out of the city at night like an alien hive looming silent around him until the thing from the maze comes back and it runs him down through the abandoned streets, and it is wrestling him and huffing from its animal nose as it blinds him with its thick thumbs and jellies his eyes and he screams and cannot see and only has the confused tactile sensations of its human limbs and its wet bull face and when Kierk finally awakens he will not remember any of this but will have the feeling that his waking life is only one among his many.

WEDNESDAY

KIERK WAKES UP TO the urgent feeling of needing to be somewhere, but not knowing where. How long has it been since he's woken on a mattress? Then he's up, remembering the world, rummaging through the shopping bags; he picks out slacks, a belt with matching brown shoes, an olive-green shirt, hesitates over tie color. Swearing because he forgot to buy socks, he uses the ones with huge holes he came with. After dressing and making sure he's gotten all the tags off he stands in the bathroom trying to wet down his hair. Leaving, he's careful to blow his cigarette smoke away from the new clothes.

The route to work is from Union Square Park to nearby Washington Square Park and takes him down Broadway. Myriads of smells ride in boats, the sick pine of roasted nuts, the trash blown about, the scent of sweat perfusing into the air. On Washington Place he finds the blocky brick tower reaching twenty stories, with only small and sparse murder holes for windows. Inside it is dark and cold as a cathedral.

In the elevator up he's tapping his foot nervously, one hand pulling down his shirtsleeve to cover the writing on his forearm. But Kierk ends up wandering lost through multiple intersections of corridors. The room numbers aren't in the right order, and he grows more and more nervous until he catches a group of people entering a glass-walled room.

Kierk is mildly late to the orientation. There is a man standing behind a small podium preparing to speak to an almost full room. Separated at the front sit a handful of people whom Kierk assumes are the other seven

Crick Scholars. He grabs a seat among them as his eyes slide over, drawn to one of them, a young woman who turns in her chair to look at him, who is brushing the strands of blonde hair from her face, who has strong, flashing teeth when she smiles briefly at Kierk, like a ping of sound in the middle of a quick searching glance of curiosity that flits away on contact—all this in an instant before she turns back away and he sits, adjusting, nearly knocked into his seat. A young Indian man, tall and steady of movement, bends his mane of black hair slightly in greeting to Kierk.

The man behind the podium begins to speak. Kierk recognizes the voice from over the phone.

"Welcome to the official start of the Francis Crick Scholarship Program. I'm Norman Bennett, the director of the program. To me this is a truly momentous day, because when I was just beginning in neuroscience you couldn't mention the word 'consciousness' without drawing derisive laughter or strange looks. This skepticism began to end due to the efforts of Francis Crick, whom I counted among my close friends. After discovering DNA he figured he could do whatever he wanted. He also noticed we don't actually have any scientific laws that relate consciousness to neurological states. So in the early nineties he started a research program to investigate this mystery, with this working definition: by 'consciousness' we mean the inner domain of sensations and perceptions and thoughts, all centered around a self, that make up your life. The world of experience that begins when you wake up in the morning and vanishes when you enter a deep dreamless sleep. Your consciousness is what it is like to be you. Now Francis was smart enough to avoid being bogged down in philosophical arguments, so he called it 'the search for the neural correlates of consciousness.' Neuroscience can start by merely correlating brain states to particular conscious states. It's a mark of how far this research program has come that we are being supported by the Department of Defense, specifically the Defense Advanced Research Projects Agency, DARPA. It should be obvious why they're interested: solving the mystery of consciousness might lead to general artificial intelligence. Or discovering how to directly intervene on people's minds. And there are other fantastical possibilities, like brain uploading, brain-to-brain communication, and curing long-standing diseases. They've recognized that being ahead of other nations on this problem is a national imperative, and thanks to them, we're going to have the first group of young researchers in the history of the world that are all explicitly focused on the science of consciousness. Let's give a warm welcome to the eight new scientists!"

Light applause, and Kierk claps with the uncertainty of someone clapping for himself.

"You'll be based here, at the Center for Neural Science, or CNS. This new generation has tough questions to answer. Why do some physical systems have what philosophers call 'qualia,' the qualitative, what-it-is-like aspect of experience? Is there a way to solve the explanatory gap, what some have called the Hard Problem, of squeezing mind out of matter? Two years is provided for in terms of funding. There will be an advising committee with four members on it for each Crick Scholar. Your committees, of which I am a member of each, will oversee each Scholars' research. We've taken the liberty of assigning every Crick Scholar to a lab. Additionally, we have been working with the department here and DARPA to get funding for two tenure-track positions at NYU in consciousness science, so two of you will be sticking around permanently! Let's see if I can go from left to right here, I have a list . . . That there is Atif Tomalin, he was just at Oxford doing electrophysiological recordings of neurons in primates."

The tall man with the mane of black hair gives a thin-lipped smile.

"And we have Mike Benson, from Harvard, who's done work in linguistics and neuroimaging." A square-headed guy with a crew cut wearing a crimson sweatshirt that reads HARVARD waves.

"Jessica Lem, who's from McGill University, who also has a great record in neuroimaging." A pretty black girl gives a friendly smile while nervously playing with the bracelet on her wrist.

"Greg Monroe from MIT does work in artificial intelligence." Greg has a shaggy bowl cut which makes him look like a teenager. He's sallow and doughy, and does an awkward little dip when he's introduced.

"Alex Luce, who did his graduate work at Caltech on action potentials and single neuron dynamics." Alex flashes a smile; he's blond and slim of stature.

"Carmen Green, from Columbia University. She just had a paper out in *Nature* arguing that the whole cortex participates in conscious experiences, so we expect great things from her." The young woman waves to everyone at the table, grins. Some of the men in the room wave back reflexively.

"Leon Schmidt, an MD-PhD from the Max Planck Institute in Germany." A large bearish fellow nods solemnly several times.

"And finally Kierk Suren, who decided to accept this position, um, rather last minute, but we're very happy to have him as he comes from Antonio Moretti's lab in Madison, Wisconsin. A theoretician, his last paper was called 'Mapping Consciousness.' And that's it! We'll be giving tours of the facilities later, and you officially join your hosting labs bright and early tomorrow."

Norman steps off the podium to polite applause. Quickly people break into small islands of conversations. Kierk is approached by a woman radiating the kind of youthful professorship achieved only by those who go right to tenure track. She smiles and offers a hand to shake.

"Kierk, right? I'm Karen Moskowitz. You're in my lab so I'm on your committee by default."

"A pleasure, Karen. And I know you, I've read some of your papers," Kierk lies.

"I'm glad you decided to accept our offer, even if it was last minute." She winks at him. "Anyway, where have you been since you left the Moretti lab?"

"California."

"Working with?"

"Actually, I wasn't doing research."

"Oh, what were you doing?"

"Not much. Writing, really. I had a car but no money, so I just drove across country." Kierk affixes a friendly smile to his face.

"Well good for you! Taking a break, I know how necessary that can be." Karen pauses for a second. "Anyways, tomorrow you can get back into the swing of things and I'll give you a tour of my lab. If you ever need to send a strong electromagnetic pulse into someone's head, I'm your gal."

"That all sounds good, thanks."

A man joins them. Broad-shouldered with a strong chin and dark hair, he introduces himself as Max Pierce.

"So you're our lost discovery who caused so much drama," Max says to Kierk. "If I remember, you left your PhD close to finishing? That took some sorting out with the University of Wisconsin. You're going to complete your degree here, correct?"

"Yes, it was great of the committee to get everything organized, I really appreciate how flexible you've been. Really."

"Well, whatever happened between you and Antonio Moretti, your research was quite good. Interesting stuff."

"Thank you. But it wasn't really going the direction that I wanted it to go in."

"And what direction was that?"

"Well," Kierk gives a helpless laugh, "a theory of consciousness."

"Ambitious. Doesn't Antonio Moretti already have a theory of consciousness? Seems a bit presumptive to want your own."

Kierk idly wonders if the plastic fork could break through the cartilage of Max's throat.

"Therein lies the rub. Indeed he does. I helped develop it when I was there."

Max shrugs. "All that theoretical stuff is beyond me. Too mathy."

"Yes."

"Hey, Max," Karen says, grinning at him. "Be on Kierk's committee with me."

Max looks Kierk up and down. "Alright," he says gruffly.

"Great! Oh!" she exclaims, "Kierk, you should meet Alex." She beckons Kierk over to the other Crick Scholar standing by a table lined with breakfast, then excuses herself. Alex and he nod at each other, clasping each other's outstretched hand.

"Do you remember the time at that conference when everyone was drunk and singing in the hotel lobby?" Alex asks.

"Berlin, right?" Kierk replies, chuckling. "And then when the security was called all the principal investigators were trying to get the PhD students to take the fall for them. *Schnell*! *Schnell*!"

"Glad you're here," Alex says, laughing. "I think you'll make the program more . . . interesting."

Around them everyone is very upright, studious, eager to please, and Kierk starts to get sick looking over at Mike from Harvard and Jessica from McGill, who are laughing at something Max had just said like Max is the only source of valid humor in the whole damn world. There's a pinch of nausea at the phoniness of the whole enterprise and under his dress shoes he can feel his big toe sticking through the hole in his sock. The conversation moves off by itself as various professors come to join the small group: hello, it's a pleasure, really, yes, the building is quite the maze, I've read it, yes, elegant work, no, I've never lived here before, I'll be sure to check it out, it sounds wonderful, yes, of course it's no problem, yes, that's always been an interest of mine, yes, no, yes, yes, yes.

At noon Kierk, who has been charming, a self-deprecating but promising *enfant terrible* to the professors, goes to the empty men's room, and, looking at himself in the mirror, both hands gripping the edges of the sink, pale under the fluorescent lighting, wants to shoot himself.

Someone opens the door and Kierk pretends to be washing his hands. After a moment Alex says—"So a prominent behaviorist in the 1950s meets this woman and they go back to his hotel room where they screw. And after they're done, they're lying there and he says: 'I know it was good for you, but how was it for me?'"

Kierk begins to laugh as Alex scans the wall and ceiling for a smoke detector.

"Listen, I really thought I would get through this. But I just need to calm down a bit, and this always relaxes me so is it okay if I . . ." Alex uses his fingernails to pull out a joint hidden amid a pack of cigarettes. "I know it's a bad habit. I picked it up two years ago from a boyfriend of mine. But it really helps me out . . ."

"Fuck it, you don't mind if I . . ."

"Abso-fucking-lutely."

As Alex lights up, Kierk says—"What does the *B* in Benoit B. Mandelbrot stand for?"

"Who's that?"

"The inventor of fractals."

"So what does the *B* stand for?" Alex says with pinched breath, and then exhales a thin cloud.

"Benoit B. Mandelbrot."

There's a silence. Alex passes him the joint, which Kierk accepts solemnly. But then slowly the chuckles build and soon they both can't stop laughing, the kind of laughter that incubates in the serious career moments of academic conferences or corporate meetings. Kierk is coughing at the same time, hanging onto the bathroom counter, passing the joint back to Alex.

"Oh god, is that going to be our future?" Alex says, gesticulating in the haze. "I get so nervous at these things. I always want to do something ridiculous to break the spell. Have them stop talking about grants."

"Seriously," Kierk says. "What does any of this have to do with consciousness?"

The door opens slowly, hesitantly, and Alex expertly hides the joint as Atif's smiling and befuddled face peers in. After a laugh all three of them talk in the hall for a while. Then back in the conference room Kierk exists in a stream of placid small talk until the conversations lie like flags on the floor.

The pot has definitely helped. It lasts him all the way until midafternoon when most of the rest of the room has cleared out, leaving only a few small exhausted groups milling about around the chairs and tables. Carmen has finally shed the crowd of professors that had trapped her between the podium and the wall, and now she walks over to the table and greets Alex and Kierk.

"Carmen and I have met but you two haven't. Kierk here," Alex says by way of introduction, "is coming in out of the wild. Returning to civilization."

She tilts her head at him like a curious stork.

"I thought you were from the UW in Madison?"

"I've been out in California for the last six months or so."

"Is that where you got that lovely bruise?"

"I got hit in the face."

"Um, by accident?"

"No."

". . ."

Once the rest of the Crick Scholars wander over, Carmen addresses them all, clearly stepping into the role as ringleader—"We should go out Friday night! There's a really good place to play pool around here. I'll try to get everyone together."

People begin pulling out their phones. Carmen, after getting Leon's number, looks expectantly to Kierk, who shrugs.

"You don't have a phone?"

He shrugs again. Alex begins laughing—"Yup, I think Kierk will be good for the program."

Norman Bennett, the director, comes over to them all, accompanied by a smiling man and woman both sporting blue nitrile gloves and a bag reading BIOHAZARD.

"I didn't mention this before," Norman says, "but it should only take a few minutes per person." Everyone waits—Norman doesn't seem to realize that the Crick Scholars don't know what he's talking about.

"Oh! Ah, yes, we're growing cerebral organoids in the building."

Kierk, Carmen, Alex, Atif, and Leon all let out a collective "Ahhhhhh" but Greg, Mike, and Jessica all look confused, so one of the researchers jumps in. "We take some of your skin cells, then reprogram those cells back into a pluripotent state. Eventually we coax the new stem cells into growing nervous tissue, a little mini-brain, a cerebral organoid."

"Why make these mini-brains from us?" Jessica asks.

Everyone looks at Norman expectantly, who finally says—"They wanted to do eight mini-brains and I had eight consciousness scientists. Serendipity. It'll only take a few minutes each. And you can visit your cerebral organoid later on."

Calling over Atif first, they wipe down a spot on his forearm with gauze soaked in alcohol. He asks questions in his deep-voiced Indian-English accent as a local anesthetic is injected. It's followed by a punch biopsy where calipers pinch off a bit of Atif's skin, and then medical scissors are used to cut away the base of the small tag of skin. The sample is stored in a labeled test tube and placed in a small Styrofoam box filled with crushed ice. The whole process takes less than two minutes. Atif is stoic throughout while the other Crick Scholars crowd around in interest.

"Jesus!" Jessica says at the end, looking at the dot of a wound on Atif's forearm before it's covered up with a gauze wrapping. Carmen looks critically at Jessica's expression, then steps forward and offers her arm.

Twenty minutes later everyone has gone through it except Greg. He's saying—"I mean, do you really need us, specifically? And shouldn't we be like, aware of any health risks?"

There comes an overlapping chorus of voices:

"It's just a punch biopsy."

"Come on, Greg, we all did it."

"Greg, it's just a punch biopsy, you'll be fine," Carmen says.

Greg looks at Carmen and after a moment acquiesces in a quick nod, proffering his arm to minor cheers.

When an afternoon break is announced Kierk finally escapes alone, leaving the building to stand relieved in the obliterating sunlight. He feels like he just ran a marathon of human interaction. He's out to buy a phone and get a haircut during the downtime. As he runs his errands he can physically sense the weight of himself returning. An apparition is solidifying, becoming substantial again, returning to the world.

· · ·

LATER IN THE EVENING half the Crick Scholars, including Kierk, are scheduled for a tour of the primate research center at the basement level of the CNS. Over eighty primates are housed underground on the edge of Washington Square Park, a kind of surreal inversion of the constant stream of pedestrians above. Kierk, Atif, Alex, and Jessica assemble in the glass room that serves as an annex to the main animal lab. There is the thick musk of primates, dung and souring grapes, biscuits soggy with piss, cut carrots and stale green beans.

All four of them finish shrugging on soiled lab coats and strapping on face masks, pulling on thick bite-proof gloves, hopping on one foot to fit the little blue booties over their shoes. Soon Norman Bennett is leading them amid the veterinarians and technicians, yelling over the clanking and grinding.

"We're splitting the tours because monkeys are so sensitive to crowds. They're rhesus macaques, of which we have forty, and then twenty bonnet macaques, and a smattering of different species. We 'chair them' to move them up to the electrophysiology rigs upstairs for experiments. The chairs are those rectangular glass boxes that you're right next to, Atif. Their heads poke out so they can look around. But we can also fix the tops of their heads so they only look straight ahead at whatever task they're doing. They can be devils to get in."

Amid the cages and occasional hiss from their occupants it is Atif who moves with the most certainty, a knowing look in his eyes, coolly surveying equipment. He's worked in a primate lab the last several years and knows fundamentally they're all the same. Mostly he spends time eyeing the other Crick Scholars, especially Kierk. Before the program had started Atif made a point of reading all the other Crick Scholars' work. He'd been particularly impressed by Kierk's attempts to develop an actual theory of consciousness; last night after reading a paper by Kierk he had gotten carried away late into the early morning with his own musings. Atif feels a competition brewing: which of them will get the tenure-track positions at one of the best research universities in the world, in one of the best cities in the world, at such a young age? No more being shipped around countries and programs, showing up in some strange city to work in a lab for a year before heading to the next, participating in the great global migration of postdocs. If this is indeed a competition Atif wants to know the other players and is already forming a ranking in his mind.

". . . telling you now because that group is dangerous, and they do target individual researchers. They might threaten you, or try to scare you by coming to your apartment. One time a researcher was ambushed at night and chased by someone in a creepy costume. Some shamanistic monster outfit. We're sure it was them. This SAAR, the Students Against Animal Research, they're real and extremely serious. It's not a legal student group anymore but they still picket outside a lot of our talks. They have a real fetish for neuroscience. It started when PETA filed a FOIA, a freedom of information fishing expedition. We happened to be developing a new surgery at the time, something for Professor Melissa Goldman. Atif, I know you've met her because you're based in her lab here in the CNS. The surgery was done on one of the macaques here, whose name was Double Trouble. And unfortunately Double Trouble got an infection in her skullcap from the surgery. We're not going to waste a brain so of course the vets decapitated Double Trouble and made brain slices. Pictures from the surgery were exposed when PETA filed the FOIA, which really got SAAR all riled up. So then of course both PETA and SAAR went crazy and accused us of killing Double Trouble. PETA even requested OLAW at the NIH to do an official investigation for violations of the Animal Welfare Act. This continued until SAAR actually distributed the addresses of some of the veterinarians and Melissa. PETA officially backed off, but SAAR didn't. A few lab members were threatened personally. Then the chase by the monster, the costumed guy. Real serious horror-movie stuff. But what finally allowed me to get the president of the university to come down hard was what happened to Melissa Goldman. She found a bunch of supplies outside her house. Her child actually found them in the morning. A little girl. All these household items piled up in the driveway, things like orange juice, laundry detergent, baking powder and so on. Turns out it was all the ingredients you need to build a homemade bomb from scratch."

Jessica gasps. "Her daughter found it?"

Norman sighs wearily. "SAAR's funding was cut. PETA officially broke ties with SAAR and publicly condemned the group but it didn't matter, because SAAR still holds meetings."

"Did they catch who did it?" Jessica asks.

"No, and it got very political. The student body was really riled up. You know how they are now. This is why you cannot take any pictures, ever."

Cages line the wall stacked on top of one another. Most of the monkeys lay unmoving, enervated and sunken. Almost all have recording
apparatuses attached to their skulls—after being anesthetized the monkey
is scalped, the top of the head removed to bare the skull. Then the skull
is softened, a portion removed, and an open grating is installed through
which the scientist can peek in at the brain. Finally this grating is sealed
from above with a removable cap, to provide easy access, and a kind of
plastic concrete is spread over the naked skull to cover it and support the
recording chamber. Eventually electrodes can be lowered during behavioral experiments to listen to the pop-pop talk of neurons. The monkeys
thus wear crowns of concrete, often with blood or pus ringing the annulate
barrier where the skin meets the installment, with little plastic caps at the
summit like miniature chimney tops that can be unscrewed.

"What are those?" Kierk asks, pointing to reams of crumpled tinfoil in
several bins.

It's a veterinarian who answers. "The city is always generating electromagnetic background noise. To keep it from influencing the data we wrap
their heads with tinfoil during the sessions."

"You make them wear tinfoil hats?"

"How come some of the monkeys have problems with their hands?"
Jessica asks, and Kierk notices what she's talking about—the monkeys palm
the floor with flat hands, try to scoop up their toys with their wrists.

It's Atif who answers from across the room in his deep voice—"Because
the recording chamber is at the top of their head. Often right over their
primary motor cortex. And since you keep moving a needle down through
it . . ." He makes repeated stabbing motions.

"Oh!" Jessica's eyes widen.

"Anyway, as I was saying, some of these monkeys share cages . . ." Norman continues as Kierk and the others move about the room. In the far
cage-cleaning room, through the door, Kierk can see powerful hoses oper-
ated by undergraduates foolish enough to sign up for research credits spray
animal feces, fur, drool stains, pus, and food remnants from empty cages
into a wide drain in the floor. In their cages the proto-humans squat around
him, alien in their familiarity and the uncanny valley of their dark beady
eyes, their imploring hands held palm out for food in a manner that is
disturbingly human. They stare out at Kierk like things before language,

guttural expressions begging for meanings, all of them lined up with ebony eyes turned toward him. He imagines them in their natural state as dark rustling shapes in the forest of home, in a play of chiaroscuro and canopy, with their mischievous haired limbs turning over logs and leaves and rot and excrement, all dug through with black nails, the echoing screech of excitement, defending, offering, proffering, the curved kowtow of submission, the occasional portentous spark of altruism, the small fingers stripping a dirty avocado of its broad peel, and in the twilight of the jungle floor a small creature is looking with its black eyes at him, hunching its back, what is that in its arms?—recognition—it is cradling a baby rhesus that has been dead for days . . .

Jessica nudges Kierk, who has been looking lost into the dark of a cage. She enters a single gloved finger slowly through the mesh. On seeing Jessica's finger the macaque, which had been curled up in the back, lopes curiously up to the front, then turns to face the opposite direction and presses its back up against the mesh, its fur now sticking through the grating in tufts. Jessica scratches the small patch of exposed skin, and Kierk follows suit. Their smiles show in their eyes above their face masks, scratching away to happy grunting. Then the macaque whips around viciously, banging the cage, causing Kierk and Jessica to jump back and Jessica to quiet a shriek behind her face mask. With the same immediacy the monkey resumes its previous position, waiting to be scratched. Kierk shakes his head at it and turns to a pair of the smaller bonnet macaques that glare at Kierk with red eyes from their shared cage. One erects himself in his cage above the other, his little sex hanging in the air. He looks Kierk straight in the eye and begins to piss in a long stream as Kierk jumps back, avoiding it. The other macaque in the cage, servile and slinking, hunkers down in front of the pissing one and in a quick motion takes the stream and the organ itself in its mouth. With his thick glove Kierk taps Alex on the back to get his attention.

INSTEAD OF SLEEPING KIERK is out grabbing beers at a bar, sitting at the open window in the breeze and watching the late-night groups of people walk past in fits of laughter or discussion. Then he's out to join them, meandering past the bright lamplights and shuttered store windows of New York City at night. To be a scientist again, to be working on consciousness again—he can't believe it. He is a secular priest once more. In this he feels the possessor of a great secret, a thing unknown to everyone he passes, a thing that buzzes inside him and keeps him from bed. No longer is he on the outside looking in. It is happening again. He is a man catching fire. Eventually this feeling grows until his path becomes directional, purposeful. He can now enter where others cannot. Stalking through the darkened trees of Washington Square Park he veers sharply toward the CNS.

The building stands as a dark windowless tower, which he approaches in the night. A single light is on from somewhere far above. The ID card he'd been given makes the door flash green and he enters the cool artificial air with the smile of one entering a sanctum. He wants to see again the familiar sights of the graduate student making a midnight dinner, the postdoc mid-experiment listening to music, the long rows of waiting workstations, the nocturnal mice now up to play while the scientists sleep.

But in the dim lobby everything is silent, and his fingers linger on the handle, the glass, the empty lobby desk. Where is the guard? Kierk had thought entry to the building was constantly monitored, even this late. He goes to drink at the water fountain but bending down the water never touches his mouth. The metal under his hand is vibrating subtly but forcefully. He puts his palm on the cold tile of the wall. There it is stronger, almost a hum, and he can feel it moving through his entire arm now. Moving a few steps, hand still on the wall, he finds it increasing in intensity. There's some sort of incredibly loud droning vibrating through the entire building's foundation. Maybe there's construction in the basement?

Following the hum through the dark corridors, he passes no sign of anyone else on his way to the stairwell. As he descends, the metal railing shudders perceptibly under his hand. At the very bottom he finds himself back at the door to the primate labs, the annex of which is illuminated only by red light. The hum is no longer just a hum but has become an alien sound vibrating through his skeleton like an ocean of white noise. The locus is beyond the annex. Above it he can now hear what sounds like a jungle of screams and cries, howling, shrieks, the clatter of cages as the monkeys inside go mad.

Fighting the urge to clamp his hands to his ears in the dim red light Kierk gropes wildly for the light switches beside the glass door. On finding it the main primate room beyond blinks into medical brightness, and at the same time it is as if all the sound in the world shuts off. The overpowering sound is gone. The vibration is gone. Everything is still. His heartbeat now the only sound.

Kierk walks cautiously into the long room. In the stacked cages on either side the monkeys all stare at him. As he moves forward they track him, silent and totem-like. Around him the various stations of scientific equipment have been trashed. Something is so wrong but he keeps moving like a dream to the other end, past the broken glass, the shattered slides, the twisted monitoring equipment, the lab chairs that seem violently torn by some immense and impossible strength. It is as if a great force has destroyed everything. The normal musk of the animal room is present but also something sickly sweet like rotten flowers.

At the end of the area is the closed door to the cage-cleaning room, its glass portal pitch-black. The lights are still off inside. In the eerie silence he hears movement, as if some great bulk is shifting inside the darkness. There is some kind of grunt, or exhalation, but at a monstrous register, and then a low drawn-out hiss that ends abruptly, followed by a slithering of something being withdrawn. Then there is a clanging so loud it makes Kierk startle. A distant sound recedes. Slowly, extremely slowly, he reaches out to flip on the light switch outside the door. With a click he finds himself staring through the portal into the bright cage-cleaning room, which has only rubber hoses and overturned empty cages on the floor, bare walls on all sides. In the center, with the floors sloping toward it, a gigantic metal drain glistens and drips.

THURSDAY

KIERK WAKES UP TO an echo of sound abandoning him—knock knock—
before his eyes blink open. Only a hint of the dream comes back to him.
Kierk had been sitting at an ornate dinner and opposite him, so tall in the
dark he could not make out its head, some giant being had been seated. It
had rapped one of its human hands against the table. Knock knock.

Body slick with night sweats, he brushes his teeth vigorously, as if he
could purge himself of last night's events via thorough oral hygiene. After
discovering what had happened in the primate lab, staying to talk with
the security guards who eventually showed up, giving a statement, and
then walking back home in the early morning, Kierk is exhausted. And his
forearm aches. Unwrapping the gauze he sees a decent-size scab from the
shallow excision.

Breakfast comes from a baker's cart, hot dough on a hot day, a scone to
munch as he walks. But a chill washes over him when he sees what's written
in spray paint on the blank concrete wall he's passing. In great dripping red
letters it reads: DOUBLE TROUBLE LIVES. TORTURE FOR TOR-
TURERS. Recalling the director's anecdote about the bomb materials and
his own experiences last night he's at first surprised this hasn't been taken
down, but then, looking around at the nonchalant students, he realizes tags
like this must be common in NYU territory.

At the CNS he's scheduled for a tour of the lab, and he finds Karen
bent over a computer talking quietly to a graduate student. While

waiting he surveys the graduate students working at their computers, and watches as a group of researchers wearing lab coats slip booties on their feet and peel on gloves and head to the doors marked ANIMAL ELEVATOR. Carmen waves briefly to him from the far side of the lab. She gestures—one second—so Kierk prepares himself. Yesterday Kierk had noticed the effects of Carmen's looks, both on himself and also in the obvious paralyzation of others. He too had felt mesmerized by those impossibly blue eyes, that perfect grin. Instinctively he knew he would have to approach Carmen from sideways on, never for too long or too directly, like she was a monster he could look at only in the reflection of his shield else he be turned to stone.

Karen greets him with a surprising hug.

"All the faculty heard about last night! I am so sorry that happened to you. What a crazy thing. Just horrible. We have the police investigating and the university is going to crack down. What those people will stoop to!"

"I'm not sure it was . . ." Kierk trails off when he sees her face. "Yeah, it was terrible. I'm just glad I was there I guess."

A hand on his arm, she shows Kierk his computer terminal.

"I'm going to have to make some modifications," he says, examining it.

"Why don't you have a look first . . ." but already Kierk is hunting around for CPU towers to drag over to his desk. Carmen comes over and clears chairs out of the way as Kierk lugs over the last one.

"We're in the same lab!" she says, brushing off the desk as he sets it down with a grunt.

"Yeah, it's great," Kierk says, sorting out a cord, then diving down underneath the desk into a forest of wires.

"So," Carmen says, perching up on the desk above him, "what exactly are you doing with all these?"

". . . network . . . neural sim . . . need . . . blue wire? . . . little doohickey on the end . . . look?"

She opens the drawers of nearby desks until she finds a tangled bunch of different covered cables to hand down to Kierk.

"So what are you doing?"

Kierk comes up for air. "I'm networking the computers together. Then I'll model different regions of the cortex independently on each." He brushes the dust off the top of one of the hard drives, then goes back down.

Carmen nods solemnly—"So the hardware will mimic the architecture of the neural network being simulated. Since there's more intra-regional connections than inter-regional. Clever."

Kierk immediately sits back onto one knee and looks up at her, surprised. "Yes, that's exactly right."

He's been staring just a second too long when Karen saves him by tapping on his shoulder. "I come bearing MATLAB keys."

Later Karen takes them on a tour, detailing the available equipment: electroencephalography (EEG), functional magnetic resonance imaging (fMRI), and transcranial magnetic stimulation (TMS). At the same time she launches into her standard research spiel. In all scientists this is a practiced presentation as worn and automatic as a politician's stump speech. Carmen gives Kierk a subtle look and he whispers—"Call Stockholm," to which she stifles a laugh.

". . . and using fMRI we've shown that changes in consciousness are accompanied only by changes in the dorsolateral prefrontal cortex. Meaning that only a tiny, evolutionary-recent frontal part of the brain is actually doing any *experiencing* . . ."

Kierk lags behind, thinking—what a ridiculous and old hypothesis, that the entirety of mind is just a play of sartorial metaphysics, as if by adding a hat the entire outfit became conscious . . .

Carmen tugs his shirt, and Kierk, breaking from thought, follows her into the room dominated by the giant white children's toy of the fMRI. Karen is talking about the time that she, as a graduate student, had the surreal experience of giving H. M., the man without a hippocampus and therefore infamous for his inability to form new memories, a similar tour of the lab, knowing that he would forget it all in several minutes. Carmen is reminded of the anecdote about what H. M. had kept in his wallet. A small, well-handled slip of paper that read—DAD'S DEAD. That struck her so hard she had nearly cried in class when her professor told them about it. But with Karen holding court she doesn't mention it.

In the next room a medieval contraption occupies the center. It consists of a leather chair next to a table, and on the table is a buckled stand of hinged joints, like the bottom of a hideously heavy lamp, a base that rises up into a maw of metal and a wired-up football helmet with a tube-like tongue. Long hoses of wire snake around in loose nests. Arrays of monitors surround the homiletic contraption like withdrawn worshippers.

"It uses a fluctuating magnetic field to excite the neurons in the inferior temporal lobe. Subjects report feelings of religious hallucinations. We have another standard one for regular experiments, but this one is specially designed. It's called the God Helmet."

The three of them stand at the entrance of the room but do not enter.

"Did you know," Karen continued, "that this machine simulates what some neurologists think happened to Saint Paul? On the road to Damascus. His conversion, his revelation. Just epilepsy. A localized temporal lobe seizure."

"So do you want to try it?" she asks Kierk, who is staring at her.

He examines himself, searching.

"No, no. I don't think I would, actually."

Karen looks at him with sly eyes, as if he has told her a great secret.

"What about you, Carmen?" she asks.

"No. I guess I don't want to either."

Karen sighs. "Neither did I," she finally says, and turns off the lights. As the door closes and the contraption is left to blink alone in the dark of the room its slavering outline looks to Kierk almost biological, like a creature crouching on its haunches in wait.

LATER IN THE STANDARD TMS and EEG lab Karen assesses Carmen's technique as Carmen maneuvers the mesh net of recording electrodes onto Kierk's hair, which leaves tufts of it sticking out like a captured sea anemone. Then Carmen pulls down the coil that is attached to a suitcase-size battery.

"Where are we going with that thing?" He eyes the coil.

"You don't have any history of seizures, right?" Carmen says playfully.

"No, but—"

"Don't worry, I'm just calibrating it." She flicks on some dials. "I'll start with a low, subthreshold pulse, very weak, in your motor cortex. Then build up slowly to find the right threshold until we get a motor result."

Kierk makes a face. "Okay, but just keep that damn thing away from my Broca's area. It's a fucking cathedral in there."

"I'll just get to motor threshold and then we'll quit." With the coil set against his skull, the click of its activation is incredibly loud. They both stare down at his unmoving hand.

Karen watches the two of them lightly flirt and Kierk regales Carmen with the incident at the primate lab last night. At their banter Karen's thoughts go to Max, and how she will sit across from him later today in a department budget meeting and slowly, very slowly, his foot will make its way over to hers, violating the stiller air of the committee, both their faces unchanged. Under the table an observer would see their shoes begin, like an alien life-form, a strange and silly and titillating courtship dance.

Yesterday she had showered at Max's house in the morning after staying the night for the first time while his family was away. Standing beside him under the hot water the many bottles had stared at her like those statues on Easter Island. Even his son's SpongeBob SquarePants bottle seemed solemn. She, in her presence, had violated a tight, closed space. Max had handed her his Old Spice bar (his wife's soap, she couldn't help but notice, was all the way on the other side from his) and as she stood lathering her body she wondered what he would do if she reached out casually and squirted some of his wife's product onto her hands. She wanted to use too much of it, leave it noticeably lighter. But she didn't. So yesterday at work she had often paused while walking, while in the elevator, or sitting in her office chair, and she would smell him and for a moment be so confused before realizing it was just the scent of Old Spice. When she had gotten home she hadn't showered but instead had purposely climbed into bed and nestled about to lie in the fans of her hair like a primitive mammal, making a small nest of herself, a home of minute, comfortable movements, until she couldn't smell it anymore.

There's a loud click from mid-center-left above his head and Kierk's right index finger jumps all on its own.

KIERK'S ID CARD GETS him through the automatic gates of the gym near his apartment. As he passes the wide-screen TVs and upscale juice bar he feels like an imposter in his new running shorts and bright squeaky sneakers. First he heads to the weight room and lifts, feeling joy as his body assumes the proper forms, the burn and rush and release. After an hour he heads up the stairs to the indoor track to start jogging. About three or four laps in he begins to get that jouissance, that exuberant flushing all over, and he laughs wildly as he starts to push himself. There aren't that many people on the circular track and Kierk has been smoking past everybody, breathing hard, yes, but there's still that internal engine. Then there's a rush of clothing and an undergraduate blasts past him wearing an NYU track-and-field sweatshirt. The kid gets about fifty feet ahead of him before Kierk growls and takes the lead once more. Kierk holds the pace a while, hearing the footsteps behind him as the two do a few more laps almost in lockstep, and then the frequency of footsteps increases and the young man easily sprints ahead. Kierk, now feeling the riptide of each breath surge through him, catches up, and for nearly a mile they run side by side, the pair thundering past the other runners who scamper out of the way, close to a five-minute-mile pace, and Kierk, his legs wobbly, his lungs on fire, feels everything inside shutting down but musters one last burning push and starts truly going all out, sprinting as fast as he can, and just as he gets around the bend out of view of his competitor he wheels off the track and through the nearest doorway, frightening a girl who leaps out of his way, and he's gasping so loud it sounds like he's screaming as he makes it into the men's locker room, his vision narrowing to a blurred tunnel as he's heaving trying to get air, a shaking figure busting open one of the stall doors and, every part of his body trembling as he kneels, vomits up a clear stream into the pool of the toilet bowl.

SORE NAKED MUSCLES ON smooth sheets, stretching out. Around the bed a fleet of cardboard boxes stuffed with his books, arriving now from California. Kierk's taken out an old dog-eared copy of *A Confederacy of Dunces*, which is currently splayed out on his thigh. Keeping him from reading, haunting about his memory like the machinations of a ghost, is the God Helmet, the low bother of an existential itch. Coerced belief. These are precisely the kinds of things that can work themselves underneath Kierk's skin—even the idea of solipsism had nearly destroyed him, hadn't it? His first introduction to it had been amid the woodchips and hours of recess, after some skinny child boasted to a group of other children—"Well, what if the world was created just a second ago, huh, what if it was created just in the last second and then all your memories were made, how could you tell, what if God created it just now?"—and the little boy had snapped his fingers and Kierk's young eyes had gone wide and he'd had no answer.

That same wonderment returned later when he, as many children unknowingly did, rediscovered the inverted spectrum argument with one of his friends. A sleepover with two forms lying on their backs whispering—"But what if my whole life my red has actually been green. And I still say 'red' when you say 'red' even though I actually see red as green. How would anyone ever know?"

It was trivial . . . and yet . . . not trivial. Kierk could now use technical terminology to describe it as a certain lawlessness in any proposed correlation between neural events and conscious experiences, or "qualia." Because really, why couldn't one neural firing lead to green instead of red? Why would some neural activity correspond precisely and only to a particular experience? Merely because it's going on in the area that gets statistically excited when the eye is presented with red stimuli? Or merely because the area is hooked up, somewhere, to saying the word "red"? Is it really red only because the signal from the area, through a near-infinitely long feedback and feedforward—that one-two step dance, that shivering oscillation—originates from precisely those neurons and jazzes over to Broca's pub, puts quarters into the arcade games to activate the pinball levers of a tongue and the forge bellows of the lungs, and some great mechanical machine far beyond sight or knowledge moves its comically large mouth to say slowly and deeply and with the blazing eyes of the Wizard of Oz—"Red! Red! Red!"

Kierk dozes in imagery. A still-verbal homunculus, a split part of him, thinks—let us reframe the intuition. We have our subjective world, and the objective world. Can one ever fully envelop the other, or do they only have, displayed on their surfaces, the distorted reflection of the other?

Two marbles are put next to each other. They touch only at an infinitesimal point.

FRIDAY

KIERK WAKES UP PLEASANTLY tangled in sheets. Legs over fabric, sliding to the smooth, cooler parts. Groaning, everything hurts, but it feels like things inside him are being knit back together and there is a very old joy in that. On his way to the bathroom he nearly trips over *A Confederacy of Dunces* lying on the floor by the bed.

At a cafe on Broadway the barista starts making him an iced coffee and Kierk has to explain he wants it hot. The barista lifts an eyebrow—"You know we're in the middle of a record heat wave, right?"

Carrying his coffee Kierk finds a convenience store. In the cool aisles he grabs a pack of pens and then he browses through the notebook selection, which is minimal. The only ones left are bright pink Hello Kitty notebooks. After a dour moment he chuckles, slapping it on his knee, remembering early on in his California period when he would buy thick packets of printing paper and tear them open and fill the loose-leaf sheets with pages and pages of prose, diagrams, ideas, equations . . . And he feels something he hasn't felt for a long time: words stirring like small birds in his chest waking from a westward dream.

KIERK SETS HIS TRAY of sushi down as Carmen looks up from securing a lid on her iced chai tea, a tray already in front of her.

"Do you know what I saw on the way here?" she says. "That Double Trouble graffiti. 'Torture for torturers.' Reminds me of what Norman

Bennett said about how that researcher got chased by someone in a monster costume. And then whatever it is you saw! That creeped me out. And I think I got spooked from it all, because yesterday after lab, I left late, so it was dark, but I thought I was being followed. Like when someone walks behind you for too long, you know? This guy in a costume. Like a mask with horns or whatever. He was behind me the whole way home. But he must have been going to a costume party because he like, turned off right before my building."

Kierk looks over at her sushi stuffed with avocado—"Wouldn't they leave you alone since you're a vegetarian?"

"I still do animal research though. Sometimes. Besides, aren't a lot of people vegetarians in the field?"

"I'm a complexitarian. Only eat things below a certain neural complexity."

"You would be. So clearly shrimp don't make the cut." She points at his rolls with her chopsticks.

"Delicious and dumb. Just the way I like them."

"What would be an example of something that would make the cut?"

Kierk gestures to the bar. "Among the things here? Octopus. But of course being a complexitarian is just a stand-in. Ideally, we'd all be unconscioustarians."

"Nonconscious creatures only?"

"Exactly. But without a theory of consciousness we can't even decide what to ethically eat. Barbarians at the gate."

"That's why I stick to vegetarian. Playing it safe."

"Plants can form associative memories." He points at her rolls in a mimicry of her. "And they can communicate with each other. How sure are you? Even bacteria colonies trade electric signals."

"Alright, wise guy," Carmen says, laughing as she chews. When she finishes—"So anyways how close were you to completion of your PhD when you left?"

"Extremely close. But I'd rather be a lens grinder, and confront real problems, than sit pompously and comfortably among fools and partisans."

"Your problem is academia, or the way that it's run, or what? I mean, I have my days, believe me."

"Fuck the publication-and-grant game most of these people are playing. All that shit is just repetition, just banquet and vomitorium all at the same time. All minor ideas, the majority of them wrong. What I want is a theory of consciousness. That's it. And after I get it, I'm done. That's enough for a lifetime. I could live in peace."

"So you want to be a scientific one-hit wonder. You'd really just publish and . . . leave it?"

"Testing it can be someone else's job. We need firm theoretical foundations to start it off, and there's only a handful of people in the world doing that seriously."

"And you're one of them."

Kierk coughs, and Carmen notices he's already wolfed down half his sushi. "Honestly, yes," he says, finishing his bite.

"See, I don't think it'll even be in my lifetime. If it is, I suspect it won't come from anyone I've ever heard of."

"If it is in our lifetimes it won't be anyone we've heard of yet because of Occam's broom."

"Not the Occam's household item I am familiar with."

"It's when smart people unconsciously sweep inconvenient facts under the rug to support their own pet theories. That's why advances are usually made by the young. Not because they're more intellectually agile but because they have less accumulated self-deception."

Carmen realizes that she is grinning at Kierk. Talking to him feels novel, refreshing, weird.

"Well, whoever makes noticeable progress goes down in history as the next Einstein. Is that what you want?" Carmen had put too much wasabi on her sushi and her eyes begin to water so she dabs at them with her napkin.

"I don't know. I want that insight, you know? I mean, if I had some inkling, something to go on, some idea for which I could live and die."

"But by working with Moretti you've already contributed. What was that like, anyways? Alex was telling me you basically disproved the very thing you were working on. He must have been so interesting to have as your mentor."

"We were trying to develop a theory of consciousness so working with him was . . . intense. When Gertrude Stein met Alfred North Whitehead, she said a small bell went off in her head, informing her that this man was a genius. It only rang once more in her life, and that was when she met Pablo Picasso . . . When I met Antonio Moretti my own bell went off for the first time. It has not rung since."

"But see, even a disproof is a contribution!" she says. Kierk's face collapses. "No really," she continues, "It's an accomplishment."

"I don't think of it that way. It was against my research as well."

"Then you're not looking at it right. Listen, when I was in graduate school I did research I didn't believe in. We didn't lie or anything, but I'm a coauthor on at least one paper that's unconvincing even to me. But it was a learning experience."

"A learning experience? I wasted four years of my life. And the only thing I have to show for it is that I falsified one of the infinite numbers of false theories."

"You don't think it will help you if you're actually looking to come up with something original?"

"Not yet . . . I must have generated and thrown away a dozen theories. I've got old notebooks filled with them. If I could . . . if I could find a solid surface on which to stand I could lift the earth from its axis. But I can't."

A waitress sets down a hot bottle of sake and Carmen pours it out into the little ceramic cups.

"So, where does that leave you, Archimedes? Back with us mortals?" She raises her cup.

"Me, I don't know what I'm going to do. So fuck it, you know, I can find something else. I can be happy doing something else. I'll be fine." He grins widely as they touch the rims of their little trembling cups and drain the hot liquid, tilting their heads back. Kierk sets his cup down and stares out the window, and for a moment Carmen thinks his profile looks infinitely sad.

But she herself is happy to be sitting across from him, in this program, having discussions that stimulate her. It is moments like this that she wonders what the other Carmen would be doing, had her mother gotten her way. Who would be sitting across from her? It was the closest possible world to her, so close that occasionally she felt she could reach out and breach the barrier to the universe abutting this one, and that one day, on waking, she might slip streams into the other, into some different but similar bed somewhere nearby in the city, unaware that she was a point discontinuity in a continuous curve.

Kierk and Carmen's phones buzz simultaneously: a group text from Alex. Carmen's glad that an inchoate social group is forming. She's turning twenty-seven this year, so she, Alex, and Kierk are all around the same age. This summer has been the loneliest she has experienced in the city since those long-ago days when she was an undergrad at Columbia. Recently all her close girlfriends had left New York after getting their PhDs, scattered to the far corners of academia. And so, despite all her changes, the work she's put into her close friendships, her self-perspective and self-consciousness which have been carefully cultivated since her early twenties, Carmen is alone again.

Laughter as they both read: TIME TO GET DRUNK NERDS!

MIKE PUSHES THE HOOD on his Harvard sweatshirt back, watches Kierk and Carmen walking down to the corner of Union Square to where some of the Crick Scholars are supposed to meet. Mike had gotten here five minutes ago but has been hanging back, not wanting to be the first to arrive. Watching Kierk and Carmen he wonders if the two are sleeping together yet, and feels like maybe he should have actually intervened in the situation, but at this point he's just going to pretend he didn't care in the first place. Plus Kierk already had all that mystique from being the person who had discovered the break-in to the lab. What had that weirdo been doing in the building that late anyways?

Stepping out beyond the shady street corner where he's been lurking, he waves, then realizes that Alex and Jessica are with them as well. A reevaluation takes place as he watches Jessica laugh at something Alex says.

Apparently this is the full set of Crick Scholars for tonight. Mike has no idea what the others could be doing instead. He hopes they aren't in lab—a terrifying thought. The five of them head to this bar that Carmen recommended for pool: Amsterdam Billiards. Mike doesn't like how Carmen and Alex already seem to be the social center of everything, and how they've adopted Kierk like a stray puppy. But after talking to Jessica for a while Mike is starting to feel better as he notices that Jessica, as long as Carmen doesn't stand directly next to her, is very attractive.

While waiting at an intersection Carmen shows off the Band-Aid still on her forearm, and soon everyone is comparing the scabs on their arms. Jessica complains they're probably going to have scars but Carmen is delighted—"It's like we got matching tattoos or something!"

Then everyone is inside getting beers and chatting. Except Kierk, who's lounging on a barstool looking at nothing. Mike thinks he must be so incredibly high right now. Alex is talking to some guy—no, scratch that, Alex is flirting with that guy. Mike, surprised, realizes that the weird thing he's been sensing about Alex is that he's gay, which is, in hindsight, totally obvious. Maybe Alex and Carmen are both in love with Kierk—who else could stand him? Mike buys a drink for Jessica, and then soon after everyone circles around a table on fast-forward drinking and talking, except, Mike notices, Kierk, who seems to be in some sort of fugue state. Eventually something Jessica says makes Kierk suddenly perk up, lift his gaze, actually acknowledge them as people speaking words in a language he understands.

"Wait, what did you just say?"

"She's talking about how anesthesia functions. You with us, Kierk?" Mike says.

"No, she said . . . something, what was it?"

"I said, anesthesia prohibits communication. It blocks feedback in the brain, like between frontal to posterior regions. It causes you to lose consciousness."

"Ah. Yes, that's it. Delectable."

"So?"

"Anesthesia blocks feedback, making you lose consciousness?"

"Yes," she says slowly, as if expecting a trap.

"Do you know who Molière is?"

"No."

Kierk looks down for a long second, then up with a smile.

"One might even say that anesthesia . . . has a dormitive principle!"

"Umm is there a joke here or—"

"Ah, well, it's all explained then," Kierk says, draining the remainder of his beer in a long swig. "*Virtus dormitiva*. No feedback! Four hundred fucking years and we've added one step to the causal chain." Somehow his words clearly aren't addressed to any of them, said even as he is standing, moving away. Kierk feels the centuries spin by like marbles on a frictionless surface.

But after a while the colors of pool balls are also moving like marbles across the flat green in a dream of Newtonian Laws. Orange lighting, sea-like surfaces, the grain of wood, a pocket of talk. They are three games in of partners play: Jessica and Kierk against Carmen and Mike. Alex had said he is awful at pool and refuses to do things he isn't amazing at, and so has been watching the games while drinking a series of Manhattans.

Carmen and Mike have won two games already, and as Mike sends the cue ball rolling toward the eight Kierk lets out an anticipatory groan before the eight sinks into the called pocket.

"Ouch," Jessica says, "three for three."

"God, Kierk, you suck at pool," says Carmen.

"Well, Jessica over here is killing me."

Mike scoffs. "Oh, really."

"Actually it's Carmen, she's too good."

"What?" says Mike. "I'm sorry but I have been on fire tonight."

"I would not describe it as such."

"Let's play again then."

"Alright, boys," Carmen rests her cue against an empty chair. "I think Jessica and I are going to sit this one out and drink Manhattans with Alex." Alex cheers from the corner.

"Next game's loser buys what, two pitchers of beer?" says Kierk.

"No, you guys are not betting over this," Jessica says, waggling a finger.

"No, no, it's fine," Mike says, grinning. "If Kierk wants to buy the next round, he can."

"Rack it," commands Kierk, suddenly serious, walking to the far side.

"So after the program is over, what's everyone going to do?" Jessica asks.

"Well, no one wants another postdoc," Mike says as he racks the balls. Kierk makes a face in response as he chalks his cue.

"What, Kierk, you agree? What's wrong with another postdoc?" Jessica says.

"Stay in neuroscience? Are you crazy?"

Mike finishes racking, and Kierk, still talking, begins to line up the break. "The whole field is pre-paradigmatic. The reproducibility crisis is going to hit us hard. We're just waiting for enough scientists to die. Most of this so-called 'research' will be incommensurate with whatever's next. We're all just too stupid to figure out what that is right now."

He lets fly and with a thunderous crack the balls careen all around the table too fast for the eye to see. Kierk walks around, pulls out the red three from the pocket, drops it back in, even now half of him musing—so many more disordered states than ordered ones, Boltzmann, you genius . . .

He eyes the baize, and then lines up an easy shot of the two ball.

"You can't just look at something and declare that it is pre-paradigmatic,"

Jessica says. "I mean, people publish, I publish. My results, my data, they aren't meaningless."

"Actually," Kierk says, releasing in a sharp snap so that the two becomes a blue streak that disappears into a middle pocket, "no offense but they probably are."

Mike makes a parodic sweeping gesture. "You can't just say to her, to her face, that her research is meaningless. You don't even know what it is, right? Honestly, dude, it's insulting."

After just missing his next shot, Kierk gestures to Mike with his cue and says—"I'm honestly not trying to be. Until we have a theory of consciousness we're physics before Newton, biology before Darwin. It's just that no one can build a career on admitting this and the bureaucracy is already in place so people get grants and self-perpetuate and metastasize. They're playing the science game, not doing science."

As he says this Kierk feels the hum of shifting into intellectual high gear. For the past six months his dialogues have been muttered to himself on the beach, addressing fake audiences, giving the James Baldwin lecture in philosophy to a half-buried log, a sloping section of wet sand, a distant girl under a beach umbrella.

"But we've shown—" Mike begins but Kierk interrupts him, speaking so fast it's like the words are liquid pouring out of his mouth.

"You've shown what? In neural terms we still don't know what a thought is, or what a feeling is, nor an action or decision. To really figure any of that out you need to recognize that localization of all but the grossest modular function is wrong. Then start paying attention to mesoscale dynamical trajectories through continuously remade and shifting neural attractor ruins, which makes predicting or decoding brain activity as difficult as long-term prediction of the weather, but these positive Lyapunov exponents are blowing up the prediction at the order of milliseconds, not weeks. You can't take the thing apart like a combustion engine. It's been mathematically proven that no one can understand in any precise way the workings of even small artificial neural networks and yet everyone still thinks they can understand the brain? The only real question in all of neuroscience is: why are some neural states correlated with conscious experience? Why is any physical event accompanied by any subjective experience at all? That's how you carve the brain at its joints. And once you have a fundamental theory of consciousness, you should be content. Let it rest. The best kind of neuroscience is the kind of neuroscience that lets you stop doing neuroscience. Why stay in the field when it's all over, when the theoretical underpinnings are established? Why be a glorified cartographer when the borders are always changing, plastic, fractal, individuated?"

"Take a chill pill, Kierk," Mike says as he lines up his shot.

"Take a nootropic, Mike," Kierk bites back.

Mike makes a face like: what the fuck does that mean?

Carmen quickly calls out—"Kierk, listen for a second. Biology didn't stop when Darwin and Wallace invented the theory of evolution by natural selection."

"Yeah, the whole thing isn't going to be over when we figure out how consciousness works," Alex says.

Mike sinks the ten, but he ends up with no line of sight and is forced to split a pair of stripes and solids sitting against the far wall.

"Why not? The main task of the brain is to be conscious," Kierk says as he looks around for a shot. "The categories cognitive neuroscience places on mental activity are just the latest in a series of fads that has been the history of psychology. Now it's medieval humorism all over again, but this time it's levels of dopamine, serotonin, oxytocin. An imbalance of the humors made me do it!"

He positions himself into a tight bow, his cue at a steep angle, and bounces the cue ball over the eleven to gently nudge the five into a pocket.

"Oh, what the fuck," Mike says, his face flushing.

"You can't get at what's going on in the brain without talking about consciousness." Kierk circles the table. "Neuroscientists talk about things like concepts, cognition, memory, attention. But they don't exist in and of themselves, they only exist because a conscious process expresses them. I'm just pointing out that these terms don't define a playable game by themselves. They're just the shadows consciousness casts."

Mike is shaking his head, incredulous. "There are plenty of really fucking smart people in this field, and you're just dismissing everything they do and the arrogance is astounding. That's all I'll say."

"But that doesn't mean he's wrong," Carmen interrupts. "I mean, you can't believe that there are no serious fundamental problems in this field, unless you're wearing, you know, your research blinders."

Kierk bounces the one off a wall at an acute angle such that it traces a slow lazy yellow line into a middle pocket. Before it even sinks, Kierk is

crouching down and surveying the table at eye level, talking. "Let me put it
another way. If we didn't experience it for ourselves, and instead just had to
rely on the current literature that makes up the field of neuroscience, would
we have any idea, any idea at all, that mental events are bound into a single
internal world of experience and that this world is egocentrically oriented
around a self? Would you be able to deduce, at all, the structure of human
consciousness from what we know about the brain?"

Carmen shakes her head so hard she nearly unbalances herself and falls
off her stool. Alex is the only one who sees this and both Carmen and Alex
are now laughing at each other, drinks clinking.

"What about my research, Kierk?" Carmen says, recovering. "Want to
analyze mine? Say it's all bullshit?"

"Nah, I read your *Nature* paper. You're arguing on my side. Trying to
show that consciousness isn't localized to any part of the brain."

"And," Carmen adds, fluffing herself up, pretending to deliver a grand
lecture, "that the vast majority of the brain participates in any one given
conscious moment. Irreducibly."

Kierk's next target is the four, which is sitting snug against the far edge.
The cue ball barely touches it but somehow, as if tugged by an invisible
string, the four drifts perfectly sideways for almost half a meter along the
wall, losing momentum and stopping just in front of the pocket, blocking it.

"Holy shit," Jessica says. Mike stalks around the table angrily looking
for a shot. Kierk clears his throat theatrically, as if taking stage.

"I'm sure you've all heard of Momus's indictment of Hephaestus; if not,
you will hear it now. Momus was asked to judge a contest between Athena,
Poseidon, and Hephaestus, on who could construct the best artifact to present to Zeus. Poseidon bred a bull. Athena erected a house. But Hephaestus
built an entire mechanical man who could walk and talk. As the other gods
clapped and congratulated him, Momus, the god of writers and tricksters,
said—'Why Hephaestus, it is clear that you are a master craftsman. But
what is also clear is that this is the worst present in the competition. You
have failed in representing the fundamental nature of the thing. Would not
this mechanical man be vastly superior if upon his skull there was a window
through which one could see his thoughts?'"

Alex does a little golf clap. Carmen from her stool gives an exaggerated
look of unbelief, somewhere between astonishment and mock astonishment.

Kierk continues. "Installing a pane of glass that lets you look at the gears, that's the neural correlates of consciousness. It won't tell us anything, just as Momus slyly pointed out. Francis Crick was wrong."

Mike's scoff is quieted as his attempt at sneaking the fifteen past the guard of the four instead goes wide and the four meanders inexorably into the pocket.

"The house of neuroscience will collapse," Kierk proclaims like a priest, walking around the pool table. "In the ruins nothing will grow."

"Then it'll crush you and your ego as well." Mike's hands are white on his pool cue.

"No," Kierk says, lining up for the only remaining solid. "See, I don't plan on being inside of it."

A dream of chartreuse loses itself into the waiting netted mouth.

"You don't have the authority to dismiss an entire field."

Kierk smiles devilishly—"Truth is always in exile. Don't think that if a theory of consciousness were offered tomorrow everything everyone at the CNS does wouldn't disappear in a puff of smoke. Calling my shot: far right pocket."

"So what's next then?" Carmen stirs her drink. "If you've got it all figured out, Kierk, which apparently you think you do, oh please let us in on the secret."

Kierk, eye level with the cue ball, takes a deep breath, and everything slows down. He can hear himself talking, and then calling his shot, a thing apart, but he is here, with this long field of baize and the dynamics of these reversible mechanics, in this dream of a physics that never happened. Words, his, are spoken—"Perhaps nothing will grow. Like the fields of Carthage after the salt. *Carthago delenda est*."

With a clack the cue ball traces a line across the table, tapping the eight toward the right pocket. But as it rolls the eight instead comes to rest at the trapezoidal edge of that pocket's mouth while meanwhile the cue ball itself listlessly meanders into the far left pocket, tips in, and Kierk scratches.

For a moment there is silence. Then Mike, laughing, throws his hands up in victory.

"Good game, buddy!" he says loudly, already putting up his pool cue.

Kierk is still staring at the leather pocket as if expecting more from it. He can't believe he lost.

Alex calls out—"Kierk, funny how the first three games you were shooting with your left hand. And this game you played with your right."

This time, Carmen does fall off her stool with laughter. "You were robbed. You were robbed," she says, recovering.

Reaching over, Kierk takes her Manhattan out of her hand, cheering her—"So it goes." Finishing his sip—"I'll be back with your winnings, Mike."

Eventually he returns to the table bearing a tray full of pitchers and shots. Everyone does one. Mike is red-faced and avuncular. He keeps clapping Kierk on the arm, saying, "Good game," again and again.

In no time at all, Carmen and Kierk, leaning in to hear one another above the din, have separated off and are talking in fast tones about life, literature, science, language, purpose. How a personal worldline is guided by both teleonomy and teleology.

Finally Alex interrupts them, informing them that they have been huddled up together for an hour, that it's unfair, particularly to him, and that they simply must do another shot with him.

Soon after that the bar becomes a toy workshop that Kierk is moving through, drunk on airs. Carmen's face floats in his field of vision, too much stimulation for Kierk to make sense of. Fuck, he needs a cigarette. Intentions are brighter than lights. Kierk, outside somehow, maybe he left for a cigarette, he can't remember, is inhaling the deep, aquatic air, and thinking—not me, not me, I can see things clearly, can't I? I am the fish who learns.

Drunkenness takes him away, a dark carriage of smoke and gestures, one thought still echoing, bouncing off the buildings and into the streets, slipping down the drains, finding its way to the sea—I am the fish who learns.

KIERK IS WRITING IN his Hello Kitty notebook by the light of a lamppost. He doesn't know what time it is but he's taking burning swigs from a small bottle of whiskey he bought from a corner store because he doesn't want to sober up, no, not yet, not when words are flying off like colored scarves from a magician's hat; he's spastic, impulsive, expunging sentences in rages, generating more in rapture, not realizing people passing down the midnight steps of Union Square are looking at him as he smacks his forehead and pulls his hair and mouths words aloud, shouting to feel them leave him like Flaubert, standing up and then sitting back down, clenching his fists in self-loathing and belletristic anger. He rips up the page he's working on, stuffs it in his mouth and chews it in anger, shreds the soggy mess between his teeth, grinding it and feeling his jaw muscles work, and then it's spewing out of his mouth as he starts laughing hysterically. He keels over and sprays the inky mush over the concrete steps. Making a face, he picks the bits of remaining paper out of his mouth, then, still laughing, gets unsteadily to his feet. He knows he is a dense knot of metaphors faking at being a man, that he is the mere shambles of an apology with nothing to apologize for—no theory of consciousness, no writings—a mere strawman dissolving into parts, a pile of clothes on the floor, a poor synecdoche, a thing like that can't impact the world anyway . . .

SATURDAY

KIERK WAKES UP TO music. His shoulder blades ache as he rolls over on the floor. Hungover, he opens one eye onto the expanse of the carpet. His thoughts begin in a sluggish smog, gray themes and colors, but then, like breaking cloud cover, a thing rising and set free into the blue—in drinking he has reset everything, he feels, his mind is scrubbed, tilt-a-whirl, all of yesterday's habits gone. The music is coming from his damnable phone.

Soon, still nursing his hangover, Kierk is underground and everything is shaking about and screeching. Following a trail of text messages he's meeting Carmen and Alex at the Bronx Zoo, but right now he is standing amid an incredibly crowded train, a hurtling hot metal box making its way beneath the earth. He's pressed up against the glass windows of the door staring out at the stream of passing earth, metal, odd lights, brief glimpses of entire subterranean spaces. At one point a wall ends and for a second Kierk thinks he's staring into a mirror but it's just another packed train traveling alongside them, with people other than him staring back, strangers staccato blinking in the chthonic yellow light so that they look sickly, like dream people. Expressionless the two sides gaze at each other, neither one moving. Yet both move. If even motion is relative, what isn't?

Interspersed into his stream of consciousness, like frames spliced into one movie reel from another, he thinks of Carmen. He feels this lust is entirely absurd, doesn't make any sense for him. He had thought his life was all charted, that the ouroboros could be traced again and again, that he would die before thirty. In the lurching and heaving of the mechanical turns he thinks hot, dark thoughts of relativity, of sex and death.

Just one subway car behind Kierk, unknowingly thundering down the same tunnel, Carmen sits statuelike amidst the dense crowd. She is in the neutral spine position on the edge of her seat, one hand searching around in her purse beside her, discriminating objects by touch, moving past and over lip balm and a Nabokov short story collection to take out some gum, thoughts drifting. She watches herself in the moving black planes of glass opposite her. As they slow down for the next stop she sees, in a flash of illuminated yellow underground construction, a lit alcove, a concrete wall on which is spray-painted in red: DOUBLE TROUBLE LIVES. TORTURE FOR TORTURERS.

Pulling into the platform she's craning her neck, even briefly fighting her way out to look down the tracks, but she gives up and slides back in as the doors are closing. This is midtown, well beyond NYU-student territory. Doesn't make any sense. One thin pinky goes up to smooth an eyebrow as she sits back down, confused. It's a further addition to the already merry-go-round nature of her thoughts.

She'd spent the whole morning feeling like a stalker as she searched the internet for signs of Kierk. There'd been no social media presence, no personal website, no pictures of him, none of the usual information about places he's lived and weight fluctuations and fashion changes, and for some reason this lack of information intrigued her greatly, and she knew she was acting strange—she had actually smashed a glass while rinsing it in the sink from scrubbing too enthusiastically, like there was this building kinetic force inside her.

It's been a long time since she felt anything like this, and it's never hit this quickly before. Relationships, Carmen thinks, are only sensible when they're over. During, the fog of war reigns. In the plastic seats of the swaying metro, Carmen handles the last time she had been in love in her mind. The memory is not narrative in structure, but geometric. It exists outside of time, a faceted gemstone of movements and greetings and sex and food and holidays and plane flights and phone calls and parties and moments of early-dark animal warmth. Carmen turns it over in her mind, seeing the beginning, the ending, all of it at once. She would think that time is an illusion, but she knows that's a poor metaphor. Rather, Carmen feels that time is a solid; that the way God would see a life is as a solid geometric shape of a billion dimensions, a diamond shaved and smoothed by the tides of eternal return.

It had all started the beginning of her senior year at Columbia University, when she was deciding whether to apply to PhD programs. It had been the crux of her young life, but its seed had been present from the very beginning. For one of Carmen's earliest memories is of her mother, a huge head of plastic-perfect blonde hair and dangling jewelry, presenting her before some man (in the memory the man has no face) in some nondescript hotel ballroom and saying—"Here she is. I told you! She could turn you to stone just looking at her." It had been at one of those pageants her mother used to drag her to. Little Carmen would stand up on stage in her frilly dress and talk about how she wanted to be a scientist, and how she actually liked doing math in school, and all the while the judges would nod with wide-smiling approval. Carmen got the sense that her statements were taken about as seriously as the other girls' requests for world peace. And she had hated the smell of hairspray and the fake eyelashes with their tacky strips of adhesive. She hated the hotels she and her mother stayed in, with their double beds and her mother's elaborate nightly rituals of face masks and scrubs. Generally Carmen placed well in the competitions, but never Grand Supreme. Somehow everyone could tell she didn't want to be there. And so, as her mother's dreams to see her crowned Miss America disappeared with each runner-up performance, a new dream materialized: one of glossy editorials, billboard ads, and runways. Her mother stepped nimbly into the role of de facto agent and began to book Carmen as many gigs as possible. The two would travel to go-sees, cattle calls, and test shoots together; her father, a quietly supportive but overworked engineer, never came along.

To Carmen, modeling wasn't nearly as distasteful as the pageants. Solitary affairs spent mostly around adults rather than girls her own age, she'd pass much of a shoot's requisite downtime lost in a book. As a teenager she learned a lot about how to classify her looks through the conversations that happened around her. A natural projector. A downward-turned mouth that revealed just enough teeth. An emotive pout. Cheekbones a high arch. If anyone had ever bothered to use digital calipers they would have discovered that Carmen has perfect bilateral facial symmetry, as in completely zero fluctuating asymmetry within human measurement error, and that additionally her features are perfectly proportioned; that the distance between her pupils is exactly half the distance between her ears, that the distance between her eyes and mouth is exactly one-third the distance from her hairline to her chin. You'd have to do an MRI to find any asymmetries in Carmen, and that would only be a minor differential in the thickness of her sternomastoid muscles, due to tilting her head to the left when listening. To this day Carmen has never found out exactly how much money her mother made from the gigs, but occasionally a magazine, like *J-14* or *Teen Ink*, would arrive at the house, and there it would be on some glossy page—her face. At school she tried her best to hide what she thought of as her second life, and in turn her secrecy was interpreted as pride. Her mother, in contrast, would frame at least one image from every shoot, hanging them all, dozens of them, until eventually they filled up the entire wall by the staircase. And a teenage Carmen would ascend past them to her room and put on loud music and read *The Picture of Dorian Gray . . .*

At the end of high school the compromise had been this: Carmen was allowed to major in a hard science rather than fashion or business, and her tuition would be paid for, but she must go to college in New York City, with official representation through an agency. And so at eighteen, having fitted meetings with IMG and Elite between campus tours, Carmen had moved to the city to attend Columbia University and study neuroscience. In addition to a full course load, to comply with her mother's demands Carmen was working as many shoots as IMG could book. Once she actually started getting her own paycheck from the work, she was making more money in a month than in a year of being a part-time barista or work-study assistant like some of the other girls she knew. But friends at Columbia were impossible to find. As a part-time technician she stood out from the other members of the lab like a single masterwork sculpture among a lumpy amateur gallery. An Ivy League student, a scientist with a modeling job, sometimes she could almost hear the sharpening of the nails of other women. Her sophomore year she cried nearly every afternoon after classes, an infinite pit of loneliness in her chest, followed by sitting with icepacks pressed up against her eyes to prevent puffiness so no one would know.

But it was not that she truly hated modeling, for she did find some solace in it. She enjoyed being a success at something, the busyness and rhythms of it all, and in the modeling world she wasn't treated like a freak. She made sure to curb her vocabulary, eschewing and dissecting her speech prior to parties. Fashion magazines began to accumulate next to her collection of William and Henry James, and she was quick to develop the kind of high-end taste that impressed at meetings and photo shoots, which of course separated her even more from the sweatpants-wearing girls struggling to get by in the difficult neurobiology courses. Carmen, in an absurd balancing act of scheduling, would sit at the front of the class with her different colored pens and take notes in perfect handwriting. She read vignettes from Oliver Sacks to the makeup artists during shoot prep. She began attending show weeks and shoots in Europe and got used to studying textbooks in the back of the airplane next to the mephitic stench of the bathroom while the other models were nursing a bitchy hangover from alcohol and cocaine. Backstage at shows, the other girls called her "doctor" to her chagrin, even though the doctorate she was always talking about applying for would be in neuroscience or psychology, not medicine. Yet still they came to her with their problems; for cramps in their feet Carmen would prescribe them bananas for potassium, for headaches suggest that they stop staring at their iPhones 24/7, or buy a neck pillow to avoid sleeping wrong during flights.

Her senior year everything had come to a head. Once the fall fashion shows began everything became pressured, tightly wound. Abnormal Psychology was known as a GPA-buster, but Carmen had taken it anyway, and that fall the class was always the small thing making everything else impossible. She had been hectically absent for weeks, in Milan and Paris, then New York, then Milan and Paris again, transforming her life into a haze of emails to professors, of fitting into dresses, of sitting still while makeup was applied, of trying to find a place to print out case reports while tottering around in high heels on foreign streets in the liquid soup of foreign languages. In the back of the airplane the abnormal psych textbook pages blurred as she read about trichotillomania or pica or, with a grim survey of the other models, bulimia and anorexia. Her TA in Abnormal Psychology took pity on her. When she'd first seen him lounging at the front of the class she hadn't given him a second thought—Josh was tall, with big ears and thick eyebrows, and he had a mild lisp when he spoke enthusiastically about schizotypal case studies, famous depressives, cognitive behavioral therapy. His TA hours at a coffee shop were sparsely attended, and one day Carmen just unloaded on him about how she wanted to apply to graduate school, the difficulties of modeling, being alone, everything. And Josh, the big-eared, smart, and kind goof that he was, had done his best to comfort this beautiful creature that had landed in his lap as neutrally as possible. Eventually she was coming to all his TA hours to chat straight through them, and when another student came Carmen would move to a different table and read until Josh was free again and then they would pick up on the exact sentence they left off on.

They first slept together a mere one week after Abnormal Psychology was officially over, at a house party his roommates threw. She attended it even though she didn't know anybody else there, but then it turned out that all his friends were just so goddamn sweet and smart, a succession of witty science-filled conversations, and she had been wondering where these kinds of people were her entire time in New York; everything just felt perfectly natural as they played drinking games and Carmen helped Josh make cocktails in the kitchen and then the party dwindled and Josh and she each met the dark form of the other in the corridor and an arm met another arm and a hand a hand and lips, lips. The first time that night she had been at her normal level of nervousness, but then the second, no, third time in the morning it had gone from the usual—am I going to or not, is it now, no not yet he knows I'm not going to god what is he thinking why can't I—to a revelation, that with humor and no pressure, orgasms followed. And the more she had with Josh the easier they became—Carmen couldn't help but think of it like a railroad town being wired up for electricity, everything becoming more and more connected, more and more lights flickering on in surges—oh such surges!

In those heady days of the early relationship a subject she and Josh always came back to was Carmen's future. They even developed an ironic pet name for the inevitable decision, calling it "the mind-body problem." A running joke, it would pop up, with Carmen holding her coffee, or leaning against a doorframe with a glass of wine, saying—"I've had some thoughts on the mind-body problem." For a while she had been trying to tell her mother that she wanted to do science full-time, and that this would necessitate graduate school, and that it was impossible to juggle two careers at once, and so on . . . But her mother had this insidious way of slowly working away at Carmen's defenses, wheedling, marshalling her father, and, when that didn't work, she'd get so worked up that she became the real victim of the fight. On top of that, modeling had become unignorably lucrative for Carmen, and unexpected sums poured easily into her bank account. Her reputation in the industry grew and she got on more flights, spending more nights away from Josh and her studies. It was not a career she had set out to choose, but she was in fact good at it, far more able to intuit what the industry side wanted than the other girls. At the same time, graduate schools had gotten back to her with rounds of interviews, so she got on more flights. Yet she couldn't imagine leaving New York for these cold and lonely campuses, and therefore also leaving Josh, and so was banking everything on being accepted by her soon-to-be undergrad alma mater, Columbia University.

At Josh's birthday that spring they had sat with his friends unwrapping presents around a bar table. Carmen had planned her present in secret for a long time, gathering the correct measurements for the blazer while keeping him oblivious to her true purpose, all so that he'd have something for job interviews as a research technician, which Josh said was a break before graduate school. Unwrapping the Armani blazer his face had fallen to the "oohs" and "ahhs" around the table. Afterward he'd been withdrawn until Carmen had prodded him enough for him to yell about how embarrassed he'd been—she had given him a thousand-dollar blazer, dammit, right in front of all his friends!

The next week Carmen was officially accepted into Columbia University for graduate school. The same day she called her agency to terminate their representation of her, knowing what it would bring. Then she had called her mother. Josh held her hand as they both sat on the edge of the bed and co-listened to the tinny sounds from the phone, starting with—"It's going to be so hard, honey." which eventually turned to —"You should really consider keeping modeling as a side job just in case." to —"The amount of work we've put in, for *you*, for your career, is something that not everyone gets, not everyone gets parents like us." to —"Well, your lifestyle is going to change completely and don't count on any support from your father either, that's over." After the call Josh had sat holding her as they watched TV late into the night.

The next day on waking beside him she felt she had snapped into focus suddenly at the age of twenty-one, as if a scene had been set and a movie had begun to play of their lives together. She knew exactly what she was going to do with her life, and who she was going to do it with.

Possibly she felt this way because, prior to that relationship, Carmen had never been in love. She had, of course, osmotically absorbed a great deal of information about love from popular culture, from TV shows to pop songs. And she was an avid reader. So she had been exposed to countless explicit in-depth descriptions, from Tristan and Isolde to Anna Karenina to Romeo and Juliet. She knew everything there was to know about love, all the facts of it, long before she experienced it for herself. But when it was her, when *she* was the one in love, each moment had somehow been completely new and unexpected, perfectly unpredictable—the irreducible indexical fact that it was *her* experiencing all this blasted away all the prior facts and models and the knowledge she had accumulated and left something raw, fragile, alive. In his company, in their funny and sweet little life together for the next few years, everything became as sensible and obvious as Euclid's axioms.

And graduate school itself went well, almost easy, really, in comparison to the chaotic juggling act that had been her undergraduate experience. Looking back she felt distant and empathetic to her old self, but also embarrassed. As ridiculous as the whole charade of it all was to her, the glamour had been real. There is something it is like to see yourself on a billboard, or in the September issue of *Vogue* modeling coats, or tell a group of people at a party that you work as a model. It was a powerful, competitive draw. In graduate school she defended modeling from attacks by her friends who dismissed it as solely misogynistic, objectifying, and unhealthy. But most didn't even know she once worked in the industry, as she learned to keep it to herself, and spoke of it almost solely with Josh in their insular couple life that took place in small apartments sprinkled over Manhattan.

So when Josh broke up with her with no warning in her fourth year of grad school she left his apartment like a bat undone, without echolocation, flopping hysterically from surface to surface, in purposeless flight across the pinwheeling lights of the city at night all overloading her as she spun in a centrifuge, his words coming, speaking themselves to her again and again—"You are leaving and you don't even know it yet. I'm doing this to protect myself. When we started you were this student who came to me for advice. I loved lecturing to you. I loved watching you learn. But now you've surpassed me in everything. You're going to breeze through a postdoc and I'm going to end up some fucking research tech somewhere. When was the last time I won a debate with you? You contradict me about everything and you don't even notice. But what's fucked up is that you're always right. You're a better scientist than me. And that makes you a monster. Because, also, I mean, *look* at you. Sometimes I can barely stand it. So what do I have left? Nothing. Just my damn dignity. And I can't take watching you fall out of love with me. You're going to settle with me and you're never going to forgive me and then one day you'll leave me. I have to do this to protect myself . . ." All as Carmen tried to just remain upright, tried to comprehend what was happening, because her insides had clenched up into a spasming wall and she had waves of nausea coursing through her, while an abstract small voice, an academic part of her somehow divorced from her, was commenting—isn't absolute mental anguish neurologically quite interesting? She had cried uncontrollably on the subway while people avoided looking at her. In her apartment the noises she made were barely human, so far from language it was as if she had become an animal wrestling with an injury.

In the breakup the same enigmatic indexical knowledge appeared: Carmen had known that it was possible to cry for two days straight, but she hadn't *known* it. She received copious deliveries puffy-faced and in pajamas. She spent her time ignoring calls and emails and instead sat in the bathtub and watched dumb TV shows with her laptop resting on a fold-out chair beside the tub. In the hot water she had cried and cried and cried until she became delirious from dehydration. A few times it was Josh's number on her phone. Each ring tore her apart until only pride remained. She bellowed and splashed around in the bathtub as if she were cauterizing a wound. Alternating in affect between vengeful and overwrought with loss, she shouted aloud one-sided conversations over the echoing tiles, cycling through invective tantrums where she accused him of just wanting to fuck other women, to stick his dick in someone else, always followed by reconciliatory begging sessions. She replayed that final night a hundred times over in the proceeding weeks, looking for a hint, a sign, a place where if she would have acted differently it would have changed everything. Finding it, and finding that everything he said had been true—this had been what really let her begin to recover, a long scarring process ending with a tender gratefulness for the existence of one self over another.

KIERK GETS BACK TO his apartment after the zoo, his mind full of lions and chimpanzees and the bat exhibit and the bar where he and Alex and Carmen had drunk pitcher after pitcher of beer. He fumbles with his key and then the door is open and where the hell is the light switch and the only visibility is from the city coming in like a machinery of light through the window and then in the bathroom he turns the faucet on full blast and rapidly cups water into his hands to drink, again, again, the roar of the sink and the hot, hot, hot water, the water burning up his throat and he's just standing there leaning over the sink and wildly drinking hot water for a good minute before he violently and drunkenly hits the sink off and strips off his shirt over his head on the way to the bedroom and then slams into the pillow and sleeps.

At first there is nothing. But then, later, a body, a place, distinct spatial relations. The body is huddled and curled and slept in the folding of itself upside down, an upside-down world around it, and it is dark and warm here amid the mewls of the young and soft ticking motions of bodies around, all the bodies around, this small crevice from which I hang, fold, still, still as the rock and the cave, as within the belly is no longer full of movements ended, things caught, no longer full of catching of chasing of eating, the black shadow of anticipation to fall on the moving tastes of crunches, keeping nose from the cold, tucking it under the arch of leathery wings which belong, long fingers which belong, warm but empty belly which belongs, lets long fingers curl hard and naturally and instinctively, thoughts of hunting, yes, amid the black here, the black and calm of waiting, seeing the small twongs of sound bounce around and give the world, yes, it is safe, safe, cousins, brothers, sisters, yes, the other black bodies as soft as underbellies of night, rubbing, an expanse of skin, a thousand skins, which all belong, all love and strife, the true world is here in the cousins which belong, the brothers which belong, the sisters which belong, the world inside which belongs, while the world outside is a great loft of flyings and huntings and smellings and here is the home of the all, the home, the cave, and now the great belonging is moving, is rising, rising now, touchings of skeins of leather yes, now it is time to hunt to find the night to be amid the tall and the open and find find find the little wells little treasures of food food food, cousins around yes the smell of flying the quick beats of hearts, twongs, hear all movement, here, spilling out into the outside all of the all the escape of the cave the mouth the dark the home, emerge into the open, all of us, to spread to cry to mark to move to hunt to feed, yes, yes, to be bat bat bat bat bat bat bat bat.

SUNDAY

KIERK WAKES UP WITH the expectation that he is seventeen again. That he has to get to high school, which means driving in the glare of morning across the salt marshes, then leaving surreptitiously during lunch to get high in his car, to come back and take a calculus exam disheveled, to have a free period in the library and spend it with his feet up, balancing his chair on its back legs, reading Heinlein, to run with his track teammates that evening along roads as basic to him as blood, an entire day of seventeen-year-old life waiting as thick as water, as edible as bread. Everything had been potential.

But when he finally realizes what self he's in he just groggily props himself up on an elbow, his thinning and matted hair clinging to his forehead, and, surprised at his lack of hangover (a vivid sensory memory of a mouth filled with hot water), rolls and drops out of bed and does his now-daily exercise routine, breathing heavily as his life up to now recedes away along tracks.

Outside Kierk isn't really watching where he is going—he has his Hello Kitty notebook in hand and a pen is burning a hole in his back pocket.

CARMEN AND ALEX ARE out for a stroll, passing between them a whipped mocha. Carmen is in shorts with her hair up in a ponytail and sports pink sunglasses, while Alex is wearing a tight V-neck and cargo shorts and sandals. It's beautiful out, though every time they pass from the rectangular shade of a building to the brightness beyond Carmen lets loose a series of uncontrollable sneezes, and finally has to explain that it's due to her photic sneeze reflex. Two years ago she had gotten herself genotyped, and fifty percent of the reason for getting her genome read had been to prove to her disbelieving friends that she really is genetically disposed to sneeze in response to bright light. Normally the sunglasses help but today it's so bright that her genes are having a go of it and so she keeps sneezing wildly and Alex keeps laughing every time she does.

It's on the tree-lined paths of Washington Square Park that Carmen spots the figure standing on one of the benches next to the dog park. He is facing away from them, looking instead at the cavorting and speedy to-and-fro of dogs. There are cries and shouts and showers of woodchips. Carmen leads Alex silently up behind Kierk, whose back stays to them as he cranes this way and that. Carmen can see his grin as he takes in the whole scene. The dogs have between them a big red bone that they keep stealing from each other, and then, as one of them takes off across the park bearing the bone in its mouth, it is like the platonic realm itself has opened up as a pack of dogs of all shapes and sizes come rough and tumble after. A merry chase of dog bodies and dog thoughts commence.

Carmen stands up on the bench beside Kierk as he is following the game. Before he turns back she nudges him with an elbow and he, in surprise, nearly falls off. His laughter fades when he sees her expression, which is like she had just caught him performing a musical instrument she hadn't known he played. Alex waves at him.

"I wouldn't have pegged you for a dog person," Carmen says.

Kierk shrugs, squinting, watches the parabola of a thrown ball.

"I had them growing up. What are you two doing here anyways?"

"Weeeee are in the process of exploring, so you should come! That is, if you can stand another day in our company."

Alex holds the Hello Kitty notebook that had been lying on the bench forgotten, already flipping through the pages.

"This. Is. Amazing." He backs up and begins to read aloud. Kierk just sits down on the bench and sighs.

"'How is a metamorphosis of thought preceded? What augurs summon a breakthrough of this scale, what omens and signs and eyes? Is it all poetry before, is it all madness? Is such a vision preceded by passion? By failure?

By belief? As with Saint Paul, does it come upon a traveler as blindness? Could it be preceded by love?'"

There is a pause. Carmen is looking at him anew for the second time.

"Hey, wait a minute, this is actually . . ." Alex starts, he keeps flipping. "What's this?" The page is filled with strange arrows.

"Category theory. It's a branch of mathematics that—you know what, just give it back. Give me my, my, hey, give it—Okay. Let's go."

"Achoo!"

Walking to the East Village they slow as they approach some sort of commotion in front of the CNS. There are protesters outside the building, shouting, blocking the sidewalk, holding signs that say STUDENTS AGAINST ANIMAL RESEARCH. In the back, one student in a ski mask holds up: TORTURE FOR TORTURERS. A scene is already unfolding as a man, a researcher whom Kierk recognizes from the hallways of the CNS, is trying to enter to the increased rancor of the crowd. The researcher looks defiant, about to move forward, but then takes a step back in shock when an utter silence descends. One by one the protesters begin to collapse like a depressive wave spreading outward. Strings cut, the clatter of signs, the looseness of lifelessness, until all of them are splayed out on the ground in a hush, legs entangled, faces blank at the sky. The entire street is still as the organismal mass lies protoplasmic on the cement. Kierk, leading the way, is the first to move through them all, stepping gingerly around the limbs of the still figures. He looks down at their faces in vain, as if hoping to recognize one. Only their eyes move to watch as he and Alex and Carmen pass through to Broadway and beyond.

At first they can talk of nothing else, nervous about what they just saw, but then the easiness of the evening takes over and they relax into the day, moving abreast through the concrete and light and wail of passing ambulances, walk signals bleached out from the sun, sandals thwacking in synchrony, St. Marks Place a rush of small stores and trinkets and skateboarders and tattoo parlors and jangling beads. They try on hats from a display rack on the sidewalk, which is followed by laughter as the young woman secures on one of the young men a Mets cap, from which his hair sticks up in a willful column. They lean together too long before pulling away. —"Oh lady! For you lady, I will give your boyfriend the hat, yes, sir, you look good in the hat. Take care of your lady!" Laughter, cars, a bicycle whizzes by them on the sidewalk. Hands bend the bill of a Mets cap. —"Where are you taking us, where is this place?" The heat from an open brick oven compounds in the thick air as they handle paper plates made translucent from grease. —"You are destroying all my natural defenses against carbs." Then the taste of garlic and cheese and artichoke. —"Give me a bite, pleeaase." Waiting for a walk signal while a hundred pigeons take flight and swoop low against a sky so blue it has become a solid, blue through and through, an infinite bowl of blue. —"Did you see that guy? He had a cat balanced on his head. My hand to God." Nudging and laughter, a cigarette is passed around, savored illicitly. That ache in the flat pads of feet from pounding around on concrete for hours. At a small terrace looking over First Avenue sighs of relief are breathed as feet are elevated and the three lounge around as a server brings beers so cold they must be from another planet. Sweating glass. Male and female fingers touch as they both reach for napkins at the same time. Did he notice? In the advancing day the hot liquid fishes of thoughts swim upstream with the traffic. One of her hands is laying on the tablecloth in the square of sunlight. Look at how small and perfectly shaped it is, moving by itself. —"Where did you get that bruise anyways?" —"I was mugged." —"Oh." One of the young men laughs heartily. —"See, I told you, coming in from the wild." Smiling at nothing, why am I doing that? —"How do you manage to get so much ink on your hands?" —"Practice." —"I'll get the check." Chairs screeching back. Footsteps. Streets becoming tinted with evening colors. A stall of fruit, buzzing with itself. —"Okay, where should we eat?" —"Come on, let's eat oranges in the sunlight." Fingernails pick away at the skin, fingers become sticky with pulp, orange peels are discarded onto the step below where they are sitting. Three figures are sitting on stone steps outside a brownstone apartment building. The sun is setting down the west side of the street looking like a drop of blood hung between the buildings. Everything is cast red by it. The young woman puts her sunglasses on, smiles contentedly. The occasional warm gust stirs everything like an idle chemistry set. The day retreats, and in the vanilla red of dusk the electric nightlights of the city come on in uncoordinated blocks, beautifully out of sync. Every surface radiates warmth when a palm is put against it. There must be a world beyond this world. In the waning red a young woman leafs through a Hello Kitty notebook while the two young men converse, throw pebbles, until one notices and snatches it back from her. A pink tongue sticks out. Dogs pass, their owners dragged along like afterthoughts. Pigeons retire, cede the night to the bats. —"Most of the neuroscientists I meet are just . . . really boring, actually." —"Haha, same." —"I've met a lot, and if asked why they're in the field they say the mind-body problem. But none of them end up actually researching it. You two guys are the first people I've met who actually do what you're supposed to be doing and it's . . . I don't know, it's just really great." —"Thanks, Carmen." —"You too." —"I'm just glad you're in this program, is all I'm saying." —"We know. Us too." Smiling, the young woman sitting in the middle puts her arms around their shoulders, rocks back and forth. Breathe in. Breathe out. A thought swimming up over a young man's head, passing by her resting arm on his shoulder—when was the last time I felt promise? The remaining rind of sun is swallowed by the horizon and the gloaming makes all things soft. Everyone and everything bows out after having one really good day.

A SOAPY ARM EXTENDS over the side of the tub, sets down a book, and then withdraws. The wetted-down crown of Kierk's head sinks even farther into an aquatic, steamy meditation. The bathwater is opaque with soap, and from his point of view his legs are stuck out far beyond him, partially submerged, the hair on them plastered down—how incredible it is that these are my legs! That I am the thing that owns them! How responsive they are to my commands, how my toes leap to wiggle, how my ankles flex in response, how one leg lifts out of the water at a mere whim and then drops back below! How good it feels to be so submerged in this warmth but to have my feet, *my* feet, on the cold porcelain edge of the tub; how the sensations differ if the point of contact shifts from the pads of my toes to the expansive roundness of my heel, the change in the texture. How different it would be if these were a young woman's legs instead of a young man's! How different but how the same.

Sinking down until he is fully submerged he enters a warm world filled with the background hum of being underwater. From his mouth he releases a few peaceful bubbles. Then comes the knock.

His head rushes out of the water and he pauses for a second, his body totally still, the tub now rocked by waves. The knock had been unhesitant, aggressive and loud enough to shock him. Could it be Carmen or Alex? They probably would have called first . . . or maybe it's the mailman, or a neighbor, or someone confused, or some other improbable event, people come to doors all the time—the knock comes again but much louder this time, like some huge fist is slamming at the door. After a frozen moment Kierk rises out of the tub and wraps himself in a towel. Everything is slowing down. He leaves wet footprints behind him on the tiles to the short corridor leading to the front door. A few steps forward on the cold, slippery wood and then another knock booms and he can see the door shudder on its hinges. He can't take his eyes off the lock which had vibrated violently but held. Then from the other side of the door there is a guttural grunt, the shifting of some large bulk, a huffing snort. A broad shadow can be seen blotting out the light, a dark line wavering. A form. There is the stamp of something large and almost hoof-like and another snort. Kierk's eyes are wide, his hair still plastered down, his skin frigid from convection and fear. He is suddenly sure that it is happening again. He braces for sound, for that unearthly hum, but none comes. In the waiting silence he wants to look into the peephole but he can't, he can't close that distance and peer through. What would he see? His heart is beating like mad. Paralyzed, he watches the shadow shift with a corresponding creak of weight. Three booming cannon-loud knocks in rapid succession are followed by a tortured vibration afterward. The door holds but now looks as if it is about to splinter into pieces, or the locks rip from their hinges. Then there is an angry huff and the sound of a departure, the quick fading of heavy, plodding footsteps. Kierk suddenly begins breathing again, not knowing he had stopped. He slowly approaches the peephole and looks through to the empty optically curving hallway, and then he turns and sinks down to a sitting position, his back against the door, his flesh wet and flush with goose bumps, his hands trembling, his mind racing over dark, impossible notions.

MONDAY

KIERK WAKES UP GASPING, vexed to wake by nightmare. Something had been trying to get at his face, at his eyes, and he's trying to shove it off but already it's dispersing into amnesiac dream vapor. Blinking and sweating, he realizes that he must have left the air-conditioning off as the entire room is sweltering hot and stuffy. Running cold water he takes a shower, but keeps going back to the knocking late last night, and has to remind himself that he did not dream it. It was too surreal to be real, too strange. Yet not a dream. Going over it in his mind he acknowledges some possibility that it had been someone from SAAR, or maybe even a Crick Scholar, even just a random stranger trying to break in. The other possibilities were too fantastical even to consider, and he kept aborting those halfway through. And finally the equally dark thought: that this is not a problem with the world, but the observer of it. Both now and perhaps earlier, that first night at the break-in. After all, auditory hallucinations are the most common, and a knock on the door is syntactically and semantically simple enough to be such an early mirage, the preface of something more dire.

Out on the streets he's still playing around with these notions but soon the reality of the hot complex world sandblasts them all away, almost like he really had dreamed the knock, and there were daylight explanations for everything; his worries were dissolving in sun. Outside the CNS he stops to squint at the bloodred spray paint near the front door: DOUBLE TROUBLE LIVES. TORTURE FOR TORTURERS. He watches the snub-nosed toy of a plane drawn steady across a perfect blue far above . . .

. . .

DURING A BRIEF MEETING LAST Thursday Max Pierce had been skeptical that Kierk had done animal research previously, despite Kierk's insistences. In response Max had asked Kierk to perform two surgeries, one implantation and one decapitation. It was an obvious challenge and Kierk, pissed off, had claimed he wouldn't need supervision, and is now regretting it.

There's a knock on the lab door, and Carmen peeps in at the scene: a stainless steel expanse, the thin alien elegance of surgical equipment, reflective pans, maneuverable lights, tubing and optrode-preparation kit, and Kierk, looking very serious in his white lab coat, sitting in the middle of it all. He glances up from the mouse he just anesthetized, which is shifting about on the metal tray it lies splayed on, its little feet flexing as if dreaming.

"Came in right at the worst part," he says.

Her hands in the deep pockets of her lab coat make her look like a child in a too-big suit. "I assume this involves some kind of pissing contest between you and Max?" Seeing Kierk's surprise, she says—"It was inevitable. Want some help?"

"Pull up a chair then."

They both look down at the little animal slowly breathing under Kierk's hand, its small pouch of a stomach rising and falling. Whenever Carmen sacrifices an animal she says a little prayer, like a Native American kneeling over a kill—thank you for giving yourself so that we might gain knowledge about the universe, and I'm sorry little mouse you had a short and confusing life and here we are at the very end of your mystery but maybe really it's not ending because time is an illusion created by our primitive mammalian consciousness, yes, that would be nice, then nothing, not even you, would be lost . . .

Kierk puts his thumb in the hollow on the back of the mouse's neck and grabs its tail with his other hand and with a simultaneous push on its neck and jerk on its tail, breaks its neck, which sounds like stepping on a small branch in the woods. The legs scramble around for a while as Kierk presses it down on the table. As the neurons within the mouse's half-gram brain necrotize and burst their ionic insides out into the interstitial space, the state-space of neural activity flexes into wild impossible shapes, a hallucination, the smell of its mother, the first and the last scent, her great mouse body curled over him and he is small again and blind in a richness of warmth and wood shavings and his siblings heaving around him like an ocean of belonging—neural networks are structured to be the most creative when they are dying, as if evolution was trying to ease the countless deaths it was built on.

Finally the legs stop convulsing and it lies still under the lamplight.

"I hate it when they do that," Kierk says, looking down at the still body that somehow already looks smaller. Here is the machine but where is the ghost?

Carmen hands him the trauma shears, which he holds in one hand while the other expertly stretches out the ruff of the neck. He snips the head off. Carmen notices how the muscles in his tanned wrist flex during the movement. He takes the head between gloved fingers, red and slippery now, and walks to the cryogenic storage. A single fat drop of blood hits the white floor.

Chatting as they do so, Carmen and Kierk go to get another mouse, trundling the anesthesia cart down the halls, pushing a little too fast, both laughing as the gas tank and monitor sway dangerously around corners and through doorways. Another mouse is retrieved, fished from its cage sleepy with droppings and shavings, put into the glass box, and goes under from the gas while scrambling against the sides. This time they harness it on the surgery table to keep it absolutely still. It looks identical to the last one, as the mice are as close as non-clones can get to a genetic monoculture. It's also transgenetic, bioengineered from conception to be a tool in research. Kierk opens one of its little milky eyes, uses a penlight to check that it's deep under anesthesia. First, as Carmen's gloved fingers pinch the ruff of the sedated mouse, Kierk uses surgical scissors to scalp it, cutting off the top of the animal's head skin all the way out to the ears. The bloody flap is removed, revealing the pink interior bulb. Carmen swabs away the little rivulets of blood using Q-tips dipped in alcohol diluted in water. Then both begin to scrub, clearing away not only the welling blood but also the slice-thin veneer of muscle and fascia that clings to the skull. Occasionally their hands meet as they both reach for something, sharing space perhaps more than necessary, occluding one another, bloody gloved fingers touching, a digital dance done in red. After a few minutes the mouse looks totally obscene, the most naked an animal can be with its revealed skullcap of solitary bone a shiny bulb reflecting the surgical lamps. Carmen forages for a bottle of bone softener while Kierk uses a scalpel to etch lines in the skull, digging little troughs that will help the bone dissolve easier. It's the same technique used by construction crews to break up a road. Carmen takes the bone softener and applies it liberally to the etched bare dome. While waiting for it to work she prepares the multi-array optrode implant, which will sit in the mouse's parietal lobe, serving as both a recorder of neuronal activity with its micro-tetrode core, as well as a diode which will shine light onto the local brain region, perturbing the genetically engineered light-responsive neurons around it. When the timer dings Kierk scrapes away the weakened bone like he's chipping away the flaking top of an egg. Together they follow the laminated notes over the desk (smeared with blood) for how to lower the optrode in. A complicated claw controlled by dials is used to descend the array to the appropriate cortical depth. Carmen gets the giggles at one moment when both of them are holding three different things in each hand, steadying the limbed machine that positions the electrode, just as the mouse briefly stirs, showing signs of waking, and so Carmen, still giggling, has to lean over and uses her mouth to dial up the anesthesia dosage knob. The knob is cold and awkward in her mouth, both of them laughing now, and Carmen then stands up, not letting go of anything, and, stretching, spits out the metallic taste in her mouth into the sink at her side, getting ready for some flirtatious banter as she turns back. But she finds Kierk lost in thought staring as the little mouse's belly settles into a steadier rhythm—what marvelous skin and globular eyes you have, and your splayed feet, the obsidian of your claws, the dome of your skull, and, inside that, the oracles of peduncles and ligaments and cranial webbing, and all the textbooks and anatomical drawings unfold before Kierk like a flip book, all primary colors of the capillary structure and strung-out webs of neurons, and then down at the cellular level, a galactic exchange of ions, those millions of little Maxwell demons of transport exchanging one for two, one for two in a steady windup of available work, and beneath that the equations and stochastic mechanics of thermodynamics and the exchange of heat, motion, energy, and below that, still flipping the illus-trated pages of the book of existence, the arcana of the collapsing wave-form, the quantum phenomena stuck in their multiple coexisting tracks, and Kierk knew that he could spend a whole life, an all-too-short span, sifting through the tottering and holed web of concepts stacked on top of one another in supervenience without ever ordering them correctly . . .

that all these levels dropped away like the sea floor, farther and deeper than anyone could hold their breath for—and then he looks up at Carmen.

"Hi," she says, smiling. From his gaze she knows she has interrupted something, and as he returns he pierces Carmen with those green eyes, a locust whine of green, sleeves of it in a thunderous forest bringing forth a memory long forgotten. Carmen has seen those eyes before . . . It had been dawn, and she, blushed with herself, in her yellow raincoat of youth and on her way to school hopping over puddles, all pink notebooks and ballpoint pens and report cards, had been confronted on the road by a fox not five feet in front of her, a fox with green eyes just like that. It had been frozen waiting for her to notice until she pulled up short and they stared at each other, speaking no language at all, Carmen's central faith shaken by such a thing, her unspoken belief in only bodies and languages had been uprooted, all done away with by those eyes screaming that within me is something else, an entire simulated world, mental phenomena living and birthing and dying in ferocious, pullulate growth, a whole ecology but internal, like it's climbing the walls of a space without walls, a presence looking out from behind the biological wet of those eyes. Kierk, in his motions and speech, points her toward this same basic question, somehow making it obvious that beyond her own enclosed world there was a whole other world, but this one was inside him. Biting her lip she considers—should a fox have such an effect on my ontology? Should a boy?

"Hi," he says, finally returning her smile. But now they have been staring at each other too long and the moment becomes self-conscious, so they busy themselves until it dissolves.

After finishing the electrode placement, they use a kind of liquid concrete to create a skullcap on their little patient, just like those on the rhesus macaques, molded around the long wrapped snake of wires that now sprout up from the mouse's head and connect it permanently to the recording equipment. The mouse is put back in its cage, a sleeping, healing husk. They wash their hands thoroughly, pushing each other a bit for space over the sink, which escalates into soapy water throwing. While hanging up their borrowed lab coats Carmen notices through his dress shirt the tattoos on his back and becomes insanely curious, but doesn't mention it, storing it for later with a small pulse of satisfaction. Instead she gestures as he rolls up his sleeves.

In small dark print up the inside of his forearm it reads: *Where Do We Come From? What Are We? Where Are We Going?*

She looks at him questioningly.

"The title of a Gauguin. It's hanging in the Boston Museum of Fine Arts. I only saw it once in person, and I got this immediately after at a parlor in Cambridge."

"It's beautiful . . ."

"It's the second question. It's that second question that has captured me."

"Okay, I'm going to show you something, but you have to take it to the grave, okay?"

Carmen, with a quick look around, wiggles down her jeans a bit, presenting to Kierk her left hip where there is, peeking out from behind the surprising red lace of her underwear, the black outline of a small dolphin.

"That. Is. Fantastic."

"I got it when I was modeling with my girlfriends in Paris. Nobody actually spoke French but we were in a French tattoo parlor. It was a mess. I don't know. I like it now because it reminds me of who I was. And who I am now."

"I'm so telling Alex."

He blocks Carmen's kick.

"So do you want to play hooky?" she asks.

They report back to Max and let him know everything went (Carmen's word) "swimmingly" and tell Max not to forget the mouse head waiting for him in the freezer. Kierk feels like he is the victor of this game and so he grins his best shit-eating grin at Max as they leave.

When Max hears their high-five before they get on the elevator his anger fades. Thinking of office romances brings only sadness. Karen's been avoiding him. Karen who up till now had always been drama-free, had always been wet and humorous (a sense of humor, when had his wife lost hers?), and it was that sense of humor, that thrown-back horse laugh, an equine whinny, even at her own jokes, that attracted him so much. Without her he feels like he is slowly reentering some sort of prison, that gates are closing behind him . . .

After their last liaison, Max had left to pick up Chinese food for his family. Then at home he had watched his son try to open the white box of fried rice, and Max had insisted—"Let him do it himself." And his son, who at that age should have been in school learning trigonometry, instead couldn't open even a simple takeout box, and after fiddling with it for a while (hands along the top, then the sides, then even the bottom) had just stopped and stared at it like it was the greatest puzzle in all the universe.

THE TWO FORMS BRUSH past Karen as they exit the CNS, so wrapped up in each other they don't glance up to acknowledge her. She watches Carmen double over laughing as Kierk is gesturing, and then they are out of view. Maybe just a year ago she would have disapproved, but now since Max and she had begun the affair (even though it feels clichéd to even think the word) she just wants people to do what makes them happy.

On Friday they had "stayed late to work"—Max had bent her over her desk and she had felt his hand searching her, a single probing finger that caused a whelming and responsive moan, the onset of her tic of shifting her weight from one leg to another uncontrollably as she waited, her ass in the air squirming, and then she had heard the zip of his zipper and his slow, teasing entry accompanied by slaps and gasps. Unknown to them a janitor had stood outside her office door paused in mopping. After they were done Max had, as always, slapped her ass one last time in appreciation and kissed her roughly, and then slowly that retraction of emotion had begun, that withdrawal like an undersea animal into its shell, a calcium carbonate composite of clipped words and clothing, and she'd still be hugging him to her nude body while he was fully dressed as he dialed enough takeout to feed three. Most of the time she tries not to think about it, not to think about his wife, or his kid, the morality of it, whether it was right or wrong, but just to be with him, when she could, when he could, because this intensity of being stood unsupported, un-needing of justification. Such thoughts keep occurring to her today; she's finding it hard to think, everything seems to whizz past. But then occasionally something like seeing Kierk and Carmen together slows it all down into an almost indefatigable beauty and stillness. Karen is so regular that just an absence of three days is enough to get the test. She touches her stomach. She is pregnant. All is phenomenon.

TUESDAY

KIERK WAKES UP, ROLLS over, painfully slaps his hand on the wall next to him, and comes to consciousness cursing. His alarm did not go off. Hastily he dresses, grabs his notebook, dons his new Mets baseball cap, and thunders down the stairs without waiting for the elevator.

Walking, he spills some spots of coffee on the burning pavement. Everything on Broadway dissolves in the omnipotent light—the smoke from his cigarette, his sneakers jutting forward in front of him, and people become whitewashed outlines; even the butt that Kierk flicks away vanishes into the light.

KIERK SITS AT HIS desk professionally, mulling over the meetings he's had so far this morning with Max and Karen. He'd told them he wanted to delve into pure theory, examining consciousness from a fundamental perspective. They'd disagreed, and now Kierk was thinking about the compromise they'd landed on for a first paper. The idea is to write up a review paper of the extant measures of consciousness, using his old computational model of the cortex as a test case. If the measures fail in application to give sensible values for a model of the cortex, such measures cannot be correct and a new one is necessary. So Kierk just needs to adapt the handful of measures invented by other theorists into heuristics he can apply to his simulated network. Since most had never been subjected to a test, the idea was to separate the wheat from the chaff in the literature. According to the committee, Kierk must complete this first paper to receive his PhD. But he knows the paper is pointless. Everything in the literature is chaff. Trying to communicate that . . . had been difficult. It's been too long since he's had a real professional conversation. Being alone for so long with only his note-books, Kierk's wondering if he has become an island ecology unto himself, if the population of his thoughts had become isolated, if the genetic bot-tleneck of founding effects had amplified into a full-blown speciation event and all that remains are centaurish forms, hopeful monsters.

He gets a text from Carmen that tells him to meet her and Atif. After hunting down the room Kierk finds the two sitting on a couch facing an empty chair, which Atif gestures at, smiling. Instead Kierk squeezes between them on the couch, the three now sitting in a row awkwardly.

He immediately leans down to tie his shoe. "We wanted to talk about—" Atif leans forward, then backward, to get line of sight, "—about doing some kind of joint project."

"Why ask me?" Kierk calls up.

"We have both read your papers. Obviously, we think such a pairing would be beneficial." Atif's voice is tinged with amusement.

"It would look good for the program if people coauthored," Carmen says as Kierk finally comes up, everyone shifting their weight on the squishy couch. "And—excuse me, Atif, sorry—also our skills are well matched."

"What would it be about?"

"Well. Atif and I have been discussing your research." She holds up a heavily highlighted printout.

"Why bother?"

"Fine. You don't want to look back. That's fine. But let's come up with something, the three of us. We have Atif's experience with primate research. My experience on decoding brain signals. And your experience on the the-ory side of things. Let's do something outlandish, attention-getting."

"What, like hook up all the monkeys' brains to one another?" Kierk says sarcastically.

"Actually . . ." Carmen pauses. "Actually, Kierk, that's an incredible idea."

"I was joking."

Atif says—"No, I agree with Carmen. Online communication from one animal to the other."

"And what would I do?"

"Well, what's your thoughts on it?"

Kierk sighs, but then his hands begin moving as he riffs—"Setting up a big brain made of smaller brains is probably best modeled based on natural brain development. In development brain regions have to come together, integrate themselves into one mind. How do they do that? Feedback. Like a baby finding its foot. All brains start out as many brains. All minds as many minds. They become integrated, rewired into a single entity, through feedback and reward. So we need to design it so that the, ah, monkey group mind, is constantly getting feedback and reward from doing joint tasks, and slowly their brains will interpret the noise they are getting via the implants not as noise, but as signal."

"*How to Build a Hive Mind* by Kierk Suren."

Atif, nodding along—"Starting such a research program would be no small thing."

Carmen's eyes are bright tunnels of light. "Listen, people have done brain-to-brain communication stuff but never as part of a systematic research program on consciousness. What's the bandwidth needed to form one consciousness out of many? And coming from the Crick Scholars! The history, the program, it's all there. A new frontier in the search for the neural correlates of consciousness."

Kierk shakes his head. "This stuff is just better and better mapmaking. Or worse, magic tricks."

"You act like everything is so incredibly problematic," Atif says, still half-amused.

"Do you know what a pitcher plant is?"

Atif nods. "Of course."

"Well," Kierk smiles grimly, "I think some ideas are like pitcher plants. And how happy do you think the one ant is that figures out they're in a pitcher plant?"

Carmen flings his own paper at him. "God fucking damn it, Kierk."

Atif looks shocked and unsure, but Kierk just glances down at the paper in his lap, the askew pages with his name on them. Carmen is waiting for him to say something.

"It's a career move."

An exasperated sigh. "It's starting something. Providing a reference point in the literature. Maybe it's flashy but that isn't inherently negative."

"This isn't how it gets solved."

Atif—"Do you think we will solve it in this room, now?"

"No."

"Then why not take the time to do this?"

"If you have strong enough arms, you can bail out a boat with holes in it forever. Even if it's unsound it never sinks."

Carmen, visibly frustrated, says—"So you'll just let it sink?"

Kierk looks down at months of his life in just a few pages of ink.

"Alright. I'll do it."

"We don't want you to do it if it's going to be—" Atif begins but Kierk cuts him off.

"If I commit, I commit. I'm in."

They all shake hands. Soon Kierk, standing at the whiteboard, is sketching out a concept tree, and it all becomes a game of intellectual tennis as the ball of the idea is bounced, served, returned, and the board fills up with diagrams of experimental designs, little monkey faces with lines looping between them, some math that Kierk came up with on the spot on measuring neural bandwidth. Quickly the whole expanse has been filled and Carmen takes a picture of it with her phone, then Kierk erases it furiously and they start on another.

AFTER LEAVING THE SHOWER Kierk picks up his notebook, flipping through the pages, looking at the dense blocks of paragraphs. It's more than he wrote in the last four months of California. Some spigot is open again, and with the notebook in hand he laughs for joy in the empty apartment. Shaking out his wrists and grabbing a pen, he flops down on the bed, his eyes burning, feeling like he is etching his thoughts directly onto the page he is writing so fast.

> *O Consciousness! To be working on consciousness again! It stokes within me a fire, it beats at my back as if the furies chase me and I flee laughing. It is my heavenly manna and my djinn lover and my assassin all at once. As I rise to its challenge strength flows through my frame, my intellect becomes a piercing lighthouse sweeping across choppy waves, and words summon themselves to me so that I overflow into prose. My cup runneth over. An energy hums in me with such intensity that I can naught but shout it into ink, all in reverberatory response to the very scope of the thing, a problem cosmic in its implications and reach. What a*

mighty thing, consciousness! What aspect of our world does it not touch? In science it shows itself across all hierarchies, all primary and all special sciences. It appears as the monarch of psychology with all other mental events its yoked subjects. Within neuroscience it hides as the intrinsic meaning of the alien popping of action potentials in the brain. It lurks in the agential equations of economics, pops up as the irreducible remainder after genetics has done its deterministic work, and down at Planck time it may even trigger the waveform collapse that transforms the mere relata of possibility into the definite fact of existence. Indeed, what other candidate for the noumenal is there? Look unto history and see all of it as the consequences of consciousnesses en masse! It is the foundation for all axioms in mathematics, the fixer of reference for all language, and the provider of the only indubitable certainty possible. It is the boundary condition for all knowledge! The domain of universal discrimination! It acts as the demiurge of all art, and yet at the same time it is also the audience, a double act as it both creates and gives meaning to the creation. If left unexplained, so far does its reach extend that no aspect of reality can be said to be truly understood. Not anything that flies or crawls. For what snapping amphibious creature first contained that divine spark? Did it first wink on in the neural nets of swimming hydras or did it slowly accumulate like dust over all biological processes? Was it brought about by predation, by the need for ambulation, avoidance, and planning on the millisecond timescale? Could it have arisen from such dark origins, as biblical as freedom arising only from the Fall? And what of its fate forward in time? What beautiful consciousnesses will one day occupy the tangled bank of our solar system if we can only persevere? Consciousness spreading the torch of its internal light from Earth to Mars, to Europa and then Enceladus then even beyond, past the Oort cloud, to that beckoning bright density at the center of the Milky Way. Beginning in one ocean and after a landlocked interlude ending in another, a wine-dark sea far more vast. Yes, the history of the world has been, and ever will be, written in consciousness, and they are the only words that matter! Imagine then what that final theory will entail, what it will give us: a sensorium syntax as pristine as mathematics, a dialect of pure consciousness. Imagine what type of alien utterances it will allow, for to write in such a language, to speak in such a language . . . No poet has ever come close. Words blow away as empty signs next to the white-hot heat of it!

There is something it is like to be! And it is not just mere being, which alone is no different from its antimony of nothingness, but rather the awareness of being, for that is sublimity itself! What greater gift can be given? I ask you this: what is a finer property? And how is it that of all imaginable properties we happen to have the sweetest? Roll the dice of all possible worlds and we stand upon the infinitesimally small face that happens to not just be but to also vividly experience being? How finely tuned this instrument of a universe! And thus with the perfection of consciousness comes its mystery, that ever-retreating hooded phantom, that which stokes the fire within me, nay, which sets me aflame.

The pen falls from his cramping fingers. His mind is a machine whirring down, and, the notebook on the pillow beside him, Kierk, spent, nods off in bed. As he approaches the edge of awareness everything becomes images, castaway dreams, the phantasmagoria remainders of the night's thoughts. His breathing slows. And somewhere in this state the thing that haunts him rears again; it comes upon him as his mind becomes less constrained, liquefies, becomes a world without a physics. And it is here that the mystery of consciousness approaches him now with its impossible body, that body which has forever fled before him, sounding into the deepest pelagic depths, but which now is a barn-size white outline distorted under the surface of the ocean; he paddles around to face it in the dark rolling sea, his hair plastered back with ocean water, his nude and pale kicking legs white in the moonlight, white as its totemic face during its massively silent approach; he can see it coming, filling his view, it looks unflappable, terrifying in its bovine complacency, its total imperturbability by any act of his, white and hanging like a mountain as it comes upon him, its face smooth and placid like that of a newborn, those wise eyes bearing incommunicable knowledge, its tight mouth keeping unspeakable secrets, a mouth that does not move even as its words boom in Kierk's mind. **O small silly fish, you have learned nothing**, says that whale, that leviathan, his muse.

WEDNESDAY

KIERK WAKES UP IN the slow sluggish pools of himself. There had been no alarm. As he flexes the long extensions of limbs there is an unfolding as feeling rushes down to inhabit each moved appendage, like an insect unfurling at dawn and rubbing its legs sticky with dew into a high whine. Kierk begins to go about the business of waking up; his feet touching the cold floor, brushing his teeth, splashing lukewarm water on his face, finding clothes—and by the time he gets to the lab it is lunchtime. He can tell because when he walks in there are twenty heads fixated on their monitors, all with earbuds in, masticating the lunches in front of them as they stream TV shows.

The scene disgusts him so much he makes a U-turn and wanders the CNS, eventually stopping in to visit Jessica, who is eating pistachios and analyzing fMRI data. They chat as she shows him the data from a preliminary study she just ran. In front of her the computer displays a heat-map of all the areas of the brain where there is a statistically significant difference in blood flow between when subjects saw a visual stimulus and when they didn't.

"What's that?" Kierk asks, pointing to an aurora borealis on the screen that stretched beyond the brain into the surrounding black.

"Oh, that's the air. There are always statistically significant differences in the air around the head. But see, I picked this as my region of interest." She points to a small patch of the brain. "I mean, otherwise you'd get responses to the stimuli, like, everywhere, even outside the skull."

Kierk rubs at his forehead, moans.

Later in his peripatetic wanderings he remembers the cerebral organoids. It takes a while to find the molecular biology lab, and the door has an electronic lock which he swipes his card at but it beeps red. Then through the window he sees the girl who had helped collect the samples at the first meeting, whose name Kierk forgets. She's pipetting something, but on seeing him heads to open the door.

Kierk holds up the small scar of a dot on his forearm. "Hi, remember me, you took some of my DNA?"

She laughs. He continues—"We're on weirdly intimate terms because you're growing neurons made from my skin cells, but I'm afraid I don't remember your name."

"Amanda. But come in, come in, sample number three."

He's ushered into the bright white lab space, which is also pulsing with loud pop music from some unseen speaker system.

"So where are the mini-brains? Or rather, where am I?"

"They're not really visible yet. Tomorrow we're going to move them to the bioreactor so they can grow a 3D structure. So maybe a few weeks from now they'll be good-sized. I can, however, show you this." Amanda guides him back to a row of shelves bearing long terrariums, the panes of glass steamy and revealing the shadowed outlines of flowers. Amanda opens a pane and Kierk, with a sound of amazement, reaches in to touch one of the fleshy petals, which is as blue as the sky on a perfectly clear day.

"But roses can't naturally be blue," he says, delicately playing his hand over them. "These must be transgenic."

"A thousand-year dream. Kind of a pet lab project."

There's the sound of footsteps and Amanda quickly closes the terrarium as another researcher arrives, giving Kierk a questioning glance. So he takes off, promising Amanda he'll be back to check on the organoids when they're fully grown.

Karen looks at him as he enters and he knows she's wondering where he's been. It's three in the afternoon. Kierk, mercurial, spins slowly in his chair. People come and go, images change on screens, pixels rearrange themselves. He's so bored he considers jumping off the roof of the building just to have something to do. Instead he finds a bathroom, and after locking the door behind him, masturbates thinking about both Amanda and Carmen, the two switching places in his fantasy like the sides of a Necker cube.

What the nature of that final stage is—how an individual invents (or finds he had invented) a new way of giving order to data now assembled—must here remain inscrutable and maybe permanently so. Let us note only one thing about. Almost always the men who achieve these fundamental inventions of a new paradigm have been either very young or very new to the field whose paradigm they change. And perhaps that point need not have been made explicit, for obviously these are the men who, being little committed by prior practice to the traditional rules of normal science, are particularly likely to see that those rules no longer define a playable game and to conceive another set that can replace them.

Kierk sets down Thomas Kuhn's *The Structure of Scientific Revolutions* and leans against the stacks in the cooler airs of the library. He repeats the passage, two, three times to himself to recommit it to memory. He's spent the last hour browsing the stacks or in the reading room with his feet up, balancing his chair on its back legs, reading Husserl.

When he heads back to the lab the passage plays on repeat in his mind. He stops on a sidewalk bisected by the sharply thrown evening shadows of buildings, completely still, as a vision comes to him. His readings have prompted a series of abstract visualizations as he realizes that science itself can be seen as a kind of continuous metaphoric riff, a poem that starts with base everyday concepts and then proceeds by mapping them onto nature in ever more complex combinations, an endless metaphor proclaiming that x is like y is like z, that atoms are like solar systems, that nature takes the place of the breeder in natural selection, that the human brain operates hydraulically via tubes like an aqueduct, or with mechanistic gears like a clock, or carries digital information like a computer . . . this is like this is like that, a staircase of mappings, with Parnassus always retreating before the canticle of science. The Long Song. And when it's over? At the end of science, when all the questions have been answered, is that not when humankind's work truly begins in the construction of the one true religion? What will those cathedrals look like? Erected on strange worlds, against skies so different from our own . . . Looking up at the blinding coin of the sinking sun Kierk imagines a firmament filled instead by the dense cluster of the center of the galaxy, against which grand temples stand in sharp twilight silhouette.

At that moment, if you zoomed out above Kierk, the surrounding city blocks would be cinemas of motion, with the blurs of people flowing like red blood cells through an artery as the shadows retreat and lengthen, and at the foci of the camera would be Kierk, an unmoving dot, a fixed point.

SEVEN STORIES UP IN the CNS Mike Benson is staring intently out a window holding a can of soda. On his way back from the vending machines to the fMRI lab something had caught his eye. Mike is pretty sure that motionless figure a block down is Kierk. He's just standing in the middle of the sidewalk, looking down at . . . nothing?

"What the fuck?"

Mike shakes his head and mouths something under his breath. At Harvard he had met plenty of people who thought they were smarter than they were, but none of them had pissed him off quite as much as Kierk. And at least at Harvard there had been the great equalizer, those widely used study drugs like Modafinil, Ritalin, and Adderall. Before midterms or finals he would take a handful in the afternoon and study straight into the night, taking breaks only to do drum solos with his pencils. It was like catching fire. The neuroscience major had both a hard-core advanced calculus requirement and the GPA-destroying organic chemistry. Classes that seemed intractable but which he burned through with Adderall. Taking it was as if a fog he didn't know he'd been living under his whole life cleared briefly and the goal of studying and academic testing crystallized into what it truly was: rigorous rule-following. The point of it all was to manipulate the symbols given to him (they could have been Chinese characters for all he cared) in a way that conformed to the rules given by the textbook or professor. And the Adderall gave a pleasant tingle when the grind of rule-following led to correct answers. Nearly everyone he knew took them, so he never gave it a second thought. Everyone was just neurons, after all. So who cared if those neurons were in a natural or artificial chemical bath?

Comparatively, Mike likes to imagine that Kierk would have dropped out of Harvard. In his mental rant he'd say—You know next to someone like John von Neumann, you would have been nothing, a gnat, let's see how you feel when measured up against someone who was really a genius . . . but then the imaginary Kierk, whispering back at him, grinning like the Cheshire Cat—Ah, but there aren't any John von Neumanns anymore, are there? There's just me, now why is that? Kierk, now raving against him—And whose idea was it to ensure maximum destruction by dropping the bomb kilometers above Nagasaki? See, I like geniuses who only destroy themselves. You know you'll win in the end, Mike, I'll self-cannibalize, and the last thing to disappear will be my smile . . .

Mike finishes the last of his soda with a gulp, looks around to make sure he's alone, then angrily crushes the can and drops it into a nearby recycling bin.

THURSDAY

KIERK WAKES UP AND immediately knows that this day will be a dance with the noonday demon. He had felt it building yesterday, in his discontentment and restlessness. This has all happened before. Like the first organism crawling onto mud and into air from the sea, he attempts to make it to the bathroom. On the way he gives up and lies splayed out in the center of the room, examining the grain of the carpet. When it hits Kierk like this it's just something he wakes up, not an exogenous force but rather (and this is much worse) completely internal. He tells himself that is what happens when he turns his intelligence inward, like a microscope warping back around to examine itself, seeing without the gauze of delusion—and what a fucking pathetic mess he is. Some small metacognitive part of him knows that this will pass. But right now he cannot see how one can make only finite moves when bookended by infinities in both directions—Dante would not even let me into hell, I without fame or infamy, no, I would contribute only to the howling gale of the angels who remained undecided.

Forcing himself to stand, he takes a hot, steamy shower in the complete dark. With the glass shower door shut from the outside, it is shaped like a sarcophagus. He sits with his legs drawn up and begins to sob, his chest shuddering for air, a few burbling gasps, but no tears come. One hand comes up and with a vicious slap of impact rocks his head back against the slick wall. Around him in the dark, a crowd of ghosts stand. They were also the ones who slaved and obsessed, but for them there was never the chance encounter, the lucky break—the Kants never woken from their dogmatic slumber, the

Wittgensteins without a Russell, the William Jameses without a brother to compete with, Darwins without John Henslow, Matisses without Stein, Wolfes without Perkins, Carvers without Lish, Eliots without Pound, all of the poor, poor dreaming patent clerks—the faceless ghosts stretch out into the steam, a nameless legion standing over Kierk, severe of countenance, dressed in all clothing and all manners from antiquity to the present, ready to embrace him like an army from Hades. Silent of judgment, they merely watch him sitting there with his legs drawn as he speaks a mantra with water running over his lips—"I am twenty-seven and I have done nothing with my life. I am twenty-seven and I have done nothing with my life."

Two years ago during a hot summer in Madison, Wisconsin, Kierk had developed a swollen lymph node in his neck. Concerned about lymphoma, a series of tests had revealed nothing, but the ENT doctor had strongly suggested removing Kierk's tonsils. A week into the healing process, Kierk, clad only in his boxers, standing in front of the sink getting a glass of water before bed, had felt something give in, cave away, at the cauterization in the back of his throat. And blood had come fountaining up, forcefully spurting from deep in his throat against the mirror in front of him, and he, thoughts wild, had rushed downstairs, trying to gurgle to his roommates to call 911, but the two had just stared at him in frozen shock until Kierk had dialed himself and spoke through the gurgling stream. Blood trailing behind him, he had made his way downstairs and outside into the hot summer night. The dark street was lined with quiet houses and there was a warm breeze. A roommate of his called to him from the steps, but Kierk, his naked chest covered in blood, stood in his boxers alone in the street. With every beat of Kierk's heart there was the high-pressure squirt of blood, a hiss from the back of his throat, and he forced himself to calm his heartbeat, to be unafraid, to confront the paradox here—the more I react to the current situation, the more afraid I become, the faster my own heartbeat will kill me. He thought of Keats, who in his medical training knew that the telltale drops of bright arterial blood after his cough were a sign of consumption, that there was a fatal flaw within himself, that something had cracked and could not ever be repaired, and that he would die and die young, all from flecks of red against an embroidered handkerchief. The whole of the human body only contains around four quarts of blood. Calculating out the loss, Kierk estimated he'd be dead in less than thirty minutes. He felt immensely nauseous, all things surging, and knew he was swallowing incredible amounts of the stuff, but if he vomited he would

almost certainly tear the artery further and then he would surely die. So from
the ambulance to the hospital, where a panicked ER doctor sat with his knees
straddling Kierk's chest and with a metallic instrument shoved down Kierk's
throat trying to pinch off the spurting artery, to the wheeling blurring room
that was rapidly being prepared for surgery, Kierk's entire will was bent to a
single aspect, an iron thought: Do. Not. Vomit.

Lying on the table in the white room, clinging to consciousness as anesthesia had pumped through him, Kierk had heard clearly and loudly a
man's direct but gentle voice address him. It spoke as if from inside his
skull—Don't worry, remembering how to die is just like riding a bike. You'll
be fine. It's just been a while since you've done this.

After waking up in the hospital with his throat re-cauterized, no one
could say if it would ever reopen. Even now he can feel it, the raw spot in
the back of his throat, a ticking biological time bomb. He thinks—at least
Keats, by the time he was my age . . . It is my name which will truly be writ
in water.

Standing outside the glass box of steam, one would see only his hands
moving up and to the sides, as if seeking a way out, as if exploring the contours of this trap, the trap laid for him by passion and ontology—that his
impossible muse existed only within the strictures of an environment he
hated. To be cursed is to be drawn to something that vexes you to madness.

After some interminable time he manages to stand and turn off the
shower. He doesn't towel himself off but merely returns dripping wet to
his bed and lies under the covers, his hair plastered to his forehead, naked
and wet as if just birthed. Under the damp covers, he begins to slap himself
in the face. Again and again the sound of flesh striking flesh. Tortured
breathing from the rumpled mess as hands, one after another, hit with
blinding speed at his cheeks, his eyes, his forehead—"I hate you. You weak,
pathetic—I—Hate you—You are nothing—Stupid—Stupid—Stupid."
Over and over until his face aches and his hands burn and then, right at
the climax of it, he pauses and his hand curls into a fist. He eyes it for a
moment. A brief thought—this is ridiculous. And then in punishment
for the detached irony of its tone he punches himself right in his eye as
hard as he possibly can. The impact sets everything to white and yellow
for a moment and he curls up, cursing, burning. He lets out a few sobs,
buries his head in the pillows, groans. He stays there. The tension in him
slowly unwinds, ebbing away along with the pain. Eventually he enters a

state which is half dreaming, half waking, and there, amid the changing languages and settings, the props and actors, he is not himself, and he can watch the stirrings of memories play across a screen not his own . . .

WISCONSIN IN WINTER WAS a whole planet removed from the sun, a frozen globe of thought. Kierk was a riding phantom blowing past the dead Midwestern cornfields at 100 miles per hour in the night. Already drunk, he'd been swilling beer for the entire ride, the interior of his falling-apart car lit only by the dashboard, opening bottles between his knees, the grain silos blurring past. Kierk had felt irreducible, violently American, and young.

On Kierk's arrival outside the huge house Antonio Moretti came out and greeted Kierk with a welcoming handshake, taking the bottle of wine Kierk bought and giving a small frown at the label. The modern house was made entirely of glass with walls that unfolded into the surrounding nature during summer. Impressive square footage. There was a garage with a hanging kayak in it, a projector screen for interviewing postdoctoral applicants for the lab, a CD collection that took up a wall, a fireplace, a sauna, a Jacuzzi, an outdoor brick oven, a small shooting range, a barn with the ass-end of an SUV protruding, a liquor cabinet that stretched across shelves, and a wall-to-wall glass atrium filled with trees and plants. Antonio Moretti himself was unnaturally tall, and bald, and always impeccably dressed. European and old-world cultured with an MD in psychiatry, he was like a benign Hannibal Lecter.

That night Antonio brought him upstairs alone, and they talked next to bookshelves which spanned the entire length of the study . . .

"And did you read his autobiography?"

"Yes, one of the best."

"You are young. Did you read Schopenhauer—"

"No, I never did. Excerpts though. The world knot. After all that's what we're trying to do. Untangle the world knot."

"You never read him?"

"This is a beautiful house, by the way, I can see—"

"Thank you. More cognac?"

"No, no, thanks, I'm good. I'm still working on this one. Oh hey, is that Will Durant?"

"Yes, I read all of it."

"All of it?"

"Yes, all eleven volumes. Yourself?"

"I read, ah, the Egyptian one, I remember that. Ancient hieroglyphs, so interesting, a language no one could understand but it was all around them. Like something aliens would write in."

"I called you away from the others to talk, man to man."

"Oh, okay."

"You read literature, Kierk? You write? Do you chase many girls?"

"I'm not sure—"

"Because you're distracted easily. You would rather talk about problems than publish. The papers must be published. Carthage must be destroyed. It has not even been invaded."

"It's taking . . . It's taking longer than I thought."

"Carthago delenda est."

"Every time I go to write all I see are the holes."

"What holes?"

"I sent you that review, by William James, of Spencer's notion of the conformation of inner relationships to outer relationships. James's critique is pretty devastating."

"It's a hundred and fifty years old."

"But we're just retracing the same ground all over again. We're just repeating history. Over and over we keep making the same mistakes. Every-one who works on consciousness does."

"You are lazy."

"I've been trying to get a clear view of all this—"

"To be a scientist, to be anything of caliber is difficult. In fact, it is nearly impossible. You wish to study consciousness, you must, as they say, do the time. You must do boring, menial work, sometimes. You must finish papers."

"I'm trying. I stopped writing fiction, like you told me to. I haven't written a word since you told me to stop."

"You are clean. As drug addicts say."

"Yes, I'm clean."

"Good. One cannot be an artist, and a scientist, and a philosopher. To be that is to be a monster. A centaur. A freak."

"I understand."

"How many times have we had this conversation?"

"If you'd let me do it my way I could—"

"You must stop reading as well. No literature. And you must not, must never, read philosophy. It is especially dangerous for you to read philosophy."

"I'm just trying to help, to shore things up, to focus on the foundations."

"The foundations can be reexamined forever, an eternal return. We must progress. Or what are we doing here? Or more specifically, what are you doing here?"

Later, back in Madison, Kierk trudged across the dark frictionless expanse of the Capitol Square at some late hour of the night, craning his neck to occasionally look up at the golden angel. Beneath her the dome of the capitol building was breaching snow and wind like the rounded head of a great white whale. There was a notebook clenched in his cyanotic fingers. Not dressed for the weather, Kierk couldn't stop shaking.

"NOTHING LESS!" Wiping at his nose with his sleeves, his eyes darted around in the freezing dark of the square, chasing phantasmagoria.

"I WILL ACCEPT NOTHING LESS. AND YOU DON'T HAVE IT. BUT INSTEAD OF LETTING ME SOLVE THIS PROBLEM YOU MAKE ME POUR WATER INTO BOTTOMLESS JARS. BOTTOMLESS—" Coughing. Kierk couldn't stop coughing. His lungs felt like they were burning up from the cold.

Trudging back to his apartment he was a solitary figure weaving down the emptiness of State Street. At the door his hands were so chilled he couldn't put the key in. Finally inside the building, he had a violent shivering attack on the concrete stairs, sprawled out, biting down so hard he thought his teeth might crack, his legs kicking and curling in an automatic attempt to generate heat, followed by the intense cramping pain of blood coming back to every limb and digit.

Then on to his little studio apartment he'd moved into just the month before, where the sink always dripped and the kitchen countertop was peeling off in rusted strips. Nothing on the walls, no posters or pictures, no furniture, just a nest of clothes spread out across the floor between tottering towers of books. At the center was a yoga mat with a comforter laid over it. Tiredness had hit him like a wave and he collapsed. In the closing of his eyes, there was the unhearable sound of a choice being made by someone young. Tomorrow he would confront Antonio about the irresolvable problems in his theory of consciousness, telling him the truth Kierk had kept hidden so long, and damn the consequences.

FRIDAY

KIERK WAKES UP AND the world imposes objects and is in turn filled by them. The first thing he does is lie quietly and inspect himself, examining his mind. Right now it's merely a dollhouse set in plastic, and while he knows the basement is flooded and heaving with crocodiles, they are confined for now. This is not depression but realism. Bouts of realism that can last anywhere between a day or a week. Once one stretched into a fully agonizing month. In the mirror he examines the bluish hue that is a half-moon arcing along his right zygomatic arch.

Of course he knows that he could be diagnosed, that there was some box in the DSM that, once checked, would allow him official approval to oscillate between periods of euthymia and dysthymia. He knows what the research on the statistical link between creativity and depression or bipolar disorder is. But Kierk thinks that drugs for mental illness are more like chemotherapy—the medicine was not actually targeting what was wrong and correcting it, but rather both the mind and the disease were poisoned and it was hoped that the mind could withstand more than the disease. Besides it all seemed rather non-neural and pretty psychologically obvious: Kierk's capacity for self-hatred was as expansive and powerful as his ego. In fact, one necessitated the other.

It's already late afternoon, so when he does finally get to work Karen has left for the weekend. Kierk just sits down in his chair, seeing only a few other souls in the office, and right after he sits the lights automatically wink off for the weekend and he is illuminated only by the blue light of his computer screen, his head now hanging in his hands. There are seven missed messages on his phone.

THE STROLLING GROUP IS a slow aggregation of bodies, a disordered row, an isolation of some, a coupling of others. Eventually all the Crick Scholars are present. There are many lights and suddenly they are all very young. Mike walks with Jessica, both laughing easily. Alex lights up a joint and passes it around. Only Greg turns him down.

"There's a hookah bar south of Houston that's supposed to be good. Follow, boys, follow." Carmen leads the way. In front Atif is so tall he has to bend underneath the low-hanging crossbars of construction scaffolding. The rain begins to play its small hands against the pavement. Everyone's hair gets wet as they traverse the glistening pavement, the piles of trash and crushed cans. Alex nudges Kierk and smiles.

"I heard you weren't in lab today. Or yesterday."

"Yeah, I was, ah, working on something."

"Are you okay? Just because, I mean, you did leave the top research lab on consciousness. In the entire world. I heard, well, many rumors. Was it some kind of conflict? Or something else?"

In front of them Carmen has focused her hearing laser-like behind her. Kierk looks over harshly at Alex. "What you know, you know."

"So," Leon interrupts in his thick German accent, "do you find the curriculum of the program appropriate?"

"The required course we have to take on professional development is pointless," Kierk replies, "if you haven't noticed already."

"It is only every other week. You do not believe it will be useful?"

"I don't believe in professional development."

Leon smiles an ursine smile. "Yes, it is nice to be younger."

Now the storm has passed itself off as a mood of the sky. Their speech increases in volume as the sky thunders a bit, as the cars honk off into distances. They all pause at a stoplight, waiting, looking up sporadically. The deep oil spill of a summer storm is spreading over the city. Carmen's hair flashes around in the warm wind. Atif pulls up his hood, a tall shadow dreaming up rain. The pressure of the air is a vanguard, lifting the hairs on the back of Kierk's neck. Carmen's delighted face is upturned, she sticks her tongue out briefly, a quick dart, smiles.

The hookah bar is under a mirror of itself. Two callers yell for them, beckoning north or south. Atif leans his tall frame over the steps and begins a raucous dialogue with them in Hindi. The rest of the group mingles on the concrete until Atif emerges from the conversation and ushers them up to the top hookah bar, the bottom caller now shouting insults, the top caller shouting back.

Inside everyone sits down in a circle. "Pomegranate, let's get pomegranate!" Jessica says amid the low chatter, to which Carmen rolls her eyes.

Atif orders several rounds of a drink that Carmen doesn't recognize, but after three her opinion of them becomes quite high. The Crick Scholars quickly begin to amass empty glasses. Eventually they turn to discussing how they ended up in the program, going around the circle. Greg is last.

"I got my PhD in computer science from MIT. But since the brain's the most complex computer, my principal investigator encouraged me to apply to the Crick Scholarship."

Kierk is looking at Greg the way one might look at a hideously deformed child, pity and disgust warring on his face.

"What did you just say?"

"That my advisor—"

"No, about the brain. Being a computer."

Carmen shaking her head "no" at Kierk. Alex puts his head in his palms.

"Well, like, okay maybe it doesn't have von Neumann architecture, but instead like a parallel processor. It's definitionally an information processor."

"That's totally vacuous. Everything can be described as an information processor. Literally any system. Information processor just means change occurs."

"But, hmm, but computers systematically transform inputs into outputs."

"Again, totally vacuous. Rocks do that."

"What, how do rocks do that?"

"They take in all the forces acting on them and produce an output based on their previous state."

"Yeah, but those aren't symbols. Like a symbol processor."

Kierk's voice is slightly slurred. "Oh come on. The representational structure of those symbols is only there because humans designate it. Because consciousness fixes it. You could read out Shakespeare from a rock with the right reference codes. Brains are about as much computers as rocks are."

Greg, flushing a bit—"But computationally brains are much more complex."

Kierk sighs, shaking his head—"Greg, something being a computer or not has nothing to do with complexity. You can build a universal Turing machine out of like a hundred Legos."

"I know that!"

"Do you think a Turing machine made out of one hundred Legos is a mind, or a brain?"

". . . No."

"So why would you claim any kind of an identity relationship?"

Mike has purposefully started up another conversation with Jessica.

"Listen, I see what you're driving at," Greg says over them in his adenoidal voice, rubbing the carbuncle on his nose, "but, well . . . I'm an eliminativist anyways. Consciousness is an illusion."

When the server comes up Atif waves him away. He wants this to play out.

"And I stand by that," Greg is saying, defiantly.

"How? How can you possibly?" Carmen is replying, exhaling hookah smoke.

"Listen, don't ah, don't treat me like the enemy. I just think consciousness is basically an illusion."

Carmen, after passing the pipe—"Greg, you just denied the very thing we are all here to study. An illusion for whom? Illusions are perceptions."

"People used to think the Earth was at the center of the universe too!"

Carmen is shaking her head—"That doesn't follow at all."

Kierk sets down his glass hard. "Galileo took observers out of science on purpose. He bracketed them to the side to make it simpler. Now we're the ones adding observers back in."

"But I would say that—"

"I would question your ability to say anything once you have denied your own consciousness. You must not cut off the branch you are sitting on."

Greg is shaking his head ruefully—"But how can you really believe that there's fairy dust sprinkled onto brain states and that it's just magic? Is that what you actually believe?"

"Oh! Oh yeah, Greg, yeah, that's what I believe. That's the appropriate response when I accuse you of begging the question. That I must believe in fucking magic. *Petitio principii,* Greg, *petitio principii!*"

"Kierk, you are so loud right now, just like, tone it down, man," Mike says, leaning over.

Kierk stares at Mike, but then looks down at his drink. Much more calmly—"Consciousness is a natural phenomenon. It has properties, scope, character. It's the world in which you live day in and day out. It is unlike, in kind, anything else in nature. It has a greater claim to existence than anything else. Consciousness is not the hypothesis. The outside world is the hypothesis. If you cannot accommodate consciousness in your natural order, then the natural order must expand. Your reality is too small. The sole reason anyone wants to eliminate consciousness is solely to keep materialism, which is a metaphysical position, intact. While some philosophers may warp themselves that much, a true scientist could never throw away the obvious, in-front-of-their-eyes evidence. People who say consciousness does not exist are like Parmenides arguing his way into believing that change does not exist. But change is undeniable. Or Zeno making his argument that there is no motion. Yet motion is undeniable. Consciousness is undeniable. And since it exists as an undeniable natural kind, then not all things are physical, therefore physicalism is false. *Ex cathedra.*"

Jessica laughs, defusing everything, drawing everyone to her. "Another lecture, Kierk! And you say you don't want to be an academic. But it doesn't answer the most important question. What's the next flavor of hookah we should get?"

The conversation moves on. When no one is looking Carmen winks at Kierk. Atif orders more drinks. Greg tries to bring up the subject again, but both Kierk and Carmen simultaneously (not quite however, Carmen moves first and Kierk copies her so fast as to appear simultaneous) ball up their napkins and throw them at Greg, and in reply Alex throws his at Kierk, to general laughter. Kierk stands up jokingly as if to leap over the table at Alex and Alex makes kissy faces at him. Kierk goes out for a cigarette and most of the other Crick Scholars join him, leaving just Greg and Leon at the table.

Sitting back down with everyone, Carmen recognizes that it may be difficult to ever get back up. She hasn't eaten dinner (a yogurt only, scarfed down standing before she headed out tonight), so four drinks in she begins to gulp water in an attempt to make that feeling of weightlessness leave, that spinning where she circumvolves around an internal axis. Carmen wonders abstractly whether she would go home with Kierk if he pursued her tonight. Her expectations have a color to them now and she can feel them in her body.

"You are all very rambunctious," Leon says, adding another drink to the glass castle he has raised around him.

"Leon, we are not splitting this bill up evenly," Kierk says in laughter. The waitress brings over a tray of shots, starts distributing them to rising noise.

Carmen—"Alright, alright, shot time. Hey! Hey! Shot time. Everybody. Everybody. You ever do a neuroshot?"

"This is so sad and uncool I want to die," Kierk gets out before Carmen hushes him.

"Okay!" she says, looking around brightly, everyone's gaze on her. "You take the shot, and then, for a chaser, you recite the twelve cranial nerves." To all the protests—"No, no, it works, it works! Alright. Ready. Set. Go!"

The whiskey burns down their throats, and then, in a drunken chorus searching for synchrony:

"Olfactory, Optic, Oculomotor, Trochlear, Trigeminal, Abductens, Facial, Vestibulocochlear, Glossopharyngeal, Vagus, Accessory, Hypoglossal!" they finish together, wiping their mouths, making faces.

"Oh Oh Oh, To Touch And Feel Virgin Girls' Vagina And Hymen," Carmen yells, doubling over.

Alex holds up a hand, waits for marginal silence and then says— "On Occasion Oliver Tries To Anally Fuck Various Guys. Vaginas Are History." Leon finds this particularly funny, pounding the table so hard the drinks dance.

Atif, kindly, turns to Greg, who hasn't spoken much since his last attempt, and asks him what kind of research he was doing lately. Greg has been nursing a sweating glass of water, and sips it nervously before answering.

"Um, the first project that kind of got me where I am was on artificial neural nets and learning, we were—" the hose is passed around him, "—trying to get the neural networks to be able to distinguish between male and female crabs. Like, photographs."

"Wait, wait," Carmen says, leaning in, looking around. "You trained neural networks on crab porn?" The table explodes into laughter. "Like, what grant paid for this? Did they know they'd be giving you money to make neural networks that can watch crab porn?"

Greg has become quickly uncomfortable, and instead of answering he just blushes violently—the conversation sees it, turns away.

"Are you excited to meet some of the guest speakers?" Jessica kindly asks into the air, with Mike immediately answering in the affirmative.

"I heard that Antonio Moretti might speak," Jessica says. Everyone looks over at Kierk, who shrugs his ignorance.

"There's some philosophers too, I heard. Dennett might give one next year," Alex says. Kierk mimes vomiting all over the table, making the requisite noises, and keeps at it, growing ever more dramatic, until everyone is hysterical.

Atif keeps ordering more of those drinks, and soon the tent of the conversation collapses under its own laughter. Kierk watches in a kind of gross fascination as the empty glasses around Leon grow into a small colony. Carmen keeps lightly touching the arms of both Alex and Kierk. Whenever she does, Jessica lets out a small, barely audible sigh and vigorously stirs her drink with a straw. Greg excuses himself early and there is a minor commotion as he attempts to extract himself from the table. Nearly free, he trips over Mike's foot and Mike tries to apologize as Greg nods and leaves in a hurry.

"Poor kid. I seriously did not mean to trip him at all."

Carmen bursts out laughing. "Crab porn! He made neural networks watch crab porn." She sighs wistfully. "That's all they knew, the poor things."

Later, after extracting themselves as a group, they open the door and step into summer night air charged by the storm.

Carmen looks up just as lightning splits the sky into halves, breaking the roof to let in its fingers, and she jumps a bit and then is still, thoughtful, listening to the echoes of the low roll. She rarely thinks about the obvious fact of the matter. Drunk, the idea of a universe that contains both the subjective and the objective electrifies her, awes her, all these miracles living out the minutiae of their days, like markers, signs put out by some greater power saying—KEEP LOOKING! And there is the further thought behind that one: if something as strange as consciousness is real, what else is real? Couldn't then God be real? How can a universe brought into existence randomly have such a spectacular property?

To Kierk the city has become a dream machine, the consciousness of cars and people and dogs and pigeons and the on/off binary thoughts of streetlights—Fuck, I am so drunk . . .

Carmen is slowly twirling in place.

"Alex, fuck, we're drunk," Kierk says.

Alex puts his arm around Kierk's shoulders, sways with him. Kierk looks over at him, his solemn face barely containing itself.

"No homo."

Alex collapses on the steps laughing, steadies himself on the railing. Kierk thinks about finding a place to piss, dismisses the idea.

Mike and Jessica grab the next passing cab, and Alex has another immature laughing fit with himself as he watches them get into the cab together.

"Carmen!" Alex yells, hugging his knees while sitting on the concrete steps. "We're getting rained on! Carmen! Do something!" A gust of wind nearly bowls Alex over and Kierk comes out of a nearby alley zipping up his pants. The city inhales and exhales in great whooping winds. Kierk watches a trash barrel go clattering down the sidewalk, a sight he finds inexpressibly beautiful. Leon stands by the curb, a solid statue of drunkenness.

Carmen, giggling in the street, her shirt clinging in the wind, hails down another cab. Atif has been standing in the same spot looking skyward, and now he turns to get in the cab with them but the other four are already piling in.

"Whoever is going north or northeast!" It is unclear to any of them, even the speaker, who says this.

Leon is in the front seat and Kierk, Carmen, and Alex have all piled into the back.

"No room?" Atif calls from outside.

"Hey driver, room for one more?" Carmen says, leaning forward. The driver shakes his head, so Carmen scoots up on Kierk's lap—"Come on, I'll sit on a lap, pleeaaasse." The driver shakes his head again, so Carmen leans out the window.

"I'm sorry!"

"No, no, it's not going to be a problem," Atif says, before he waves to everyone, then moves off into the storm, a tall stumbling hood of rain.

The interior of the cab spins like a washing machine. Kierk rubs his eyes. The three of them sit with knees brushing in the back seat of the cab, watching the lights blur by, driving past reaching trees. Kierk runs his hands through his hair and realizes he is far drunker than he thought—those trees really look like they're reaching out toward the cab to grab it. He rolls his window down so it all becomes summer air. Droplets of rain spurt in and Carmen reaches over him and splays her hands out to catch them.

Then her hands go to his face—"I didn't want to say anything but I noticed this." Hands at a tender place above his eye, cold and wet fingers, small, against heat. "How? Why?"

The cabdriver tells them to roll up the window.

Kierk suddenly knocks on the cabbie window from the back and leans forward under the gaze of Carmen and Alex and the driver. Kierk smiles a half-smile, a wry smile he smiles when he knows he is being charming as fuck.

"Hey buddy, you know the ducks here in Central Park. I was wondering if you knew just where those damn ducks go in a storm like this?"

There is a pause.

"Kierk, that's not Central Park."

SATURDAY

KIERK WAKES UP WITH an awareness that something is present, some source sitting at the center, warping everything like the Great Attractor, but his minimal consciousness cannot distinguish between modalities so he can only make out that there is a thing attending the stage, a giant object of unidentifiable geometry, and then as the buzzing of the phone drives him open more fully he realizes that this great central thing is pain, that there is an ice pick being driven out from behind his eyes, that everything is exploding and this pain is omnipresent, a brute fact, irreducible. He is hungover. Groping and groaning, he tries to find the buzzing sound somewhere in his bed.

It had been Carmen but he hadn't gotten to it in time. Kierk considers going back to sleep but he knows that he can't under this siege, his head is full of marching orders, of things going off everywhere, watercolors splashing against the bone walls.

Before calling Carmen back he's got to do something about his head. On the way down in the elevator he's leaning against the back of it like it's the only solid plane in the entire universe. Then, three donuts and two coffees later and a close incident in the restroom where he ran the water and stood by the sink and debated making himself vomit just to end the nausea, he staggers out not feeling any better, and now on top of everything else he's full of greasy donuts. Crossing through Union Square Park, Athena and her chisel go to work again. He nearly screams aloud at the sudden tap-tap burst and sits down clutching at his head on a still-wet park bench.

An old lady covered in pigeons on the opposite bench watches him as he fumbles out his buzzing phone and answers.

"What? Sorry. Hello."

". . ."

"Are you as hungover as I am? What the hell happened at the end of last night? You and Alex got home okay, right?"

". . ."

"Is this a joke?"

". . ."

"How? Where?"

". . . . . ."

"Yeah I'm here, I'm just—fuck. Are you sure? They reported his name?"

". . ."

"No, I don't, I'm in a fucking, I'm in a park. How did it—"

". . ."

"He fell onto the tracks?"

". . ."

"Because I have the worst hangover of my life and I'm not really processing this. Are you sure this is true?"

". . ."

"Well, yeah, okay, that's pretty sure. And there's not some other—"

". . ."

"Point taken. Fuck. That's just—"

". . ."

"Do you need anything, are you okay?"

". . ."

"Well, what should we do? I mean, he didn't have anyone here, right, no relatives here. Everyone was back in India. He said he had some friends from Oxford."

". . ."

"Yeah, that's fine, let's meet up. We can get lunch. Is it weird to get lunch? It's weird."

". . ."

"No, thanks for calling me. Talk to you soon."

Kierk sets down his phone. The air turns to stone. The birds of talk fall about him. All around the park the colorless green ideas are out sleeping furiously, making their beds amid the abandoned top hats of rain, spouting stalks, maybe Atif's soul was out as well, out in that quiet haunting of mist, the sound of words on a tin roof. All around him dew evaporates, rising up to heaven. The old lady surrounded by pigeons is still looking at him from the bench opposite his. His migraine is no longer a migraine. It is something else. The interplay between the light and fine mist becomes a study in thanatology, as do the words, the heartbeat in his ears, the pain in his skull that he is suddenly so incredibly grateful for, the slow-motion movement of people, violins of thought going off quietly in the background, everything is rising into evanescent form, the world is a ballet dancer doing a slow leaping grand jeté as gravity lets go and then everything is rising, rising, and right then he feels the violent vibration of a passing subway train underneath him. The pigeons, their rounded bodies steaming with *élan vital*, make a collective decision and all arc to sky.

KIERK AND CARMEN SIT in a local deli, the surreal bustle of customers around them. Hunks of white processed chicken glisten up at Kierk. His sandwich is a tombstone of meaning that he can't stop staring at. They'd shared a quick hug when they both arrived. Carmen's face is puffy from crying, her hair secured up in a short bun by a big blue hair clip, and she's wearing a faded T-shirt that reads COLUMBIA. Her stainless steel water bottle sits next to her sandwich, which she also hasn't touched.

"How did you even find out?" he asks.

"The local news sites were reporting that a neuroscientist at NYU got hit. My friend forwarded it to me. I don't even think the department knows yet."

"So, how did he . . . He was drunk?"

"The station was empty, there was nobody around. I feel so guilty . . ." She takes a long sip from her water bottle.

"Christ."

"What time did we leave the bar, do you remember?"

"We took a cab, right? I think I remember a cab." Kierk is rubbing his head.

"I think it was around two . . . I don't really remember either. We took the cab, and Atif walked."

"Right, he walked . . ."

"This is what I can piece together," she says. "We get in the cab, and he walks. But the storm is really bad, so he takes the subway. He goes to the Bleecker Street Station, which is only like, a block or two away. He probably wanted to take the 6 uptown . . . and that's where it . . . happened."

"Christ. I mean, do you think he'd just never . . . like, what, taken a subway?"

"Listen, we all need to go to the police together and make a statement."

"A statement about what? He must have fallen in. He was drunk. It happens to dozens of people every year. And he was just monstrously unlucky."

"We have to tell them. Like, how are they to know he was at that hoo-kah bar?"

"Why do they care?"

"So they can do their detective thing. So that they can detect."

"Carmen . . . What are they going to detect?"

"So you think it was an accident?"

"Wait, so you think it *wasn't*?"

". . . He could have been pushed."

"Don't do this."

"Listen, let's just think about it. Okay, it's like 4:00 a.m. in this station. There's nobody around. Very few subway stations have cameras, by the way. I looked it up online. So let's say somebody comes up behind him. Atif's drunk. That person shoves him off the platform just as the train is approaching, just as it's coming down the tunnel. It's basically the perfect crime. Everyone thinks it's an accident. The police don't even investigate."

"Jesus, thought a lot about it? I can barely deal with this hangover." Kierk rubs at his face, massages his temples.

"No, but this is odd: I think there's almost two hours between the time we left, or when I'm pretty sure we left, and when he gets hit and the ambulance responds."

"How do you even know when the ambulance responded?"

"The police file everything online now. It's all available. The ambu-lance responded at 3:47 a.m. but we left the bar at like 2:00, as far as I can put together."

"Poor guy probably just stopped to puke."

"I'm afraid that's what the cops are going to think. But they wouldn't—"

Carmen leans in, whispering, "—they wouldn't understand the sensitive nature of his work. So of course they're not going to suspect anything."

"What's there to suspect?"

"Don't do that."

"No, I want you to say it."

There is a stalemate as they both stare at each other.

"Fine, I'll say it," Carmen exclaims. "They won't suspect he was murdered because of what he does, what he did, what we all do. He's a scientist who studies consciousness. Was. Studied."

"Carmen, this is . . ."

"How can you of all people say that? You saw what they're capable of. And you heard about what happened to Melissa Goldman, right? She got that box of bomb materials. What if SAAR was involved?"

Kierk shakes his head. "Atif had just arrived. He was barely part of Melissa's lab."

"But that's just one possibility. Like, we know a little bit about what he was working on what with our joint project, but what if he had been doing more than that? Maybe he wrote somebody an email with something in it, something that would cause somebody or some group to . . . terminate him."

Instead of responding Kierk takes a long drink of water.

"Come on, it's not so far out there."

"It's pretty far out there. Okay." Kierk keeps rubbing at the chisel in his head. "And, well, to be honest, I don't trust it because it's a view that relieves responsibility. We got him drunk, okay? We took shots and drank all night and he walked home and got hit by the goddamn subway train. Like being hit by lightning. Totally random but possible. But if someone murdered him it's not our fault, you see. Because you pleaded with the taxi driver, right, but we couldn't fit any more and we let him walk home and he died. It's Nagel's moral luck. But we still feel guilty. And it sucks. But honestly, I didn't even know the guy. Not really. Someone who could have been maybe a friend, a coauthor, he's dead. I don't know what to say. The universe is purposeless."

Carmen stares out the window for a moment, silent, but her mouth is working and she's shaking her head slightly.

"Listen, I didn't mean to imply you are, you know, making this up."

"Fine, fine, you believe whatever you want, okay?" Carmen begins getting her things together.

"Oh come on, I'm just trying to prevent—"

"Listen it's okay, I just need some space right now, okay?"

"Okay. Hey. I'm sorry."

"Okay. Bye."

"Bye."

He watches Carmen leave, her water bottle clanking. Kierk's sandwich glares up at him accusingly, demanding an explanation for its own obscenities of meat. He can't eat it. He feels he might never eat anything again. Perversely, at the same time he feels the need to move, to exercise, to run himself down.

Wrapping up the sandwich in a napkin he exits the deli. It's not long before he finds a homeless woman propped against a wall reading a mystery novel to give it to. As he walks away he begins to speed up, first walking quickly around other pedestrians but soon he's jogging, lightly at first, and then running, then sprinting, all the way back to his apartment building, racing up the stairs and throwing open his door and scrounging around for his running shoes and exercise shorts, breathing heavily.

Kierk takes off down the watery streets, the air hot and compressed and wet in each breath. He runs without a destination, progressing randomly, taking side streets and looping back, stopping to orient himself only occasionally as his endorphins battle his queasiness. He waits for the cross signs at streets, jogging in place with the pedestrians. Soon he begins to run straight out, zigzagging across streets to avoid having to wait, his sneakers throwing up flecks of water that wet the back of his shirt. Kierk feels that he is always flipping between two modes of thought when he is running, like looking at a Necker cube. In one mode, he is a homunculus guiding the machinery of his body faster and faster, driving it to ignore its small complaints, a small squatting demon behind his eyes. In the other his thoughts expand, lose precise form, bind with his flushed body to become a single identity, so that he is every aching muscle and gasp for breath, embodied and expansive. Today is like that—his sneakers are soaked through, he can feel his toes squish with each step. He sniffs deeply, smelling morning petrichor. His hangover throbs with each step, but he actually likes it now; the dimensions of his hangover are in some ways appealing, a presence he knows, and he's never stopped to appreciate exactly how maximally annoying and painful a hangover of this magnitude is, how it has a warp and a shape to it, a distinct brutish thing unto itself, and isn't it morally obvious that something is better than nothing?

As he runs Kierk's thoughts wander to Atif, whose departure is so sudden it feels like something as delicate as a soap bubble was popped. When Kierk imagines the underground scene, the suddenness of it, he sees Atif's skull coming apart sensibly, like a jigsaw puzzle hammered in midair, and then through the open remainder of the head would pour a parade of images and thoughts, all the silk Technicolor memories from childhood cartoons to personal sex scenes, all slinking and bursting forth in a great cavalcade, a world compressed like pressurized air inside a skull. But then he thinks about what really happened. Just a bunch of gray mucus expelled.

Soon he finds himself inexorably approaching the rain-washed sign that reads BLEECKER STREET STATION. It sits in the wet air like an eye, an omen, and Kierk spends some time in front of it with his hands on his knees, breathing hard. There are a few people milling about, coming up from Lafayette Street, but mostly the rain has driven everyone away and the streets are quiet and humming with a humid heat. He imagines the way Atif must have seen the sign in the drunk dark. After walking around the different entrances he finds the one that would be closest coming from the direction of the bar and Kierk takes the stairs down.

The subway station is a jar of hot air, a yellowing chamber halving away at the sides. Kierk, trying to look casual in his shorts and sweated-through T-shirt, descends into a thing organic with heat and grime. The hot air down here hasn't been cut by the rain, so he's flash sweating and it feels like he's breathing inches away from a pot of boiling water in this stuffy annex that empties out into just a few turnstiles. He imagines Atif coming thundering down here drunk, lightning like shuttering camera flashes behind him as he stumbled from one side to the other, a hand went out, caught the wall by the staircase, lingered on the spot that Kierk's glance lingers on now.

Kierk leans over the turnstiles with their blinking green lights, looking out. He doesn't have his wallet, so he cocks his ear for sound, hears nothing, looks behind him, then backs up a good ten feet and sprints forward and hops over one of the turnstiles with the ease of a former track captain.

The platform he emerges onto extends far to his right, only eight feet wide, a thin curving line all the way to the end, and is devoid of all but a single figure, a homeless man wearing a tan trench coat and a red baseball cap, slumped down. Across the crisscrossing black beams and dark tracks on the opposite side, isolated as if on a distant moon, a few forms sit on benches.

It's even hotter here on the platform. Wiping his forehead, Kierk turns and begins walking down the long curving platform. He realizes why it's so empty: it must be 105 degrees down here. Nobody in their right mind would be down here if they could avoid it. He wonders—if he had heatstroke now on this deserted platform and collapsed, how long it would take for that lady on the opposite side to notice and call the EMTs. How ironic would it be if he cooked his brain like a pan of sizzling eggs just feet away from where Atif had bit it just hours before—what the fuck would anybody make of that? He almost laughs, but pants instead, thinking about everything Carmen had said, but now the emptiness and the heat adds a dimension of seriousness to her claims. He looks warily behind him to the lonely turnstiles. The air is subterranean here, a thing made of ground-up earth, fresh from the city's granite bowels, and Kierk could detect the aural stink of decomposition, but thinks he is probably imagining it. He wonders where along the track Atif's body had been obliterated—kinetic energy deposited on a scale that would do nauseating things to a rag-doll entity like a human body. The remainder of it would be smeared the length of the track. How did they even clean that up? Hoses? Spear up all the bits and pieces with trash pickers?

He reaches the other end of the platform, which totals by his estimation maybe three or four hundred feet in length. But the entire thing is very narrow. If Atif had been standing not with his back up against the wall, and someone had come up behind, there was very little room . . . Kierk shakes his head, looking around. Immediately past the turnstiles on this side of the platform a wall ends the pedestrian section, but the platform ledge actually continues, cut to only a minimal span of less than a foot. The man with the red baseball cap is hunched against this nearby wall, not looking up at Kierk. Around some wooden benches Kierk sees dozens of scattered purple pamphlets. He picks one up, reading the blocky yellow letters on its cover, THE THREAT OF SCIENCE, which continue haphazardly on the inner folds: SCIENTISTS SAY THEY WANT TO REDUCE HUMANKIND TO BIOLOGY. BUT EVOLUTION IS UNSUPPORTED BY THE FACTS! SCIENTISTS WANT TO SAY THAT FAITH IS JUST A CHEMICAL REACTION IN YOUR BRAIN. BUT THE HUMAN SOUL CANNOT BE REDUCED TO THE BRAIN!

Holding the pamphlet, Kierk turns to the man with the red baseball cap, who has stood and begun to shuffle toward the end of the platform.

"Hey! Did you see who left these here?" Kierk shouts over the rumble of the train passing on the far side. The hunched figure speeds up, and, as Kierk watches, vanishes out onto the thin continuance of the platform edge and into the catenary mouth of the tunnel. It is as if the man just pierced some veil of dark and disappeared.

"Hey!"

Jogging forward, Kierk slows as he approaches, growing wary. Looking around, the platform is still almost empty. So Kierk places one foot on the protuberance, has a hand against the tiled station wall for balance, and leans out into the tunnel, trying to see how far the ledge extends into the tunnel. It continues as far as is visible, hundreds of feet out, until being lost from view, and is almost hypnotizing in its curve. He expects to see, in the dark, a figure hugging the wall far down, slowly creeping away. But instead he sees nothing. Had he hallucinated the entire thing? No, the man had been real. Kierk hears a squeaking directly beneath him and looks down. Locating the sound in the mess of sundry takeout and pulped newspaper waste stuck up along the tracks, he sees the rats, three of them, suddenly foregrounded, two paused in movement, the third scurrying amid the garbage, and it's one of the paused ones that draws Kierk's attention, one of the little dark forms that Kierk can't quite make out—it's on top of something, clutching its little paws and mouth around it, gnawing something glinting like the head of a mushroom, something with the nail still attached, a small stub, a brown big toe, and it comes to Kierk in a revelatory rush that there must be many little unaccounted bits still out there, being gnawed upon, taken off to chthonic nests, serving as rotting birthing beds for hosts of hairless rat litters, mewling cannibalistic nibbles out of a rotting—

The crumpled pamphlet dropping out of his hand in shock, Kierk is backing up, he's turning as the leonine roar of the subway train approaches, he's beginning to run, hitting the turnstile so hard he bounces off one of its edges, lets out a yelp at the pain in his hip, rounds into the empty corridor, takes the steps three at a time, nearly losing his balance on the slick top step, then is off like a shot down the street, where he loses himself among the people, the vendors, the bicyclists, and Kierk is slowing now, calming, still breathing heavy but just walking now, until, several blocks later, he pauses and, leaning against a brick wall, comforts himself in the propinquity of the crowd.

It couldn't have really been a toe. Nor could the man with the red base-ball cap actually have vanished. The heat had to have created a mirage, a short hothouse dream, an underground nightmare; the poet in him said *ignis fatuus*, the scientist said not color constancy but thematic constancy, the philosopher said it was nothing but the mummified gauze of expecta-tion, and if he unwrapped it in slow trepidation he would find just a collaps-ing emptiness underneath as nothing was holding the form to begin with. And what of the knock at his door last week? Perhaps another symptom . . .

Standing outside, rubbing at his hip and wincing, a smiling college-age girl hands him a glossy pamphlet protesting NYU's aggressive buying up of real estate and its effect on the local community. Kierk thanks her, but once he's a bit past her he limps over to a recycling barrel to throw it away. As he crumples it up he realizes that the pamphlets in the subway had all been brand new, shiny, like someone had been handing them out there and had dropped them. The man who disappeared into the underground? If that hadn't just been a symptom of the heat? Maybe he had also been handing them out there late last night, and Atif had come up, said something, they got into an argument . . .

Kierk limps about for a long time as night comes down, all the way to the docks. By then it is dark out, and the city lights have switched on, and in the still-hot blackness he looks out on the lit figurine of the Statue of Lib-erty. His thoughts are like the bodies of black waters making their way down streets, alleys, across cobblestones and pavement and concrete, submerging street signs, a wash of mannequins and paper and garbage and trash barrels and eaten-away photographs and that creased pamphlet, all slipping softly in the night into the Atlantic, a dark sheet bending over the dock and into the sea. What is it like, to see that bright headlight thundering down, to be doomed by clockwork and automata? What is it like to be struck and be so violently done away with, to know that it was all leading up to this, that every choice you ever made had led you here, to this absurdity of fear? What is it like to be? Turning away from the water, he looks into the trees lining the dark, the streetlights, and beyond the city howling in steel and glass, the backlit stumps of gargoyles leer down, whole skyscrapers have become obelisks of light. Something swoops above him, dark forms, a whole cloud of them, a sentence of wings, the arcane and familial lives of bats. In their movements they are an unbreakable code.

SUNDAY

KIERK WAKES UP IN the long troubled highways of dreaming's end, and, rising, nearly sleepwalks to the bathroom and only comes to himself fully with his hands on the sink. Some time is spent admiring the deep blush of bruise, a spreading purple stain across his right hip.

It is upon checking his new NYU email that Kierk finds it, addressed to all the Crick Scholars as a group.

> **Subject line:** *To Whom It May Concern*
> **Subject body:** *You are very far in a strange land. This is where my boy died in a strange land. The school did not have air-conditioning when he was a child. Think on this. He loved cricket as a boy. Then he discovered computers. He begged me to buy one and he spent so much time learning. His first love is here with me. She helps me write this. She cannot believe. He was the most intelligent, kind young person. I hope you got to know some of that. What happened to my boy? What happened with my boy I am talking to everyone. Asking everyone. No one will tell me anything. Accident! He was so smart. Nothing makes sense. Please help me. I need help now. I need help now God. What happened to my boy?*

Kierk takes a deep breath. He is surprised to find his eyes watery. Then—what can I say? Your boy has been turned into a smear underneath New York? He shudders at the harsh language of his own thoughts, closes the email, then opens the window, smelling the humid air of the city.

It's Sunday, so Kierk, in jeans and a V-neck shirt with the Mets cap Carmen bought for him pulled low over his eyes and his notebook at his side, walks around for a while until he finds a brunch place with outdoor seating. There, amid the chatter of couples and families, he orders an omelet, a stack of blueberry pancakes, three cups of coffee, and a glass of orange juice. Strangely, Atif's death has stoked his appetite, a hunger not just for food, but for everything. Hungry hungry living hippo. Smacking his lips contentedly as he finishes, and still flush from the stipend money, Kierk tips forty percent then drains the last of his coffee. He heads up Broadway and finds himself back near Union Square Park, in which an art fair is being held. He is quickly immersed in the panoply of colors, tents, and people.

The tent city holds a throng of amateur artists displaying their wares. Kierk sits in the middle of the art fair, quickly getting lost in the maze of his notebook. The best writing Kierk does is always when he completely forgets himself, becoming only a vessel to pour words through, and at the end of such a period, after the deep immersion of a paragraph or a page, he'll look up and it's like he is coming up from being submerged, a sensorial beaching—what whales must feel when they break sea and sky.

It is in this manner that he writes furious and unusable sentences on the steps, too pure and unrefined to be sensible, all keenings of language, bellows of description, words like birch logs falling from the sky as white as the cataracts of dreams, decimating the park around him, and he builds rickety ladders as high as siege engines, things of an unknown purpose, absurd, words dedicated to the people around him, the stone they walked upon, even the mundane, hell, even the fucking squirrels that come and peer and jeer and run about in primal mischief, all in an effort to manifest an intentionality which would allow him to transcend himself, become a true artist, an immanent being of perfect empathy, and only as the sun sets and the quiet death of day descends does he come crashing down, human once more, nearly broken, sunburned on his arms and the back of his neck, the pages of his notebook flapping in the wind, crushed cigarettes discarded in a circle around him.

Nothing he wrote that day is very good, he thinks. Soon the day has gone to the dogs, run off with itself, and Kierk is left still and alone at an outdoor cafe, lighting his umpteenth cigarette, exhaling the evening. The haunting of the day by Atif's ghost has made the world a beautiful sensorium. Brief studies and prolegomena on thanatology are scratched out, rewritten, played with vaguely. He picks at his fries, throws one to a brave albino pigeon. He thinks about Atif's mother, the coffin, the prodigal son returning to his homeland in pine . . .

Is there anything worse than for a parent to lose a child? And then with a sharp intake of sadness as if cold water had doused his chest—where does she think I am? She must think she has lost me.

At a secluded section of a nearby street he paces up and down before working up enough courage to dial an old number from memory.

"Hello?"

Her voice, the first voice, hits him so hard and so fast he immediately begins to blink away tears, a sudden buildup of glottal pressure in the back of his throat, and in an instant he's crying, turning away from the street to face the brick of the building.

"Oh, Mom, it's me, I'm so sorry. I'm so fucking sorry. I should have called six months ago. I shouldn't have cut you out like that."

"Where were you? Where were you? Honey, where were you?"

"I . . . I was . . ."

"What happened to you?"

"I got . . . I got lost somehow. I just . . ."

"Oh, honey, you're okay, you're okay. You're okay, right?"

"Yeah, I'm okay. I'm in New York . . . and I have a job now."

"A job? And you're okay? You had me, I was so, I couldn't—"

"I should have called you when I came back east. I'm going to come up and see you, okay, I'm going to come up and see you the moment I get a break here, I'll get like, a week off and I'll come up. I was just so ashamed about leaving Madison and disappointing you, and the fight we had then, and everything. I was just so ashamed. I'm so sorry. It was all just too much, it was too much. But I'm back, Mom. I'm back."

"Honey, the things I said, I think about it every day. I didn't mean them. I love you and your life is your life, and you can come up anytime." Even over the phone it is clear she is shaking with emotion. He can see her perfectly, sitting in her reading chair and tearing up, probably in her old ratty robe and pajamas, the TV on mute, the small terrier a half-moon of fur poking up from the dog bed.

Even long after the conversation is finished Kierk is still seeing her, imagining her rinsing her cracked feet in the sink before going to bed as she always had, all the protections built up around his heart breaking and washing away.

THE SOUNDS OF NEW YORK City at night boom in ambulance wails that seem purposeful attempts to demonstrate the Doppler effect, which mix with the sounds of conversations outside her window, and Carmen is listening to it all while lying on her bed, a book splayed in front of her, as, unknown to her, the phone in her discarded pair of jeans is buzzing because Kierk is calling her.

She has spent a lot of time contemplating Atif in the background of her day. Reading the email that had come from Atif's mother had caused her to feel like her chest was collapsing into itself, and she had put a hand over her mouth and sobbed. She had written and deleted and rewritten again and deleted again. Nothing could answer the question.

So instead that morning she had called her parents for a long conversation, mentioning nothing, reveling in the sameness of their complaints and concerns, their well-worn tracks. Then she had taken a walk around her neighborhood in the East Village, where even the trees had seemed mournful, the day overcast. She'd spent the rest of the day holed up in her apartment, filling the hours doing yoga naked on her yoga mat while listening to NPR, making coffee. Everything tasted very good and the yoga made her body feel useful and functional. Now she's reading one of her favorite books, the correspondence between Descartes and Princess Elisabeth of Bohemia, which ranged in topic from the mind-body problem to fluctuations of their health and fortunes to the punctilious dissection of Descartes' theories of atomic vortexes. Carmen reads this the way some people Bible dip, finding random things of relevance, adumbrations of their daily lives, poetry. When she shifts her weight on the bed she leaves stamped outlines of her sweat on the sheets. Her fan is on full blast, and she could really use some frozen yogurt, but the thought of putting a bra on seems infinitely difficult so she's meandering between Descartes' belletristic linguistic bows and winking compliments and Elisabeth's occasional playful teasing to thoughts about death and how quickly life can change, how precarious everything really is. Occasionally she perceives an aural hallucination refusing to fully manifest, an acknowledgement of the K-sounding specter that is haunting her thoughts, mondegreens of his name in the clicking—*kah*, *kah*—back-and-forth movements of the fan, but she is refusing to ruminate on him, she is relaxing, happy, a thing alone and content with herself, with her body, her body that is like a hot collection of parts discombobulated about her, hair sticking to her forehead, unconsciously a fingernail is picking lint out of her bellybutton, one of her legs is up and stretching itself using a bookshelf on the nearby wall for leverage. Next to the bookshelf, are postcards announcing various art exhibits from the local galleries, along with a black and white NYC calendar, fitting the theme of her whole apartment; even when the city was separated from her by only a brick wall she still had gifts from it, a mute boyfriend expressing its love via fliers for concerts, found playing cards, little knickknacks from the city. Some people Carmen knew who lived in New York City for awhile become ironically muddled in their relationship with the city, but not Carmen, she loved in a pure fashion. A few of the things that hung on her wall were the products of taking art classes early on at Columbia University, amateur but talented drawings of buildings, courtyards, and her favorite, which hung by her bed: a negative-space self-portrait of just her own form, posing, one leg slightly behind the other.

Covered in sweat, Carmen finally drags the standing fan closer to her bed as far as the cord will reach. The air blasts her in the face and she sighs, the pages of the book now flapping wildly. The book itself had actually been a gift from a philosophy of mind professor whom Carmen had appreciated and thought of as an excellent teacher. He had even written her a graduate school recommendation (this is in contrast to the professor, who, in talking to Carmen after class one day had experienced a devastating attraction—a seismic mental event that had tilted his mental life on axis, had nearly led to the dissolution of his marriage, and had made him late for class several times because he was sitting in his office crying and occasionally pounding the desk in tortured abstinence, all of which Carmen still knows nothing about). When the professor was first explaining Descartes' theories, Carmen, a freshman, had apparently posed the exact same question that Elisabeth (a potential intellectual equal of Descartes, being adept at mathematics and severe of beauty and thought) had originally posed, the primary objection: If the mind and the brain are different substances then how can they interact? Minds and bodies. Bodies and minds. Two substances which Descartes had never been able to reconcile to the Princess' satisfaction. And so the professor had given Carmen the book as a gift. On receiving the correspondence between a princess and a philosopher, Carmen had thought that this was exactly the kind of fairy tale she was interested in. Reading the letters always begat a strange sensation in her, and it was this sensation that kept her coming back, rereading. It is perhaps too strong to name this sensation as déjà vu, but each sentence unfolded so naturally to Carmen that the motives and similes and metaphors and metonyms and the overblown compliments and obsequious mannerisms were all hiding something so clear: that these supposedly platonic letters between the princess and the philosopher were a code written so large they could only be read from a great height, dug in deep trenches into the earth like the Nazca Lines in Peru, and, given the right altitude and perspective the true message jumped out—Love! Love! Love! These were love letters disguised as letters of philosophy, and as she read them she would catch herself, unexpectedly, almost absurdly, crying over them, or having that tingle spread down her spine over them, because she could see this deep implicit longing on both sides, two people who had connected across historical events and social structures, both equally amazed that the other existed and expressed interest in them, yet they had missed each other, could never reconcile their different positions and worlds. An impossible situation, neither ever married, they had only a dozen visits between them but so many words. And every time when Carmen got to the end and read of Elisabeth's reaction to Descartes' death, when Elisabeth claimed that she had lost the only true friend she had ever had, Carmen would always break down and weep for an epistolary love affair four hundred years gone. But it is so lovely and sad that she reads it when she can't sleep, like now, because her mind has been spiraling lately, concentric, always beginning with Atif but then jumping out to the suburbs of history, and then the whole of the pale blue dot, to all those who have lived and died—Descartes and the princess in love but kept apart, primitive hunters dying far from their beloved gatherers, all one hundred billion souls that have existed on this planet, until Atif became a semiotic signifier for the entirety of the sadness and the too-soon-ness that was human life . . .

A group passes her second-story apartment and their conversation breaks her from her meditative state. Stretching, lissome, she reaches over to the bookshelf and reshelves the book of letters, then says aloud to her apartment—"Whatever, I'm still alive"—and gets up to pull on her pants. Checking her phone she sees that Kierk called but judges it's too late to call him back now, and she can't decide if she's angry or pleased that he called.

She pulls a shirt over her head, still braless, at this point unable to bring herself to give a shit whether it will turn see-through in any kind of harsh lighting. Shuffling on her sandals and grabbing her purse she heads out into the wasting heat of the night to get frozen yogurt and take a walk while it melts, to perform those small daily things which are the rituals that separate the living from the dead.

And it is there she will resolve to do all she can to answer the question that has been put to her.

MONDAY

KIERK WAKES UP FULLY aware and feeling an urgent need to move. Rising, flipping sheets onto the floor, he does a set of exercises until he is panting red. Breathing deeply in the bathroom light he looks at himself. He's always been able to put on muscle quickly, filling out his frame to its natural proportions. Patting his taut stomach he goes to shower. Under the water he soaps himself, pausing when he gets to his hip. Its bruise is in full bloom, still painful from his collision with the turnstile, and it is only then that he remembers everything that had happened over the weekend.

KIERK LIMPS HIS WAY to the CNS, an occasional hand going down to check his hip. Upon arrival he finds the halls eerily bustling, graduate students and technicians waiting for the animal elevators, the professors and administrative staff energetically popping in and out of rooms in what all seems a rude assault on mortality. It was as if Atif's death had never occurred. Karen waves at him as he walks in, as does Carmen, but she doesn't get up from her computer. His hip is so bad that he nearly lets out a yelp when he sits at his desk. He checks his email and, besides the unanswered one from Atif's mother that he avoids opening again, finds only a bland departmental missive detailing a "tragedy among the staff." It goes on to give a short biography of Atif and express its deepest condolences. He spends a while looking up the few short articles pertaining to Atif's death on local news websites. There is nothing on there that Carmen hadn't told him, just a low-resolution close-up of Atif's grinning face. There is no mention of the police, or any investigation.

The picayune events of the day pass him like flotsam; his hands move by themselves, doing without doing. It doesn't feel like he should be working. It's this feeling that eventually draws him inexorably to Melissa Goldman's lab. There he finds a more muted atmosphere. Only a few hushed whispers float over the maze of cubicles and computers. Atif's desk has already been cleared. On it is a cardboard box with ATIF written on the side. Inside there is a stack of printed-out documents, a small wrist cast for carpal tunnel syndrome, a number of pens, a set of headphones, a framed picture of an older woman—it must be of Atif's mother, who is smiling manically with her arm around a younger Atif in a graduation robe, both of them on the long and well-kept lawns of Oxford, romantic Gothic buildings soaring behind them on that bright summer day. Kierk takes one of Atif's pens from the box.

He's also extracting the stack of papers when Melissa Goldman, wrapping a scarf around her shoulders as she exits her office, catches sight of Kierk and approaches him with a questioning look on her face. As she does Kierk is thinking about what it must have been like to find the bomb materials outside her house, leering and obscene in her driveway out in the suburban wind.

Kierk gestures to the box. "This for the police?"

"Actually some university employee is going to send it home. They said they'd be down about twenty minutes ago. You're one of the Crick Scholars, right?"

"Yeah, hi, I'm Kierk Suren."

"So you knew him?"

"I was one of the last people with him."

"I'm sorry. I only heard last night, I packed up his effects. I've never done anything like this. What a sad thing."

"Listen, I'm sorry, but I was working with Atif on a project—"

"Oh, the one with Carmen?" Melissa says. Kierk opens his mouth, closes it again. "Because Carmen already looked through this stuff for those notes."

"Sorry, I should've mentioned, I just talked to her, actually, and she wasn't sure she had gotten everything of relevance. You know, making sure."

"Well it can't hurt, go ahead, just don't actually take anything. I have a meeting to get to."

As she leaves Kierk quickly scans the room, looking at the other work-stations, some of which are occupied by the stooped forms of graduate students. Then he's striding through the lab surreptitiously snatching up printed-out documents from the various unoccupied desks, keeping an eye on the door and the seated lab members, a few of whom glance at him, and he seriously nods back at them, and in a minute he has a stack about the same size of that in the box. He replaces one for the other, and with Atif's documents under his arm he walks out with purpose. He passes two people in the hallway. One is pointing the other toward the lab—"Atif's workstation was down there"—and Kierk, not looking up, hurries out into the stairwell.

He goes up a few flights. Pausing, he thumbs through the documents, which from a brief perusal are mostly just science papers but contain, to Kierk's surprise, all of his papers as well, which Kierk raises his eyebrows at and smiles, pride mixed with melancholy.

Eventually he goes back to his lab, walking past rows of heads whose names he's never learned.

Carmen, seeing him coming, turns in her chair and looks expectantly up at him, waiting for him to speak.

"So I've been thinking, and listen, I'm not saying you were right, but I am saying that it's not so far out there it shouldn't be considered."

"You're apologizing for yelling at me?" she asks, with some coyness.

"I am. I was wrong."

"Okay, good."

"Melissa said you read through his notes and papers."

Carmen holds up her phone—"I tried to take some photos. Didn't get everything though."

Kierk pats the sheaf of documents he's holding. "I grabbed everything."

"What?"

"I stole them. Purloined. Pilfered. Absconded. Shanghaied."

"Jesus. Okay, but smart."

"He has everything I've ever published. Some of which is not exactly easy to find. There were philosophy papers too. He was more knowledgeable than I thought . . . I should have discussed more with him. Point is that I changed my mind."

"Why?"

"Let's just say my priors were significantly updated."

Carmen kind of just pats his leg. "Great. Have you thought about where our, um, investigation should focus first?"

"I figured I'd let you do the honors."

"Well, a certain acronym comes to mind."

"Atif did work in Melissa's lab."

"And I heard that last week they staged some kind of an 'occupation.' They disrupted a neuroscience class. And they do have meetings."

"Are they open to the public?"

"It's every Wednesday."

"I'm in."

"Okay, do you need any help getting ready?"

"I'll pick something up tomorrow."

"I already have my disguise, the origins of which will remain unspoken. Let's just say there was a phase."

"Listen, it wasn't just the email from his mother, or what he was reading about, that changed my mind. There's something I need to tell you. Just, ah, bear with me okay? This is going to get . . . a little weird." Kierk pulls up the side of his shirt with one hand and pulls down the belt of his pants with the other, revealing a deep purple bruise that contains whirls within whirls.

APPROACHING THE DOOR TO Karen's lab Max prepares himself, all the things she'd said to him on Saturday ringing through his head. — "I just really need to be alone right now, Max." —"Just let me be alone for a couple days. That's all I need, a couple days." —"Max, I'm . . . I need to go."

Half hoping to avoid her, half hoping to run into her, he peeks in to see Kierk talking to Carmen, his shirt pulled up. Shaking his head Max continues to the elevator. He's running late. Apparently, his son, Jared, is having one of his bad days. Not that this wasn't near routine at this point. It's been four years since Max had, with the manner of those cursed by the gods, watched his child, his precocious and beautiful boy, who had loved *Goodnight Moon*, loved talking and being read to, who for two years had been normal, even bright, begin that terrifying regression into his autos (which Max learned was Greek for "self"), which led eventually to the oubliette of severe autism, that trap of a self, as all his son's attention seemed to turn inward. Jared no longer looked out on the world but merely into the mirror of his own consciousness. The first symptom had been when he stopped looking Max in the eyes, followed by the lexicality that had marked Jared's early childhood beginning to vanish daily, words gone, slipping away, replaced by—what? Betrayed by expression, his mimetic skills failing, his child took to rocking back and forth, endlessly, an interminable movement that was so easy to associate with helplessness, with hopelessness. Animals pacing in their cages at a zoo. Max speculated that the reward systems just got off track. The world is a thing to be decoded in a certain way but his son's brain was using the wrong key. Max had been horrified at these ideas that occasionally fled like bandits across his mind—at another time this child would have been left out on the cold slab of rock on a mountain and we would have had another. That other child that his wife said she didn't want—because it would apparently detract from Jared, she was too busy making sure Jared got to cognitive behavioral therapy twice a day, making sure he had his allotted floor time, his glucose-absent meals, his immersive activities, all the failed attempts to create any kind of paracosm for him to inhabit. Max knew his desire was selfish, and couldn't help it, couldn't do anything about it, the want was so deep it was everything, biological, spiritual, mental, and so after six years of faithful marriage he found himself with Karen, and knew it was wrong and that he still loved his wife, or still loved the idea of his wife. Max knows that couples who lose a child often get divorced and no one blames them, and he would never say it out loud but to him it was as if his beautiful boy had been murdered as surely as if he had been shot. Something in him just never reached escape velocity, instead retracting. How far had it retracted? It was impossible to know, but as he watched Jared follow simple but alien goals, like moving certain objects to a certain corner, or yelling at a particular window, or rocking back and forth, Max sometimes couldn't help but think the most hideous thought of all—that even while his son was doing all these things there was no longer anything going on *inside*. That the complex actions, even the emotional outbursts, were all going on in darkness, an automated program still running after all the light had left, and that, since no one could pinpoint where consciousness began or ended, his child might truly be just a biological robot, performing its actions for no reason outside of how it had been wound up, conscious of nothing. In comparison, Max's hatred at himself for even having such thoughts burned in him like an internal flame.

. . .

RUNNING INTO KIERK IN the stairwell Alex considers for a brief second before going in for a solemn hug, followed by the metacognitive shame that he still calculates this stuff with his straight friends. Kierk returns it pretty casually, though Alex can discern just the slightest stiffness to it.

Kierk, as he disengages—"Can you believe it?"

"No. Not at all. I've been reading all about it online. I can't stop. I feel like a freak."

"Any new information?"

"Just that the operator saw him, and that Atif was laid out on the tracks."

"Yeah, I read that too. And there was nobody else in the subway."

Alex glances down at his shoes. "It could have been any one of us. Greg left earlier alone, and Mike and Jessica had already headed out. I think they took a cab. Leon, you, me, and Carmen all got in first. That's it. We all live north of that place. It was raining. Probably we all would have taken that subway line. And the email from his mother. That hit me. Harder than . . . than I would have thought. Did you respond to it?"

"No. I didn't know what to say."

"Me neither. I've been spooked, and sad, unbelieving, everything. And now guilty."

"Do you remember what happened after the cab ride?"

"Actually I don't. I pretty much remember saying goodbye to Atif and getting into the car with you and Carmen. Didn't you pee in an alley?"

"Yes. Here's a question: how is it possible that neither you, nor Carmen, nor I, remember anything beyond getting in the cab?"

"We drank a lot," Alex says, shaking his head. "Which probably was the reason why Atif . . ."

"Hey, Atif was the one ordering all those drinks anyways. We did shots but he participated in them of his own free will."

"So you don't feel responsible."

"I feel responsible in that his death was counterfactually dependent on us but that's irrelevant for freak accidents. There's no *mens rea*."

"That's really how you feel?"

"Sure. Back to the memory thing. Have you talked to Leon?"

"Apparently he remembers leaving but basically nothing afterward until his wife was yelling at him the next morning."

"Leon's married?"

"So when other people talk, what is it that you hear?"

"Did he get married today?"

"Ha. Alright, despite how totally un-depressing this conversation has been, I've gotta run to a meeting."

But Alex never gets to the meeting. Rather he ends up lying on a couch in one of the break rooms, staring at the ceiling. He's back into the cycle of mind he's been trapped in since he heard, like some crucial border had been staved in between loss and death, death and loss . . .

Three years ago, when Alex was still in the middle of getting his PhD at Caltech under Christof Koch, Alex had taken dance classes in LA at a place called Millennium Dance, where he had ended up in class with a young agile instructor with a mop of crow-black hair named Jason. After some flirting Jason had invited Alex out to West Hollywood that Saturday night to this club called The Abbey, which Alex had never been to but Jason definitely had, because as soon as they were in and had done some shots (free because all the bartenders knew Jason), Jason was immediately up on the poles, up on the bar, up on basically everything, and Alex had felt like he was being carried along by the strong current of a river, the white rapids of music and bodies and exposed flesh and Jason, ahead of him always, smiling and beckoning, swaying to the rhythm as one hand reached back and dragged Alex through the crowd, and Alex, nervous, amazed, excited, seduced, following behind, at first unsure but then, later, it became all marmalade make-outs and fog-machine gropings, Jason pressing him against the wall, pinning his arms above his head. Then the rush of Jason dragging him out into the night streets to find a little spot in the shadows up against a brick wall, which Alex had been shoved against, breathing hard. And Jason had smiled at him and then kissed downward, Alex laughing out loud at what was happening, looking around furtively, thinking about how ridiculous it would be if they were caught, and then he wasn't thinking anymore but was looking up between the buildings to the breaking black liquid expanse of the universe with its magnetic fields and neutron stars and solar nurseries all pouring like radio down on him now, his hands feeling for purchase against the pebbly surface of the brick behind him as Jason undid his belt and sucked him off as the world spun and the galaxy rotated, wheels within wheels all the way down to a tongue circling.

Four months later they had moved in together because Jason needed a place and Alex's apartment was subsidized by Caltech. Jason had just begun to get everything together to apply to graduate schools to study dance professionally, but at the time he merely taught a few times a week or moonlighted as a dancer at various clubs as he completed his on-again, off-again undergraduate degree at UCLA. Neither Jason nor Alex had ever actually lived with someone they were in a relationship with before, nor even really had a relationship of any seriousness. At first it was like they didn't know what to do with each other in the small rooms: they listened to their respective music with headphones on, they were very careful and calculating about using the toilet only when the other was out of the apartment, and for a while Jason didn't let on how much he actually smoked pot (which turned out to be a thrice daily habit). But soon enough everything began to blend—for instance the pot habit quickly became a shared ritual of morning, after work, and deep at night under the blue glow of two open laptops before they had sex. In a fast flowering, they began to enjoy the humorous freedom of living together. Near continuous nudity became the norm. Nude smoking a bowl, nude cooking, nude eating, nude movies, nude toast in the morning, nude watering of the plants. There was even nude painting, laying out the plastic sheets everywhere, shopping together and looking at color swatches, then giving their bedroom an undercoat of white, which culminated in both of them running after each other with paintbrush splotches on their butt cheeks, backs and legs, streaks on their faces, getting paint everywhere around the room, Jason laughing and defending himself with two paintbrushes until Alex had taken him down with a Judo throw, then squirmed on top, madly kissing with lips tribal white. Alex loved that Jason would sing hilariously dirty takes on classic Disney songs in the shower. Alex loved that Jason was flexible. They became inseparable, cryptophasiac in their language, known around WeHo for their antics. They were jointly invited to parties, they became fixtures of the gay scene, but were fiercely jealous and defensive. Although they never had The Talk to define any boundaries, neither of them ever transgressed, they were an item and came as a fungible unit and this was known. A year passed, the best year of Alex's life. Then the acceptance letter from the Tisch School of Arts in New York City came for Jason in the mail. They wanted him for their esteemed dance program and this was the opportunity of a lifetime, and at first Alex was jubilant; they celebrated back at The Abbey, but there was a darkness to it, because Alex still had three years to go before completing his PhD. And so it was that this knowledge began to infect everything. Every party became a wake. And as Jason's flight approached it all exploded into screaming fits and slaps and shoves. They hit and pinned each other. They woke with bruises in the morning on their wrists and arms and legs from the fights and the crying and the accusations and the recriminations, both their faces becoming grotesques, gargoyles of their former selves, their movements erratic, compulsive in their need to hurt and to be close at the same time, a dissonant dance that neither had ever experienced before, completely shocked by themselves, completely shocked by their newfound capability to be so spiteful and so uncontrollable. But the inevitability of parting settled like the clearing of sediment from muddied water, and the fights and the bruises ceased, and when the subject came up they would just sit together, together but apart, filling a room with their silence, their inability to find a solution to this problem in which they both did not lose. In such a sorrowful state they hung on for the next month before the flight, clung to each other, to their joint life. They had some nice nights out, they celebrated as they could. Eventually they hung on for just a day, then, an hour. The ending bore down upon them in Terminal 4 of LAX. Hang on for just a few more minutes. Hold me a few seconds longer. The universe is fourteen billion years old and we can hold on to each other for five more seconds before you go through security and get on that plane and we never see each other again.

The first thing Alex missed after Jason's departure was the argot a long relationship develops—the animal noises in response to questions, the soft hums of sleep, the inside jokes and rituals and faux debates. When a relationship dies a whole language dies with it, just as private and unique as any endangered tongue spoken in the deep rain forest. To avoid the pain Alex had rearranged the apartment back as best he could to the pre-Jason state. The only thing that really stayed, a little case study of mimetic transmission, was the pot smoking. Smoking at least partially dulled the green prick of jealousy, because what began to eat at Alex was the thought that there would be other people fucking Jason, other men's dicks involved, that Jason would say encouraging things—Oh, fuck me hard, Oh, you're the biggest! It drove Alex insane when he thought about it. He'd thrown pillows and kicked couches. He'd gone on revenge fuck escapades but their friend group thought that it was unhealthy and strange for Alex to be so suddenly single, no longer sessile, waving about like some obscene anemone in the current from one pair of arms to another.

Alex could not honestly say how much of his decision to apply to the Crick program had been influenced by that whispering and nudging small cacodemon inside him, a thing giddy and dark, hopeful and monstrous, saying that he would then be in the same city as Jason again and one day he would be walking down the street in fashionable clothing with a group of attractive friends, and who should he run into but Jason—"Oh my God is that you, Jason . . . I didn't know you were still living here what a great surprise . . ." —"Well, that does sound like an interesting show, maybe I'll be there. I mean, I have a lot on my plate professionally and I already have plans for Friday night, but if I can make it . . ." —"Yeah, it was great to run into you too, bye, yes, bye . . ."

LATER THAT NIGHT IN his apartment Kierk does pull-ups on a door-frame, sit-ups, and push-ups, repping each till exhaustion three times, then shadowboxes until he is panting. He throws one last haymaker punch and stops. Breathing hard he shuts off the lights and lies on his back staring at the dark ceiling of his room. In the room around him even more cardboard boxes have arrived, silent and squat, so many it made it difficult to navigate the apartment. On the black screen of the ceiling Kierk thinks about Moretti, a meeting from four years ago. Like so many of his memories it is from the third person, his own viewpoint a disembodied eye looking down on the scene . . .

Antonio Moretti was sitting behind his desk wearing a bolo tie and a boyish smile, nearly twirling in his office chair. Around him were shelves of psychiatry books, whiteboards filled by equations and diagrams, loose-leaf paper, and discarded pens everywhere. Kierk was twenty-three and in ripped jeans and a disheveled, unwashed T-shirt, circles under his eyes from reading all night. From tiny cups they drank espresso made from Moretti's new state-of-the-art espresso machine that had the sleekness of a high-end automobile.

Antonio Moretti was speaking . . . "The most amazing thing is that using my theory you can recreate someone's consciousness just from their brain's connectome."

"Basically a consciousness meter," Kierk said.

"Yes, precisely. As per the theory, all conscious experiences are essentially geometrical information shapes. Very simple to represent. Very beautiful."

Kierk, excitedly—"Yes, like you've extracted the conscious experience out of the physical system into a simplified mathematical form."

"Exactly. Which means that, given my theory, we'll be able to transmit the quale, the conscious state."

"Others could reconstruct it."

"Imagine, Kierk, if one finds a patient with a particular sensory deficit, a neurologist could send the quale, the conscious experience of that patient, to another neurologist. I imagine art exhibits of qualia, large geometric structures. The conscious experience becomes fungible. You could even instantiate it in other brains if you wanted to. Change the connectivity of a particular brain to get the sensation or sensory space that you wanted." Antonio began to sketch out on a sheet of paper the anatomy of a machine capable of such a procedure, of bending the neural connectivity of a brain to produce heightened sensation, or maybe even transplant another's experience directly into it.

"Consciousness as a commodity. You're talking about building and selling experiences," Kierk said quietly.

"Well, such things are possible, Kierk, when you have a theory of consciousness."

And maybe, Kierk had thought, leaning back in his chair, one day we'll have synaptic sewing machines with fine enough fingers to sculpt the delicate neural architectures required to replicate, precisely, the pain of Jesus Christ crucified on the cross. We can sell them at discounts and try to save all our souls, he had thought, watching Antonio continue to draw sketches of his machine.

TUESDAY

KIERK WAKES UP AND collects the rags of himself crumpled about the floor of the apartment, a difficult task now because the cardboard boxes have taken up nearly all available space, as if they were capable of reproduction and had multiplied.

Out on Broadway he can feel the barometric pressure drop that indicates a storm approaching, that tingling feeling on the skin, that wind chime of receptive bone, the way the trash skitters across the pavement as it is swept from one side of the street to the other. The sky begins to gray, becomes a low roof.

Waiting for his simulation of the cortex to run he uses the espresso machine Karen has set up (above it is the sign I'LL SLEEP WHEN I'M DEAD). Kierk sips his espresso and gazes out at the city from the tenth floor. The bright specks of people cross streets. Cars wait for them under the gathering clouds, points of clothes and handbags and faces mill about—like a great mill we walk around inside of, machines and pistons move, causality and information are transferred, and does anything arise?

The simulation run is at ten percent. He sighs and leaves, making his way through the windowless corridors. As he walks Kierk notices that the air pressure differentials in this building are very weird. There are vents in almost every room but in some corridors the temperature will be drastically different; goose bumps will form on his skin as he enters and he'll rub at his uncovered arms, while in others he will break into a near flash sweat or lean against the wall and bask like a salamander until someone walks by and he will pretend to check his phone. But the most strange thing about it is that, due to the pressure differentials, often doors will not close all the way but remain propped an inch or two open such that through them will come a strange howl of air, a constant moan whose prosody depends on the temperatures and airflows, which in turn depend on the guts of pipes that wind their way across ceilings and up stairwells, rumbling hot and then rumbling cold in a series of differences making differences, which in turn determines which of the doors at any given time are closed, or are hovering an inch or two off their frames, and how mellow or anguished the wind's moan is.

He follows a stairwell upward, exploring until he finds a door that leads to the roof. Ignoring the NO —XIT sign with the flaked away E he opens the unlocked door, propping it ajar with a brick lying nearby.

The wind rips at his clothing, then subsides. Beyond the lip of the roof the city is a spun sculpture, an airless and hot mercurial expanse. Due to the wind it's much cooler up here than down in the streets; he could almost be wearing a jacket. He stares out at the metal dream of teeth and steel and contemplates apostasy. All Kierk wants at that moment is to live a good life, no, a great life, to be a Mozart of living. Should he really be here waiting on his project, which is essentially a Rube Goldberg device for biased random number generation? Of late he feels like all the activity of himself and his peers is just playing the Science Game: varying some variable with infinite degrees of freedom and then throwing statistics at it until you get that reportable p-value and write up a narrative short story around it. The banality of it all is crippling to him, nearly sundering his will for the day, and it is all he can do to keep from hiding up on the roof forever, to ride out the storm like a mad ship captain. Still, there might be an efflorescence in store for him here, maybe, if this thing inside of him that he feels building, whatever it is, can make its way out of his mind and reveal itself as seraphim or golem or stillborn.

Looking down gives him vertigo. In his peripheral vision there is a fluttering at the base of an imbricated tin structure, near a rusted series of pipes that looks like a church organ's mouth. It's a feather, the fluffy white smaller tufts of stripped plumage. Kierk crouches down and as it is tussled by the wind and he picks it up, rolling it in his fingers, and then looks farther into the small corner—wind whips behind him, but this place is secluded and protected amid the rubble of brick and copper wire. In the dark, pressed up against brick and concrete there is a small ritualistic gathering of tiny bones—bird bones. Kierk sees the fine spread of a wing, and the skulls, some intact, others chipped or malformed or crushed, picked at, bones almost all separated out, discolored, some white and fresh and others older and yellow, a little nest all laid out. None are full skeletons, rather they are disjointed, taken apart, such that given this jumble of bones it is impossible to tell how many birds—pigeons, these must be pigeons—actually contributed to the mortuary. Or perhaps this is some sort of a nest? Kierk takes a piece of rusted wire from the ground and uses it to poke and disturb the collection, noticing as he's digging around the bones that there seems to be an implicit order in their layout, as if certain types of bones, skulls, wings, have been sorted independently and grouped together as sets. He is thinking of the ethology of octopuses, that they and humans are the only kind of predator who arrange the bones of their prey in geometric patterns, the only hyper-intelligent predators—maybe the first true intelligence that ever existed was in a carnivore playing with the bones of its food. Kierk stands back up, holding the wire at his side, looks around at the empty gray roof. Across the street from him a lower roof is thick with pigeons, sitting on structures, flying from one post to another, and on the neighboring roof in the other direction he sees even more rounded forms dart from one pipe to another. Here, nothing moves except the wind.

"Huh."

LEAVING A MEETING THAT afternoon Carmen takes the stairwell, paus-ing on the landing, feeling overwhelmed. So much has changed so quickly, and now within her there is a cacophony of feelings and valences. Every other minute she flips: Atif, the mystery of it all, the investigation, the responsibility, the occasional flit of worry about her own safety—and then on the other side, the new job, the job of a lifetime going well, all the mun-dane things are good, and, of course, the people here that she's met, the people who are new to her life promising more change. One of whom she refuses to think too much about. This whirlwind has in turn engendered within her a kind of thawing. Yesterday she'd stood in line at the grocery store face-to-face with a baby looking at Carmen from behind the mother's shoulder, all blue-eyed and mouth open, absorbing everything and every-one around it as receptively as a Buddhist monk, with a forehead as placid and calm and wise as a sperm whale's, and Carmen had let out a squeal and a wave in a way that would have made twenty-one-year-old Carmen roll her eyes, because back then she hadn't really gotten the point of babies, except as something to be observed in neurological interest, thinking of them then as these giant diffuse and basically randomly wired neural networks trying through a response-reward curve to make sense of the world, trying to define the fire hose of undifferentiated input into categories that could be used, bound together, but lately whenever she got close to a baby all she wanted to do was smell it and interact with it and basically just teach it, feed that response-curve with funny faces and giggly waves and winks, which Carmen knew made sense, because every cutesy thing that adults do around babies is not random, no, all those funny faces highlight expressions, and the tone taken is precisely tuned to stimulate a baby's developing auditory system, and the googly eyes and funny voices and little games are in-built—adults are as genetically programmed to teach babies as babies are to learn, an oscillating cycle, a generational handoff that goes back and back and back. And she finds this beautiful.

"How are you doing that?"

"Doing what? What's he doing?" The baby's mother had turned around and asked her, smiling.

"Being conscious," Carmen had said seriously, bent and gazing into the blue eyes going to-and-fro, rheumy but brilliant in their color. When she had given that blue-eyed baby a wink and wave the response was a happy crinkling gurgle that was literally too cute for Carmen to handle and she actually had to leave the line to calm down.

Maybe it was age, maybe it was something else. Everything felt so different now, even from just a few months ago, and how quickly that internal distance had grown surprised her now. Back then she had, with little hesitation, given up a sure bet for a family, a whole other life. Her last boyfriend, whom she had left seven months ago, had been a lawyer, having only just passed his bar exam but with great prospects. At thirty he was four years her senior, and what had happened wasn't her fault, not really. She, vivacious and enigmatic, concerned with her latest research study and living in a small studio apartment, always pausing to sneeze loudly as she walked outside, and he, all old money and sailboats, from a family grown bored with its wealth, passionate about becoming a public defender so he could work with the disadvantaged and institutionally overlooked, bristling at social inequity—a man who, for all the irony of espousing the benefits of a welfare state while on a yachting outing off the coast, was a good man, a decent man, which Carmen had known from the start. And she also knew from the start that she should feel a sense of promise, but instead she felt a slowly advancing sense of panic, entrapment. So without meaning to, quite incidentally really, just as a consequent of their dynamic and personalities, just something that happened without her knowing about it until it was over, Carmen had cracked his chest open and eaten out his heart, all in plain view of his friends and family, who had watched it happen, issued warnings as dire as the young man would allow and then those same friends and relatives had to look on with the same morbid fascination felt when watching one insect cannibalize another gruesomely, as this witty and skinny, smiling and blonde, charming and singularly intelligent, aloof and unpredictable young woman had utterly destroyed the young lawyer, he who had imagined her one day on a beach somewhere in whipping white mouthing, "I Do," but instead she had left after just three months, after licking her fingertips clean of her meal, her pretty mouth smeared with blood and chunks of gore, standing beside the couch in the subtly ornate living room of his family's beach home, looking around as if saying: what? what? Clearly there has been some misunderstanding, you didn't think this was going to be *it*, oh, you did (how much of her knew he thought?), and leaving the family with a corpse next to that plastic-wrapped couch (the scene of the final massacre), a corpse that would take years to revive, perhaps some five-hundred-dollar-an-hour therapy, and it was probable that even then every woman the young lawyer met ever after would be compared and contrasted, seen to fit in congruency or break in some asymmetry, to her. At first she had felt guilty, but it really wasn't her fault, she had been as clear as possible (hadn't she?) that this probably wasn't going to be enough, that she wanted something *different than everyone else had* right from the beginning, and hadn't he agreed anyways, proffered himself even, like certain species of male mantises?

RESEARCH ARTICLES, COVERED IN marks made with Atif's pen, are scattered around Kierk's bed. Books are splayed out on the floor, the ones Atif had mentioned in his notes. Reading neuroscience textbooks had always given Kierk that creepy feeling of being a machine reading its own blueprints. Now though he's just lying on his bed, a thing coming apart, pulled at a frayed edge and unraveling into spools of string. He has been thinking about consciousness, or rather thinking about Atif's thinking about consciousness, which he finds surprisingly sophisticated. Atif had been bothered by the same issues, found some of the same dead ends. And within the notes, Kierk had found the occasional cartoon drawing of a great eye with spindly human legs.

The softness of the bed is rising around him like dough. He bakes in the pleasurable heat, is swallowed, drifts off into a sea. Images come and go, some of them are of her, he's not dreaming yet, he's in the lands between, an indefinable time erased every night by retrograde amnesia, but it is here that he sees a series of doors, doors slamming shut, again and again, echoing in their closing, cutting off a sound from the other side, the babbling of an idiot, a scream, and then slam, and then silence, until even this image cannot maintain coherence and Kierk dissolves into mere associations, a million things at once, the pieces of a jigsaw puzzle thrown against the wall. Sleep is a series of doors slamming shut.

WEDNESDAY

KIERK **WAKES UP LIKE** a fish twisting on the line, struggling against the force reeling him into the world. There is already someone standing on shore, a form in the light with a hand raised to shield her eyes from the sun, hair whipping behind her. Throwing off his sheet, Kierk knows what has woken him just ahead of his alarm—expectation of her.

Among the heterogeneous pedestrians that crowd the streets of New York, Kierk doesn't look that out of place, but the moment he steps into the refrigerator air of the CNS he feels ridiculous. When he walks into the lab Carmen, turning in her seat, becomes locked in humor. A hand tries to cover her reaction as she, who is quite normally dressed, rushes up to him.

"Oh come on, you're not even wearing yours," he says, looking her over.

"I am not insane, so I didn't wear to work my costume-slash-disguise-slash whatever that is. I brought a change of clothes."

"Oh . . . right. In California this would actually be pretty normal."

"Well, it's . . . magnificent."

"Thanks."

"Here, look at this little pamphlet I got of theirs."

Carmen hands him the SAAR pamphlet. Flipping through it he sees the disturbing images of vivisections, experimental animals mixed freely with scenes from factory farms. On the front of it is a lone rhesus macaque, the photo a dense grain of color showing that it has been scalped and one of its eyes has been sewed shut. The remaining open eye is a black stone, a dark planet far beyond the others tracing out a long elliptical orbit where it is always night.

CARMEN'S HEAD POPS INTO Karen's office.

"Carmen—what can I help you with?"

"I just wanted you to know that, um, despite the unfortunate event of Atif's passing, Kierk and I are still going to be working on that project together."

"Oh, the brain-to-brain communication in monkeys?"

"Yup! Just wanted to let you know that if we're both gone that's why. Like this afternoon we're going to go down to the primate lab. But we'll be around."

Karen seems to be smiling subtly when she says—"Okay. Sounds good."

Carmen nods to her and exits, walking past Kierk, who is emitting a soft jingle as he types (there's a bell somewhere on his person), and when he looks up questioningly she gives him a thumbs-up and continues on past through the quiet working bustle to get coffee and a quick snack. The lab itself is not something most nonscientists would immediately recognize as a lab, looking as it does more like an office space well-equipped with broad-screened Macs all separated off by modular panels. Ergonomic chairs with wheels and an adjustable back are standard. There are probably about thirty such workspaces arranged in segmented cubicles. The first hints are the books—*Monkey Cortex VII*, *The Human Amygdala*, *The Hippocampus*, *Rat Barrel Cortex IV*—stacked about in the same way that works of cartographers and navigators were historically stacked on ships, but these are for charting coastlines of gyri, straights of sulci. On the computers themselves there are pretty-colored heat maps of cortical activity, the hum of Fourier transformations running away on a minimized MATLAB tab, and sometimes the neuron spike sorting from electrophys rigs that impaled the monkey's open brains downstairs like single-armed sewing machines. Programs all trying to get that signal, that signal from the noise. But the most obvious indications of the provenance of the lab come from the rarer moments—someone walks in with an unconnected EEG cap on and the thick multicolored ribbon of wires dangles down their back like an external spinal cord, or one of the lab members, not having time to change from the animal rooms, runs in wearing a white lab coat, blue booties, and a face mask, or when there is that low bouncing rumble that signifies an animal chair being maneuvered down the connecting hallway, heavy with the macaque stuffed like an embryo between the clear plastic planes. A hallway that smells vaguely of musk and strongly of chlorine. All the real scientific action happens in the recording rooms (for monkeys) or the experimental rooms (for humans). The recording rooms are giant Faraday cages, dissipative vaults safe from the electromagnetic noise of the city—although it was a running joke that nothing could keep out the subway directly below, so that whenever one of those metallic caterpillars crawled on its electric track underneath them the whole CNS vibrated minutely, and the vibrating plus a passing surge of electromagnetism or shifting masses or something that nobody could really figure out would interfere with the EEG, the fMRI, even the electrophysiology equipment enclosed by the copper aegis of the Faraday cage, which meant that the terabyte of data produced annually by the CNS had edited-out gaps at ten-minute intervals marking the subway's passing. The lab, despite being a coordinating center for all of this data collection, all this *science*, is recognizably human, what with its little kitchen with the refrigerator that always stank of forgotten food left by one of its thirty-plus users, stuffed also with big bags of frozen blueberries (for the monkeys) and refrigerated Cheetos (for the rats). Currently the whole lab is preparing for the Day in the Lab outreach tomorrow. Carmen is actually looking forward to it because she can spend some more one-on-one time with Karen, as they're going to have a booth or something together. Some confrontation between them is probably inevitable. Carmen is technically a member of Karen's lab in a sense, and so there is a weird implicit expectation of joint publication (which Carmen is dreading, because Carmen thinks that Karen's best publications might be behind her, that Karen will slow her down)—and all of this is too precarious of a situation not to collapse into some angle of response, so the only thing Carmen can do is hope that when that happens it is a steady, load-bearing heap. But such a conflict is a ways off, and besides, the Crick Scholars are in vogue in the CNS and Carmen is pretty sure that she can win, or at least not be crushed by, any internal power struggles. Kierk, though, she's not too sure about. If he's as smart as he believes he'll probably publish something amazing that'll make the rest of them look like minnows. But if he's not, or is just plain unlucky . . . She wonders if there is anything she can do to help him as she rummages around in the disgusting refrigerator past the monkeys' blueberries and the rats' Cheetos for the little plastic container filled with olives she got from a local bodega.

ON KAREN'S WAY TO lunch Kierk passes her, his flip-flops smacking in echoes, his tie-dye shirt a walking illusion. She stifles a laugh as he moves out of sight, now wondering if there's some costume party she doesn't know about. Leaving the CNS into the glare, she realizes that laugh was the first in a while. She needs fresh air. Even passing Max in the hallway earlier had caused her to flee to the bathroom. Now she takes refuge at a nearby cafe.

Karen is used to ghosts over her shoulder. After all, she had passed thirty-five. Ex-lovers, family members she feels estranged from, friends who were once like sisters whom she never speaks with anymore, all her grandparents gone now as well . . . But she's never been haunted like she has been for the past few days. And she's shocked to discover that there is apparently this whole level of regretful haunting she never even knew existed. This whole thing has been a huge mistake. And it's only becoming clear to her now. At first, while the pregnancy had still existed, she'd had no idea what to do, none at all. And it wasn't that she'd listed out the pros and cons and weighted them accordingly and then couldn't make a decision, no, it was that when she had even tried to think about it in terms of options, of choosing among alternatives, there had instead been this blankness, a white frictionless surface so smooth every thought of hers had slid off it. Not that there hadn't been feelings, but there'd been no explicit naming of the decisions possible, no enumeration; when her consciousness called for plans of action her unconsciousness simply refused to serve her up anything. When she had cast her nets of thought no fish were caught. Today she has been reassuring herself that nothing was wrong with her, and that one-third of all pregnancies ended in spontaneous abortion. She hadn't wanted it, not at all, but she felt like something darkly momentous had happened and she had been changed for the worse somehow, tainted. Even now, looking around, it is as if the city had become a playground, and sitting outside the cafe sipping her tea she watches the families stroll by and feels that something had broken irreversibly in her at the same time that the knot of blood had released on Sunday, something untied, bloody fingers unclasping from a tightly clenched fist, and synchronously something even deeper, a supporting subterranean structure, had cracked in response and wept its heartblood. She had spent the weekend drifting from bedroom to bathroom clutching a heating pad to her stomach and moaning whenever she sat down. Should she stop seeing him? Is this part of the plan, that grand plan she's had since she was nineteen to become a successful, independent woman scientist? Because this didn't feel like it was part of that plan. No, this was a sign from a God she doesn't know if she believes in, this is revelation time, this is get-your-fucking-life-together time. A mask is settling, being fitted, she is discarding things in this cafe, coming to conclusions. Behind her, on the metal chair that is hot in the sun, she will leave a molted skin. Outwardly, however, there is calm. She quietly sips at her tea, she eats the cookie in little dainty bites with one hand held underneath to catch crumbs. When the bill comes, she signs her name with surety.

"IT'S SO HOT OUT here! Yup, those are vegan, everything is vegan. Yeah, just pull up two of those chairs over there. Sorry, we're organized, but disorganized, ya know?"

"Um, Allen, maybe we could ask if anyone wants to sit inside? Like, maybe the outside is problematic if someone has allergies?"

"Oh yeah, sorry, I didn't ask. Is the location comfortable for everyone . . .? Good! Good to see everyone again! Thanks so much for showing up today, and uh, supporting our mission. I really think we have a lot of forward momentum. The student body, or at least the right parts of the student body, are energized. They see what's going on. Everyone by now has heard about the occupation we did in the neuroscience class. I was there. A lot of cries for justice, the faculty didn't know what to do, the department didn't know what to do. The professor was so funny, he was like—'What?' He tried to say stuff and talk to us about animal research but we were all banging on the tables. Disrupt and Disseminate. That's stage one."

"Achoo!"

"Bless you! So anyways, we've got, well, let's just do introductions for the two new members, or potential members. Feel free to introduce yourselves, just say maybe why you're interested in SAAR and what brought you to New York."

"Hey everybody, we're both seniors at NYU, and, oh yeah, my name is Jim, by the way, hey everybody."

"—and I'm Carol."

"Hi!"

"And we're both—"

"We're both interested in the scene, you guys have been a pretty effective force, which is rare, you know, like where I was before I transferred, they just don't take this really seriously so it's nice to find a place where people do. We heard about you because of the occupation."

"Carol, where'd you transfer from?"

"Oh, from UMass Amherst, it's in like, the middle of Massachusetts."

"And Jim?"

"I've been at NYU for three years but I've only recently gotten like, morally serious about this issue. But I've kind of always been into animal rights. I actually ran a chapter of PETA in high school."

"That's great. That's actually exactly what I did, I also ran a chapter but it was in Brooklyn, where were you at?"

"Um, New Hampshire, actually."

"I didn't know it was widespread enough to have branches there."

"I think it's rare but I was lucky. Lucky Jim, that's me."

"Okay, great, well, so Carol, how'd you become interested in this stuff?"

"Well, okay, I transferred here, I mentioned that originally I was from UMass Amherst, but it wasn't really my scene. So there I was, like, someone who worked in the biology building, like a work-study job. Well, I also ordered things for professors, and they'd be just like, hey, I want some primers from this company, here are the numbers, and I'd be like, what are primers, you know? But they'd give me like, these order numbers and the professors would just come to pick it up. Anyways, I'd been there like, a few weeks and I order this thing for this professor, I don't know what it is, it's just from this company. A couple days later I'm alone in the office and I sign for it and it's got like, air-holes, which like, okay, I didn't know we'd be ordering live animals, so I open up the box, and inside are just these little white rats, which as babies are like, really cute, and they're all moving about in this straw stuffing stuff. And you can like, enter the order number, and so I'm reading about what they are and what they are used for, and I read that what they did was that they, the researchers at this company, had injected them with some genes, like a virus with genes in it or something, when the rats were like, embryos, and these are genes from humans that grow human neurons. So these rats are like, rats, on the outside, but on the inside, their neurons are all human neurons, like actual human neurons inside these rat bodies, and I swear, one of them was like, standing on his hind legs and sniffing up at me, just watching like, making real eye contact with those red eyes. And I just freaked, I couldn't like, understand what this meant and it was like, a million degrees outside, like so incredibly hot even in the office and I just couldn't deal so I like, plastered up the box again with packing tape and just took it outside and just like, ran around with it for a while. And no one stopped me or anything, I was just outside on this brutally hot day with this incredible low sky, just so menacing and hot, and there's this pond in the middle of the UMass campus and I was down by the pond just walking around holding the box under my arm, and everyone is just walking around so nonchalantly, so normally, and I'm holding these rats with human neurons and I can't stop thinking about what the researchers there are going to do to them, like implant them with those skullcaps and stuff, but then also I'm like, holding an invasive species you know, like what if these rats are supersmart and can outcompete all the other rats? The sun was reflecting off everything, the water, the tall buildings, getting me in the eyes, it was just so hot, and I'm standing on this little bridge right in the middle of the pond with people walking by and I drop the box into the water."

"Oh my god."

"Oh, I'm so sorry."

"God that sucks."

"You couldn't have done anything differently."

"I just didn't know what to do."

"That's, oh my god, that's such an intense story. Listen, if you'd like, if you're ready, we have a newsletter that you could write something up in. Because that was also kind of beautiful. Like in a way. I don't know . . ."

"Thanks, Allen, I'd love that, thanks. I thought you all might, well . . . Oh, and I got fired, by the way, it's one of the reasons I came here."

"Yeah, they can't stand having anyone stand up to them."

"I wasn't. At the time I wasn't trying to do anything like that, but yeah, I feel that way now."

"Wait Jim, you were at UMass too?"

"No, I was here at NYU. Have been for three years. Her backstory is more elaborate."

"Oh, right, right, okay."

"And how do you two know each other?"

"Oh, let's just tell them. So Jim and I have been dating for a couple months now. Ever since I moved here, we met and it was like—bam! That's it. Keep trying to change how he dresses though."

"You guys are suuuch a cute couple."

"Oh thank you, thank you. We hear that all the time. No need to be embarrassed, Jim."

"Oh, guys, I made vegan muffins!"

"Achoo!"

"Bless you, Carol."

TONIGHT SLEEP IS ELUSIVE for Kierk. He keeps looking over at the dark of the hallway door, the maw of the bathroom door. There are far too many doors and nooks and crannies in this apartment, areas he cannot see in the crouching darkness, a slim lock on the door, an open window, a thing beyond, a stillness to make movement in. He's been tossing and turning in the oppressively hot breeze from the open window, and he keeps replaying some deeper intuition inside, a stone unspoken, dropped into a well. Because he has been dwelling with a brain close to dream on the mystery of the roof, on bones. He feels febrile, insane, he keeps clenching his teeth and hissing into the pillow, there's a feeling like a needle is being held inches from his eye and his whole body reacts, his fingers grip the sheets, his feet dig for purchase. One foot bumps up against a book in bed with him and Kierk goes berserk kicking it off. Something is wrong, he feels he has been poisoned. He lies panting in the heat. Soon all the covers join the excommunicated book on the floor. The kitchen is a whole other room beyond him, anything could be happening in it. The suicide-proof bars on the window mean that only the most deformable body could enter through it—a thing with suckers and a beak for a mouth, stinking of ambergris. He gets up and tugs the window closed, then lies back down. This is all because, he thinks, while walking back after the meeting he had passed again Bleecker Street Station. Kierk had taken up position sitting on a stone wall opposite the entrance and there he stayed as the sunset and night came on fully. With the patience of a hunter in a blind he had charted the comings and goings of those who entered the subway station, trying to note each in turn but just as often drifting off in thoughts on consciousness. Eventually, the people entering and exiting had become a slow trickle, and Kierk, immensely bored, had made his way home. But here he couldn't focus, couldn't sleep. And now he is eyeing that slit of light from the hallway, which he can see in a diagonal line of sight from his bed, because he is sure that he had seen something move, that a shadow had drifted across then stopped, then withdrew, but only slightly. He could have been followed back. From the meeting. From the subway. From both. Something just now had clearly *moved*, a person making no noise but standing outside his door, still and patient, breathing through their mouth to minimize noise. Maybe who or what had knocked on his door previously. Or maybe a thing that arranges the bones of pigeons into macabre patterns. Kierk lies on his side utterly still. There is a heavy breathing that is not his own. It is wet and deep. A protuberance of shadow moves to reveal more of the thin slit of light, very obvious, very definite, and Kierk is lithely on his feet, slipping quickly across the bedroom and into the kitchen, where he, very slowly, opens a drawer and withdraws a large kitchen knife. Holding the knife in one hand and keeping his eye on the door he locates some boxers in the dark with his toe and quietly shuffles them on. Now his anger's rising—in the dark Kierk's face becomes a rictus, a sneering grimace that exposes his teeth. He flips his grip to underhanded, for slashing, and so it would be harder in a struggle for an assailant to grab hold of his wrist and immobilize the knife. Then he rips open the door and leaps into the hallway in his boxers, the knife low and leading the way. There is nothing. The long empty corridors mock him, turn corners on themselves. Closing the door, cloaked in shadow, Kierk is silent for a moment, head cocked. He chuckles once, standing in the dark with the knife hanging at his side.

Then he hears the tiniest ding from far away.

He whips the knife into the wood floorboards by his feet and, still only in his boxers, he sprints down the length of the corridor and to the elevators just in time to hear the soft shut of the doors as he approaches and to catch the blinking numbers start at his floor and tick all the way down to the ground floor, where it stays.

Kierk leans against the cold surface of the elevator doors, breathing hard, thinking hard. He hears the click of a key down the hall and when the young woman turns toward him she freezes at the sight of the nearly naked young man breathing heavily against the elevator door, his hair straight up, his eyes changing from alarmed to amused. Kierk smiles at her, bows, and pads to his room. As he enters he pulls the knife out of the floor. He spends a little while pacing back and forth in the dark before he gives up, and, finally too tired to care anymore, he lies back down again. But he doesn't return the knife. Instead he slips it between the mattress and the box spring so that the handle sticks out on his right side, well within reach. Staring at the ceiling, he closes his eyes and there is time enough for three heartbeats before the revelation comes. The revelation is similar to one you would have if, in a museum examining an ancient mural containing a painted scene of great clutter and activity, you had, in browsing across the different sections of the enormous painting, discovered that one of the tertiary figures, arrested in some pose in the background, was a precise facsimile of a childhood friend of yours. The man with the red baseball cap in the tan trench coat that Kierk had seen vanish into the tunnel on Saturday had walked out of the subway entrance earlier that night hidden among a small group of people and had turned directly toward Kierk, watching him back, his face still obscure, just for a moment before vanishing up a side street, and this all comes to Kierk only now.

THURSDAY

KIERK WAKES UP WITH memories of last night bearing down on him. Rubbing his eyes, naked and now standing, he glances down at the hilt of the knife protruding from between the mattress and the box spring. In the morning light all the inanimate objects and spaces, conspiratorial at night, have become a toy set of innocence, sapped of intentionality, obvious. Alone but still embarrassed Kierk takes the knife back to the kitchen before going to the bathroom to urinate his way into the start of day.

APPROACHING THE CNS THE streets are full of small children heading to different NYU departments and buildings for community engagement. There is also a college student holding up a sign with a picture of a vivisected monkey on it, and one of the teachers has stopped and is arguing with him as the other teachers shepherd the children away. Next to him a girl with dreadlocks whom Kierk recognizes from SAAR holds up a placard that says DOUBLE TROUBLE LIVES. TORTURE FOR TORTURERS. He passes them while coughing to hide his face.

In the CNS Leon is waiting for him patiently, holding in his ursine arms a cardboard box labeled BRAINS. Kierk apologizes for being late as they make their way to the conference room that the original meet-and-greet for the Crick Scholars had been held in, a room that Kierk has searched for a few times during his walks and never found. Carmen and Karen are manning the next table over. Max comes in, raises up two fingers, and then leaves in a hurry—Kierk notices he avoids looking at Karen. Then the students flood in. Words and phrases used descriptively in emails surrounding this event: socioeconomic choices unavailable, urban, minority, pre-college enrichment opportunity, students of color, scientific exposure. Leon is lifting the brains out of Tupperware like caught fish, Kierk is snapping on his nitrile gloves surgeon-like, and the kids split off and make their way to the individual stations. —"So Leon, how about this. You play the mute, gravely German giant and I play the wordy and handsome court jester introducing you?" Before Leon can respond: —"Hey boys and girls, my name is Kierk and this big European guy right here is Leon." —"Are those brains?" —"Yup, these are human brains, but they are from people who wanted us to have their brains after they died, so that we could do science with them." —"They're gray." —"Yup, but in the skull they're actually very pink. Leon, can you hand me a . . . Great, thanks. Okay, let's get started. Just to begin with, the brain has got two big parts, this part in the back of the brain is called the (Kierk affects an over-the-top Italian accent) cerebellum. "Everybody say it with me, just like me, cerebellum." —"Cerebellum" (in chorus). —"Wow, you guys are so smart and you all have wonderful Italian accents, it's all very impressive" (Carmen is looking over, smiling above rows of heads in motion). —"The cerebellum helps you to move, like, if I throw this brain at you (mimes throwing brain to giggles and shrieks) then your cerebellum would be what helps you catch it. Everybody stand on one foot like me" (eight little sneakers lift off the floor). "Now say (faking balance loss to giggles, arms pinwheeling) 'cerebellum,' everybody." —"Cerebellum!" —"Wonderful! So the cerebellum has a tough job, and it does that by having as many neurons as all the rest of your brain! Do you guys know what neurons are? You haven't gotten to that station huh, well, who's fault is that" (making a face, Kierk points to the teacher to giggles). —"Okay, so just trust me then, that the cerebellum, alone, has as much capability as the rest of your whole brain. But here's the most interesting thing about the cerebellum (eight sneakers follow Kierk's down), and that's that if you lost your cerebellum in a tragic accident, you'd still be you. You'd be the same person you are now except that you wouldn't be able to balance on one foot. That's all you'd lose. If you lost half your neurons! That's different from the cerebrum, which is the main part of the brain—everybody now, cerebrum." —"Cerebrum!" (Eight Italian accents again.) —"Mwah! Beautiful! Perfetto! The cerebrum is the other big part of the brain, and if it gets damaged, you lose everything about you that makes you you. We're going to take a tour of the cortex now. Leon, will you start?"

—"Well, children . . . The cortex is all this outer layer of the brain. It's got um, sulci and gyri. The peaks and valleys, I mean."

Kierk immediately takes over—"So the cortex, the outer part of the cerebrum, is what houses most of your thoughts and feelings and memories. All the action is in this outer layer. It's only about a tenth of an inch thick. Only this big! That outer surface is where all the neurons are. Everything else, all this white stuff, is just wiring that allows all the neurons to communicate. So really the cortex is just a big sheet, but all folded up. A big sheet of gray matter on the surface, and inside is just a giant mass of communication lines, like telephone lines. And that outer sheet is where your consciousness is."

They settle into a rhythm of this for each group that passes by, Kierk and Leon play off each other to widespread amusement. Carmen keeps looking at Kierk, who always seems to be making a funny face or movement, always elastic and expansive—his is by far the loudest booth. Carmen's strategy at her booth differed from Kierk's by being based more on enchantment. She activates some deep-seated psychological response whereby the children fall immediately silent while she talks, pairs of reverent eyes following her movement as if she were a movie star. Their attentions keep darting back to her even when Karen is talking.

Eventually the pretense of organization falls apart and kids run about from booth to booth. A very small girl hovers about a teacher's legs, and Carmen waves down at her, causing her to hide behind the teacher's dress. "Oh, come out, darling. What's your name?" The teacher reaches around and picks up the little girl, who is round-faced and wide-eyed and very pretty, and Carmen says as much, and the teacher lifts her into Carmen's arms.

"Her name is Sarah."

"Well hello there, Sarah." Soon Carmen is making small talk with the little girl she's holding, swaying a bit, almost dancing, jiggling, clearly delighting in this little girl, who is clearly delighting in Carmen back.

Kierk is sitting on his table lightly kicking the front of it with his heels. His station empty, he's looking over some of the children milling about and at Carmen holding the little girl. Carmen spins her passenger, beautiful, both of them, like all the light has left the room except for this spotlight on Carmen holding the little girl and Kierk has paused mid-kick, realizing that something deep inside him has shifted—all in the time that it takes Carmen to look over at him, smile, and wave the little girl's hand with her own.

Reeling, Kierk stands, and, looking for something to do, begins to put the supplies away like an automaton. Mike has wandered over and is asking Leon something. A small voice breaks Kierk's pinwheeling analysis of his own state. A black boy with cornrows and a mild malocclusion is looking up at him, Leon, and Mike.

"Hello, what's your name?" Mike asks.

"Hi, I'm Ari."

"Ari, what can we do ya for?"

"So why do you need the other part, unlike the . . ."

"Cerebellum," Kierk says.

"Yeah, why can you lose that cerebellum but you can't lose the . . ."

"Cerebrum."

"Yeah."

Mike, smiling down, snaps on a glove and holds one of the brains out for the boy to see more clearly. "Because you *are* your cerebrum. But you're not your cerebellum, you can lose that. Like you can lose an arm."

Kierk leans over the table, takes the brain from Mike and submerges it back into its Tupperware container before turning back around, taking off his gloves as he answers.

"No. Listen, Ari, it's like houses and garages. You live in your house, not your garage. The cerebrum is the house in which your consciousness lives. But you're not your house. You just live there."

Mike looks over at Kierk questioningly. "Well, not exactly. I mean, listen, Ari, you are your brain. That's why when parts of it get damaged you get damaged as well. That's what all these stations have been showing you today."

Ari looks from Kierk to Mike, Mike to Kierk. After a second of silence Kierk leans forward until he is nearly sprawled across the table, trying to make eye contact, almost pleading. "You are at least your brain. That is what you have learned here today. Just like a painting is at least paint. You see, Ari? You are at least your brain."

"Kierk," Mike says curtly. "Let's stick with what is established." From the heated interaction a bubble has formed around them and some of the nearby tables are looking over. The schoolteacher is still talking to her but Carmen is no longer paying attention.

"Established? When, Mike? Tell me when."

"Kierk . . ."

"Listen, Ari. Imagine . . . Imagine you are a square, a two-dimensional square, and you see a sphere. But because you're a square you can't see that it's a sphere, you just see a circle. That's how you have to interpret it, because that's the only perspective you have. The brain is kind of like that. All we have is this one way to view things, as objective relations, and so right now all we see is this gray lump, this cauliflower mass. We think that's what the brain is because we're seeing it the only way we know how. But one day we're going to be able to see the sphere. We'll be able to see your mind for what it really is. And everything will be different."

Ari, his little face condensed in nervousness, nods his head at Kierk, backing away.

"Remember that, Ari. Remember that!" Kierk calls after him, causing Ari to turn back slightly as if he was going to address Kierk but then he changes his mind and shuffles quickly into the milling group, the rounded hunch of his backpack soon lost amid all the others.

Mike is looking at Kierk with a sneer on his face. He throws up his hands.

"What the hell, Kierk."

"Oh, you think I'm wrong, Mike? I bet I could squash whatever petty worldview you have with one hand tied behind my back. Want to talk population coding and macro causation? Chaos theory and computational irreducibility? Copenhagen vs. many-world? Supervenience and negentropy?"

"Kierk, you were basically yelling at that kid. What the hell is wrong with you?"

"I wasn't yelling, I was correcting you. You, who somehow solved the mind-body problem and didn't bother telling anyone."

"We're not here to confuse them."

"No, we're here to protect them from morons who—"

"Kierk." Carmen, who's come up behind him, puts a hand on his arm because the two are now within a foot of each other.

"Come here, help me with this, we need to break down our table." Kierk laughs suddenly and explosively, claps Mike on the arm so fast and hard that Mike flinches, then the humor vanishes from Kierk's face. He and Carmen walk away as the remaining children trickle out the door, leaving a mess of a room with people dismantling their stations.

"It's not worth it, Kierk, it's not," Carmen says.

He stops, grabbing her arm. Turning her to him and looking her deep in the eye he says—"It's not?"

Kierk upends the nearest heavy table in a single movement, blocking its momentous downward swing with his foot, then, the table on its side, he shoves in those metal rings that keep its legs from collapsing, getting one up before moving to the next, but it won't budge, so Kierk, with a grimacing glance up at Mike, slams it in with his heel to a resounding clang.

DEADENED LIGHTS. TROUBLE WITH the microphone. Kierk has his Hello Kitty notebook over his knee. The lecture by Max (who introduces himself as "Dr. Pierce" to a scoff by Kierk) is on optogenetics and *in vivo* controllability. Kierk already knows this stuff so he sits in the back and amuses himself by writing avalanching sentences that come down the mountain and flatten the tree line.

Max is describing the full process that Kierk and Carmen had initiated in the surgery of the transgenic mouse last week—a virus is injected into the mouse embryo which inserts a gene into the DNA of neural precursor cells, a gene which is eventually expressed in the development of those cells' ion channels. This gene makes channels express rhodopsin, the same molecule found in the light-sensitive rods of the eye. These mutant rhodopsin sit like tiny alligator eyes all over the surface of the neurons. Kierk imagines the ever-dark of that organic jungle, the nocturnal glia, the thoughts curled up like napping jungle cats, a thousand sleeping thoughts with their claws retracted, the little mutant channels doing nothing in the natural dark of the brain. But one day there is a loud drilling and bone dust sprinkles down and then—for the first time—light coming in through a crack in the world, something beyond (but what could be beyond the world?) peeking in, the giant faces of Kierk and Carmen wearing surgical masks, a view which is immediately swallowed up by a snaking fiberoptic cable, which descends like a predator and then waits. Weeks later, after the healing process has run its course, some sleep-deprived graduate student says—"Let there be light." And with that the fiberoptic cable blinks on, illuminating the fibrous cave, and those rhodopsin channels open and the genetically designed neurons start firing. Max shows a video at the end of his lecture of a rat with a cable snaking from its head, and everyone chuckles as it runs around in clockwise circles.

"And to the left . . . annnnd to the right now. It's remote control."

The chuckling breaks into laughter as the rat pivots, its little body heaving with exertion. Kierk looks around at the crowd, mouth agape, and thinks about what it must have been like to sit in the room while the physicists and engineers were taking bets on whether the first nuclear bomb would be a "boy" and set the atmosphere on fire or a "girl" and not. To control something without understanding it . . . He feels sick. But then the lights are on to applause and everyone heads out in groups to get lunch.

SLEEP REFUSES TO CLAIM Kierk even as he lies still, all the rituals of going to bed completed. Instead he is lost in a cycle of mind, a tumbling over of the same problem. Getting up in the hot dark he flips on the light, yellowing everything, and starts to unpack the boxes that have taken up his bedroom floor. It becomes a slow browsing process that stretches on into the night—the unpacking is done as reverently as if lighting candles for Christmas mass. His hands touch spines, check inscriptions, flip to sections he knows. He lights a cigarette and takes a drag while looking down at the growing piles stacked around him, evincing an order only he can see. Slowly a bibliophilic recrudescence takes place, a real resurrection. My soul, he thinks, has been untethered by so unorganized a library.

He picks up a neuroscience textbook marked by odd stains, realizing where it's from—a neuroanatomical lab his first year of graduate school in Wisconsin, back when Kierk, ennui laying on him in a grime of nicotinic soot, had seen clearly his difference, his eventual end. One day he had gone to get the supplies for the neuroanatomy class: human brains. They were crowded in a white plastic bucket, suspended in formalin, bumping into one another like a school of marine life set to dead dreaming. They bobbed back and forth as Kierk had removed two, one after another. Each time his gloved hand had to cup the corralled reef of the cerebellum to keep it from detaching. He laid them delicately in a metal pan and took them glistening back to his lab partner. Then Kierk had stood posed with a scalpel in hand, staring. The classroom, the people, the voice of his partner reading aloud the lesson plan (step one: identify the central sulcus) entirely faded to the periphery, and instead all Kierk could do, sound and light and thought red-shifting in recession, was stare in deafness at the two brains, one bisected mediosagittally, the other still whole. In the buzzing deafness Kierk felt the problem was presented here so starkly, the problem he was most attuned to, his intellectual resonant frequency. How could such a gelatinous structure, suspended in fluid, sloshing to-and-fro under the force of acceleration, stabilized by the plush dura layer, the silky strands of the arachnoid layer, the skin of the pia matter, hold within its electrical storm the thin and definite and complex geometry of thought—of feeling, of blues and greens, of orgasms, of dying, of Jesus' time on the cross, of every possible experience—the naked axe of phenomenological realism cut through materialism like a dream of shattering clocks. If such a graying and solid object, wrinkled with sulci and gyri, something you can hold in your hand, could be conscious by just the erotic swap of chemical packages, this is followed by the more terrifying awful amazing thought—then what isn't conscious?

"Light is both a particle and a wave," Kierk had whispered, and, his partner paused in perplexed expression, Kierk stripped himself of his nitrile gloves, muttering the mantra over and over, in his haste to leave nearly knocking over an empty beaker at another pair's table. An aggressive question was thrown at his departing back. Thinking to himself—Both a particle and a wave. Both a particle and a wave. A particle and a wave. A particle and a wave. Some things have a dual nature. Subjective and objective. Subjective and objective. The brain is both subjective and objective. It's a paradox. For how can a thing be both subjective and objective at the same time? But perhaps paradox is merely an opportunity for transcendence.

Ignoring everything, he shrugged on his black peacoat and stalked out of the Medical Sciences building and across the pavement of University Avenue, which was windy with leaves, moving off under a sky that was gray-white and infinite in all directions.

FRIDAY

KIERK WAKES UP TO a concave whiteness, his body strangely placed, and in his slow movements of coming to he's shifting his arms and legs about in this slick technologically alien cocoon, above him, a ceiling stretching out in the bright clinical light, and around him, the curved surface cupping his body. The light above hurts his eyes, one hand going up to rub his face. Then he's suddenly fully awake and fully clothed, startling in his slouched position. Kierk is in the tub.

". . . What? Why the fuck?"

Amnesiac, he digs around to check his phone. He's late. With half of him pondering, worrying, the other half rushes from his apartment all the way to lab, sitting down at his desk pretending to be working, still wearing the clothes he woke up in, just as Karen comes out and waves him over to her office.

"How's everything going?" she asks as he closes the door, still blinking away sleep. "I wanted to catch up because I'm leaving for a conference. I'll be back next week."

"I've, ah, run into some problems. There's the issue of exactly how few measurements of consciousness can even be applied. Most are so ill-formed they don't even make sense to apply."

"Any good news?" Karen says with a chuckle.

"Actually I've been working on this little theory, more like an equation or two, to measure consciousness. Just something new to toy with right now."

"That doesn't sound like the first paper that the committee decided on."

"It might go into a second paper. Maybe where I'm able to present some of my own ideas."

"I'd like you . . . we'd like you . . . to focus on the first paper for now. That's what the committee talked about. That's how you'll be awarded your PhD. Or alternatively the collaboration you were planning with Atif and Carmen. Everyone would love that. I bet you could get a first-tier journal."

"One of my coauthors was hit by a subway train."

". . . Well, yes. Of course. But Carmen mentioned to me that you two were still working on that project? She said you were brainstorming together."

"Yup."

"How's that going?"

"Real well. Real well. I think we're onto something."

"Well okay then. Good to hear. So that's what you'll work on when I'm away?"

"Definitely."

FOR A REASON HE doesn't wish to explicitly consider, Kierk is attempting to find the roof again. The bones. But upon reaching the top of the stairs and finding no rooftop door, he realizes he is in the wrong stairwell. He backtracks and wanders around the top floor for a while, trying to find the other paths to the roof, but runs into doors to which he does not have access to: his keycard merely makes the locks beep red. He passes the breathing machinery, all organic with pumps and fluids and the ticks of recorded electricity. An autoclave sits like a dragon and boils the entries in its belly with loud clanging. Finally, he finds the door at the head of a stairwell with the flaked NO —XIT sign. Shouldering it hard, he bounces off to a loud clank. He looks over the edge of the railing all the way down and neither sees nor hears anyone. So he kicks it as hard as he can, once, twice, three times before his heel explodes in pain and Kierk hops up and down—Fuck fuck fuck—now leaning against the stairwell wall, one hand on his hip too, eyeing the door vehemently. Defeated, he limps away from his search.

Against his better judgment Kierk buys another pack of cigarettes at a bodega and, looking up and down the busy street, lights up in the braggart heat. Sigh of relief. The palindromic drone of cars. People talking on cell phones. Night is the old Indian woman discarding wilting flowers on the sidewalk in a heap, looking up at him from dumping the cut stems from an old white plastic bucket. He feels he is already forgetting California, that everything prior to this was a dream someone else had. Today he's been toying with the idea all day that consciousnesses are tautologies tied in nature—he's taken Schopenhauer's "world knot" seriously in his wondering at exactly how one might tie such a knot: through reentrant cortical connections, or through some kind of meta-mappings of sensory maps, and so on, but it's never enough, it's never radical enough to produce phenomenology from mere wrappings and recursion. Just another thing to add to the scrapheap. His shoe pokes at the pile of cut stems. He's reminded of the infinite theories of Adolf Lindenbaum's work, who showed that Boolean operators could make a lattice out of the infinite set of all possible theories, all possible models, every thinkable thought of the world—the vast majority of which are wildly incorrect. Lindenbaum showed how to order (but not to search) this vast library, which holds all truths. Somewhere, lost in that tower of Babel, that library of Borges, was the theory of consciousness. The one and only correct theory an infinitesimal needle in an infinite haystack. To see a glimpse . . . It would fit in how many English words, how many sentences? Half a paragraph, for those with the right vocabulary? Would it use information geometry? Thermodynamical work? Autopoietic symbol construction? Algorithmic complexity? Computation? Symbolic recursion? Stacking of hierarchical receptive fields all the way up to grandmother neurons? Quantum physics? Would any such theory give the tools necessary to describe exactly the inner life of the same Adolf Lindenbaum on that beautiful summer day in Lithuania, 1941, as he was rounded up by Nazis along with hundreds of other Jewish intelligentsia, all marched under that cheerful summer sun to a place of deep ashy pits and tall trees and faraway bird calls. Stand around the pit. Line up. Don't look behind you at the deformed faces amid the ashes. Pray. Know that the idea of God is a member of your ordered set of infinite theories, but hope now that He is a member of the by-definition true theories, the set of tautologies, the theories that must necessarily exist. Your heart is impossibly loud and the sky is impossibly blue. You are so afraid but cannot move. When it comes it's sudden, loud noises accompanying a rough push back like being shoved hard but in many directions at once and your body isn't really your body anymore. Then you're lying there mortally wounded among the dead, and all the theories in all the world bleed from you and slip into the sea of ash. All the dark embers are set to flame, a cigarette sparking against concrete, a heel crushing it out.

"YOU KNOW IT'S ONLY been a week since . . ." Jessica trails off as she shuffles off her coat and hangs it on her chair at the bar.

"God, I know. It feels so much longer than that," Carmen commiserates, setting down their beers on the table. As Jessica picks one up she says—"Should we be drinking again? I feel weird."

Kierk raises his glass. After a moment so do Carmen, Jessica, and Alex, and all four put them together to clinks.

"To Atif. May we honor his memory with deed," Kierk says. Carmen and he make eye contact as they sip.

Carmen asks—"So, Jessica, I haven't gotten to really talk to you about that night."

"Oh, God. No, Mike and I didn't hook up. Sorry. Too much information."

"Well, how much do you actually remember about that night?"

Jessica makes a face, shakes her head. She looks reluctant. "I . . . I actually don't remember much. The hookah place. And I remember the cab I got with Mike, kind of. Like a blur, or like, the sensation of walking. I must have been really, really drunk. And then the next thing I know I'm in my bed and it's morning and I have the worst, I mean, the worst hangover I've had. Ever. And it's weird because I never get hangovers. My dad is like that too. I didn't learn about Atif till Sunday and the email. God, his poor mother."

"So you don't remember how you got home?" Alex asks.

"No," she says, hesitantly.

"What about being with Mike afterward?" Carmen asks. "Does that fire any neurons?"

Jessica pauses. "Well, I don't really remember, but I asked Mike. Apparently he and I took a cab back to my place, where I, just like, collapsed. But he, like, helped me to my bed and there was a pot beside me when I woke up. Which was really nice of him."

"So he was there for a while?"

"Yeah, I guess. I haven't like, talked to him too much about it."

"And you were still in your dress?" Carmen asks.

Jessica set down her beer. "Why? What are you asking?" she says defensively.

"No, listen, okay, nobody remembers anything about that night."

"None of you remember either?"

Alex and Kierk shake their heads and Carmen raises her eyebrows as if to say—see!

Jessica puzzles her mouth. "Weird. Because it's like, if he was drunk, and that's why he . . . fell. But when we were leaving people were drunk but not like, *drunk* drunk. Were we? How did we all go blackout?"

"Perfect blackouts," Carmen says, "for at least five people. What are the chances of that?"

"Wait. So all four of us, plus Leon?"

Carmen is nodding. "That's right. But apparently not Mike."

"But we all drank the same drink. Like most of it was shared," Jessica says.

"Does anyone remember what Mike drank that night?" Kierk asks.

Everyone pauses.

"Because I don't," he says.

The other three shake their heads. Jessica says—"But I'm pretty sure we were all drinking the same thing."

"Okay. Well let's assume that's true for a moment," Carmen says, excitedly digging around in her purse and pulling out a slip of paper. "So I went and found out what type of alcohol we had, what those drinks were. It's something called kallu. It's a palm wine: wine made from sap."

"You went there?"

"I went there. I talked to them and this stuff, it's just wine. It's a little bit less alcoholic, actually."

"That's impossible," Alex says. Everyone is silent for a moment.

"Rohypnol," Carmen says, and then immediately looks around at everyone's reactions. Jessica gasps. Alex, after a moment of reflection, rolls his eyes. Kierk is inexpressive, thinking.

Alex says—"But . . . But what would the motive be? That's the thing. There's no motive."

Everyone looks over at Jessica, who's shaking her head—"I'm fine, guys, I'm totally fine! Besides that hangover the next day."

Kierk gestures a swift cut, stopping the quick back-and-forth. "Look, it could have been a known drug like Rohypnol. But it also could have been anything that does a short-term block of protein synthesis. Like Beta PMZ. Which stops the formation of new memories. Shuts down the strengthening of synapses so there's no more plasticity. You could go into any of the wet-lab freezers of the CNS and rustle up a whole host of cocktails. Stuff that's only used in research to block the memory formation of rats and monkeys. Stuff that wouldn't show up on a tox screen. Any one of the people who were out that night could mix that up easily. Dilute it in some water, put it in an eyedropper."

Carmen is nodding excitedly—"And that could account for the killer hangover we all experienced. Who knows what a short-term protein synthesis block feels like the next day? I'd guess it would feel like the worst hangover of all time."

"Maybe we all have cancer now," Kierk says. Everyone chuckles uncomfortably except him. He continues—"Let me tell you what I'm having trouble with . . . exactly what Alex said. Without motive there's no reason."

"Well there's SAAR," Carmen says. "There's implicitly a motive. It's happened before. Here, with Melissa, whose lab Atif was in. And in other universities too. It's plausible. I'm not saying it's true. It's a hypothesis."

"But you think they're connected to the memory thing?" Jessica says. "That's just so elaborate."

"Maybe not. We don't really know how the brain stores memories," Alex says. "We don't know how variable that is. There's been somnambulist cases of people driving without having memory of it, or even murdering someone, and obviously alcohol drinkers get blackouts or brownouts in which people can also drive, hold entire conversations, or have sex with someone. I mean god, I know I have!"

"How can this be natural. It's so strange!" Carmen protests.

"But not strange enough," replies Alex, "to overturn the null hypothesis. That this was all an accident."

Carmen, gesturing her doubt with her hands, continues—"What if this was something else gone awry? Like maybe Atif's death was indeed an accident. And the reason a smart top-tier young neuroscientist fell onto the subway tracks was because he was drugged, and originally there was a different target."

"Are you saying it was one of the Crick Scholars? One of us?"

"No!" Carmen says. Then—"I'm not saying it. Okay. I'm just listing hypotheses."

"Fine. Just don't go accusing people of things," Jessica says.

"I'm not! There's just a lot that's odd. Like something happened to us. Has anyone . . ." she says, "experienced any . . . continued effects?"

The table is silent.

"I'll go," Jessica says. "Because I didn't connect any of this until now. Um, the day before last I was walking around the city and it all . . . Sorry, I don't know how to say this. All the buildings were teeth. It creeps me out to even say it. I've been trying not to think about it. It was like a dream. But I was . . . I was awake."

There is further silence. Jessica lays her hand on her chest. "I keep losing stuff. I don't know. It didn't used to happen. And it's umm, pretty weird. Like I couldn't find the milk. And then it turned out I had put it away in the cupboard. I don't know, it could just be a coincidence."

Kierk pauses. "I heard something. At my door. Twice. But once was before Atif's death. And this morning I woke up in the tub."

Alex, eyebrows raised, shaking his head—"I'm fine." But then he cocks his head to think, frowning. "Well . . . There was this one thing. I was at work. This was like, two days ago. I sat down in the morning and then it was the afternoon. But it all happened *really* quickly. Time passed like it was a blink. I thought maybe I was just really busy but now . . ."

"Has anyone felt like they were being followed?" All eyes turn toward Carmen, who asked the question. Then, slowly, Kierk nods. So does Carmen. Alex makes a considering face, like he's internally debating, before making a gesture of unsure confirmation. Jessica puts a hand over her mouth, eyes fearful, almost crying. She nods. All stare at one another wordlessly.

"Hey, Jess!" All of them jump as a coat is thrown over the table and Jessica is wrapped up in an embrace. Two girls, one white, one black, come in a flurry to the table, shattering the spell.

"I didn't know you were inviting friends," Carmen says, then makes a face that Jessica can't see but Kierk can, causing Kierk to darkly laugh-sputter into his beer.

"What is this, the attractive academic support group?" the white girl who'd introduced herself as Jen says.

"Yeah," Carmen replies, "we're having T-shirts made."

Soon, the other girl, Chelsea, is deep in conversation with Jessica and Alex, while Jen has integrated herself with Carmen and Kierk. Jen is good-looking in a girl-next-door kind of way. Kierk notices that she wrinkles her nose when she laughs, which he likes. Soon they're hitting it off. Jen is apparently getting her MFA in creative writing at NYU, but knows Jessica through Chelsea, and the two of them go back to high school. Jen and Kierk end up talking about literature.

After some time she says—"Are you sure you're a scientist?"

"No," Kierk responds, drawing a laugh.

Eventually Carmen gets up to go get more beer, and Jen hands her cash.

"Just get us whatever." Carmen pauses for a moment before nodding her head and as she turns and walks to the bar she mimics under her breath—"Oh just get us whatever!"

At the bar the lone bartender is taking forever to service some forty people, and Carmen is stuck behind all of them. Two men have already approached in just the time she's been waiting here, each independently asking if she'd like them to muscle their way through and get her whatever she is waiting for, on them of course. Carmen wonders if people knew how predictable they really were, thinking of that Borges quote, something like—"the universal history is the reapplication of a limited set of metaphors." You could say the same thing about people.

While looking at her phone and trying to project unapproachability she keeps glancing back at Kierk and Jen, who are leaning in closer to hear each other.

"Hey, are you waiting for a drink? Want me to wade through? It's on me," someone says to her, and Carmen looks up to see a well-dressed man. Glancing back, Carmen sees that Kierk and Jen are still head-to-head. Turning back to the guy, she flashes a smile, bites her lip. Ten minutes later, they each carry a tray of drinks, maneuvering through the crowd. Approaching the table, there is some kind of a scene going on. Jen is standing up angrily.

"Oh, I'm sorry, am I boring you? Am I boring you?" Jen is saying. Kierk is kind of slouched back, looking up at the ceiling like he cannot believe what is happening. Jen continues—"I'm sorry, sorry that my fucking opinions are so inferior—"

"I didn't say that."

"Yeah, you basically did. Jessica, where did you find this guy?" Jessica kind of looks helplessly around. Both Chelsea and Jen are gathering up their things to leave. Kierk rolls his eyes, acting exasperated.

"Real nice sociopath friend here, Jess," Chelsea says.

"That term hasn't been used since the seventies. It's technically a psychopath."

"Fuck you!" Jen says.

"You would have," he says, smiling. "But I'd have died of boredom from your cadaverous taste in literature before we got that far."

Chelsea and Jen both give him the middle finger, to which Kierk shrugs. After hugging Jessica goodbye they pass Carmen and the guy she's brought with her.

"This is ah . . . Rob." Carmen lays out the drinks, mentally cursing.

Rob sticks out a hand. Kierk reaches past the proffered hand and picks up one of the gin and tonics and drains the entire thing, his Adam's apple bobbing. The empty ice-filled glass is still vibrating on the table as he wipes his mouth and says loudly—"Thanks, Ken!"—and then disappears into the crowd toward the bar. Carmen calls his name once before he vanishes.

Rob turns to Carmen. "Who the fuck was that?"

Carmen ignores him, debating internally, watching the crowd for sign.

THE NIGHT IS FULL of eyes, inhuman, a peacock's tail. Momus would have laughed. Everything left, even the city. Carmen comes out of the bar wearing Rob's hat. Alex pirouettes down the steps like an acrobat. Kierk is across the street already, had been for some time, sitting on the curb with his head in his hands. Distant voices call his name, looking for nothing at all. Kierk is thinking that materialism is a clock wound up by a macrocephalic god. The group is soon standing around him, including Rob the investment banker who has been hitting on Carmen all night with remarkable persistence and, so far, considerable charm. He hands out cigarettes to everyone. A lighter is passed around. Kierk shrugs off a hand on his shoulder.

"What's his story?"

Looking up from his hands—"This has all just been a terrible misunderstanding. Thank Galileo for that, that old fuck, for establishing some goddamn assumptions that are going to fuck us over in the end. He took the observer out of science . . ."

Kierk's head lolls about like a puppet with its strings cut. He shrugs off another offer to stand. Talk goes over and around him. A wall of legs, jeans, slacks, a dress. Some shoes are nicer than others.

"Materialism is a chrome clock wound up by the palsied hands of a macrocephalic god!" Kierk says loudly.

There is a drunken silence.

"Is this guy for fucking real?"

Carmen shoves Rob the investment banker into the street. A taxi honks as it swerves around him.

"Whoa! What the fuck! You could have killed me! You can't just shove people into the street to get hit by a car. What the fuck is the matter with you people!"

"FUCK OFF." Carmen gives him the finger.

"Hey, hey, I didn't start this, and—"

"YOU FUCK OFF."

"Christ, you frigid cunt, take a fucking pill."

Kierk, dark deeds on his mind, tries to get up, but instead, betrayed, becomes a caving scarecrow of night, tumbling back on his hands. The investment banker recedes offstage. Nervous laughter comes from Jessica until Carmen gives her a hard look.

Carmen, bending over him—"Here, Kierk, you want another hat? Take this hat."

With a green baseball cap that reads AIG firmly secured to his head, the three of them enter a process of lifting Kierk to his swaying feet.

"Just leave me here. Just leave me here."

"Okay, Mr. Dramatic," Alex says, "we're not leaving you anywhere. Let's go. Come on."

"This is all second-order reality anyway. The only really real thing is consciousness."

"Kierk, I never know what you're talking about," Jessica says, moving to help, but Carmen gets between her and Kierk. With a hand under each arm Carmen and Alex prepare to lift.

"Kierk, we're going to lift you up okay, and take you home. You ready?"

Kierk says upward at them—"To a materialist there's no beginning and no end to a Rube Goldberg machine. Trace its history back to the big bang and forward to heat death. Nothing starts and nothing ever stops for them. It can't be true. It's too absurd."

Carmen pauses. "Maybe I'm drunk too, but that just made a lot of sense to me," she says.

"Alright, let's get him up . . ."

SATURDAY

KIERK WAKES UP AND rubs the salt of sleep from his eyes, rolling over, his horizon the pillow. Maybe he's still drunk because the dream had been drunken, loose with imagery.

Some sort of Grecian monster, a surreal nightmare of a thing, had chased the fleeing Kierk into the benthic dark of the CNS, its stamping hooves following close behind, hide and seek, the thing behind him closing in, and he knows that if it finds him it will dig out his intestines, turn him into spilling offal, so Kierk keeps running until he's deep down in the basement. There he had flung open a door and found waiting for him a pale rubbery white wall, betraying a giantism that went back and back, revealing what was actually a great whale literally *under* the entire building, in fact *holding up* the entire structure that was resting on its monstrous bulk. Kierk, thinking beyond the curvature of his pillow now, the dream fading like an afterimage, wonders at the lack of realism. Not concerning the dream's events, but in his own reaction—that if you are being chased by a monster the most vivid thought would be that monsters existed *at all*, that up until now you've had the ontology of the universe entirely wrong. That's how he knew he hadn't really been there, because in the dream world you're dreaming up a self too, it's not you in the dream at all. . .

THE BUSTLING DUSK STREETS are so hot and humid Kierk feels his blood might curdle as he lugs his grocery bags and dodges through the crowd.

As much as Kierk might protest at the characterization, the grocery bags attest that he's really more of an aesthete than an ascetic. In California he ate only cheap sandwiches, pizza; he picked through cans of vegetables using plastic forks, ate handfuls of spinach directly out of the bag. Not just because of his meager budget but also it seemed a metaphysical statement, that this was fuel, just fuel, for an engine that sputtered the more he tugged on the pull cord. Now his three heavy bags are filled with figs, lobster salad, truffle oil, arugula, several cow's milk cheeses, a half pound of sea bass, extra virgin olive oil, garlic and fennel, some cooking wine, parsley and rosemary, polenta, garlic and herb crackers, salt, pepper, butter, a lemon. In another bag is a bottle of Riesling from Alsace.

At the steps of Union Square a small crowd has gathered around a street preacher standing on a wooden footstool, one hand raised in oratory. Most of the crowd appears to be accidental audience members. Kierk, passing through, stops to set down the bags and tie his shoe and wipe the sweat from his brow.

"And it is not JUST that they ask us to take a knee, and say that science is salvation, but that they force us to embrace it with open arms! Should we embrace the ATOM BOMB?! Should we embrace CLONES?! Should we embrace drugs that create ARTIFICIAL HAPPINESS?! We fund this research but give no money to those suffering on the street! We fund scientists who say they want to reduce humankind to biology!"

Kierk straightens up and looks over the crowd. He moves to the front concrete steps where there is clear line of sight. The street preacher is around Kierk's age and is wearing a red bowtie despite the heat. Sweat stains are clearly visible under his arms against his white dress shirt. A poster stands next to him with the words in blocky yellow letters: THE LIE OF EVOLUTION.

When the street preacher shouts the words he spits them out like he's been masticating them for a while, waiting for this. Kierk imagines in his personal life he would be shy and avoid eye contact, a bent head with a clean haircut, but once he's on his little footstool he spits and seethes. While examining him head to toe Kierk is also realizing what has struck him, a thing making its escape, a dark association—words identical to those on dozens of purple pamphlets spilled out over the subway floor.

Kierk sets his grocery bags by a tourist couple and moves through the crowd to the front. The street preacher is yelling out the running prose of himself—excising bile like the draining of a medieval humor; he's all spleen, lip spittle, and theological tax returns.

"—too long have our children been taught the undignified lie that we evolved from apes. But there are IN PRINCIPLE reasons to deny evolution! Yet this is not taught. The corruption prevents the return to the fold. The fight against modern science is done with the sword of faith. The rule of Christ is at stake, and unless these deceits are cast down—"

A few of the more downtrodden have separated themselves from the cosmopolitan passerby who are clearly taking this as entertainment. Three men in the front are ragged, unhealthy, moving in an offbeat tempo to the preacher's speech.

"—and it is only through coming to THE LORD that you can defy such forces, that we can become human once again, not animal, but human, without the—"

Kierk, in the front of the crowd now, begins to shuffle and nod along, hesitantly at first. Then, committing, he closes his eyes and lets the words rock over him, swaying to the preacher's rhythm. He's now with the other devotees, undergoing this strange public conversion. Kierk begins to shout—Amen!—during the downtime between sentences to punctuate the preacher's points. The preacher, emboldened by this new buttressing and vital force, responds in kind, becoming more vitriolic, more enthused. Kierk feels the eyes from behind, the members of the crowd disdainful, but he keeps clapping and shouting, nodding his head in agreement. Luckily he is wearing one of the few T-shirts that survived the purging of his old clothes, and although his new sneakers squeak cleanly against the pavement his movements and general attitude are convincing enough. The couple sitting on the steps looks on in confusion at this whirling dervish, this repentant sinner, and then back to the Whole Foods bags he'd set down beside them.

Kierk twists like a cobra in front of a snake charmer. Even the street preacher now seems impressed by Kierk's personal passion, the other desperate souls are egged on, and they continue this kind of dance to the preacher's rant, which itself winds from the evils of science to the glory of service to the giving away of all wealth. A small part of Kierk, blasé and impassive behind his eyes, is impressed at the oration. He wonders if afterward the preacher trembles as he washes his face in the sink of a public restroom. But as the preaching drags on long beyond Kierk's expectations, it begins to change from annoyed to snapping anger. He wonders what would happen if he went up and planted his fucking foot into the street preacher's little stool and kicked it out from under him. Mostly he is annoyed at himself: he did not count on having to maintain the charade so long. The preacher, as if sensing Kierk's approaching boiling point, stops, gumshoe mouth and all cylinders fired, and becomes again a man, pausing, glancing around at the traffic, blinking, and Kierk knows that look—it's the same look on Kierk's face when he finishes writing a scene, feeling precisely how Brahma must feel at each new creation of the world as he emerges from the center of it all blinking, looks around, lights up a cigarette, holds it up to his mouth with blue hands, takes a drag.

The preacher is gathering up his little stand and Kierk walks up to him looking like he just came out of a dance club.

"Amen, man, that was great talk."

Kierk had been right. The preacher does tremble afterward.

"I'm glad you liked it. But it is not me speaking. Can I provide you any assistance?"

"You said you were a member of . . ."

"The Following Brothers of Christ. An organization devoted to promoting the word of Christ as a shield against the corruptions of the modern."

"Well, I'm ready, I'm ready to change, you know? Like I've been reading a lot of stuff online. So many ways that scientists distort the truth."

"Good!"

"Do you have like, a pamphlet or something, a meeting or something? Like, how do I join?"

"Right here," he says, and after digging around in a bag hands Kierk a purple pamphlet with blocky lettering reading THE THREAT OF SCIENCE. Kierk flashes a dark glance at the preacher.

"We hold weekly meetings at a chapel on Fifth Street, between First and Second. We welcome all those who come to us before Christ and agree with our mission. To get involved go to that address."

"I'll definitely do that. So what do you plan on doing about all the corruption from science, all the lies?"

"Well, you'll see at the meeting."

"Have you considered like, action?"

"Action?"

"Against science."

"It is our duty to expose the hidden underbelly of flaws that rule over—"

"But more direct actions. Like outreach or picketing or something. Or like taking it to them, you know." Kierk makes a punching motion.

"Stop by next Monday. You should find it very interesting."

"Like I was reading about how they are going to like, map the human brain. Like a big brain map. What do you think of that?"

"Well obviously that would be against God, as he gave us free will."

"Exactly."

"You should come to one of our meetings. Fifth Street church. Most nights. The coffee is free. But right now I have to go."

"Wait, let me tell you of my path to God."

"Listen, I'm glad my message reached you, but I have to go now."

"Tell me—"

"I'm sorry, I have to go."

Kierk considers following him. Instead, he watches as the preacher waits for the pedestrian walk signal with his sign and little stool. People are staring at Kierk. He pockets the pamphlet, finds his untouched grocery bags sitting on the steps, and then heads home.

In his apartment he is deep in thought weighing possibilities as he unloads the groceries. The Riesling could now almost burn skin if gripped long enough. And on picking up the small plastic container, which is aglow with a sickly warmth, something globular is dissolving. Opening it, Kierk's upper lip sneers in disgust. The lobster salad has turned rotten from the heat.

SUNDAY

KIERK WAKES UP, COMING to awareness amid books, notes. Last night, there had been something important. He had stayed up late reading, thinking, sketching things out about consciousness, until it had all become a dreamy blur. Yet he remembers being sure he had made some sort of breakthrough. A hand goes out, finds a piece of paper which had been torn out of a notebook lying in bed with him, with large handwriting sprawling across it. Sitting up in bed he holds it up in front of him, squinting at the hasty and excited writing.

"Consciousness . . . is the . . . stone of the world."

Looking around for anything else, he puzzles his face. Finding nothing, he repeats the phrase. Standing, Kierk shuts off his alarm and meanders to the bathroom to brush his teeth. He laughs in the mirror, toothbrush in his mouth.

"Consciousness is the stone of the world!"

His phone buzzes on the dresser, next to the pamphlet from the preacher last night. Rushing back with his toothbrush in his mouth he looks at the name of the caller.

CARMEN AND KIERK ARE sitting in a coffee shop on the Lower East Side. Neither is sure if this is a date. On arriving they both apologize for Friday night simultaneously. Then, standing outside, they had shared a cigarette.

Carmen, after realizing that she never smokes but always does with Kierk, thought—bad sign, Carmen, old girl. She'd also done something today she almost never does anymore, and so currently her face is made-up, her lips a violet matched by her eye shadow, her hair straightened.

Inside they have a little corner to themselves, drinking coffee in two plush chairs, a low round table between them. There is a large open window at seat height right beside them so it is basically like they are sitting outside, and the temperature is perfect, a rare day where there is a playful breeze and a cool blue sky vividly streaked with clouds, as if they are sitting next to a large mural so realistic that tickling gusts are drifting over from the world of the painting.

First, they talk about Kierk's encounter with the street preacher, and the pamphlet that he found, which he shows to Carmen. He wants to go alone, but she convinces him they should go together to the next meeting of the Following Brothers of Christ to check it out. The conversation moves on to other things between refills.

"I was deciding between grad school and modeling, which was what my mom wanted me to do. Even if you're doing it part-time it takes up your life. I knew I wanted to go to graduate school for neuroscience but I didn't have a subfield yet, I didn't have any specified interests. After all, it's not like the textbooks even mention consciousness. Anyways, the decision was made after a fashion show at a party. Everyone, I mean, *everyone* was drunk on wine and shots. It's like this cream over everything, that's how it was at those parties. I didn't go to many but I went to this one. I had this friend, Sheila . . . God, I haven't thought about her in years."

"You were good friends?"

"Probably my best in the modeling world. We worked for the same agency and we kept each other company. There's an unimaginable amount of downtime while you're being a human canvas. Anyways, everybody in the house was drunk as hell and there were these uppers being passed around and I had a few. Probably a trigger for serotonin-release, like MDMA. And I'd never really done that before. I thought I was really daring, early twenties you know. It's not like I had a bad trip or anything. I do remember that I could see myself walking around past all these beautiful, drunk, sexy people. The kind of party where upstairs all the doors get closed and you can hear people having sex in them. All models and rich international pricks. Anyways, the party goes on and I do more shots. And later, and I remember this vividly, I was walking through the house, which felt like a mansion, and I was like gliding around."

"What were you doing?"

"I was trying to find Sheila. I wanted to leave or something. I finally get to this like, big decadent bedroom, and there's Sheila and this other girl, Samantha, Sam, also a girl who worked for our agency. On the big bed everybody's naked and Sheila is getting fucked by this dude. Another girl I didn't even know was giving a blowjob to this guy on the other side of the bed. Sam, she's also naked, is holding a glass bong and jumping up and down on the bed as the other four are having sex. And she's just bouncing there in between them, giggling and hysterically laughing and falling over. Sheila sees me by the door and she's literally having sex as she calls me over because Sam keeps falling on her as she's getting fucked, and she's like—'Sam, what the fuck I'm trying to have sex here, like, Carmen, come get Sam.' So I like have to grapple this laughing girl between these people having an orgy, get her to put the bong she's waving around down, and everything just smells like sex and sweat, you know, and this guy is like literally coming on the face of the girl next to me. At one point I fall over on the bed and land like right near Sheila's snatch so that I could smell the wet plastic condom with that, that acidic undertone. Hear everything, you know? It was just all bodies, all around me. Just all this flesh. And I . . . Sorry, this is probably way too much, but I was like, responding, you know? And at the same time I just felt like, disgusted with myself at that moment. Getting Sam out of there I nearly threw up in the bathroom as we left. Not because I'm a prude. I swear. It wasn't the number of people, or the openness, or anything like that. It was that it struck me as inexpressibly empty. And leaving that party I knew that I wanted what was missing. The problem is with our whole culture. There's no mind anymore, it's all just . . . flesh. Just half of everything. Just the material, that's all that anyone believes in. And not that there shouldn't be the material aspect of life. There should be bodies and mechanisms. Engineering diagrams are useful, good. Computers are useful, good. Psychiatric drugs can be useful, good. But somehow the information age, it's just body. Just syntax and mechanism. And we, humans, we're not just mechanisms and syntax. Like, real sex, real orgies, involve minds. Because we're something more. And we've forgotten the other part of us, the consciousness part of us, so everyone's life is now some kind of half-life. It's like the legend, I think it's from Aristophanes, where humans used to be creatures with four hands and four feet and two heads and we all got split in two. And we spend our lives looking for our other half. That's us now."

Carmen takes a deep breath, giving a quick glance to Kierk, sees him with hands clasped, face serious, looking like a psychologist bent forward in his chair in a way that feels natural, cultured, expectant.

She continues—"And I didn't want to be representative of that kind of ontology. I didn't want to be a body in a culture where everything was just body, just extension, even if those bodies were beautiful, but without a place for mind anywhere. To present only one face. At the time, my ex-boyfriend and I, we called the decision to give up modeling for science 'the mind-body problem.' Just a joking thing. But that night I realized I didn't want to just have a mind-body problem, I wanted to *solve* the mind-body problem. It took me a while to articulate it to myself like that, but I think it was true in the moment and it's still true. I don't regret leaving."

"And that's why you study consciousness now?"

"And that's why I study consciousness now."

"Fascinating."

"I don't usually . . . tell anyone that."

Leaning back in his chair, Kierk looks like he is appreciating a delectable wine, a psychic swallowing which is then gone.

"Don't worry, people tell me things all the time."

"Well, now you owe me a story," Carmen says, laughing nervously also in relief, her fingers dancing on her coffee cup. "So what about you? How'd you get into this?"

Kierk smiles wryly, looks down, clears his throat in preparation. Outside, beyond him in the window, Carmen can see a single cloud splitting in two like it is undergoing mitosis.

IN THE SUMMER AFTER they graduated from college, Kierk Suren and Mike Hogan—friends, classmates, and intellectual competitors in many late-night dorm-room debates—had gotten into Mike's messy black jeep, their science poster, "Neural correlates of bistable perception," secure in a plastic tube rolling around in the back. Together they had road-tripped up from Amherst, Massachusetts, to Toronto, Canada, so that they could present their poster at the fourteenth annual meeting of the Association for the Scientific Study of Consciousness, held by some clerical error on the exact same weekend and only blocks away from the main site of the G20 economic summit. As they drove, around them a legion of other cars bore protesters heading to the economic summit, protesters who were equipping themselves with an armament of balloons filled with paint, who had signs clanking around in their trunks instead of science posters, many of them listening to radical podcasts and communicating to one another via encrypted text messages. The occupants in the thousand cars around them were preparing for war.

The conference's opening reception had come with the smell of cigarettes. Mike was already back out on the balcony, smoking. Mike, thin, tall, with Jewish curls grown long, unkempt, talked and thought fast in a way that Kierk appreciated. In college they played chess with each other while running subjects in neuroimaging studies, and as the research subjects a room over watched the Necker cubes flip in bistability Mike and Kierk would exchange black and white pieces in rapid movements. At the time, the two college friends were also roommates for the summer, living in an apartment absent of all furniture except for yoga mats in each of their rooms for sleeping, and piles and piles of books on philosophy and science they passed back and forth, until even Mike's smoking habit had been transmitted to Kierk.

The welcome seminar to the conference was an affair of Brazilian coffee and glass chandeliers, plush leather chairs and bite-size berry tarts. A few people whose books Kierk had read welcomed the crowd. One of the first seminars was run by a member of Antonio Moretti's lab, which Kierk would be joining in the fall, so for three hours Kierk took copious notes. Next was an array of seminars held in large presentation rooms, which Kierk bounced back and forth between.

There were pathology talks:

"—a blindsight patient acts blind, they use a cane, their family members say that they're blind, they live the life of a blind person. A lesion to their primary visual cortex severs the main visual input stream to the brain. Yet if you toss a tennis ball at them, they'll catch it—"

Neuroimaging talks:

"—as you can see, we're showing this whole-brain ignition, which is very rapid and occurs after the stimulus is presented. So basically, instead of something being processed in a specific region, it's more about how the signal becomes integrated with the ongoing process that already dominates the brain, but this process is itself a mystery—"

And philosophy talks:

"—while no one has yet solved the scientific mystery of consciousness, it's worth noting that theories are currently substrate neutral. There's nothing special about neurons, no magic fairy dust that makes them consciousness. Because of this, we don't know where consciousness ends or begins in nature. What about complex systems? Or computer programs? Artificial intelligences? Or networks of interacting agents? After all, you yourself are merely a mob of neurons, all acting in concert, and somehow those neurons collectively generate experience—"

In the late evening everyone left the hotel, their black dress shoes and heels shining wet across concrete, oblivious to the watchfulness of the citizens they passed. After a few hours the same polished shoes all stumbled back to the hotel, as did Kierk and Mike after taking shots with some of the grad students, and it was only when they got back and drunkenly switched on the TV that they saw the cop cars on fire and the police in their riot gear marching in lockstep, and protesters called the Black Bloc, who wore ski masks and all-black clothes, and were smashing windshields and throwing Molotov cocktails into empty police cruisers, all of which had happened just blocks from the conference hotel.

The next day Kierk and Mike were standing around their poster, smiling vaguely and hopefully at each passerby. The two of them were wearing their nicest dress shirts and ties, looking out of place for how young they were. Then came the mind-numbing hour of explaining their poster over and over to passersby in thirty-second sound bites.

They ended up outside just after noon, with Mike smoking and Kierk throwing pebbles against the side of the conference building. Far away, sirens wailed, coming and going.

A young man about their age walked past them wearing a backpack. They both noticed that it was unzipped and a black mask peeked out. Sharing a look and in silent agreement, Mike flicked his cigarette and Kierk threw his last stone and then they began to follow him.

As they traveled deeper toward the areas of the previous day's protests the police activity grew around them. People were walking in odd paths on the sidewalk to avoid the shards of broken glass from payphone booths and bus stops and bottles. Kierk paused in shock when he saw the arm lying on the ground in front of him, before realizing it had been disembodied from a shop mannequin, and that other parts were lying about: a leg poised on a bench, a head tilted skyward in a tree. Shop owners were out boarding up windows. Unmarked white vans blasted down empty roads and through red lights for no discernible reason, a sea of tinted windows moving and crisscrossing in a higher order that looked random from the ground.

Mike and Kierk were swept away with the crowd, and soon began to see the first gangs of riot police dressed in black body armor with opaque, light-reflecting helmets, their badge numbers covered up with black flaps of fabric. The two ended up following a thin stream of people through lines of standing cops containing and directing the flow. They realized that they were surrounded by an army, and it was closing, shuffling closed, everyone flowing in the suggested direction, walking quickly or jogging down the only available route, and then they were funneled out into the south end of Queen's Park.

The statue of John Macdonald looked like a focal point for the protesters. There were at most a thousand, congregated densely in the front with a long petering tail farther back into the park. Behind Kierk and Mike, from the direction they had just come from, there was truly an army of police, almost as many police as there were protesters. Cop cars were parked sideways in the street and, far in the back, a division of Mounties patted the sweaty flanks of their horses outfitted with blinders and equine armor. The protesters, skewed toward the young, seemed motley and unorganized. Some passed around stainless steel water bottles, signs held down at their sides. A few of the protesters looked out for the hell of it, but others wore UV-resistant sunglasses and were tan and fit, like they had just come out of some protester boot camp.

The day was dipping toward boredom for all involved. A shirtless man sat on the top of the statue, flapping his arms. Signs were laid atop one another on the ground, people sat scattered and cross-legged. A few of the braver citizens had walked directly up to the police and began to chat with them, exchanging a few jokes, getting a few responsive faces, so nervously encased in glass and armor, to laugh.

A man in his thirties with a beard and forearms a deep tan shared his water bottle with Kierk, who looked fundamentally out of place in his dress shoes and dress shirt and dress pants and little laminated Association for the Scientific Study of Consciousness conference badge. Wiping his mouth,

Kierk handed the water bottle back. "Hey, man, I appreciate that. So what are you protesting about?"

The protester looked around, out at the police. "The world's pretty fucked up. What's not to protest about?"

"Actually, that's a pretty good answer . . ." But the protester was already moving off, because he had noticed something Kierk hadn't, which was that there had been some kind of change in the air, in the mannerisms of the cops. The police, arranged in a loose line a couple hundred long, twenty men deep in places, seemed to be organizing into different contingents. Somewhere in the city, a single man behind a desk, having in mind the Molotov cocktails used on empty cop cars yesterday, having heard reports of cops being sneered at or bullied and the windows of shops being broken, distilled all these individual facts together by the alembic of binary command: Do It. And the order had been relayed down the hierarchy from the original node, spreading out and multiplying diffusely along the branches until it reached an output layer thirty-thousand times larger than the source at locations all throughout the city.

Shots went off—the police were firing into the crowd. Kierk hit the ground, rolling away as the screams began to ring out. Looking up, he couldn't see anything, but people had stopped running. Kierk was one of the few on the ground. Mike was gone. Standing, he saw a haze of dissipating yellow gas, and realized that it was the sound not of bullets but pellets of tear gas. As the gas cleared people were falling over themselves trying to get out. A girl was too slow and the cops descended on her, binding her wrists as she screamed and her friends made confused half steps forward, yelling at the cops to let her go but keeping their distance as the girl was dragged by her feet back behind the lines. The last thing Kierk saw of her was her head bouncing along the concrete sidewalk as her body slipped from view.

Something in the crowd broke. It grew more vocal, more collectively responsive; it shifted with more unity, it roared with more certainty. An agreement was implicitly reached. A single plastic water bottle was thrown in an arc, splattering onto the clear riot shields and then spinning away fizzing under booted feet.

—"You call yourself citizens!" —"That was someone's daughter!" —"Take off your masks!" —"Show your badge numbers!" More water bottles created a rain of objects, most plastic but some metallic, chrome, along with balloons filled with paint. In response the army of police began to do snatch-and-grabs, performed in a regimented, almost ritualistic, manner. First the heavily armored ranks in the front would open up and out would sprint a pack of more lightly armored cops bearing batons. The crowd would react like all prey throughout life's history has reacted, surging away as those nearest tried to outrun not the cops, but the other fleeing people. The pack of police would home in on the unlucky, the unwary, the slowest, or one of the really hard-core professionals who wanted to be arrested and so stood waiting, making a peace sign, and then the baton would take them behind the knees, or at the shins, and the protester would be swarmed over like an obscuring pride of lions swarming a gazelle. A moment later the handcuffed protester would become visible again as they were dragged back behind the police army's line. Then the crowd of protesters that had surged away would refill the gap, moving right back up against the row of shields. Maybe on the thirtieth or so snatch-and-grab Kierk and Mike literally bumped into each other as they ran from a raid. They had left objectivity a while back so they ended up right at the front, chanting and screaming in a chorus with all the others.

—"SHAME! SHAME! SHAME!"

The cops' gas masks made them into armored bugs, things carrying death-wands, multilimbed. They began to move as if driven by the mask: it led them, they swiveled in unison, they beat their batons against their shields in unison, they stepped in unison, they breathed in unison. They closed ranks like centurions locking their shields together and then would push forward into the screaming, biting, shoving, crying, fighting mass of the crowd. By then Kierk had a serious antifascist psychological response going on and ended up getting too close, and so he didn't notice that from the back of the army a few dozen armored horses bearing masked riders had all been maneuvered up behind the front line. Mike and Kierk were both right up front when the ranks of the cops opened up to clear space and from merely twenty feet away a cavalry wedge of two dozen horses charged the crowd.

"Oh fuck!" Kierk managed to get out, before he turned and grabbed Mike by the arm and the two of them were sprinting away, the thunder of hooves behind them. Leaping over a row of hedges, they ended up clear of the charge, but turned in time to see a backpack-wearing man whom they had raced past be trampled by three of the horses, his body and backpack flapping around like a rag doll. The girl next to them kept up a high, continuous scream. Then the cavalry wedge wheeled around and was absorbed by the waiting shield wall. There was a shocked, low silence, but still the protesters regrouped, re-congealed. And over and over the same series of events repeated themselves as the protesters were slowly, one foot at a time, pushed out of Queen's Park and into the Toronto streets.

The two of them ended up separated from the rest of the protest by a series of police rushes and advances designed to carve up the main mass. They were together with maybe three hundred protesters on a tight little street. It felt boxed in because the only exit was the far terminus of the street, what seemed like a world away, where cars were peacefully passing. The sides were a flat wall of buildings. At first everyone relaxed. The rest of the cop army kept streaming past. Some of the protesters in the little group tried to keep the energy up but everyone felt splintered, cut off, they couldn't even see any of the other groups, just the endless passing legion of police. Then the thin strip of cops guarding the entrance of the street suddenly got a whole group of reinforcements, tripling their numbers. As the legion kept streaming past, the armored cops at the mouth of the street began to beat their batons against their shields and advance. Kierk suddenly felt that everyone in the crowd was thinking the exact same thing—There's only one exit to this street in the far back and if any of these passing police circle around and block it off then we'll be trapped in here and we'll all be beaten and arrested and so we have to get to that end of the street before they block it off and wall us in because they are probably circling around right now. The thought raced across the crowd like a neural pulse through a web of synapses, everyone sparking off at once, and in about five seconds suddenly all three hundred people were surging, running, forming a stampede. The line of police followed the running protesters at a jog, banging their shields like they were flushing animals. As the stampede gathered force there were calls for everyone to stop, to slow down, but by then it was too late because people were now running just to keep from being trampled, their eyes wild and rolling. And over the moving mass of bodies, within it, everywhere and nowhere all at once, hung a single feeling, felt by each person, yes, but also all on its own, a dull beast experiencing fear and existing only for a few minutes.

Kierk saw someone go down in his peripheral vision, and then in front of him a bicycle stand, and with no space on either side of him to move out of the way he had to jump clear over it, landing wildly before being quickly enveloped again. He saw the form of the woman running next to him stumble and he reached out and grabbed her hand, yanking her forward and keeping her on her feet. They ran holding hands and when Kierk glanced over it was a middle-aged blonde woman who looked like a suburban housewife, her hair up in a bun, her mouth a thin line, her eyes terrified. Her hand gripped his like a vice and they balanced each other amid the surging motion until everyone burst like a flood out of that thin street and the dull beast that had known only a single feeling in its brief life dissipated.

As Kierk and Mike would learn the next day, at that very instant their names were being called at the conference, and heads were turning in the well-lit and calm main room, a slow stir among a well-dressed crowd. The two of them had won the best student poster prize, but with no one to accept, the conference organizers had finally, and awkwardly, given it to the runner-up.

Hours after the mad rush of the mob, Kierk was sitting on a small brick wall off of a sidewalk in a little shady spot underneath a tree. Beyond him, small sounds still exploded into motions of people running from the aftermath or the racing forms of ambulances, shattering the glass garden of silence that had grown up toward the sky with the exhaustion of everyone, the exhaustion of the protesters, police, bystanders, the exhaustion of police dogs that lay panting in the shade. Mike was away getting them hot dogs and water from a nearby food stand and Kierk was depleted and waiting, his stomach rumbling among the people milling around, recovering in lower murmurs. A few smaller bands of riot police marched by but without a critical mass of people it was as if a truce had been called, clemency granted, and now the scattered groups were merely citizens again. A play had ended and the actors, still in their makeup, were mingling with the audience. Kierk, however, was still eyeing the loose formations warily. Across from him, on the other side of the small street, one of the riot police had stopped while the others went on ahead. The officer proceeded to draw a plastic water bottle from his belt and take a few long sips, then poured the remainder over his head and face. Finished, he looked at Kierk, noticing that Kierk, exhausted, was rubbing his elbow absentmindedly and had blood running down the side of his head because he had been whacked by a stray baton, that his eyes were red and bloodshot from the gas, the left eye so much so it was puffy, that he looked like he reeked of tear gas and pepper spray and his tie was loose and low and twisted around, that in the evening doldrums his clothes hung loose on him, that he had dark pit-stains under the arms of his dress shirt, and there was blood—not his own—splattered on his slacks. The cop, a stocky man of about forty with his hair so wet now with sweat and water it looked like he had been swimming, noticed all this and only solemnly nodded to Kierk. And Kierk, seated on his little brick wall overlooking the passing of pedestrians, thought about what that man's day must have been like, the soreness of his quads, what it felt like to have wet hair and a right shoulder on fire from swinging a baton, his visual field and his feelings toward the mess of a protester sitting on a low brick wall across the street, sharing this moment with him. Kierk thought of the suburban housewife, running beside him, the fear in her eyes. Considering these things, he was a still point in everything, it was all slowed, the water seemed to drip off the stocky cop's head in slow motion and a car moved past like a slow thrumming beast. It was only a few minutes until Mike would return with hot dogs and the news that he had decided to become a war correspondent instead of a scientist, but at that moment Kierk, still dazed, brought his hand up to his ear and felt the sticky aching spot that hummed when he touched it. Every sound was somehow both muted and loud as if the streets had become an amphitheater, unique, clear, real, and behind it all there was the double-thump sound of valves opening and liquid pumping through and Kierk could not tell if it was his heartbeat or a portent of the world spirit, but he could feel that the brick under him was a solid surface, his mind was a tuning fork still resonating, the air was a medium for prophecy, the glare of colors were bombing past him like schools of fish exploding in the setting sun—at the exact origin of this he felt he was a djinn at the epicenter of history and knew that he would be the one to solve the mystery of consciousness.

LATER, AS THE SUNLIGHT is sliding off toward the end of hours, a completion of day, Carmen has just waved goodbye to Kierk, laughing a bit, straightening out her dress, moving to stand at the street corner. The light changes. As she passes a car honks, causing her to jump. Inside, a watching head behind glazed windows. Carmen pulls down the dress more, aware of herself now, the click of her heels on the pavement. On the sidewalk groups instinctually move out of the way, each splitting as they let her carve a path through them, all turning, men and women alike, with looks of approval or disapproval or open appraisal as eyes saccade over her clothes and hair. Her body is read like it's language. Her mind is still echoing and exposed due to the story she's just told Kierk, and she is now suddenly reevaluating his attentive face, his leaning in, his interest in each word, and with this a deep and old insecurity rises: that all her relationships, both professional and not, are warped unnaturally by this biological form that cannot help but attract, a thing no more impressive and just as predetermined as a pitcher plant emitting its tantalizing scent. What she likes about Kierk is his seemingly unaware resistance to it; she feels that his disinterested intelligence acts like some kind of shield for it, but suddenly she is unsure, worrying at what she's building and how genuine this budding bridge really is.

It is a busy afternoon. On the avenues the flow of people perceptibly recognizes her, clears space. Girls with long painted nails size her up. A homeless man exclaims as she passes. A group of men lounging on concrete steps fall silent, all looking. A fleeting summer day myth, Carmen makes her way like a serpentine medusa through the Grecian columns of the city towers, the summer light clinging to her, until she stops by the glass mirror of a building to evaluate herself. At first it is merely to tilt her head and move aside some stray hairs, but then, her mask dropping, she suddenly begins to rub the lipstick from her mouth, which comes off in a violent violet streak on her forearm, and then she's smearing her foundation with her palms, tugging down her dress as low as it will go, and it is only when digging around her purse to come up with a clip with which she tries to pin her hair up in an ungainly bun that she realizes the mirrored wall of the building is in fact a window onto a coffee shop. The inside snaps into focus and within she sees the many faces that have turned to watch her, looking up from their seats or turned in the line, all paused, earbuds dangling, mouths open, frozen.

MONDAY

KIERK **WAKES UP AND** dwells for a while amid the covers, already having a coherent mental conversation with himself over the flat liquid mercury of his mind, a monologue proposing that perhaps, during the waking operations of the brain, small segregated parts of it become cut off, involved in only their own processing, and produce within them functional micro-consciousnesses, disconnected events, local dreams, perception without a self, qualia unassigned, unknown and amnesiac, whole brain circuits left in an idling conscious state, forming and winking out at a startling rate. Perhaps even this very thought occurred in one such micro-subjectivity and then bubbled up to fill the space of his receptive morning mind, and that every day's consciousness was the continuation of some lucky dream.

In the lobby of his building, as he is passing the security desk, tapping out a cigarette from a new pack, someone calls to him.

"Hey! You look like you're feeling better!" Standing behind the shoehorn desk is a smiling middle-aged black man in a dark blue uniform.

"What do you mean?"

"You probably don't remember me," the security guard guffaws. "I normally work the night shift. Last time you saw me you were, I mean, I've been there myself. You certainly had a time of it."

"Friday," Kierk says. "You're talking about the Friday night before last."

"Would have been around then. Man, you were far-gone. I feel that though, I feel that."

Kierk's manner has changed in a way that only someone who knows him would notice: now there is a different stance, an aw-shucks tilt to his smile, his sentences not rapid-fire as usual but drawling and slow.

"So . . . What can you tell me about that night? I'm missing some parts of it."

"Well that's too bad. That's something to remember. You were with that girl. What a thing. What a creature! Give me five, man."

Kierk high-fives him quizzically, his face one of confusion. "What girl do you mean?"

"The blonde one. You two were hot and heavy together on the sidewalk, man. Gotta hand it to you. Most fine-looking woman I've ever seen. I thought for sure she was going to go upstairs with you, cause you both came into the lobby, and were still going at it. Making out. Not that I minded, man. I was rooting for you. I thought that you were gonna score big man. But then you both left."

Kierk's mind is an explosive carnival of music, a round of live ammo dropped. "We left? Why?"

The security guard gives a deep-bellied laugh. "Don't ask me, man, can't believe you did. You were doing your thing in the lobby for a sec. Then you left."

"Do you remember the time?"

"Actually, I do, because we get a security check at 2:00 a.m. This was a little after that. Maybe fifteen minutes later?"

"And when did I come back?"

"Oh shit, man, don't tell me you let that get away. I was hoping you had gone to her apartment."

"No, man, I woke up here."

"Crazy night, huh. My shift ended at four and I didn't see you by then."

Kierk drums his fingers on the desk. "You're saying that I did not walk through those doors to go to bed until sometime after 4:00 a.m. that night?"

"Well, I guess that's right."

". . . Beyond the utmost bound of human thought," Kierk mutters to himself, lost.

"What's that?"

"What? Oh, nothing. Reveries. Impossible connections. Poetry and lost time. I can't . . . I'm sorry, thanks so much for your time."

As he leaves, the security guard calls out to him—"Hey man, you make sure you go after that lady!"

Kierk, having reached the glass doors, looks back and nods, then pushes the doors open.

He smokes the cigarette he's been holding while pacing the steps of Union Square. He is uniquely aware of his lips, his hands, his body seems new to him, fit, sexual. Sitting on a bench he closes his eyes and briefly reviews the imagery and memory techniques of Cicero, Ramon Llull, and the origin of the concentric circles on his back—Giordano Bruno. Then he filters out everything. The outside city sounds become a white noise. His whole mind is now laid out as landscape, passages and buildings of artful Grecian architecture, workshops cluttered with hand-drawn maps and wooden globes, beakers and trigonometric instruments, chalkboards lined with mathematical scrawl, the reliquaries of books, hanging gardens, pools with bottoms of smooth white stones traversed by bulbous-headed fish, and a room with a view and a typewriter sitting by the window. Beyond this small village of civilization are the desert regions where desire and ambition rage as dervishes of weather and sand, and where half-buried pharaonic halls contain within them the stone statues of himself, their visages worn in the timeless heat, all bearing different versions of his face. Kierk summons forth a white space where his mental avatar appears to him, awaiting attributes like at the start of a video game, and he first wraps it in the clothes he had been wearing, then sets it walking out of the hookah bar, the rain is added in, Alex is set laughing on the steps, Atif is set standing looking up, Carmen is set smiling at him. From the surrounding white infinity a taxicab drives into the little domain of color and objects. As the avatar climbs into the cab the perspective shifts and it is Kierk climbing into the cab, Carmen scooting up her butt into his lap. Rain on his hands coming through the window. Her hands over his hands in the spray. Leon in the front seat, the outline of his head shifting about. The jerk of a stop. The form of Leon is exiting, leaving just Alex and Kierk and Carmen, and Alex goes to the front, and then the lurch of a start again, Carmen ending up in his lap, thrown over him, body unto body, hair mixing so close now, their faces inches from each other, the exotica of another's breath, lips meeting, her tongue surprisingly cool, wet from rain, the incredible texture of an unknown mouth responding, everything spinning but her mouth, hands gripping at each other, trying to break free of the material world and into each other, and then there is a wall of obsidian black, perfectly smooth and texture-less and extending like a monolith up and up forever. Kierk opens his eyes to the passing lines of people, the burned-out cigarette in his hand. If any part of him remembers the further events that memory is wrapped up as tight as the higher dimensions of string theory, everywhere and nowhere in him all at once.

PROFESSOR NORMAN BENNETT WATCHES the verbose young man in front of him pick his nails down to the quick as he talks, a rolling expanse of words, a prolix assault that Norman can't quite make sense of. They're supposed to be having a meeting about scheduling participants for neuro-imaging runs (Norman has surreptitiously checked his calendar twice to make sure), but instead Kierk is talking about subtle biases in the setup of neuroimaging experiments, and something about "tracing causation in reentrant chaotic systems is a mathematical impossibility." Indeed, he's still blathering on—". . . I mean it's basically a convenient happenstance that hemoglobin responds differently to magnetic fields based on whether it's bound to oxygen. Sure, neurons in a particular brain region might increase their energy-hungry firing and therefore the vascular system initiates a hemodynamic response bringing more blood to the area with increased glucose need. In theory! So yes, presumably this hemodynamic response increases and decreases with neuronal firing. But we all know how sluggish it is. The blood takes two seconds to rush to the aid of neurons in need, and oh hey, it's variable in its intensity and timing, meaning that fMRI has a temporal resolution that's like averaging a symphony into a single note . . ."

The girl, Jessica, sitting next to Kierk and nodding, is looking more and more convinced. Norman holds up a hand.

"Thank you, Kierk, but just so I know, as a Crick Scholar, are you planning on actually doing any neuroimaging while you're here at the Center?"

"Honestly, no."

"Okay, well, let's focus on that, not on the effectiveness of neuroimaging as such, hmm. I have a meeting in a few minutes," Norman lies. He stands up behind his desk and begins to move toward his office door, a trick he has found which causes people to begin automatically retreating. Kierk and Jessica are ushered out, thanking him for his time. As the two of them recede down the hall, he hears them mention "Bennett" and "Nobel" and smiles as he closes his office door, goes and sits behind his desk. He leans back in his chair, reliving in his mind the handshake with the king of Sweden, that red carpet, redder than anything he'd ever seen, the flushed pride of his wife. Yes, her pride. His research on functional magnetic resonance imaging, the first real leader in the field, led to him sharing the prize in physiology with two colleagues.

In this, his memory is transparent crystal—he's almost there again on the plane ride back from Stockholm. First class. He and his wife are holding hands, hands beginning to vein with age. The endless parade of parties and processions is over. They have laughed together and danced together, along with the other laureates, in a ballroom of red and gold. She sleeps but he can't, so he watches the in-flight movie. It's a romantic comedy. They are both exhausted as they take a taxi from the airport back to the house. The road is dark and bumpy and hypnotic. Looking out the window their home comes up on them in the darkness. He pays the cabdriver and assists his sleepy wife out of the back seat. He worries about her. It is December and very cold. The lawn is frosted a ghostly white and their breath comes as fog as they walk up the path to the front door, their suitcases a track of noise behind them in the dark. Put the luggage at the bottom of the hallway stairs. The house is freezing, so find the thermostat and adjust it up. Get out of this suit. Get out of this dress. Brush their teeth. Put socks on. Collapse into bed, but not before resting on the mantle the gold and glamorous Nobel Prize on its stand. Then the lights are turned out and they lie next to each other in the dark. Besides their wizened forms underneath the sheets the house is empty. There is no one to tuck into bed, no turning of a small body from its back to its side, no pajamas to put on one leg at a time, no small hands, no small toes. There is no small bed frame to check under for monsters, there are no children's books on the mahogany bookcase, no toys left underfoot. There are no bedtime stories, no giggling and soft sleepy yawns, no restless visits in the blue-black of the morning, no small hands, no small toes. There is just the empty altar of the house, a piece of metal on the mantle, their age, and the haunting by a child that never was.

Carmen stands under an overhang with wet splotches all across her shirt, her ponytail now a wet rope, and she's wiping away the drops clinging to the fine hairs of her arms like ants, which had been the advance guard to the army that is now marching just beyond her little rectangle of shelter.

The street is a sheet of water. The rain has taken on its own patterns, a series of shifting frames spliced at just wide enough of an interval to bob up as discrete objects in her stream of consciousness. Cars come and go like ghost submersibles. Under the same overhang is a girl, maybe an NYU undergraduate, having taken shelter at the same time as Carmen when the sky broke with a crack and the white noise of rain boomed up the avenue and all the humans scrambled for cover. On the concrete wall behind them both are words writ large in red spray paint: DOUBLE TROUBLE LIVES. Carmen feels camaraderie with this girl—she looks as miserable as Carmen, and though they haven't spoken since they both nodded to each other upon reaching the overhang, and although the girl has been texting on her phone this entire time, Carmen feels that they are sharing this little intimate experience. She had also been wearing mascara like Carmen so now it looks like they've been crying together, two sad raccoons huddled from the rain.

Then through the shadows of rain a young man under a giant umbrella comes jogging up. The girl hugs and kisses him, casts a quick look of apology at Carmen, and then the two of them vanish into the rain, leaving Carmen alone in front of the red lettering, shivering and hugging herself.

"Oh, give me a break," she says, her teeth chattering.

She stares out into the rain at the barely visible entrance to the church where the Following Brothers of Christ are supposed to be meeting. What the hell is she doing here? Of course she can account for the material sequence of events: that night, the train, the email from Atif's mother, the investigation, Kierk's finding of the pamphlets. But these were merely the surface occurrences, not explanations of her own motivation. Carmen knows that even for a simple artificial neural network, trained by humans to, say, identify pictures of cats versus dogs in photographs, expressing the why behind any decision it made was in many cases mathematically impossible. A dark truth that made the naïve ways people tried to explain human behavior nothing more than a series of fads and post-hoc explanations, from Freud to therapy couches to the physiological analogy of "trauma"—what hubris, to think that what was impossible for a few hundred lines of code was possible for the brain! Perhaps the true prime mover of her motivation could only be found in some memory hidden deep down in the weights of connections between neurons, a delicate piece of neural lace that if held up with the smallest of tweezers would appear barely a gossamer strand of a spider's web, but if unraveled in some still-unknown way would contain a single memory: as a girl she'd been given *D'Aulaires' Book of Greek Myths*. Carmen the little girl had splayed it out on the floor almost every night, and leaning over it had flipped through those colorful pages, hypnotized by tales of gods and monsters and titans and men and women, and within those pages one had been a colorful sketch of a woman surrounded by impish monsters, a woman who had seemed the epitome of beauty to Carmen as a child, a woman who was drawn inexorably to a box, haunted by it, until she had finally thrown it open. While for the adult Carmen, approaching this mystery in a scientific way is important to her—gather evidence, be open to possibilities, rely on both deduction and induction—those scientific methods don't account for her abiding certainty that there is something to investigate, no, that certainty came from that young girl crouching over the colorful pages. There are boxes in the world that contain mysteries, and they must be opened; such irrational faith is what exists behind all of science.

"Brrrrrr," Carmen says, pacing from one side of the overhang to the other, crossing in front of the giant red letters.

Then through the rain she makes out a form sprinting across the street, and after clearing a knee-deep puddle by the curb in a giant flying leap Kierk is under the overhang, completely soaked like he had just emerged clothes and all from a pool.

"Oof!" he says, as she hugs him, laughing.

"You're freezing." He's rubbing her arms, which are suddenly lined with goose bumps as they pull out of the embrace but linger, standing close to each other, his hands on her.

"That's it over there, right?" he says, gesturing across the street.

"The meeting should be going on right now."

Hand in hand they race across the river of the street and burst into the small entrance of the church. They end up in an annex, Carmen wringing out her ponytail onto the marble, sopping and laughing.

Trailing puddles and following signs down steps they arrive at a basement room. A man is speaking, of similar dress and manner to the street preacher that Kierk had approached. Around him are dozens of folding chairs. Most are filled. All heads in the church basement turn toward Carmen like magnets orientating along a vector field, running the gamut between homeless and well-to-do, but all male. Their faces shift to disbelief as she brushes away a few stray wet strands of hair from her face.

Kierk leans over to whisper—"Great undercover work, *Frauleinwunder*."

She elbows him discreetly and he stands jokingly nursing his side as she makes her way as naturally as possible to get herself a Styrofoam cup of coffee, men parting before her as if it were Cleopatra herself approaching.

". . . not that there is any evidence of this! No! It is just assumed true. That's why you have to learn how to muster your arguments against theirs. Set side by side, one is clearly superior, as clearly as when the snake of Moses swallowed up the snakes of the Egyptian sorcerers."

As she's getting coffee Carmen smiles at an older man with a white mustache who's leaning against the coffee table.

She quietly says—"Excuse me. What exactly is the purpose of this organization?"

He's chewing gum and looks over at her with gray eyes.

"We're a peaceful organization."

Carmen pauses. "Yeah, I mean . . . of course. But I wanted to know if there was like, a mission statement or something."

The man points to the wall behind the speaker, on which hangs a banner reading THE FOLLOWING BROTHERS OF CHRIST: TO SEEK THE TRUTH, TO EXPEL THE MYTHOLOGY OF THE SECULAR.

"Thanks . . . So is there somewhere I can sign up? Like a member roster? An email list?"

The man shakes his head.

"How many people are in this?"

The man shrugs.

"Yeah, um, thanks a lot . . ." she says, then takes the two coffees and sits down next to Kierk, handing him one, shaking her head to answer his unspoken question.

"And yes, we've attempted to reach out to them. At Columbia University we picketed a month ago outside the so-called evolutionary biology building and were manhandled, yes, we were *attacked*, by the security guards. But the theme of this summer is rising a new threat. Apparently there is a program at NYU, this Francis Crick Scholarship, a program that is devoted to the supposed biology of consciousness. The biology of consciousness! They want to explain the human soul in terms of nerve cells! They want to convince the public that science can explain not just the origin of creation, and not just life itself, but also your very soul!"

Carmen and Kierk share a glance with wide eyes, each marking how far it is to the exit. Kierk cannot but feel that some trap has been laid, but the preacher continues as if they weren't present.

"... these scientists are the next threat to our faith. Just as evolutionary biology sought to destroy the notion of God's design, so does this supposed science of consciousness seek to destroy the notion of the soul. It effaces the human. It disposes of our divinity. It is our duty to stop them, under the guidance of Christ our Lord. Amen."

"Amen," the men all echo back at him.

There is a smattering of applause, which Kierk and Carmen hesitantly clap along to. Carmen tries to stop Kierk from raising his hand but it's too late.

"Hi! Everybody. I actually got interested in this by the person who sometimes hands out pamphlets at the Bleecker Street Station. I forget his name. Does anyone here know who I'm talking about?"

There's a long pause. Finally the preacher says, "Now why would you want to know that?"

"I . . . just wanted to thank him. We had a good discussion. Really helped me out."

"We hand out pamphlets all over."

"But specifically I'm looking for the guy who does so at Bleecker Street Station. Red baseball cap?"

"If you come next week, maybe he'll be here."

"Oh, okay great, I'll, ah, look for him again then." And then Kierk sits back in his seat, rubbing at his hands. He sees in the front row the street preacher, now dressed in normal clothing, who had told him about the meeting yesterday. The young man turns toward him, looking him directly in the eye, to which Kierk's knee nervously bobs up and down.

Carmen puts a hand on his knee, looks at him quizzically, mouths—What?

"Well if that's it for everybody let's break officially and then we'll start to meet and greet our new members. But first, a prayer."

Everyone puts their heads down to pray and closes their eyes. When they open them the rain-soaked young couple has vanished.

"Okay, so I guess this is it," says Kierk, both of them standing outside the CNS in the bright lamplight. The rain has stopped. The night is full of sweet sounds and cars passing on Broadway.

"So sorry I have to do this," Carmen says. "My participant is supposed to meet me here."

"Hey listen, there's something I wanted to tell you," he says, suddenly serious.

"What?"

He informs her about the security guard seeing him and Carmen at an estimated 2:15 a.m., but that they had left shortly thereafter and Kierk hadn't returned until after 4:00 a.m.

"So you're telling me you weren't home yet by the time of the murder?"

". . . Yes. That's what I'm saying."

"But if you weren't home . . . I had cleared everyone who was in the taxi. Leon, Alex, me, you. After the bar we all went in the opposite direction and I assumed the cab dropped us off at our apartments. Now . . . Anyone in that cab could have gone back in the meantime, texted him to meet or something. Then pushed Atif in. Oh my god."

"So you're suspicious of everyone?"

"Think about it, Kierk. There are just two tenure-track positions available for eight Crick Scholars. And it's not like those just come around, not at a place like NYU. Those jobs are once-in-a-lifetime offerings. And Atif was stiff competition. He had a great publication record, got along with everyone, and wasn't white."

"So now you think it was a Crick Scholar?"

"Listen, cui bono? Who benefits? I'm just saying that in some sense, everyone had a motive. Even you and me. Even Alex."

"You're willing to put yourself up to the same level of scrutiny?"

"But I have direct access to myself. I know I didn't do it."

"Do you? What if you went for some reason, somehow, and Atif tried to grab you? Grope you. And you got mad or scared and pushed him and he stumbled backward and fell on the tracks."

Carmen pauses, thinking. Then she says—"I have no text messages. How would I have found him?"

"Maybe he said where he was going before but we forgot?"

"Fine. I'm on the suspect list. But I'm low on the suspect list."

"What about me?"

"Give me your phone."

Kierk hands it over. "If there was anything, I'd have deleted it." Carmen shoots a glance upward before he breaks into a smile—"But I didn't!"

She hands him back his phone and they both stand chuckling for a moment. "Alright, you and I are both very low on the list then."

"Good to hear."

Carmen, looking at him quizzically—"So what the hell were we doing in the lobby?"

"This." And Kierk pulls her to him.

There's a quiet gasp and the two are leaning into each other, Carmen on her tiptoes, their hands immediately clasping each other's bodies, and in the wet glistening of the city at night their thoughts slipstream as their lips meet and everything becomes the violins of biology, the cool wet mouths provoking a spiritual déjà vu, like they've done this before, done this a thousand times in different ways and with different tongues—and suddenly there is just the opening of a mouth, just the electricity of a hand on my waist, touching the flesh under the clothing, yielding, the feel of a hipbone under my hand, hands designed to grip grasp and un-grasp, the heat of your body a whole other engine burning away in its chassis, how soft can anything be, the barest of her exhalations across my face, the contrast of his stubble on my cheek, a small trembling rhythm to it all, poetical flesh in the smallest friction, the exact center of reality has been located, it's your mouth—the scent of her hair a beguiling scent from another land—the scent of his rained-washed body a sharp citrus, the bloom and decay of the rising blood, arterial trees inside each of them branching deep to the heart, the softness of her lips I could kiss forever, the foreign coolness of his tongue—

There is the sound of a trepidatious cough.

The two look over in the lamplight to the undergraduate research participant who is looking back at them, standing nervously, backpack in hand.

"Umm, Professor Green?"

Kierk and Carmen pull apart, but like trees coming untangled parts seem to catch, his hand by her waist, her one finger hooked in his belt loop. Kierk is stifling a laugh.

Carmen collects herself. "Hi! Sorry. You must be the participant. Thanks for coming in so late."

She turns back to Kierk, who raises his eyebrows. Both of them smile and make gestures as if about to speak but neither do.

"So . . . Friday?" he finally says. "What if we got a drink. Just us?"

"Friday," she says, smiling, and then as Carmen leads the participant into the CNS, she leans back out the door and yells after him—"So it's a date?"

Kierk pauses in his walk—"Yeah it's a date, professor!" and she laughs and darts back inside. As she leads the research volunteer she's too preoccupied to register the CNS's twists and turns as she maneuvers to the EEG lab, only minimally conscious of the veneer of small talk. Her mind is busy handling this new object: a feeling incarnated as a velvet red cube with no hinges and no latch that radiates an organic growing heat. Her analysis continues until even after the experiment has passed in a bemused blur and she has said goodbye to the sticky-haired undergraduate and she is sitting on a stool soaking the EEG cap in a bucket of water to wash it. Looking at her soapy hands she laughs aloud for no apparent reason, her laughter leaving the one lit room and echoing out into the surrounding dark labyrinth of the CNS.

ALL THE LIGHTS ARE turned on. Fingers select music to play from the phone. A notebook is laid on the counter, along with Atif's pen. The refrigerator is opened and three cans of Red Bull are laid out like ducklings on top of a bureau. A deep breath is taken. Kierk chugs all three cans in quick succession. Soon he's standing over the sink, nauseous, splashing water on his flushed face. Looking at himself in the mirror he begins to dance to the music, first just his head moving, then his shoulders bobbing along, and then his whole body following. Leaping out of the bathroom into the living room, bouncing off the walls, spinning, arms and legs going along to the beat, grabbing his notebook to hold it like a dance partner, twirling it and dipping it and then taking it on a whirlwind foot-kicking dance all across his apartment, screaming along to the music at the top of his lungs. Then he is ready to write.

TUESDAY

KIERK WAKES UP AND in a spasm of movement turns off the alarm clock on his phone and settles back into the heat and morning shadows, trying to return. But it is impossible to sleep because of the hot quarter of light from the window pressed against his cheek.

Boxers, pants, shirt. Mouthwash? No time. Cigarettes are on the otherwise bare counter, and he lights one in the elevator and holds it hidden at his side as he passes the manned front desk.

Exiting the building is pushing into a wavering syrup of heat. People fan themselves as they walk, keeping to the negligible and contested shade. The concrete reflects the sun back onto Kierk's face and he squints along with everyone else. At the first crosswalk he stops to look directly up. Between the spires the sky is mercilessly blue.

It's like walking into a refrigerator when he enters the CNS, that mechanical cool tinged with the tin of air ducts. He searches for a while to find the room of Dr. George Williams, who's finally back from a conference. Karen had roped George into being on Kierk's committee over email last week. Knocking on the half-open door Kierk leans in. The professor is sitting behind his desk. His shirtsleeves are rolled up and he projects the confident air of a man whose life is secure socially, economically, tenure-wise, recognition-wise, and grant-wise. There's a framed fMRI scan on the wall. There's a bookshelf, the contents of which are mostly familiar to Kierk. But what attracts Kierk's attention most directly is the crucifix. The cross hangs metallic and unobtrusive between two photos, barely a pencil's length in size, yet its incongruity with its environment makes it as weighty as an old ironside.

"Kierk Suren, right?"

"Hello, Professor Williams, we said we'd meet today at 10:00. Is that still okay? I know it's like 10:30, but if you still have time . . ."

"Please, just grab the door and have a seat."

Kierk nods to the cross—"So you must be a non-overlapping magisteria kind of guy, huh?"

At first Williams blinks in confusion, but then follows Kierk's gaze and for a silent moment both regard Jesus' face orgasmic with beatific anguish.

"Well . . . I don't let it interfere with my work, of course. A bit of a private issue, actually," Williams says, obviously peeved.

"Not to worry," Kierk says. "I'm not an atheist anyways." Even as he says it, he doesn't know if it's true or not. He never does.

Williams shifts in his chair and asks—"So fill me in on what you've been up to, what you expect from your committee, and so on."

Kierk does his best to overinflate his minimal progress. Then they talk logistics for a while, but eventually Williams asks him—"You worked with Antonio Moretti?"

"That's right."

"Are you planning on continuing the work you were doing prior to leaving your PhD program, or . . ."

"I disproved most of the work I did. Turns out you're not really supposed to do that in science."

" . . ."

"So I want to start something new."

"That's fine, I guess. Do you have any ideas right now?"

"Well . . . Last night I was thinking that there are intriguing similarities between problems in information theory and the kind of problems with consciousness."

"Let me be frank. From what I've heard there's a bit of a self-indulgence problem here. With you. And I'm not sure that it's the best idea—"

"Let me explain . . . hmm . . . Take a book, for instance. Is there actually any meaning within the words themselves, or are they defined, given by, the reader? See, we know that words are just symbols, chicken-scratch. Look at text from a language you don't know and the problem jumps into clear focus. It's the consciousness of the reader that gives any meaning, any content, to the chicken-scratch. The problem of consciousness, interestingly, can be described in the same way. When we look at the chicken-scratch of neuronal firing patterns, what are we to read into them? If you see some neurons firing in, say, the medial temporal lobe, what are we to say about what they mean to the brain? Just because something responds reliably to an object or concept, does that mean it represents it? And most neurons in higher cortical areas don't reliably respond to anything in particular. And if you say that they mean what they do because there is an interpreter of brain activity somewhere in the brain, well, then we are stuck in an infinite regress, because who gives that observer their internal content, and so on? Is there some universal author who draws across all systems in the universe the epistemic boundaries needed to give consciousness definite content? Does God fix consciousness in place? Some invisible author just makes shit up, assigns this here and that there . . ."

"I, umm . . ."

". . . in other words: was it God who wrote these signs?"

"I'm sorry, what?"

"That quote is originally from Goethe, of course, and then, later, that's Boltzmann quoting Goethe. Boltzmann was already working on the physics of information way before anybody else was. He was quoting Goethe in respect to Maxwell's meager and elegant four equations, which summarized so much of the physical world with so little that they seemed divine in origin . . . from scientist to writer to scientist . . . The quote is a beautiful analogy to the paradox . . . Was it God who wrote the signs in our skulls . . . Of course that was before he killed himself for his intellectual failures."

"Who?"

"Boltzmann. Goethe, on the other hand, reconciled his genius with lived life."

". . . . . ."

". . ."

They avoid eye contact. The silence has grown long enough to be uncomfortable. Finally, Kierk, slapping his knees, stands and leans over the desk to shake Williams' hand, which is returned with a surprisingly strong grip.

"Have we covered everything?" Kierk asks perfunctorily.

"Ah, I guess we have covered some things. Certainly."

"Good." Kierk turns to leave, and it is then that he sees the back of the office door, on which hangs, long and in the shape of a man, a tan trench coat crowned by a red baseball cap where the head would be. Kierk freezes.

"Are you alright?" Williams asks. His question releases Kierk, who spins on him. At first, perhaps due to a trick of the mind, or perhaps because he was confused by Kierk's pause, Williams' face is a truly unreadable canvas, disconcerting in its blank untranslatability, but then this flits away, replaced by an expression of benign concern as he meets Kierk's eyes. Kierk examines that face, that expression, with all the detailed intensity of a portraiture artist, attempting to match it to his brief opaque memories of the man he had glimpsed in the subway.

"I actually have a few more questions, professor. Have you ever heard of the Following Brothers of Christ?"

"No. Should I have?"

"Do you ever get down to Bleecker Street Station?"

Williams is an enigmatic sphinx, paws on the arms of his chair.

"I don't know what you mean. The subway stop?"

"Yes. Were you there Saturday before last?"

A brief flicker of anger. "Today is my first day back from the conference. As we discussed numerous times over email."

"Oh. I'm sorry, professor. Forgive my absentmindedness."

Kierk continues slyly watching Williams, as if about to say something, but then, with nothing forthcoming, he just nods and nearly bows out of the room, closing the door and retreating to the stairwell where he paces about on one of the landings.

Questions in his mind: did Williams mean for him to see it? Was it a sign, and if so, what did it signify? Threat? Complicity? Informing Kierk that he knew that Kierk knew?

Rushing back to his computer he pulls up information about the conference Williams had been attending. Online Kierk thumbs through the photos of the conference, looking at the timestamps, looking up flights from Chicago (the conference location) to New York, and finally concludes that Williams really had attended the conference, and in fact had given a talk the day before Atif's body had been found. The immediate closure is disappointing to him—surely it was unlikely for someone in Chicago to appear in a photograph one day, and then to have traveled to New York the next night to commit a murder with no motive? And then pretend to be away the rest of the time? And should he tell Carmen all this? After all, this would only inflame her in a quest that Kierk did not fully believe in. It could also prove merely a distraction, more noise injected into the search for signal. Eventually he decides not to tell her, for now. Like a proper scientist he would wait for more evidence.

WAITING FOR THE ELEVATOR to go down for lunch, Kierk hears a squeaking noise. Down the hall, trundling quickly but seeming to take forever, there glides like a specter on wheels a chaired macaque. It is pushed by a scientist in a blue lab coat and face mask. The macaque is encased in a rectangular and see-through plastic box, its head jutting out from a beveled plastic top. Squat, it is turned toward Kierk during its passage; it looks down the corridor at him with intense concentration as it slides past on wheels. The protuberances of little humanoid hands grasp and press against the box, the installed plastic chimney is a pink tube rising from its skull, its irises black stones that watch Kierk like a totem. Grinning, it is an obscene magician's trick of biology disappearing around the corner.

Kierk stands watching the space where it was. He wants to rip the gunk from its stupid, primitive head. To free it, even briefly, from this attempt at understanding. He feels monumental embarrassment for it—even its thoughts will be naked soon, nothing hidden, an unclothed brain among clothed ones, hinting that our sense of agency is maybe just a sartorial illusion cast by our skulls not being splayed and violated with a recording needle, the worst kind of rape, a discarding of an entire ontology. But at the same time he knows that it'll win in the end anyway, outlast all these buildings and face masks and tetrodes—consciousness will still be here after all this is gone, undefeated, smiling as wide as the Cheshire Cat, because it's the only game in town. Experience comes before, and will last longer, than any science.

Kierk enters the elevator and watches the doors close. The floor numbers tick down and he's lost in thought—why does anyone wake up with the same consciousness they went to sleep with? Why does this "I" continue each time? It cannot be mere continuity, as that is disrupted by a dreamless sleep. So then it must be something else that maintains continuity, like memories, or the motifs and structures unique to your experience. But this leaves open the possibility of a theory of consciousness that tells us that, from within a perspective, there is no difference between one *C. elegans* and another, that the phenomenology of watching an elevator door close at the center of your field of vision is recreated a billion times a day all over the world by a billion different people watching elevator doors close and at the level of description that makes a difference there is no difference between any of them, all just amalgamations of the same motifs, the same concepts, the same memories and feelings, the same self-narratives and acts all reoccurring across history, each conscious moment constructed of subsets of others that have been experienced by others before, like dolls with detachable parts, mere bundles that share contents, and when old motifs are instantiated, or two motifs are drawn to one another into an ancient pattern, or when the same immemorial problems confronted, then phenomenological selves can skip and jump from similarity to similarity across space and time and people like a stone across water. Metempsychosis. Reincarnation, but only in parts.

The elevator doors ding open.

AT THE ENTRANCE TO the CNS Carmen and Kierk have a brief interaction but are heading separate ways. He had brought her no news, although she felt perhaps he wasn't mentioning something. Afterward Carmen is drumming her fingers on the lid of her coffee, ruminating, for she had wanted to mention what had occurred last night but it seemed so ridiculous, smaller now, shrunken in the logics of day. She had been woken in the early hours by her phone ringing from an unlisted number. Groggy and dry-mouthed she had picked up and said hello. On the other end had been wet and heavy breathing like the phone was being held up to the mouth of a bull, and she, thinking she might be dreaming, had laid there confused for a number of seconds listening as the breathing intensified. Eventually it reached a crescendo and there came a guttural welling moan, like something coming into its own hands. In shock she had hung up and threw the phone away from her in the bed, fully awake now, looking at it lying sinisterly there like a giant bug. It rang again. Automatically her hand had gone to the light by her bed but then she consciously arrested its movement. Slinking out of bed, in the dark she pulled on her pajama bottoms, and then she snuck into the kitchen and with a quiet snick took down the butcher's knife from where it hung on a magnetic strip above the sink. Knife in hand she had tiptoed to the door, checked the three locks, and then looked through the peephole into the empty hallway for a while. She slowly checked out the bathroom, using the knife to peel back the shower curtain, opened the sliding door to her closet, and then, very slowly and with her heart beating so fast she could hear it in the quiet, lifted up the covers of her bed and looked under. The street outside was also empty. Exhausted and defeated she had drifted off some time later on when the black sky had developed a tinge of verdigris. But in the bright light of today she just couldn't bring it up to Kierk, it seemed such an overreaction on her part, an event so separate from the daytime world in which she and Kierk have a date on Friday.

There's a fuss in the lab as she walks in. All the postdocs are grouped around a computer terminal in the back. Karen is calling in over Skype from the conference, her voice booming from the computer terminal like a high-pitched Wizard of Oz. Early this morning a link to an article had circulated rapidly around the postdocs and graduate students, along with exclamation marks. Some anonymous author had posted a long takedown of various contemporary theories of consciousness, Karen's included. In fact, hers especially, because the scathing review was focused on so-called "higher-order theories of consciousness" that attributed consciousness to frontal brain regions and neural representations. The anonymous article had been posted on a *Scientific American* blog. Carmen had read it, her eyebrows rising higher and higher as she scrolled down. Soon Karen's lab-wide email, hurried and terse, had come out, calling for some sort of reply. Carmen, having only recently and only nominally joined the lab, hadn't thought it her place to get too involved, so she approached apprehensively now. One of the postdocs is saying—"How the hell did he . . . or she . . . even get this up? Anonymous public peer review. We shouldn't even address it. It's just a blog. The format—"

"The format doesn't matter, the owner of the *SciAm* blog says this is some kind of supposed wunderkind that he's letting stay anonymous. When they type my theory or my name into Google all anyone is going to see from now on is this." Karen's voice shatters through the speakers and someone reaches to turn her down a little.

Carmen, however, thinks—but the reviewer is right, because there is no reason to believe higher brain regions are necessary for consciousness. There are lesion patients without a prefrontal cortex, it's not like they are phenomenological zombies lacking all consciousness . . .

The Skype icon blinks on and off. Carmen takes a long sip of cold coffee.

Finally Karen says—"Look, my theory is based on the fact that the same brain regions are involved in theory of mind judgments and internal judgments of self . . . So I don't know what the problem is."

One of the postdocs nods enthusiastically at the computer—"He's basically rejecting all of neuroimaging. Anyone else noticing that?"

"Look, he's obviously a smart guy but the way I would have done this," Karen says, "would be—listen, this area is new to me, I have certain questions. I would not have framed it as a direct attack. And he doesn't understand what I'm saying about theory of mind."

The group has parted to allow Carmen access to the computer, which she leans forward to speak into. "I think that's the distinction he's leaning on. That's why he's bringing up animal selves. The author of the post is saying that even simple organisms like bees might have a phenomenological center to their subjectivity. Consciousness is primitive. Basic. It comes before all that higher-level cognitive stuff. Just pure experiencing."

There's a pause.

"Are you saying you agree with him?" Karen's digital voice rings. All heads turn toward Carmen and her clutched coffee cup. Her mind races, outpacing the room, the earth, light. Sketches of possible worlds are drawn, scrubbed away, redrawn.

". . . No. No, of course not. He's um . . . he's . . . He's rejecting it out of hand because his main point is just that it doesn't fit his intuitions about which organisms would be capable of feeling things. But whoever said that a theory of consciousness should fit intuitions? Right? Quantum mechanics doesn't fit intuitions. There's your counterpoint."

". . . Okay, Carmen, yes, thank you, he's definitely putting the cart before the horse here."

Carmen hangs her head knowing how weak her point was. What had Kierk called it? Occam's broom . . . She listens for a while longer, standing there wondering if all of them really believe in the narrative that Karen has spun up with a few neuroimaging studies that probably weren't even replicable, if the human capacity for self-preservative delusion is really this powerful, or if they were all enthusiastic liars. Then Carmen pictures Karen sitting on the edge of her hotel bed, her laptop open, making this call, and what Karen is going to do when she hangs up and is left alone in that empty, impersonal room. Everything around her will be an uncaring alien hum, and she will have no shield against a world which takes and takes from you, unsparing even to pet theories. I want a family—Carmen thinks suddenly—I wasn't sure until right now, but I want a family. If I am making this call in ten years, I want to be able to hang up and make another call.

To CLEAR HIS HEAD Kierk has laced up his sneakers and bolted down the stairs out into dew-laced New York, the sun a white bowl hovering, the morning light angular and precise. Breathing and small-puddle hopping become priorities; everything is lost in the pace of his sneakers and the lope of his stride, his body happy to be used. As he runs he introspects on his consciousness, the majority of which is not the sense data of how hard each heel strikes or the cool air on his legs, but the feeling of control, of access, the feeling of availability composed of the fluid shifting of counterfactuals and the navigation through them—left leg, right leg, jump, lean in, go hard now, ease back, turn right—all in a realm of control far abstracted from the domain of twitch muscle-fibers and synapses calculating how much acetyl-choline to release. He spends a little while working out how problematic this is for theories of consciousness—for why would it be at one particular spatial and temporal level that experience makes its home at, why not any other, why not Planck time and space, and why these exact contents specif-ically? In what scripture are such rules written?

After finishing the subsequent shower Kierk stands in his living room where all the boxes have been torn apart and books are everywhere. His legs are achy and feel twangy and used. Kierk loves the feeling. Not just for the pleasure/pain of it, but also for the concept: having broken down, having torn and ripped, his entire frame was now riddled with micro-tears throughout—but it is only by tearing everything down that one can build anything that lasts . . .

Notes have been piling up on the floor in the form of scribbles, draw-ings, equations, the tentative tendrils of his latest assault on consciousness.

Crouching down on the balls of his feet in the middle of it all, idly turning over a page of notes, Kierk glances around before speaking to the empty apartment.

"How do you like it now, gentlemen?"

THE SCENE STARTS, PLAYS out all the way to the end, then starts again, an ouroboros. Kierk's in the elevator with that distinct vestibular sensation informing him that he is moving, moving down. The floor numbers tick in red. Everything is skipping around, his perception is blurry, focusing occasionally, a shaky camera. And as the display ticks down from impossibly large numbers he realizes that someone is in the elevator with him. Standing right behind him to his left, in the corner. There is a flicker of the lights, fluctuating power. Kierk looks over his left shoulder at the figure in the corner, hoodie on a sweatshirt pulled down to conceal the face, hands in the pockets, jeans, looking at the elevator floor. The killer! The figure remains motionless, the lights flicker again. Kierk reaches out a single, trembling hand to touch the hood—the lights go off in the elevator. Kierk jumps back in the complete darkness, retreating frantically until he feels the cold metal wall behind him. He is sure that the killer has moved from the corner. Kierk lashes out with his leg, kicking into the dark at different places and at different levels—if it approaches, he'll feel it coming with his sneakers, the blow will reveal location and give forewarning—mid-kick, the lights come back on in the empty elevator. Breathing hard, Kierk regains his composure. He has escaped, he knows this. Again he watches the floor numbers, now a melancholy yellow. He's twitchy, he paces back and forth, waiting as the countdown continues. Nervously he watches the door, now realizing it will open and that the thing will be waiting for him there, at the basement level. The tension builds, the lower digits go by, he's nearly on his knees now, crying. The elevator dings open and he cries out in anticipation. The macaque, totem-headed and grinning, sits in its plastic see-through box. Kierk falls back in mortal terror against the far elevator wall. But it remains stationary, left there, alone, rapidly breathing, its arms and legs scampering inside the box like the legs of a frantic centipede, pressing and smearing against the glass from all angles while its head remains fixed facing Kierk, looking directly into his eyes. Its lips are moving, and there is the hissing sound of syllables that reveal flashes of canines. It is whispering something. Something just beyond Kierk's hearing. Kierk steps toward it in trembling trepidation and curiosity. He leans down to listen, puts his ear right up against its whispering thin lips, hearing just snatches of mathematics and foreign scientific terminology. His eyes, at first confused, begin to widen and then change into a look of incalculable awe. Kierk's brains are blown out through the back of his skull and splatter against the wall of the elevator in thick chunks.

WEDNESDAY

KIERK WAKES UP SUDDENLY, startling. A sound is receding, unidentifiable. What had woken him? There's light through the window, but checking his phone he finds it blinking 6:00 a.m. A long low groan . . .

KIERK HAS BEEN SITTING in lab since early morning, paper spilling out over his desk, each page covered in notations and equations and diagrams, the whirring of his multiple computers heating up the area around him like thermodynamical demons. Nearby undergraduates sit fanning themselves. The first paper, an overview of theories of consciousness and the application of them to a computer model of the cortex, is a mess. The truth is that it felt like wrestling sheets of balsa wood in high wind. And Kierk wrestled those flat, wide, bendy, wind-catching sheets across a field one at a time, trying to construct something, anything. The most hobbling issue was that the measures were so vague, so nonmathematical, that it drove Kierk to fits of frustration, and he found himself trying to formalize the theories, building on them even though he knew they were wrong, just so that there would be something definite to disprove. Except even in his efforts to improve them so that he could disprove them they would give way, the materials were no good, and the balsa sheet would fly off into the field and he would watch it go tumbling away, a piece of matter so animated in making its escape it seemed almost ambulatory, wood becoming an animal that would live as long as the wind kept blowing.

So after a few hours he, exhausted, hot from the computers, had gone to take a walk in Washington Square Park, joining the congregation around the geyser of the fountain. Teenage girls take off their shoes and sit with their feet dangling over the rim of the fountain into the cool watery spray. There is a grand piano out over to one side of the fountain, and Kierk recognizes the strains of an Erik Satie *étude* floating over to him on the air. Near the piano, surrounded by a low crowd of children, a woman has a kind of string contraption that blows huge soap bubbles larger than some of the kids. The bubbles gleam their oily curvaceous nature, vary from perfect spheres to elongated spheroids, platonic entities from outside the world forced to take form within it, lose their way and their nature. It's windy and so the bubbles take flight in swarms all moving in the same direction, chased by the clapping and outstretched hands of the children, some flying low into their arms but others escaping into the air, become floating orbs passing above the piano, some even making it through the far stone arch. There they cohere, change, decohere. Sometimes two bubbles travel together for a time, then split off. Or a single bubble yearns to be three, while other times two bubbles will seek to merge into one. Sometimes a bubble will completely contain another one, unified but still with their surface boundaries intact, and carry on until they wink out together. When a bubble perishes it becomes a wisp, a vanishing string, or splits into smaller, rounded marbles, all going off in different directions. For a long time Kierk sits on a bench by the fountain watching the bubbles and the children and listening to the music, waiting for revelation to strike. He never goes back to lab. But he does while away the rest of the evening writing in his notebook with Atif's pen.

Eventually he notices that someone is watching him. Across from him on a bench there is a girl, maybe college-aged, maybe younger, it's hard to tell as she's thin and wearing baggy clothing, and as her hair is natty and wild, and she is barefoot, and has hemp bracelets on her wrists and ankles, in dirty cargo shorts and a fading T-shirt, with a dog next to her, and one of her hands is stroking its forehead while her other holds up some used stock mystery novel, the kind with a glossy embossed cover. Around her is splayed the kit of the beggar—the wicker mat, upon which sits a cardboard sign and a plastic container with some change and a few dollar bills in it. Her smudged thumb turns the page, but she's occasionally glancing at him, and now he at her: does she remind him of someone? Then he places it—Alice Waterson, a fellow neuroscience grad student at the University of Wisconsin-Madison. Three years into the program Alice had dropped out for reasons unknown, although everyone speculated. Madison was a small enough town that people from the program still saw her downtown occasionally, now with hippie tassels in her hair, zooming around on a skateboard with dirty bare feet. Everyone avoided her, and the girls in the program always gossiped about her, exclaiming about how embarrassing it was to see her downtown, how they always had to hide to avoid saying hi. But to Kierk it had seemed like maybe she had found some kind of inner peace. A few months after Alice left, Kierk had run into her one evening at the public terrace overlooking Lake Mendota. Over the sound of the live band she had talked about her renewed Christian faith, been energetic and engaged, happy to be outside, if a little thin and grubby. He didn't see her again, and neither did anyone else, until a year later the next summer, when Kierk was driving back from getting groceries, his windows rolled down as he cruised the back roads. He spotted Alice again, walking over a hill toward a bus stop, wearing a shabby backpack. Kierk pulled over and approached her. She didn't have her skateboard anymore, and though she lit up at seeing Kierk she struggled through their conversation, her gaunt face slow to respond to his comments, and she smelled bad even in the sunny breeze. She tried to summon up a brave face, dismiss everything, crack a few jokes, but after chatting with her for a bit Kierk told her to wait right there. He went back down to his car on the side of the road and lugged back up five or six full bags of groceries. The bus had come as he trudged up the hill. The driver idled with the door open. Kierk and Alice, who had once been paired together on a project about the evolution of the neocortex in a graduate-level course, stared down at the bags of groceries. Embarrassed, finally she took them, apologizing to the driver as she lugged them onto the bus, waving to Kierk as he walked away down the hill. For a while Kierk followed the bus, as it was headed the same general direction as him, but then its blinker went on and it took a turn and he never saw her again.

He thinks about going over to talk to the girl, see what her story is, but he wouldn't know where to start. And he's running late anyway.

For the last few weeks Kierk and Carmen have spent the majority of time within one square mile of each other, moving about. If you tracked their movements across the map of Manhattan, they would appear like figure skaters always crossing the other's tracks, entering a store as the other exits, taking parallel paths down neighboring avenues, making *X*'s of parks. Now they converge again.

". . . BECAUSE THAT'S EXACTLY WHAT we at SAAR care about. Sometimes it's like everyone is always putting these things into boxes, into causes, that they care about. But that's really problematic. 'Cause it's all intersectionally connected."

"We should have brought Alex. He'd love this."

"He'd have died laughing . . ."

"—and so I just wanted to thank everyone here for fighting against all the intersectional institutionalized forms of oppression like animal research."

"Wow. So amazing. I love it. Totally non-problematic. And with that I think we'll wrap it up because we're running over time. This was a really good meeting. We'll pick a few of the visiting speakers that use animals. Focusing on primates like poor Double Trouble, but also like, cats and rats. We'll narrow it down next meeting and protest those. Alright. Till next time everybody. Stay out of the heat."

"Hey, Allen?"

"Oh yeah, excuse me, hey, Carol. And Jim."

"I just wanted to ask: is it really enough? Just to disrupt some speakers? I mean, what about doing something more real? More impactful? Something that sends more of a statement, you know? That this kind of oppression is so unacceptable."

"What I think we're trying to say is that she and I are getting a little restless—"

"A little bit fed up."

"—yes, a little bit fed up, and we are kind of thinking about how to implement something big, considering that Carol has access to the neuroscience department on campus. You grok? We've got an 'in' at the department."

"Really? How?"

"I'm doing an independent study with one of the professors in the building. Who's like, a psychologist. But I have building access because she lets me work in the EEG lab. So I have access."

"Wait—you never said you were a science student."

"Um, no. Not at all. I'm a sociology student but I need research credits and um, it's human psychology so it's not that bad."

"Oh, okay."

"Like, obviously humans only."

'Uh-huh."

"But I really do have access."

"Hey, I mean, I can feel that you two are serious. I can see that. I think that's great. But we've already got stuff covered. See, we've already got someone on the inside in that department."

"You do? I don't recognize anyone from here . . ."

"They don't come to meetings. It's too dangerous. Even if you were seen here, Carol, that could cause some trouble. So be careful. We don't want it to get out that there are people in the CNS that sympathize with our cause. Who respect our mute brothers and sisters enough to keep them from being tortured. People who believe in justice."

"Wow, that's really great. Really great. Maybe I could help them."

"With what?"

"With, you know, whatever it is that they're doing. The strategy. The move. Disruption."

"Not a good idea. You're new. Just keep coming to meetings. Besides, we're in serious down-low mode. We recently pulled off something big. Took a lot of planning. And there's still no heat coming our way."

"Is it something we would have heard of?"

"Why?"

"Just wondering."

"Just keep coming to meetings. With your enthusiasm, I'm sure we can find a use for you. So I'll see you next week?"

"We'll be back."

THURSDAY

KIERK WAKES UP AND a murder of books slide off him, one from his stomach, another from the crook of his arm, and a third which had lain clasping his lower leg like a giant insect. They fall to the floor in successive thwacks, lying spine-broken and covers upturned—a book detailing the derivation of the laws of physics from Fisher Information, poems by e. e. cummings, and *Philosophical Investigations* by Wittgenstein. The noises shock Kierk fully awake and he sits up on the edge of his bed, groggily closing their covers with a toe. Stretching and standing Kierk yawns and yaws his way to the bathroom, on the way shuffling and kicking the clothes he had left lying on the floor from yesterday, then, having compiled them in a clump, picks them up and pulls them on, hopping one leg at a time to get his pants on.

IT IS FLAT AND bright yellow in the sun. Occasionally it is turned over and a fresh yellow replaces the diagonal loops and small mountain ranges of black ink. Behind it are tufts of wilting grass amid dirt, the puckered prepubescent nubs of anthills. Ants in swarms like around the mouths of holes, armies amid the sparse grass. Visible also is an oblique curve, the rubber tip of a sneaker. Kierk has snuck out to lunch with a yellow legal pad pilfered from the department office because he'd forgotten his notebook at home. Pen in hand he is sitting on the grass of Washington Square Park. The pages are filled up with discrete probabilities distributions, calculations of the Earth Mover's Distance and diagrams of causal models; some even have rings around them of possible worlds ordered by Hamming Distance. He's been trying to figure some good way of measuring emergence in physical systems between bites of a pastrami sandwich in a Styrofoam to-go box. He leans down like the face of God over the busy lives of the anthills, observing the patterns of the insects running to-and-fro like strings of zeros and ones, making in their movements a superorganism, a living thing built of *other* living things. And not only that, but a thing consisting only of pheromone trails, the scent paths that allow ant colonies to forage, learn where food is, respond to threats, retreat, rebuild, migrate . . . similar then to neurons releasing their chemical packages of neurotransmitters, because, after all, what was the brain but a huge network of micro-plants entwined together communicating in puffs of chemicals, which of course foregrounds the much bigger question: if organized groups of small living cells can somehow create/instantiate/express a consciousness over the entire group, couldn't organized groups of small living creatures create/instantiate/express a consciousness over the entire colony? If so, what would the qualia of an ant colony be like? Would it feel, in its temporally slow manner, sluggish thoughts of success, being hungry? Angry? Horny? All just from the lingering traces of pheromones, literally a conscious smell. And what happens to the micro-consciousnesses of the ants? Are they unaffected or somehow subsumed, replaced, by the colony . . .? And if this city, Kierk thinks, finally rises to consciousness, what happens to the consciousnesses of the people within it? Would we all carry on, unknowing, as we might be carrying on now? Or would some great sublimation occur that left everything different in some imperceptible way, everything in the same place but with a different meaning? A similar kind of subtle change to if you woke confused, but unsure what you're confused about. Because your love is at your side. Your child is in its crib. Stretching after this restful sleep feels so good. You move your legs to the cool section of the sheet. You notice in the calm night that the whole house is silent and illumed with moonlight. You can see the alarm clock blinking. You can hear your lover's breathing and hear your child turning. You wonder where you were before you awoke. Are you somehow out of time? Hadn't things been different? Surely that had all just been a dream, a dream of you aging . . . Everything around you makes so much sense you don't question it and so you just smile at the moon and turn to your sleeping lover as your child shifts safely again—unaware you are now in heaven.

Such thoughts racing through his mind, the mathematics on the page dance beyond all bounds of reasonability, devolving into only the purest fancy—but then his time is up. He licks the tips of his fingers, making sure he doesn't disturb any of the anthills when he stands up. He makes his way back to the CNS, stopping in the communal kitchen on his floor. He proceeds to wash his hands, distracted.

"Hey there!"

Kierk startles, looking over his shoulder at what he assumes is an undergraduate, a guy standing behind Kierk, waiting to use the communal sink. A larger, sweatpants-wearing, enthusiastic and shaggy senior, probably volunteering for lab time. Kierk had seen him around before, carousing with other people in the lab, leaning on tables and laughing. He was part of the contingent that always went out to eat lunch together. Several of them had asked Kierk to join his first few days here, but he had said no each day and they had quickly stopped asking.

Kierk dries his hands, mumbling something in an apologetic tone. As he turns, he feels a grab at his arm. The undergrad is gripping him.

"I said, 'Hey.' My name is Ben by the way. Ben."

There is no one around and Kierk is looking down at the undergrad's arm gripping his.

"Listen, I just want your acknowledgment that there is another human being in the room with you. Okay? You've been in the lab for like a month or something and you haven't learned anyone's names. Like at all. Did you even know my name?"

Kierk, first taken aback, is suddenly ice-cold, his eyes narrowing, a smirk forming on his face.

"No. I don't. And that's because you're irrelevant. This field you think exists, doesn't exist. You're wasting your time here, and more importantly you are wasting my time, which is like gold to your cobalt." He rips his arm free and glares. "If you touch me again I will break all the fingers in your hand."

Ben takes a step back, horrified. "Jesus Christ, dude." He retreats back along the corridor, his face a mask of incomprehension, turns around the corner and is gone.

Kierk stalks off the other direction until he finds a restroom and angrily pushes it open. He slams the door shut and hurls the legal pad against the wall. Turning the sink on full and gripping the edges of it he splashes his face with the rushing water.

Looking up at himself in the mirror—"Fuck. Fuck. Fuck. Oh fuck."

KIERK IS AT A bar on the Lower East Side. It serves his purpose: plenty of table space, a live singer who isn't too loud, good lighting and comfortable chairs, and air-conditioning. Outside it is a hothouse. People's glasses fog up when they enter the bar and all heave deep sighs of relief.

An hour ago he had switched from coffee to wine. He's again been wrestling with that first paper, and as a result his Hello Kitty notebook is covered with expunged diagrams, scribbled-over equations, X-ed out experimental designs. All these supposed theories of consciousness are impossible to even hold his mind anymore. They are mere metaphors and illusions, and he can only gesture in disgust at them.

This afternoon Karen, just back from the conference, had called him into her office, and he had gone, shooting a glance at Ben, who sat stiff-backed in his chair looking straight ahead. On entering the office Kierk sat and Karen had adjusted her papers, looking dour and serious and hassled. Before Kierk could speak she began.

"I don't like adjudicating disputes, Kierk. I'm very busy, I have a lot on my plate, there's this stupid anonymous review . . ."

"We didn't—"

"Well, Ben, who has worked for me for over a year now, told me that you told him that he, and I quote, 'didn't exist.'"

"Not what I said."

"You said something similar."

"I said that the field didn't exist and therefore he is wasting his time."

"What does that mean?"

"It's complicated. But I did not say that he didn't exist."

"Did you also tell him that you would, and I quote, 'break every bone in his hand'?"

"Listen, he grabbed me. I wasn't expecting it. It was the heat of the moment. I accept responsibility for—"

"You damn better. What makes you think that you can just yell at a research assistant?"

"Look, the guy, I mean, Ben . . . was just mad because I didn't know his name. He came in looking for a fight because I won't go to lunch with him."

"It doesn't matter, Kierk. It doesn't. I've heard . . . reports from other people, and there's been some talk among the other Crick Scholars and the professors, that you've been . . . disruptive. That you've instigated some situations and yelled at people. That you talk down to them and ignore them."

"That's exaggerated."

"But it's been mentioned to me multiple times, Kierk! And honestly coming from that many sources there is clearly a problem. So I don't know what to do with you. I really don't. I mean, you tell me. Tell me what you think the appropriate response is."

"Free meals at the Prytaneum?"

"What the hell is that?"

"What Socrates suggested his sentence should be for corrupting the youth."

"I don't care about Socrates right now, Kierk. I don't. I need to know whether or not you can function in a healthy, open, work environment."

"I take full responsibility, Karen. There won't be any more problems."

"Just focus on your own research. Ignore what everyone else is doing. You're a smart young man, just stay out of trouble. Keep your head down. Okay?"

"I can do that. Thank you for your patience. Truly."

"Okay, Kierk. Okay."

So Kierk had ended up in this bar, scribbling away, trying to make some kind of progress he could report. He wondered if Karen somehow knew, unconsciously, in some animal way, that he had written the blog post dismissing all those theories.

Around him in the bar gather young professionals his age, and he's uncomfortable until remembering he's one of them now; that he fits in with his dress shirt and haircut and discerning look and that his form had filled out and he now looks closer to athletic than starving. He orders another glass of wine and dips at the spots on his table with a napkin.

Then the lights begin to flicker and surge. There are gasps and oohs and aahs. The singer stops. Everyone is craning their necks up. The lights go out.

For a brief second the world is only language. Remarks and cries and laughter, the sound of women grabbing and shrieking for their partner, and then a single bright emergency light blinks on near the door. The manager stands on the little stage and announces that it's just a power outage and that there's been public announcements that this could happen sometime soon, and there is nothing to worry about. And with that the room breaks into whooping, and calls for more drinks and food, and celebration.

The performer, after a look of wonder, begins to play again, now without a microphone, and the whole room has been set by the single bright emergency light to a deep chiaroscuro, the bar suddenly over-crowded with both shadows and people clapping, standing up, hugging one another, draining their drinks. Under the emergency light the back wall has become another bar populated by their outlines. People become more open and vulnerable. A young woman who is also sitting alone glances over at Kierk, smiling. Patrons are standing, leaving the bar, they want to see what's going on in the streets, and Kierk, after smiling back an apologetic goodbye at the girl looking his way, sets some cash down and grabs his notebook and follows the wanderers outside. They spill out the entrance onto the street, entering the unlit obelisks of buildings and primitive airs of a Manhattan without power. Block upon block are in blackness, and although Kierk can see, peering uptown, the great lit beacon of midtown, everything else is dark except for the bright sweeps of cars, one of which bears down on the crowd and illuminates all of their smiling faces briefly in passing, and Kierk, wheeling on the sidewalk, separates himself from the others and begins to wander into this astrolabe for giants, this Stonehenge.

Kierk walks the streets in this new darkness that is occasionally scattered momentarily by headlights, as well as by the occasional hanging bulbs of light coming from backup generators. With its nemesis air-conditioning fully vanquished the heat seems to be relinquishing its hold on the city, broken by a natural breeze. The lack of light seems a balm. And it is under that calming blanket of absence that everyone comes out to this new city. An entire subnivean world is being carved out of the darkness; passageways are opened up and labyrinthine flows of pedestrians construct tunnels and junctions. It is a new world intense with childlike emotions. There is trep-idation at each intersection as people pick their way across voids of total darkness, and voices become hushed, aware of those around them, yet now forced to address them directly, to focus their attention on those they are passing, to nod, to speak, to reach out to. Around Kierk the streets become small dramas: merchants give away their merchandise for free, strangers embrace, men and women who were just friends before the blackout stop in the middle of the street to kiss, phones change from information-processing devices to flashlights bobbing up and down. Unfriendly faces appear out of the darkness, startling those they approach, only to break into smiles after eye contact. As if, Kierk thought, everything could be rolled back, and when we lost power we also discarded all our postmodern irony and practiced apathy and solipsism and empty physicalism and we found again the rough sensuous core of the human.

In all the windows lining the street one by one a candle is placed. People are smoking out on fire escapes, calling to those below them. From the sidewalk he looks up to a second-story window across from him and sees a girl gazing out, probably younger than him, college-aged, illuminated by a single candle she's holding. She opens her window to let the air in, sets down the candle on the sill, and then strips off her shirt and unclasps her bra, looking out with defiant seductiveness.

Kierk, wheeling from everything around him, grinning madly, continues on his trek into those tunnels, that subnivean world underneath the darkness, thinking—all these consciousnesses don't need manufactured light. They make their own.

He ends up sitting on the steps at Union Square having been given a cigarette by a passerby. Away in the dark he hears the chants of "Hare Krishna" as outlines of robes move back and forth. Craning his neck up he can see that there are now stars over Manhattan. Exhaling smoke, listening to the babble of the human river around him he thinks that he's close. Closer than he's ever been since leaving Madison. After all, he's really been doing his own research on consciousness since coming to New York. His claiming to do anything else here has been merely a halfhearted ruse, he knows now. Maybe this time with the right momentum he will jump the explanatory gap on the horse of the city, and so with the blackened outlines of gothic spires looming around him Kierk decides that from here on he will only work to solve the mystery of consciousness, and damn them, damn them all if they didn't like it.

FRIDAY

KIERK WAKES UP AND immediately regrets it. He's actually unsure exactly how long he has been awake. He may have come to consciousness moments ago or maybe this is his second or third resurgence. There is a timelessness to his thoughts, such that he begins one only to realize he's already thought this thought and arrived at its conclusion and is starting it again. Beyond him, threatening, the day promises pointless toils, and there are umbrages of the quotidian menacing from yonder his blanket, taking form before his sleepy impossible-to-open eyes in the image of the busy lab, with people bustling about and sitting down and standing up and then sitting down again and looking at screens and moving pixels of light around on the screens into different configurations, and it seems so pointless and stupid that there is just no reason to do anything but drowse within this warm pool of sheets and comfort. Kierk does not want to get up.

But he does. He has to. After flipping the light switch up and down to no effect he brushes his teeth in the dark before leaving for work.

About a block away from his place the power is already back on, but it's spotty; he sees at least two blocks with no power during his walk. The streets are so hot that everyone has their lips pulled back like the day is performing oral surgery on them. The light lances at everything, stabs at the city on its table.

At the CNS Kierk spends the entire day sitting in front of his computer, reading article after article, catching up on everything he's missed in the field of consciousness research. It feels like unhinging his jaw and sticking a fire hose in his mouth. After hours of marking up research articles and philosophy papers he slowly begins to categorize the dozens that he's read today, beginning to start some short notes, the making of connections: he sees several which could be made into papers but he feels that this is a waste of his time, too small fish, so he does a catch-and-release program and keeps the ideas for himself on pieces of scrap paper, knowing that they might service something greater. At three in the afternoon he realizes that he hasn't eaten all day so gets takeout and returns quickly, eating heaps of Thai food at his desk as the articles continue to play across his monitor like the pages of some alien codex.

BLEARY-EYED AND SPORTING A headache from the long assault of his low-Hz monitor on his visual system, with one hand massaging at his lower lumbar because of his non-ergonomic chair, Kierk is trying to find Alex, who just texted him TRAPPED ON 11TH FLOOR WITH WEIRDO PLS HALP, quickly followed by JUST COME SEE. After asking some PhD students Kierk finds the bank-vault-heavy door with the blinking sign above that reads EXPERIMENT ONGOING in computronic green. Outside hangs a whiteboard reading COME IN below an evocative draw-ing in red marker of a mouse's anthropomorphized head with a cartoon sword and a pirate patch over one eye.

Inside is a windowless boxcar-size room full of shelves of equipment, or rather pieces of equipment, like the entire room had been caught in flagrante during a promiscuous act of creation. Alex and another man are standing in front of a computer screen positioned at standing height on a messy shelf. The heavy door slams shut behind him. Alex beckons him over in the small space—"Kierk, this is Vlad, Vlad, Kierk."

After shaking hands—"So what did you want to show me?" Even as Kierk says this he hears the briefest of scrambles and his attention is drawn to his left. There is a mouse at chest level to him, not even two feet away. It is crouched on a flat disk that rotates and wobbles with its movements—it is affixed at its head to a metal beam that gives enough space for the mouse to crouch between the beam and the disk, while the disk itself is on top of an adjustable stand, all of this part of what Kierk recognizes now as a giant amped-up microscope, nearly as large as Kierk himself, a thousand times as large as the mouse, towering above the scrabbling mammal trying to keep its balance with splayed-out feet; a machine with so many buttresses and overhangs and protuberances that the mouse looks like a biological outgrowth of the machine itself, a fact especially vivid because the top of the mouse's skull has been scalped away, even the bone, and a glass skull has been surgically installed instead. The technological eye of a giant camera extends down to just a few inches above the affixed mouse. The mouse with the glass skull, thrust into a surreal situation beyond its ken, is surprisingly calm and adapted—it follows the movements of the pink giants with glass black orbs.

Vlad's accent cuts out rough Russian syllables—"It's a calcium imaging setup. Since the mice are transgenic they express green florescent protein intracellularly at the synapse. It fluoresces when it encounters calcium. So neurons fire, calcium is released internally to trigger synaptic vesicle release, the florescence gets triggered, and I can watch in real time the neural activity of thousands of neurons with the microscope. It's a ten-hour operation to replace the mouse's cranium with glass. And I can see activity across all six layers. See, I also embedded thin prisms in its brain when I performed the initial surgery. The prisms span the entire cortex and reflect up whatever cortical layer I want onto the 'scope. I can image millions of neurons, in theory."

"I remembered your story, Kierk," Alex interrupts. "One of the reasons I called you up here. The one you told about the Greek gods making a robotic man with a window in his head? Look at what we can do now. Greeks gods got nothing on us."

Kierk leans over to get a view directly over the mouse and there it is, the transparent curving pane, not bone but pure glass, the open wound of a craniotomy clearly visible underneath, the rosy pink of the tiny brain within.

"Let me show you some of the raw data." Vlad summons up various videos. "First is when the animal is under anesthesia. See, I put the mask on him." Vlad gestures to a plastic tube that protrudes toward the mouse, mounted on small wheels with a hose sticking out the back, calibrated in size to be pushed forward and encompass the mouse's face. The playback under anesthesia is just a grainy image flecked with white against a black background. "So nothing, right? But then, see, the animal is waking up." On the recording a spot on the grainy surface lights up into a small white blob, small tendrils snaking out. Nearly all at once, hundreds of other white blobs flash and then fade—and then they are firing intermittently against the background gray of the interstitial space, and under each wave of firing the dendrites and axons come into view briefly like the structure of the network was being photographed with paparazzi flashes as groups go on and off. The whole thing looks as random as the blinking of white Christmas tree lights.

"Mmm," mutters Kierk.

"What's that?" Alex points to a two-prong device that looks like it can be medievally wheeled in.

"I show it images on the screen here. When it sees one type of image, it is trained to lick to the right, and for the other it licks to the left." Vlad's tongue flickers out in a mouse-like slurp, testing the air one way and then quickly darting the other way. Alex laughs, catching his balance on Vlad as he's righted. Under the florescent light Kierk frowns, and as Alex continues speaking to Vlad, Kierk bends down to closer investigate the mouse, which causes it to scramble at its wobbling wheel. To Kierk the whole setup seems almost ontological in its significance—the mouse is crouched, splayed on the wheel, which rests on the adjustable pedestal, which rests on the microscope bolted to the table, which rests on the floor of the boxcar-size room, which rests on the entire superstructure of the CNS with all its levels and rooms underneath, which rests on the underground sewage and waterways and abandoned pneumatic tube systems and ossuaries, which rests on the Manhattan bedrock, which rests on sight-unseen worm-ridden earth until even that fades away and there is just an endless nothingness that somehow in its black bulk supports the whole edifice, a great layered tower, a biological totem that ends in this pinnacle: the small, fast-breathing, eye-darting form of the mouse with the glass skull. All of it hangs in blackness . . .

There is a squeak that breaks into a tinnitus-inducing hiss. The mouse is contorting, as much as it can with its head still tightly affixed, and then it suddenly freezes, not even breathing, its whiskers rigid, the wheel underneath it trembling.

"Whoa! What's going on, guy?" Vlad says, looking around confused. "That's a fear response. As if there's a predator around. These are human raised so I've never seen one do it unless you expose them to cat urine."

The mouse, they all realize, is not actually still. Despite its pinioned head it is attempting to crouch lower and lower until it is in complete supplication, its eyes rolling up so that there is pink exposed underneath those black orbs, and it is shifting, trying to flatten even more, but since it cannot it only engages in a slow undulate movement, tracing out a circle one creeping haunch movement at a time, its eyes rolling ever upward.

All three humans crane their necks to stare perplexed up at the totally empty and unthreatening expanse of the concrete ceiling.

"What's above us?" Kierk asks.

Vlad shrugs. "Just the roof."

OF COURSE IT TAKES Kierk forever to find Williams' office again—where he had thought it located is now occupied by a janitorial closet. But Kierk has found that the best strategy for locating anything in the CNS is not a purposeful search but rather a random drunkard's walk. Only after he's been meandering about does he find the door with Williams' name on it. But as he goes to knock he realizes that he has been hearing something as he approached in the background of his consciousness, a stream of steady sound from behind the door. It's oddly constant, not like a conversation at all. Leaning in at first the mumbling is indistinct. Then Kierk crouches down and presses his ear directly against the keyhole, and the mumbling, which is actually more of a chant, comes into aural focus. It is definitely Williams' voice but speaking strangely in low constant tone:

". . . to lay with the sinner is to eat of the apple and smote the tree of knowledge and to eat of the sinner's body is to enter the womb of the earth for there is cultivated the sin of cannibalism of the worm of one's own self and so it is from our birthplace we will travel through the black gulf to bring the song of warning to stop the fruit being plucked and stop the worm of self from being eaten as we bear wisdom beyond ken that lo shall put an end to a terrible mewling and striving that must not be . . ."

Kierk pulls away in shock. It is definitely Williams' voice but quickened and nonsensical. He doesn't recognize anything but vague biblical allusions—what it had sounded like was the free verse of a man possessed. His face puzzled, he withdraws, the mumbling becoming a continuous low drone, until Kierk, backing away, leaves the portent of the door. Everything but suspicion forgotten he searches for a way out.

Later, Kierk is browsing the internet for the snippets he remembers from the stream-of-consciousness chant, but the specifics of it are quickly fading from his memory and each variation gets no results. No origin is forthcoming. Indeed, he thinks at his desk, nothing is lately—

The lights automatically shut off, causing him to jump. Looking around he's alone. His confusion clears when he remembers how late in the day it is. Outside the windows of the dimly lit lab there is void as dark as deep space.

KIERK, HAVING GONE HOME to change into one of his new shirts and wash up and shave and load up on deodorant, heads to the martini bar near St. Marks Place where Carmen suggested they meet. He arrives early. The general theme of the bar is prominently displayed on the walls filled with old crumbling historical maps. Kierk picks a seat at the bar under a large map that he likes, with beautiful arabesques scalloping around its edges and in the blank frayed territory where the Indian Ocean should be is a large-snouted sea serpent entangled in a banner on which is writ in stylish lettering: HERE BE DRAGONS. He spends a while playing around with a few ideas in his notebook before Carmen taps him on the shoulder. She is wearing a blue cocktail dress and looks radiant. Kierk instinctively pulls out a stool for her. They order two martinis and watch as the drinks get made in front of them. They spend a little while catching each other up on things. Carmen tells Kierk about the blog incident when Karen was away at the conference (Kierk is conspicuously silent as she speculates over who the writer of the post was), which leads to them discussing Carmen's grand dream: to show that the entire cortex participates in each conscious experience, like a large spider's web where every part vibrates in response to the smallest perturbation of any part. That the apparent modularity that ruled current thinking was just an illusion brought about by the coarse-graining effects of neuroimaging and lesions. But she can only do one or two experiments at a time and so Carmen feels frustration at the limits of it, like she's always cleaning a smudged glass with a rag that is itself dirty. There are so many variables beyond the experimenter's control, so many background assumptions have been made, and consciousness is always squirming away, impossible to isolate as an experimental variable. When Kierk keeps asking about experimental designs—"Yes, but what does it *really* tell us?"—she can feel her own skepticism rising. His questioning in this is like some monomaniacal alembic, distilling things down to their essences. Carmen freely admits that her experiments and methodologies aren't going to offer up a theory of consciousness, but maintains that they might tell us something if the string of assumptions that the field has constructed holds up. Yet it all suddenly seems so tenuous. Alex has spoken to Carmen about this before: Kierk imparts this sense that all you have been doing in neuroscience is useless and pointless and it's like this contagious mood of depressive realism that can't be shaken off. At the same time Carmen greatly enjoys these types of conversations because there is the sense of movement to them, like eventually everything, the departments, the grants, all could be torn down and the two of them could stand looking at the naked brain, erased of all assumptions, and consciousness would be suddenly as obvious as if the brain's folds were lit by the light of a clear summer day.

After Carmen has stuffed the napkins containing summaries of their conversation into her clutch they order another martini and Kierk fills Carmen in on what happened between him and Ben, which he tells in a humorous manner, but it is clear that he intends Carmen get the serious subtext of it. He also tells her about what he overheard at Williams' office door, to which Carmen perks up, fascinated, and then Kierk tells her that he confirmed that Williams really was at the conference, news that disappoints her. Finally, he also tells her about his revelation during the blackout last night.

"As long as you're still doing that first paper you said you'd do, right?"

"It's just not what I'm focusing on right now."

"Because I think Karen is kind of pissed at you right now."

"I know, I know. Don't worry about it."

"Well, while you were deciding all this, during the outage I was just sitting in my apartment reading. To candlelight. It was very romantic."

"What were you reading?"

"Some of Descartes' correspondence, actually. But anyways, tell me some of your preliminary ideas."

They spend some time going over some of Kierk's thoughts, sketching things out in the notebook that he brought, their eyes serious as they talk.

"In the end the problems go back to Hume. We can observe the brute physical objects of the world, but we can't directly observe the relations they have, only infer them. Relations like function, or computation, or representation. The world is like this big user interface that we read into. Take the brain and its neurons. That description, the neuroscientific one, is just one functional description of many. A physicist might see the same pinkish blob as a quark cloud, an economist might see it as an agent. All performing different functions."

"So something that always bothered me was how many different kinds of neuroimaging techniques there are, and how, um, diverse they all are. Across space and time. A correlation at one level might not be there at another."

"Yes! A neuron could be firing an action potential or not. Are these its states? What about its physical location, its temperature, its receptivity, the damn . . . the damn internal decay rate of calcium signals. So its states depend on your level of description. Which *you* chose! And what function is it performing? Depends on how far back you look and where you look. Maybe it's firing so you think it's 'on,' but then you zoom out, and as part of a group of neurons, or a module, it's actually 'off.' See, it's like we, as conscious observers, are highlighting some set of relations. And by imagining them—"

"Wait, imagining is a strong word. How about selecting?"

"Okay, by selecting them, we form our model, but at its heart it's still based on us conscious observers."

As they talk Carmen asks fundamental questions with an acuteness that Kierk finds startling. Unnoticed by them the bartenders are lurking nearer to them, attempting to overhear the strangely fascinating esoteric conversation of this young couple.

Carmen gestures over to the bartender. "Two more martinis, good sir."

The ordered martinis long gone, both of them have excused themselves to go to the restroom. Kierk, pissing into a urinal, uses one hand on the wall to steady himself. He cannot believe this is happening between him and Carmen. He feels feverish from not having had sex for months. If they don't go home together he will have to tie himself to a mast like Odysseus. But it's not going to come to that, some barrier has been breached and Kierk thinks of those deterministic model systems he used to study, where once some invisible line is crossed an attractor sucks the system forward into a future state. He looks down at his penis and smiles like a munificent master.

Six feet away through a wall Carmen pops a squat to pee and stares at the side of the graffitied door, having that out-of-body experience of drunkenness: she is both squatting and watching herself squatting. She thinks—bracketing just like Husserl. Then she snort-laughs while peeing. After wiping off and washing her hands she spends a brief moment looking in the mirror, thinking that if he doesn't make a move ASAP she is going to shove him into some dark corner and have her way with the boy.

When they both get back Kierk says—"Hey, want to get a drink somewhere else?"

To which Carmen immediately replies—"I have wine at my apartment."

"Sold."

On the way over everything seems to be alive with gender, each building leaning on the one next to it, rubbing; spaces are tight, occupied, waiting, each small thing become so biological as to breathe.

At Carmen's apartment they spill in through her door, both laughing because it takes her so long to find the right key among all the others and Kierk pretends to die a little each time she tries the wrong one. The railroad apartment is a long rectangle covered in photographs, many are of New York City, and there are explosions of color in the form of carefully cut-out medical illustrations framed and hung up: the colored blues and reds of enzyme activity, the shaded regions of the brain stem, Kierk even recognizes the intricate trees of Cajal's drawings of cerebellar Purkinje neurons.

As Carmen heads to the bathroom Kierk sets his notebook down and heads for her bookshelf. It's always the first thing he does upon entering a home, go right for the library like a bloodhound. His fingers play over the spines, past a few popular science books, stuff on philosophy of mind. He stops, finger-walking back to a specific title stuck in the middle of a shelf, pulls it out.

"What's this? Is this the selection of Descartes' correspondence you were talking about?" he says over the distant sound of running water. "I mean, I know the general story . . . The princess raises that objection of interaction to Descartes' substance dualism . . . and the two of them—the princess and the philosopher—they fall in love but they never get together . . ."

Carmen spits out mouthwash, adjusts her hair in the mirror, looks at herself from several angles, flares her nostrils to make sure they're clear, examines her pores, winks at herself, comes out of the bathroom smiling and a little bit wobbly.

Closing the collection of letters Kierk puts it back in its home nestled between Nietzsche's *Thus Spoke Zarathustra* and Kundera's *The Unbearable Lightness of Being*. Kierk, charmed by the synchronicity between the two covers, is drunkenly struck by the repetitions and cycles of history, imagining how within individual lives the same choices are presented again and again like notes in some grand song . . . and that there must be a Hegelian synthesis between Eternal Return and Unbearable Lightness, that maybe there is a road not yet taken, that lives were lived again and again but sometimes a choice was made and this time around everything was different; that history was a giant chaotic system of attractors, different versions of the same identities living over and over like Buddha's previous reincarnations in the Jātaka tales, each one building and cycling on the ones that came before it, sometimes identical but sometimes coming within a hair's breadth of their previous incarnations until a single choice changes everything . . .

"Lost yourself?" Carmen says quietly, standing beside him.

"Oh, hey." He collapses back, a rain of thought coalescing again into form.

"Hey."

The lights flicker, then surge and go out. There are cheers from outside.

"Let me get some candles." She paws through a cupboard, Kierk gives her his lighter, and soon the apartment is thrown into flickering relief. Out the windows they see, one by one again, candles being put in other windows. To which Carmen puts a candle on the sill over which they lean, watching more and more small points of light flicker into being.

Then their leaning forms are suddenly very close, and that same deterministic force is now drawing them together, the city itself conspiring to bring them in slowly until their lips meet, and there is the hesitant movement of hands unfamiliar, and it seems to last forever, just their lips touching, their hands hovering about the other's body, then one hand goes to the back of one neck, another hand locates soft and burning skin underneath a shirt, and the two close completely. There is a soft bite on a lip and there is laughing as shoes are removed without the kissing stopping and then it does and an immediate seriousness takes over as a shirt is slowly unbuttoned and a cool small hand slips inside through the breech, and it is now that the other's body becomes a buzzing drug absorbed on contact, every touch two shots of gin, the air becomes breath, and a billion years of history is immanent in a departing shirt which sails across the watery air of the apartment, a hand literally shakes as it tries to unclasp a belt, and where the hell is the bed, and where are your lips I want to bruise them, I can't get enough of everything about you, you are my missing shade of blue, please, put your hands here, there, the small curve of her back is a cool arch, his chest is broad plane of heat, I want to feel your body in my body is the thought as she pulls back briefly and the bra falls to the floor and the whole-skin embrace that follows after the jeans and the socks and everything else sheds off in the darkness ... if we can just get a little bit closer we'll breach flesh bone thought maul me with your hands all over me a push a shove a kick back a reaction an action up against the wall and then after a time back to the other wall another push a hand pressing against my lower back and slipping lower, yes, I haven't forgotten how to do this just like riding a bike and I feel the hot pebbles of nipples under my palms and she licks me on my collarbone and we fall back I fall back she falls back onto the bed yes I run my hands up her legs back on top now her legs wrapping and grasping behind me I push my hands past the titillating barrier of his boxers to find an outpour of flesh yes, to grasp what I want to grasp—I don't have a condom ... —Fuck it, I can pull out ... —Oh really can you control yourself when I do this ... A bite of his ear and then I am pushed back onto the bed and we are separate for a moment again and his hands slide up and hook a thumb on my panties and both his hands caress down my leg and the panties are cast out into the darkness and I open my legs and I run my hands back up her legs as she opens them and then lower myself down on top of her biting at her nipple with my mouth his mouth is hot his teeth tug out I arch out my hands behind her back and pull her close as I begin to enter the hot deep core of the world and she makes a sound like she's being murdered and then says—Oh god yes put it in, and he does and is now heavy over me, yes, push me pin me grab my wrists bite my neck own me fuck me, there's that feeling of stiffness penetrating me and the heat of it as everything is opening around the grinding core of the world, the stretching and filling and shifting, the securing of a position, the thermodynamics of skin, the rhythm of a feedback loop as the movement begins to fill and open me and all I can think about is this movement and gasping and moaning and the weight over me and pushing away this pillow corner obscuring my mouth and my sticky strands of hair and then his one hand is cupping my ass and the other up against the wall far above me for counterforce and my body is lying underneath a thrusting body and moving to the thrusting body and it all makes sense because the universe may not have been made for us but we were made for the universe and this here is proof.

· · ·

CARMEN, MUSCLES LANGUID WITH pleasure but mind awake, looks up from the notebook she has been reading to candlelight over to the sleeping form of Kierk in her bed, who is pleasingly naked except for the thin tussled sheet that covers little. Is he waking? Around her the room is a blue eye dissolving in liquid, materials left around, the shucked remnants of clothes, everything has gone soft, physics has left them alone for now and only the delicate birds of thoughts lie roosting. Kierk, still near-dreaming something sinister and sweet all at the same time, moves a foot, finds nothing but sheet. His head turns away from an empty pillow, looks around for her. Maybe just the occasional flip of the page had awoken him, or had he sensed her absence? Carmen is a few feet away on the small couch, reading his notebook by the single remaining candle on the end table. Her expression as she looks up from the pages is one of consternation, no, revelation, while his look is one of unkempt waking, small shock, bleary, propping himself up on his elbows. She glances down at the notebook in her hand.

"Kierk, you know . . ."

"Come back to bed."

"But these aren't just some random notes. This is a whole journal. And it's good."

". . . Yes. I know."

"I want to finish this part."

"Come back to bed."

"Okay, in a second . . ."

"Just . . . come back to bed."

Kierk holds the blankets open for her. They settle in together, afraid to inconvenience the other in their movements. Eventually, after he has done so, Carmen falls asleep, and dreams of blue dissolving, of sounds and pleasures, of strange happenstances, primitive feelings with only bare visuals, and for the first time in a long time she does not have the dream of the subway train light impossibly bright and impossibly close bearing down with the sound of screaming metal.

SATURDAY

CARMEN WAKES UP. **A** slow and refreshing waking without the beep of an alarm, the natural waking point of a dream comfortably ended, and as REM sleep slides away Carmen opens her eyes. Her familiar apartment cciling. She comfortably moves a knee and finds a startling heat, and, smiling, rolls over to find the still, sleeping form of Kierk, his mouth open. She pauses, oscillating between intense melancholy that this moment is already passing, and an ebullient joy and nervousness.

"Kierk!"

"Mmm . . . hey."

"The power is back on."

The apartment is a palladium of sunrays now—there are clothes everywhere, the bed is clearly askew, diagonal now, and she has no idea how that pile of books was knocked over, maybe when—Carmen smiles idly. An arm reaches out and pulls her sitting form back into bed. His face up against hers.

"Well," she says, in close, "would you like a latte or something?"

"That sounds great."

"Alright," Carmen says as her hand plays over his shoulder, tracing with her fingers the geometrical designs there. "Buuuut first you have to tell me what these tattoos mean."

"No."

"Tell me!"

Kierk slowly props himself up. "They're designs from Giordano Bruno."

"Oh! He was the guy, the monk, who was burned at the stake for suggesting the universe was infinite? Right?"

"These are combinatoric wheels for his art of memory. They were supposed to combine to create a perfect language. It preceded the Turing machine by three centuries. Same idea, really."

"Why'd you get them?"

"Besides being twenty-two? I had just gotten back from Toronto. I told you about that . . . I got it because, if you had a theory that would really describe consciousness, the how and why of it, its content, its level . . . that would truly be a perfect language." He smiles. "And because I thought there was dignity and romanticism in impossible projects."

"Do you still?"

Chuckling, but a sadness to it. Carmen shares a long kiss with him—"Alright, you get your latte now."

She hops out of bed and looks over to see Kierk looking at her. Pulling on panties as she sticks her tongue out at him, then walking bare-breasted to the kitchen, she puts a large cup under the nozzle of her espresso machine that she starts up to a familiar mechanical hum, a tune she hums along with, kind of dancing. Her dance takes her to the refrigerator, where she pulls out a mason jar, unscrews the lid, pours in some 2 percent milk, then shakes it back and forth really hard, her butt stuck out and wiggling, and she hears Kierk laugh from the bedroom where he still has line of sight. When it's done she unscrews the top of the thick now-foamy milk and sticks it in the microwave for thirty seconds as she takes out two big saucer cups from the cupboard and sets them out on the counter. The microwave dings. Taking a big spoon out she sticks it in her mouth concave side down, where it is cool and wide against her tongue, the handle projecting into her field of vision, and, still humming, she first pours the espresso that has accumulated in the original large cup into both saucer cups equally, then, taking the big spoon out of her mouth and using it to keep the milk foam at bay, pours a pattern of milk into each with zigzagging movements so it looks like a Christmas tree when she's done.

She turns holding the two cups and sees Kierk, fully dressed and leaving the bedroom. Carmen is suddenly extremely aware that she is not wearing a top.

"You're . . . clothed," she says, as he takes one of the lattes from her.

"So I had . . ." He pauses. "On waking today . . . and maybe it was you, maybe it was the talk last night, or last night in general, but when I woke up today it was like . . ."

". . . Like what?"

He pauses to sit down in her kitchen chair, taking a deep swig of the latte. "Like Saint Paul on the road to Damascus."

"Wait, Kierk, are you saying that you—"

"I'm not claiming anything," he says up at her, shaking his head. "I'm not claiming anything right now."

"Let me guess. You have to go."

"Yes. But only because I have to get it down, just make everything clear."

"So . . . I just want to make sure," Carmen says, sitting down on his knee, "that last night was, I don't know, that you're okay with all this? You're kind of running out on me here."

"What?" Kierk looks up at her. "No, I mean, believe me, this is amazing. You're amazing." He kisses her long and hard. "But this idea is just nagging at me, I really think . . ."

"Maybe we could brainstorm it together?"

"Maybe . . . but it's not . . . it's more like seeing a pattern but you can't . . . If you go to describe it too soon it'll fall apart. Like marring the dust on a butterfly's wings. Like Fitzgerald."

"Hmm?"

"I'm just gonna need the day. To investigate this."

Carmen is nodding in his lap. "Yeah, I mean, that's totally fine obviously. I've got a lot of work to do anyway . . . I think I've got an idea for a . . . lead. In our case. Or whatever. That we could pursue. Maybe tomorrow?"

"Sure. We'll meet up tomorrow. Text me whatever you come up with in terms of our murder-mystery stuff."

Kierk kind of picks her up and sets her down as he stands. Now Carmen can't decide between seeing him off and going back to put a shirt on but she's worried he might be gone before then. He's already putting his shoes on and she's still standing there in her underwear with her untouched latte.

Finally she just says—"You're an elusive man, Kierk Suren."

Grinning up at her—"Yeah, but I make up for it in other qualities."

After a quick goodbye kiss Kierk disappears out the door and she hears his descent down the chairs. At first she laughs but then it turns into a frown. Her phone buzzes. Alex has texted her HOWD THINGS GO LAST NIGHT and has also sent her a bunch of kissy emojis. Carmen sends him back an emoji of a thumbs-up and some fireworks and an egg-plant, followed by a string of question marks.

There's still a lingering contact high from Kierk. Maybe it's the nicotine. Or maybe, Carmen thinks, she can blame evolution for making humans pair-bonding mostly-monogamous primates. After all, there's Kierk's intel-lect (showing an ability to plot on behalf of his genetic material), his broad shoulders (capable of brutish brawling with other male humans for domi-nance), his long legs and lack of adipose tissue (good for hunting, tracking, warfare), his combination of aggression and empathy (willing to commit violence to protect the genetic material he cherishes). And he makes her laugh (sexual market value). Of course she knows it goes both ways: her intellect also demonstrates an ability to plot on behalf of genetic material, her lithe and dexterous form (excellent for gathering, crafting, stealing), her facial and musculature symmetry (indicates lack of parasites and strong immune system), her beauty (as sexual selection becomes its own tauto-logical self-reinforcing phenomenon wherein beauty is attractive because beautiful children are attractive), and her fat deposits are all in the right places (good for the creation of the brains of more genetic material, which are mostly made of fat). But at the same time Carmen hoped that all these things were merely expressions of something else, that the deep structure of the universe rewarded this reciprocal altruism between consciousnesses, that as one traced the physical to the biological to the psychological to the spiritual it was obvious no one description captured all of it—that there was the underlying abstract truth that two are better than one, that unification was primary in ontology, that all of metaphysics was love and strife—the evolutionary was just one level of description, a single-dimensional slice of a high-dimensional object.

Regardless of its origin or ontological status she really does feel dif-ferent. Beyond the exchange of saliva and flesh and friction and cum and the pressing of our bodies and all that other truly excellent stuff there were other, deeper things at work, from the exchanging of the species of fungi that live in our lungs from our breaths, the microbiome of our mouths and urinal canals and in our eyes and hair and the colonies on our flesh, there was even the exchange of human cells, the development of microchimerism wherein genetically different cells from other people are found throughout our own bodies—while cells are often thought of as this strict matrix, the bricks we are made of, actually organic cellular structure is not like inorganic

architecture at all. Cells migrate and move, the whole body is always shifting, a thing with its own currents and eddies and tides. And Carmen knows
those cells with different DNA are taken up in our permeable bodies and
end up in our brains as well as our bellies, our genitals and toes, our lips
from kissing. We are destined to become a cellular chimera made out of our
mothers and fathers and lovers and children, monsters all.

AFTER SOME YOGA AND then taking a shower, Carmen begins to do
what she has done for the last two Saturdays: investigate the case, as she
thinks of it. First she cuts up a banana and sets it in a bowl with cream
and sprinkles brown sugar over it, and then she sits by her open window
looking out at the street with her Moleskine notebook, occasionally taking banana-slice bites, listening to the city sounds. Opening to a series of
pages with names, times, and locations on them, Carmen flips past those to
one titled "LEADS." Alone with her thoughts this notebook has felt both
funny and dark and necessary all at once, but when Kierk was here it suddenly seemed paranoid, ill-humored, and vaguely pathetic, like she was a
bored suburbanite concocting a fantasy about a neighbor. The organization
helps her consider the main points of the case: Atif, herself, Kierk, Alex,
Jessica, Mike, Leon, Greg, SAAR, the Following Brothers of Christ, the
kallu, Bleecker Street Station, the taxi, Mike taking Jessica home, Kierk
and her kissing in the lobby then leaving, the aftereffects, all forming a
set of conceptual points that she arranges and rearranges into different
constellations trying to make the outline into a shape she recognizes. She
enjoys doing this—after all, isn't the fundamental plot of a mystery identical to the fundamental plot of science: distinguishing the true causal structure of a series of events? Untangling correlation and causation? Coming
up with the simplest theory that explains as much as possible? Was the fact
that none of them had clear memories a mere stochastic event with no ties
to Atif's death, or was it central? What about Greg leaving early? What
about what the leader of the local SAAR meetings, Allen, had said about
there being an insider in the CNS? All accompanied by the remembrance
of a bit of trivia she recalls: that the English word "mystery" comes from
the Greek word *muein*—to close one's mouth.

She also remembers an article she'd read about an animal rights spy who
had infiltrated one of the top primate labs in the world, the Max Planck

Institute. Carmen flips to a new page in her notebook and writes at the top CANDIDATES FOR THE INSIDER/DOUBLE-AGENT OF SAAR IN THE CNS. She chews on her pen. It can't be one of the Crick Scholars. They arrived too recently for any sympathies or effective collusion to be established. That leaves faculty, an unlikely option, and staff, which is much more likely. A janitor or security guard? No, she thinks, the ideals of SAAR are too abstract to gain serious blue-collar converts. She can't imagine anyone not educated at a $80,000-per-annum school nodding along to "the intersectionality of animal research and multiculturalism." Which leaves students. But not graduate students, for the same reasons that excluded professors and postdocs. Which leaves undergraduate researchers. Plants. Looking up the process online it certainly seems pretty open. You just had to declare a science major, which you could do at almost any time. But what science undergrad is going to appear to be the perfect little scientist for their entire undergraduate career, while at heart believing the moral calculus worked out firmly against research? So applying Occam's Razor she knows that spy must be an undergraduate staffer or research assistant, or someone who very recently switched over to the neuroscience, psychology, or biology major, i.e., someone with an incongruence between what they are doing now and their previous classes.

She flips to a pristine page and draws out her deductions in logical form from premises, listing where she applies the Razor, which facts are contingent, and after the whole structure narrows down to the conclusion of her semiformal proof she writes *Quod Erat Demonstrandum* in big elegant letters at the bottom. She takes a photo and texts it to Kierk.

Carmen puts on some NPR and gets into her comfy underwear. It's getting dark out but she makes herself another iced latte, realizing that the CNS departmental website should have a list of student research assistants if it's up-to-date. Carmen gets into her bed, turning on WNYC with an outstretched toe. With the soft voices in the background, she balances her laptop on a pillow so it can sit on her lap without burning her, the air-conditioning a stuttering hum going on and off at intervals and only rippling at the surface of her attention, one hand going out to touch the handle of the iced latte habitually, not even picking it up but instead occasionally just hovering near it or gently touching the sweating glass and then retracting. Sitting at an incline, her legs out beyond her so that she can see her toes peeking up from behind the pillow/laptop construct that takes up most of her vision, the air-conditioning and iced latte a welcome contrast to the intense outside heat that she can, even from here, feel pushing in through her street-facing window like a forceful invisible beast—it is in this manner that night comes on and the room goes from gold to red to blue to black around her until the only light is from her computer screen.

By the end, Carmen has investigated every undergraduate working at the CNS, stalked each of them online, found their social media accounts and comments and blog posts and looked up old class websites to see what courses they've taken, slowly pruning the list. Occasionally, while doing all this, a detail of the night before with Kierk pops into Carmen's mind and she smiles to herself in the blue light of the screen, excited but confused about this morning. At the end she circles a name in her notebook: an undergraduate research assistant for Professor George Williams: Skylar Davis. A sociology major who had signed up to get research credits by working on the fMRI. The ongoing project she had requested assignment to? Getting the macaques into the fMRI scanner so they could be neuroimaged. Carmen drafts up an email demanding Skylar's presence in the CNS tomorrow afternoon, even though it's the weekend, claiming that there is an urgent issue concerning usage of the fMRI by the macaques. She also sends an email to Kierk asking him to meet her in the CNS tomorrow afternoon a bit earlier so they can coordinate.

Stretching, Carmen is restless from being in her apartment all day today. So she puts on some shorts and a T-shirt and grabs her purse and heads out into the summer night, into a city hallucinogenic with neon, the lights of cars, everything melting in the heat. Kierk still hasn't responded to the previous text, so she sends him another one. Looking up from her phone she realizes where she has been unconsciously walking toward like a somnambulist, drawn. Carmen descends into Bleecker Street Station like Persephone into Hades.

In the microclimate the air itself is so heated that when it gusts those strange underground currents it doesn't cool but heats, the stirring of a pot, and Carmen is sweating profusely as she swipes herself through the turnstiles. The thin platform goes like a yellow brick road on a long arc. Distant figures on the opposite side of the tracks are all fanning themselves. A metallic scream announces a train. When it pulls away the opposite side is empty. Carmen begins walking the long platform, which is only about six feet wide from the wall to the drop to the tracks, and finds herself hugging the wall, shying away from that tubular dark, almost dizzy with vertigo from its close presence. There are just one or two forms on the far end; the only person close is the man coming toward her now. She can hear the building sound of an approaching train. She's in the middle of the long empty stretch as the man approaches, haggard, beer-bellied, wearing cargo shorts and a stained T-shirt, a big guy. There's a long moment when he's staring at her as the two close, and she finds herself shrinking back toward the wall as they pass each other. Right as they are side by side he explosively moves up on her and, grabbing her shirt in one hand and her struggling arm in the other, even as she screams and tries to pull back, the man whips her staggering form around, once, twice, her legs trying to find a way to resist as he grunts this low, bull-like grunt, his face buried in her hair and on the second time around the centrifugal force is enough and he makes an animalistic guttural snort of effort and releases her clawing body into the black gulf off the platform, everything slowing down as she hangs in the impossible air and impossible circumstance, followed by the fall into the dark that takes forever, feeling the thump of her head but not quite losing consciousness, the screams just beginning from somewhere far away . . . All she knows is she's on something uneven and needs to get up but the coming train is barreling down on her scrabbling form, her mouth of hair and blood, she knows she has to get up, is trying to move but there's no air in her lungs and her mind is a long high scream of denial as everything gets brighter and brighter and louder and louder . . . a vivid sequence that flashes by in her mind when the bullish man passes her by, muttering to himself. After taking a deep breath and peering over the edge to the tracks to the dirty rails, Carmen exhales slowly, then chuckles at herself as she watches the shambling man wipe at his nose, say something to himself, find a seat back near the entrance she came from. She finishes her walk all the way to the other entrance. There the platform shrinks to a little ledge maybe a foot wide and winds off down into the tunnel for as far as she can see. She keeps eyeing it even as she finds one of the little wooden benches and sits down by herself. Sweat trickles. Even the wood underneath her radiates warmth.

After each train leaves, the subway is empty except for Carmen, and then about a minute later the first person descends from above until the slow trickle fills up the platform, then another train comes and clears it out again, and Carmen can't help but think of the filling and draining of calcium in a synapse, the molecular beat of the thing; that this part of the city is like a chthonic alien organ with some opaque function. Occasionally the perceptive among those who pass notice with a quirk of interest the beautiful young woman planted in the middle of it all, biting at her fingernails, fanning herself, watching, waiting for something unknown and unsayable. And ever so often the automated voice addressed independently of listeners—"Stand clear of the closing doors, please."

Eventually the people become less numerous. In the lateness of the night her mind begins to imagine scenarios, to play them out again and again on a loop, as if some part of her is daring something to happen, is waiting for something drastic. Instead the night just gets later and later and the people fewer and fewer, until finally entire trains are coming and going without the entrance or exit of a single soul. And Carmen is becoming half-terrified of the menacing long platform next to her, which extends into that subterranean realm . . . The scenario she imagines is that of a creature, something huge but lithe, something with an animal head, peeks from the side out onto the platform, a bull's head maybe, leering at her, its mouth gaping and panting, its eyes impossibly dark and lewd upon her, and eventually the image becomes so strong, and the expectation so intense that she suddenly bolts from her wooden seat, pushing through the turnstiles and in her flight continually whipping around to look until she reaches the safety of the surface.

CARMEN STICKS TO LIGHTED paths all the way back to her apartment, deriding herself for being silly but also deeply glad when she arrives back in that cool safety and closes the door behind her, locking it. She is wiping the sweat from her brow, is adjusting the thermostat even further downward, when, turning, she pauses. Kierk's Hello Kitty notebook sits on the seat of one of her kitchen chairs. It had somehow gone unnoticed, the sly thing. Kierk, in his rush, hadn't taken it this morning. Or maybe she had unconsciously hidden it last night in her sleepy state? She picks it up gingerly and thumbs through the pages, blocky with text. It was strange that Kierk hasn't contacted her about it, tried to get it back.

To rid herself of that grimy feeling that comes with being out in Manhattan for a long time, she starts a shower. Just as she gets ready to begin the long process of conditioning her hair the phone rings. Thinking that it might be Kierk she darts out, grabbing a towel for some instinctive reason and wrapping it around her as she leaves puddles all the way to her cell phone in the kitchen.

"Hello?" she says, smiling, one hand clutching her towel closed.

There is the sound of a deep exhalation, a guttural pant.

Carmen is frozen. Dripping wet she is suddenly intensely cold, her whole skin flushing with goose bumps.

With far more courage than she feels—"Who are you?"

The guttural breathing begins to intensify, breaks with a huffing snort, then goes back to the deep breathing. Why now? Had someone followed her back from the subway?

Carmen's face contorts—"If we ever meet, if I ever find out who you are, I am going to kill you. Do you understand? I will kill you."

The breathing seems unfazed, or maybe even excited, continuing to ramp up, working toward something she didn't want to imagine; it sounds like spittle is flying with every breath and the tone has grown even deeper, guttural, a heaving thing beyond language. Then there is a moment of dislocation, a doubling. The sound is both coming from the phone but also, somehow, it is near her in real life too. Her whole body reacts in the sensation of utter terror. She freezes completely. It is here. It is near her.

Her apartment is small and she's standing in the middle of it in a towel. The sound, that horrible moaning, is far enough away that it's nearby, but muffled, like it's through a wall. The window with the fire escape. Slowly she sets down the phone as the impossibly low moan begins to build, both through the phone but also, beyond. The window. It's outside the window. The light inside makes it impossible to see outside, where there's only a black plane. Then there is creaking, a motion. The fire escape. Dripping, one hand holding the towel. One foot back, then another, to the kitchen. The drawing of a knife, her hand shaking. It is impossible to move in all but the slowest movements. It is impossible to think. Another sound, more creaking, a shudder of massive weight shifting. Oh help me. Someone help me. The hand holding the knife goes up to flick off the light switch. The apartment is plunged into darkness. There is a frantic series of motions, the sound of someone moving about outside, of clanging metal, but quickly fading away, and then all the sounds stops. Her eyes are adjusting. The pane of dark glass. One step, then another, her feet still slippery. Still almost impossible to see. Something is there. A human form. She shrieks. It is stilted, to the side, lying there on the fire escape, propped up, sitting, looking in. She's gasping and screaming, clutching the towel, the knife. It is unmoving. It sits propped on the fire escape looking at her scream. She can't find her phone in the darkness but doesn't want to turn on the light. Why is no one coming? She screams again and again. The figure is motionless. She stops screaming. Nothing moves. There are only the mute city sounds. It's a person looking in. No. Her eyes have adjusted now. It's not a person. It's a mannequin. A female mannequin, legs splayed out, resting back against the railing. It is inert. Someone left this thing here. Oh god why? There's something wrong with its face. Carmen cannot quite make it out. She moves closer. Its blank face looks back at her. It has a blonde wig on but no clothes. There. A handle. Something has been impaled into her face. Under her eye. An ice pick. An ice pick under her eye.

Just like a lobotomy.

Carmen screams again, more like a sob. The dummy stares at her. Whoever had left it had left themselves, she had heard them go. Hadn't she? She can't turn on the light. She's close enough she can peer through the window to the rest of the fire escape, which is empty. Slowly, she unlocks the window. She might still be able to see whoever left it departing. Carmen's upper body leans out, creating a mirror to the mannequin. There is no one on the ladder, above or below. Some deep instinct causes her to push away at the dummy, push it through the railing, and it falls in a heap to the ground a dozen feet down. She hears an exclamation from somewhere down the street, someone walking who had seen it fall.

Closing the window quickly and locking it, Carmen, groping around in the dark, throws on some clothes, finds her phone, her purse, and for some unthinking reason also grabs Kierk's notebook. She opens the door slowly after staring through the peephole and listens. The hall is quiet. She descends the stairs, then is out the door, down the steps, and Carmen flees up the street and into the city. She's headed to the most populated area she can think of near her. Turning onto First Avenue, Carmen's already on the phone with the police.

"You can come down to the station to report it. Or we can go to your apartment. It sounds like maybe it was a prank, ma'am."

"It was a death threat! And I'm not at my apartment!"

"Was there someone there inside the apartment?"

"No, they were probably outside."

"What did they look like?"

"I didn't see them. They called me."

"What did they say?"

"They didn't say anything!"

"So they called you but they didn't say anything?"

"Look, they left a lobotomized store dummy. Do you even understand what that means? That's a threat."

"Maybe. There's a lot of college students in your area and it's a weekend. Lots of dumb tricks happen. Why don't you come down to the station and file a report. Keep in mind that it may take a few hours for the paperwork. But unless you have any further information I'm afraid all we can do is get a record of the event. I'm just being honest with you about how this is going to go."

"Fuck you!"

Hanging up, Carmen experiences a surge of frustration. Did they even know what such a thing meant? She remembers a photograph she'd once seen in class. A 1950s housewife directly facing the camera. The only sign she'd had the operation were the dark bruises under both eyes. Back then a lobotomy was an outpatient procedure performed in fifteen minutes, often on depressed women. Some doctors performed dozens a day and patients would ride home in cabs after. To figure out how deep to swish around the ice pick, and when to stop, a common practice was to ask the patient to sing "The Star-Spangled Banner" as you did it. When she started forgetting the words, you'd gone deep enough. And sometimes the ice pick left behind barely anything, sometimes there was only a body remaining . . .

She shudders, rubbing her arms, looking around. As she was talking to the police she'd also been following the late-night weekend crowd, and so Carmen, with a nervous look around, shows her ID to a bouncer and follows a group of people into a bar. The music thrums around her, people packed in, drinks sloshing. Carmen jumps when someone puts an arm on her back to push past her. There's a knife handle sticking out of her pocket, her body is still wet underneath her clothes, and in one hand she still holds Kierk's notebook. She finds a backroom without as much noise and dials him. Again and again the phone buzzes to no answer at all.

·   ·   ·

CARMEN LIES AWAKE IN the hotel. At first she keeps jerking up at the slightest noise, very aware of the structure of the door, or the open glass of the hotel window, and at these times she clutches the Hello Kitty notebook to her like some kind of metaphysical shield. On the nightstand rests the kitchen knife. The door has stacked in front of it all the other furniture in the room except the bed and nightstand. Unable to sleep even in the sanitary hum of the hotel, she's instead been trying to quiet her fear by reading the journal. It is the only thing that can occupy her busy mind, and, wide awake, she reads deep into the night, finally arriving at the last entry written in Kierk's quick and spindly scrawl.

Sometimes I dream of a great tree. I dream of it at night but more and more during the day as well. I feel it may come to me in many guises, in other forms. In the dream it is a monarch of a tree, as if the land of trees had elected it unanimously to represent their kingdom. The trunk is so wide that it loses curvature up close, and only by stepping back dozens of paces does it finally resolve itself into a three-dimensional shape. A sequoia. Larger than any I saw in California. A great towering and branching sequoia, all alone in a great field. It is always night where the tree is. Thousands of years old, it spans the history of human civilization. Its mammoth trunk brachiates into knotty giant offshoots that run almost perpendicular to the ground, and this epigeous brachiation continues on and on, tufts of bushy dark green sprouting off, making the tree even greater in reach than it is tall. The body of it is huge even at the higher areas, the diameter of the branches large enough for a man to easily walk on, except at the very top where hundreds of feet up one has to climb carefully on the swaying branches, hoping they hold your weight, such that only the very tips of your fingers ever clear the tree and end up in the cold, infinitely fresh air. Above it swirl the richest stars you will ever see. The backbone of the Milky Way is a bright speckled bridge across the sky. One can almost see the hazy spun disk of light that is the Andromeda galaxy engaged in its four-billion-year collision course with us. The twinkles of stars are like pinholes poked in the canvas of the sky, and wherever you turn your head, to whichever direction you fix your gaze there is cosmic scenery, for the tree stands in some relation to the stars, but it is the kind of unspeakable relation that only deeply old and deeply natural things can possibly share with one another. Down at the base of the tree steps have been carved into its side, wrapping around, and there is occasional evidence of human engineering and controlled growth. And out along the thick roads of the branches, all over that expansive arboreal kingdom, are shadowed figures, sometimes moving about in small, lit areas, outlines of human forms. This is Yggdrasil. The world tree. The tree of knowledge. And on it wander those who have advanced it, natural philosophers all. There is an organization to it—older discoveries and more fundamental theories are medial to the trunk, and then the farther along a branch one goes, the more modern. This is often reflected in the means of illumination: the light at the base is from torches or fires, and then higher still candles, then lanterns burning whale oil, then hanging light bulbs and computer screens near the outer layers. I am simultaneously on the tree and looking at myself on the tree from the ground. How can both be true at the same time? Walking out along the branches faces come out at you in the darkness suddenly, and each is rough with a wild wisdom. Exploring at the base I find Plato, twenty-eight, only a year older than I, all in black and looking outward into the night. From his solemn stare I surmise he must be gazing out at the tombstone of his mentor Socrates. Just a bit farther down I see Aristotle with his notes and specimen samples but I don't approach. My destination is the outer branches and although I am torn with curiosity I push on, finding footholds carefully in some places, while in others I can proceed at a steady stride. The order of the tree is not always what I expect, although in general it obeys the hierarchy of the sciences: philosophy and mathematics at its base and then physics, chemistry, biology, psychology, economics, and sociology (these branches seem flimsy and enervated at the very top). I linger over Leibniz and race past Rutherford, then have to backtrack until I find Galen standing next to a cot where a diseased man clutches something—a cross? Galen is whispering soothingly in ancient Latin. After a few more figures I come to William Harvey, who stands next to the ghoulish vivisected body of a horse strung up between two thin offshoots of the tree that form an X, a Roman crucifixion, with the valved and chambered great equine heart struggling to contract in the dim light of candles, and he says to himself— "It's a pump that circulates. A pump! And the body is a complete circuit." Higher up, William James is here. He's alone and well-dressed but in near-total darkness along an empty section of a branch of the tree. Quiet

and kneeling he does not turn to me as I pass but I hear a continuous mur-
mur. I think he is praying. Tracking sideways a bit, finding a connecting
branch, I come upon Francis Crick. The confident thirty-five-year-old
is seated at a small table with a half-full beer and is sketching on a bar
napkin under a single illuminating bare bulb and I can make out the
twist of a helix in bleeding pen. And near the end of the branch Antonio
Moretti is on the tree. Perhaps him being here is just a personal affec-
tation of mine, or maybe the tree has some sort of a fractal structure,
whereon, zooming in on a branch, more branches are revealed, endless,
and in the end everyone is somewhere on the tree. Regardless, he is
here, looking just as I knew him. He has in his hands a chewed pencil
and sheets of paper which contain causal diagrams and logical mecha-
nisms and information theory terminology. He is impeccably dressed in
a sports jacket and bolo tie. He turns from me as I approach and will
not look upon me. At times I switch temporal perspectives, flipping back
to being on the ground gazing up at the tree's enormous arboreal outline
before I have climbed it—it is then that I am enraged by the tree, I
attack its base, I scream at it and tear at the impenetrable armor of its
trunk. I think of ways of chopping it down, each more outlandish than
the next. But I know that this is mere release, catharsis, as I could never
truly injure it. I have neither the tools nor the will. But I do prostrate
myself on my knees to beg, to asking pleadingly—where on the tree?
Where on the tree would a theory of consciousness be placed? On what
far and tangential branch? On physiology as it turns to neurology? Past
computer science toward the arcane side of information theory? Off of
mathematics and physics? From where would it grow? An extension of
analytic philosophy? What of the far tuft that is complexity science and
the language of state-spaces? The only question I ever ask it as I beg
or rage—where on the tree? Where on the tree? And what figure will
be paused there frozen in the discovery of it? A face illuminated by the
revelation, yes, but the eyes clouded cataract white, struck blind by the
Damascene light. For no revelation is without cost . . .

SUNDAY

CARMEN WAKES UP HAVING slept only lightly. Lying in the hotel bed she is just able to snatch at her last dream's end and, by focusing on the last scene, is able to rewind and recover it. In the dream she had been in the CNS, trying to find Kierk. Or rather it had looked like the CNS, had all the surface appearances of the normal everyday building, but somehow everything was different. The building had the same relations, the same designs and shapes and hung scientific posters and corkboards, but there was something in the deep structures, some presence she could sense not in her base perception but rather solely through whatever apperceptive means she normally identifies intentionality, teleology, mind, life. So moving through the building she had also known it was a façade for something actually organic, biological. She had been aware of this but unperturbed and unfazed and her attention had been entirely on finding Kierk, hurrying after him to deliver a message, some discovery that she could not articulate now while she's awake but had fully possessed in the dream. So she had searched through the hallways that were not really hallways and in the stairwells that were not really stairwells until she heard, around a bend, an elevator door ding open. Turning a corner she had seen in front of the elevator doors a macaque in its plastic box, set like a totem to greet the opening of the elevator. Carmen had paused, watching it from afar as it writhed within the box, the skullcap on its head vibrating obscenely as its body scampered about. And from the elevator had come the form of Kierk, a stooped and harried figure, cautiously approaching and leaning in as if to listen. For a while he just held an ear to the macaque's lips, then with a sound as loud as a gunshot he had rocketed back sporting just the ragged remains of his skull. The bang itself had woken her up, but she had experienced one last inter-regnum which had landed her back firmly in the dream where she had been standing in shock facing the monkey down the hallway, Kierk's legs splayed out as the elevator closed on them, and the monkey had oriented itself in his chair toward her and was now smiling in a way that only a human could smile.

The whole process of remembering the dream had taken a total of three myoclonic jerks.

Carmen sits up on the edge of the bed, realizing that she had fallen asleep holding Kierk's notebook. She feels it had become incorporeal and seeped into her psyche like a perverted inside-out dream catcher—there had been enigmatic hints like *This time I must swim out further, swim so far that the choice to return to shore is no longer viable*, or *Twenty-seven is the year in which I must either bloom or wilt, for this stasis has become monstrously unstable*, and other things of that sort. It was almost as if these thoughts had sum-moned the dream to her, like words on the subject of consciousness spoken in the right order could conjure something from another realm.

She calls him again, for what must be the twentieth time.

"The person you are calling has a voicemail box that has not been set up."

CARMEN IS IN A holding pattern designed to strip away the hours. She's feeling calmer now that she's gotten breakfast and taken it back to her hotel room. But all morning the absence of Kierk has been popping into her head, a question mark floating over her.

She spends an hour convincing AT&T to put a trap on her phone, so that if that . . . voice calls her again, she can get the number. Feeling slightly more secure now that an action has been taken, she dials her mom.

At the happy exclamation of her mother as she answers the phone Car-men almost breaks down and weeps. She's so close to telling her everything, but she can imagine the immense worry that her mother would have, and her ineffectiveness, fear, and lack of understanding. Instead Carmen just wants to have a normal conversation, to experience the totally safe and standard world her mom inhabits. They end up chatting for an hour about the most mundane topics Carmen can guide them to.

Eventually she's saying—"The Crick program is going really well for me. I've met . . . some interesting people. Some great people."

"Any of these 'great people' men who happen to be in the program with you? You know, someone who shares your interests. Because that's always been a problem with you, honey. You have such abstract interests. Very high-minded."

Carmen sighs. "Yes, Mom, there are also men in the program."

"You know what I meant. Don't paint me like I'm so obvious."

"I know what you meant, yes. I'll have to let you know, Mom."

"You can't blame me for asking. I'm just asking."

"I know, Mom."

"So you did meet someone then?"

"God, Mom, I don't know, okay. I'm trying to figure some things out. Some important things."

"Are you mad at me? Again? Just my asking how you are is enough to make you mad now?!"

"No, no . . . Mom, it's fine. I'm sorry, I just . . . things have been difficult here. Can I come up? I want to stay with you for a few days."

"Of course, hun! I'm always happy to have you. You know that. I know there was a time when it seemed, well . . . Anyways, I thought you said it was going well. Why come over?"

"Weird might be a better word? Like really weird."

"Like what? Like some of the people in the program?"

"Yeah, exactly."

"Well, if work itself is going well that's really good. And it helps that you had that article thing that was really important?"

"Yes. The article I published in *Nature*."

"That's the journal right?"

"Yes. *Nature*. The scientific journal."

"Well, I have it, honey. It's on the fridge." Carmen hears the sound of rustling pages, like her mom is holding the phone near it and playing with the pages.

"That's great. Did you read it?"

"Of course I read it."

"It's just like, a really big deal."

"I read it! You know . . . I mean, it's very interesting. Some of it, you know, whooooosh. To be honest, honey, I stopped trying to understand everything you did in high school. You would come home with some project or something. I used to brag so much about the books you would read. I couldn't shut up. Your aunt would be like, just be quiet and stop noticing what the girl is doing. Because if you get all weird about it it's going to change how she feels about it. And we would have debates about this. All the time. You never knew. But we did. Because different kids have different styles. Different needs, you know, to be ignored or encouraged. But you'll learn that. You'll find out all about that. You're going to be so surprised. Because it never turns out how you think it will with kids. You used to be such a little princess when you were really young. You were always running around? Do you remember that? Always wearing pretty dresses you would pick out yourself. You could be so stubborn about them. Already stylish. Do you remember that?"

Carmen can't help it—"Those were for the pageants, and it's not like I was the one out there with a platinum credit card buying them."

". . . Oh says you. And then you got to high school and like some flip just got switched! It just got switched. And everyone could see it. Your father was always saying, you know—'Where'd my little girl go? Where'd my little girl go?' Just like that. Not that he was angry or sad. Just bewildered. We never thought you'd be a scientist. And I'm not trying to be, well, you know, but you were so beautiful. You are so beautiful now. But growing up you were like an angel. Just like an angel. People would always tell me, you know, people would always say—'She's gonna be an actress. She's gonna be in movies.' People would really say that! Strangers would come up and say that! So, of course that's what I thought. That's what everyone thought! Oh honey, I only wanted what was going to be the easiest thing for you. That's why I took you to all those, those damn hotels. So that you could have opportunities and a career of your own. But you, well, you're stubborn! Like your grandmother! You had to take the harder path. But you did it. I mean you *really* did it. And now, I tell everyone that you're a scientist now. That you grew up to be a scientist, when they knew you as a little girl. And they say—'Imagine that.' That's what they say. Imagine that. That's exactly what they say. You flummoxed them all, sweetheart. You flummoxed them all. And me too! And you know I'm so proud of you. I'm so immensely proud of you my heart just breaks with it. But I'm never going to understand what you do. But I know now it's important." Her laugh is tinny and faraway over the phone. "At least I know it's important."

Carmen finds herself crying. She wipes at her eyes, surprised at this reminder of the tender-raw narrative of her life, the origins of it all. How different it had been then, how far she has come, how real her life was outside of the recent events. Not that it had been so much harder and the choices so much more devastating than any other life, but rather it had been full of hardship and choices in the way that all lives, all lives all over are, and because like every personal past of someone who has moved away and become a different person it had condensed into an almost solid structure from time passing, a beautiful but heartbreaking piece of art she sometimes forgets she possesses, a Rembrandt in the basement.

IT'S TIME. OUTSIDE IT is gray and hot, the clouds are low, trapping the heat in, a lid to the city. During the walk to the CNS she texts Kierk again, this time just a bunch of question marks. He still hasn't answered. It's been two days now since they've communicated. Thirty missed calls. A gazillion text messages. Would Kierk have walked back from her apartment to his own? Undoubtedly. Or maybe he had taken the subway . . . And there was something terrible on the news that she had missed. No. Impossible. But after this many missed phone calls it seemed completely possible. His body, that thing that was now so full of life to her, could right now be a mangled doll somewhere under the city in the dark, lost. Or the person that had left that dummy outside her window had found him, gotten him, and with an ice pick stirred apart that delicate brain of his. She is gripped with worry for him. But maybe that's not what's going on at all, maybe he's totally fine, maybe he's consciously not answering her calls, and he's decided something she didn't see coming, some part of him was an emotional cipher and had taken over and he was making decisions using some formal system unknown to her. Or what if he had missed the first few phone calls and messages and then found them all, and decided she was too unstable or crazy or obsessive and now wasn't responding at all, didn't know how to nor did he want to deal with a girl who called him dozens of times. What if she'd ruined everything? Carmen is confronted with the fact that in the grand scheme of things she doesn't know that much about Kierk. He had talked about his mother, but what about his father? He'd never even

mentioned one . . . She knew that he had left his PhD prior to its completion, some kind of fight with his mentor, but whose fault had it been?
And what of his past relationships? He'd never mentioned any, despite all
the discussions they've had. Had he ever been in love? She's just realizing
now that she doesn't know any of this. Had he just wanted to fuck her?
Maybe he'd gotten everything he wanted from her already. She'd been so
stupid not to see it! She'd misinterpreted everything. All his interest in her
had just been him wanting to check off some sort of conquest box. Who
the fuck was Kierk at all? Maybe he was just like everybody else . . . And
then the cycle started again at her worry about his safety, and she's back to
certainty that some outside malevolent force is at work.

Carmen increases her pace to the CNS, occasionally breaking into a jog
as she rounds corners or crosses streets. Hypotheses float through her mind:
that somehow SAAR knew what was going on, knew about her, knew about
Kierk . . . had found Kierk alone after he had left yesterday . . .

Entering the CNS she finds no security guard at the little vestibule. After
ringing the bell and waiting for a minute she leans over and swipes her own
card in. She presses the elevator button but it doesn't light up—probably
the power outages had affected it and it needed to be reset or something.
So she takes the stairs, which she's never done from the ground floor before.
Oddly not all the stairwells in the building go all the way up—this one ends
at the fourth floor and so she has to wander the floor, which she's never
been on, looking for another stairwell. The lights are all dim. Sometimes
she gets halfway down a dark hallway before a motion detector illuminates
the section. She wonders if Skylar is in here yet. In fact, Carmen realizes
she stupidly hadn't specified where Skylar should meet with them—stupid
Carmen, overconfident Carmen—she mentally berates herself, picking her
way through the corridors.

She stops because of a low sound, like a moan, and is momentarily frozen in place listening before she recognizes it as the change in air pressure
between rooms. She realizes that the door is resting just an inch from being
closed with wind whistling through it. She's never noticed the doors in this
structure do that before. At first she's relieved for this explanation but then
disconcerted. The building is whistling at her. It was just like her dream of
the building being alive this morning, wasn't it?

She's halfway down a long corridor when the footsteps begin. At first she
doesn't identify them as such, they are so loud and heavy in the silence. But

they are indeed footsteps. And they're on the floor above her, walking down what must be a similar corridor, booming each step. The ceiling above her echoes as the sounds approach Carmen's position where she has stopped, looking up. There's something wrong, the footsteps cover too much space between them, like it's a giant walking. They come to a stop directly above her. Carmen's hand goes to her mouth to quiet her breathing. Her mind spins. What if it's the same person who left the mannequin? Or the same . . . She wonders if there's some kind of entrance in the basement of the building to the subway system . . . maybe in the animal rooms, the large drains by the monkey cages leading down into cylindrical pits that connected to forgotten sewage tunnels. Something could definitely come up through those tunnels, something that had been moving under the city unseen . . .

When the footsteps start up again Carmen jumps. They keep going past her, down to the end of the corridor in just a few strides, and then turn the corner and all goes quiet again.

Breathing hard, Carmen becomes something slinking, primitive in her movements, like she is hunting or being hunted. And she's thinking that maybe it could come back, summoned by something being done here . . . absurd thoughts . . . She knows that she's freaking herself out but can't stop—every time she turns a corner of a hallway she expects to find some huge thing panting in the dark, crouched and monstrous and snuffling about before noticing her and turning toward her . . .

Listening and proceeding slowly, creeping through corridors and up stairwells, Carmen finally arrives at the lab. Approaching the door, Carmen hears shuffling within, something being overturned, and a small clang like something impacting. Pausing before the entrance she lets out a long breath before slowly peeking inside.

In the middle of the empty lab Kierk is jump-shooting balled-up pieces of paper into a trash barrel. There is an incredible rush of relief. Walking up she grabs a piece of paper off the desk and crumpling it up she wings it at his face.

"You haven't been answering your phone!"

Smiling, he shrugs. "Sorry, I didn't know. I've been working. I turned it off. But I saw your email this morning. So here I am, what's the plan?"

"Do you know what I've been doing? Do you know anything?" Carmen yells.

"Whoa! What's wrong?"

Carmen briefly breaks down, sinks to her knees. Kierk stares at her for a moment, then rushes over.

"I thought you were dead!" she says, and hits at his chest with her fists.

"What? What are you even talking about?"

"I thought . . ."

After a moment Carmen recovers herself. Then she's filling him in on everything from her experiences in the subway to the mannequin like she's giving a research report. Hypothesis, speculation, her own conclusions, are all laid out. Kierk listens closely, asking questions when appropriate, until he's heard everything. They go back and forth on the possibilities.

"So are we just going to speculate all day or are we going to interrogate Skylar?" Carmen finally says, exhausted in the telling. "Because we also need to find her."

"Hm?"

"I didn't exactly specify where we should meet. I mean, she's probably in Williams' lab . . ."

"Alright. Let's go find our spy."

The two quickly debate how to approach the situation while heading to Williams' lab. In the darkened and silent hallways Carmen is still kind of freaked out in the back of her mind, but Kierk's presence comforts her—he's this big loud force moving down through the silence of the CNS, opening doors and talking as if he doesn't notice the creeping feeling that the building itself is aware of them. She had told him of the footsteps she'd heard but Kierk had just waved it away, saying it was probably just some scientist running experiments on the weekend, clomping around.

Closing in on their destination they finish discussing their strategy, which turns out to be, as Carmen, finally feeling like herself, says—"Elementary."

She goes first while Kierk waits just around the corner to listen for his cue. On entering Carmen finds Skylar, who she recognizes from photos online, sitting at one of the computer terminals in the bright glow of a monitor. She's a frizzy and dark-haired girl, plump, and much shorter than Carmen. Only sections of the room are lit. And the lab is empty except for the two of them, which simplifies things.

Skylar had clearly looked up Carmen as well.

"Hi. Carmen, right? You're a postdoc in Karen's lab?"

"Hello, Skylar," Carmen says, outwardly calm and quiet. But she could barely hear her words over the beat of her own heart. "I'm sorry I had to call you in on the weekend. Thank you for meeting with me."

"You said in your email it was about the macaques and the fMRI scanner? Because I was told—"

"It's not exactly about that."

"Is it about the scheduling or, like, the equipment? Because if I like, scheduled something in the fMRI over you I'm really sorry—"

Carmen waves away the concern. She sits down in a neighboring chair. "Let's start with the macaques. How long have you been working with them?"

The two are sitting under one of the few lit bulbs and it is glaring down on them. The rest is darkness.

"Well," Skylar says, shifting around and looking puzzled, "about four months now."

"And you asked for the assignment, right? You wanted to work with the macaques."

"Umm, yeah. Why?"

Carmen leans back in her chair nonplussed—"I'm actually thinking of hiring a research assistant for my own lab."

"What?"

"Yeah, I wanted to see if you were interested. Because of your background."

"Well I don't really . . ."

"You switched over, right? From sociology to a neuroscience degree. When was this again?"

"Ummm like a little while ago. I'm in a summer research program that you can sign up for."

"So what made you switch?"

"Why? I'm not really sure I want to work for you. No offense. And besides I don't even know if I can change who I work for—"

"Why'd you switch, Skylar?"

Skylar looks around quizzically, like she is searching for a hidden camera amid the cubicles.

"I just did, okay? I wanted to switch. I, I took a neuroscience course and I just realized that—"

"Wrong," Carmen says, her tone changing. "You changed majors at the beginning of the semester, before you took any of those courses."

"What?! How do you know that?"

"Are you familiar with the Students Against Animal Research?"

Skylar stops in the process of getting out of her chair. After a second, she begins again—"Umm, I don't know what that is—"

"How could you not know what it is, they've been all over the campus news," Carmen says, almost smiling openly.

"No." Skylar is shaking her head. "I meant that I knew who they were but I'm not—"

"You know exactly what I'm here about."

"I really don—"

"I'm here to ask you some questions, Skylar." Carmen's voice is raised enough that it echoes in the empty lab.

Skylar is grabbing her sweatshirt and her phone and is standing, glancing toward the door. "I'm feeling really uncomfortable right now. I'm totally not in a safe space, so I'm just going to go . . ."

Skylar moves around Carmen, who, as Skylar passes simply says—"You can't leave until you answer some questions."

But Skylar is already hurriedly approaching the doorway. Then the outline of Kierk looms in front of her and Skylar lets loose a scream, waving her arms, backing up.

"Sit down," Kierk says darkly as she bumps up against a desk, finding a seat with her hand groping blindly behind her. Carmen has the odd thought that it really is true that people go sheet-white when they're scared.

"We're not here to hurt you, Skylar," she says reassuringly. "We're here to ask you some questions. And you are going to answer them."

"I don't know anything, I don't know anything about SAAR and I don't—" Skylar has her phone in her hand and is beginning to dial.

Carmen leans over. "We already know you're a member." Skylar stops dialing and looks up at them. "And you better start answering our questions. Because if you don't, we will destroy you, Skylar." She leans in further. "We will ensure that you are expelled from NYU for deception and collaboration with a student group that has been banned on campus. We will make sure you are prosecuted in the criminal system for conspiracy and collusion. And we *will* call your parents."

Skylar, her eyes bulging and stammering, blubbers—"I'm sorry! I didn't . . . You can't . . ."

"Skylar, if you tell us everything you know, we won't do any of that," Kierk says. "You'll be able to keep your job here. You'll have to disassociate yourself from SAAR, of course. Stop seeing them. Avoid them. Do whatever you have to. Make something up. But we won't tell anyone."

"But only if you to tell us everything you know about SAAR."

Emotions ripple across Skylar's face. They wait as she processes the situation.

"Okay . . . Okay. But you're promising you won't bring me into it?"

"We won't."

"What . . . What do you want to know?"

Carmen contains a triumphant smile.

"Do you know who Allen is?"

Skylar nods, one hand still gripping her phone but not using it.

"Allen said that you helped pull off a job for SAAR two weeks ago. Some kind of direct action."

Skylar nods. "Ever since the thing with Double Trouble they've been trying to get more photos, videos, whatever, anything. The reaction was so huge. But SAAR can't file for those freedom things—"

"Freedom of Information Act requests," Carmen fills in for her.

"Right. So I was like, supposed to get people into the monkey rooms. I swiped them in to see the cages."

"When was this?"

"It was, ummm . . . after that big storm."

"You mean Saturday before last?"

"Right. Friday it had like, rained a lot. I remember that. We spent a few minutes taking pictures and videos but then the guard came by on like, a patrol or something and we like, hid in one of the rooms. Anyways, it was scary so we all just left right afterward . . . I don't actually know who has the photos or what they're going to do with them. They might already be up on websites."

"We don't care about some pictures, Skylar. That's below our pay grade," Kierk says. Carmen catches his gaze and rolls her eyes, imperceptibly shaking her head.

"Actually, Skylar, show us the photographs. Prove that you took them," she says.

Skylar quickly thumbs through her phone, holding up a photo of a macaque in a skullcap screaming at the photographer from its cage. Carmen grabs it from her to a weak protestation and then thumbs through the photo roll, both Kierk and Carmen watching the pictures go past of monkeys screaming, baring their teeth, close-ups of their cages and the droplets of blood around their skullcaps. They recognize in the background a few of the people from SAAR meetings, and Allen is clearly identifiable in one picture with a camera in hand.

Skylar looks guilty and tired. "Allen would hit the cages. He was like, attacking the cages and hissing at them. That's why they look so furious. It was really intense."

Carmen, nodding to her, texts the entire roll to her own phone number.

"I'm keeping these as evidence against you, should we ever need to use it." Carmen looks up at her. "Do you back up your phone, Skylar?"

"I . . ."

"What's the password to your cloud account?"

"No!" Skylar says. Carmen is still holding her phone.

"Tell me or I use this phone to call the Dean of Arts and Sciences and then Professor Williams. And your parents."

Skylar responds—"And I'll tell them how you bullied me and restrained me and stole my phone!"

Carmen just laughs at her. "And who are they going to believe, two adult scientists or a kid who illegally took pictures of the research animals, which I now have evidence of?"

Silence. Skylar tells her the password. Carmen logs in and wipes the cloud, then reboots and resets the phone, handing the whirring thing back to Skylar.

"And taking those photos is all SAAR was doing that weekend?"

"Yeah." Skylar looks genuinely confused but also emotionally exhausted.

"What about the night before? Friday night. The night of the storm."

"I don't know. I mean, I don't really remember what I was doing."

"And the rest of SAAR?"

She makes a face like—what? "They weren't doing anything. That I know of. I mean, SAAR doesn't do like, things all the time. They plan stuff for a while."

"Did SAAR murder Atif Tomalin?"

She looks up at Carmen with what seems like genuine shock. "What?! Murder? Wait . . . Who's Atif?"

"One of the Crick Scholars. He got hit by the subway. He did primate research."

Nodding in recognition, but also gripping her sweatshirt in a plea—"That guy! You think SAAR murdered him? No! Listen, as far as I know SAAR didn't even know about him. And Students Against Animal Research isn't . . . It's not violent against people."

"What about the time a SAAR member dressed up as a monster and chased a researcher?" Kierk says accusingly.

"No! We don't do anything like that!"

"What about the fucking box of bomb materials outside Melissa Goldman's house?"

Skylar looks guilty, struggling with something internal.

"Tell us, Skylar," Carmen says softly to her. "We already know it was SAAR."

"We didn't . . . They didn't think it was going to be a big deal, like it was. It was supposed to be a joke. The idea was like, to just, you know, show that we could be way worse. It was Allen who made up the box of stuff. But then he was totally freaked out because the response was like, really big. But I didn't . . . I didn't have anything to do with that box."

"Oh really?" Carmen says. "So who got Melissa Goldman's home address, Skylar? It's not public but it's sure as hell on file here."

Skylar starts crying. "I'm not . . . I don't meet with the group, I didn't do the box thing, I didn't know why they needed that address and believe me, Allen is like, really freaked out and I'm freaked out and—"

"Skylar. Did SAAR leave that fucking mannequin outside my apartment?"

Skylar furrows her brow, throwing her hands up.

"Did they call me? Did they leave that *thing*? DID THEY?"

"Alright, that's enough," Kierk says. "She doesn't know what you're talking about."

Skylar nods, sobbing too much now to talk.

Carmen considers for a moment. She gets on one knee in front of Skylar, catching her gaze.

"You're never going to tell anyone about this. Are you?"

Skylar emphatically shakes her head.

"You mention anything to SAAR, we tell everyone about your involvement. Your education will be effectively over."

Skylar emphatically nods her head.

"Well, then you're free to go."

She bolts from her desk, muffling a cry, and they hear her hurried flight out into the labyrinth of the CNS.

"Well, that's that." Kierk says, watching where she exited.

"So it wasn't them." Carmen shakes her head. She'd been so sure . . .

"Well, we still don't know for certain."

"She wasn't lying. I mean, she's underplaying her involvement with SAAR but she's not lying about the lack of connection to Atif. Or what happened to me. Like with Atif . . . If you had anything to do with murdering someone on Friday, why risk a break-in the next day just to get some photos? No, it doesn't make sense . . ."

"Someone could have taken things into their own hands," Kierk offers, hesitant. "And the mannequin . . . I mean, maybe the same person?"

"I don't know . . ." she says, still gazing at the doorway. She looks down at her phone and its new gallery of photos. "No. I don't think so. But at least we falsified one theory. That's progress."

In her mind she's reordering what she considers possible, probable. Both of them are silent for a long moment, considering.

"I have your notebook, by the way," she finally says, turning her attention to him, one finger going out to catch in his jeans.

"Oh really." He raises an eyebrow. "Are we done investigating for the day?"

"Well, we could make our way back to my hotel room."

"Well . . . Maybe we should go there."

"Just to pick up the notebook?"

"Oh sure. Of course. Why else?"

In the Lower East Side they stop to get dinner and soon they are tipsy, not just on the emotions of the day but also on the combination of sharp white wine and the textures of oysters, and now both enter again into a kind of merging, two streams conjoining in a conflux, a brief meeting point where there is a mixing of waters, each drinking, and then, sated and rejuvenated by the alien other, each brachiate off again. But once two waters have mixed there is no unmixing them, they are changed forever in their constituencies and courses.

MONDAY

KIERK WAKES UP TO a slight touch, then something brushing his lips, a dream leaving him by his mouth. Carmen is kissing him awake.

"Hey," she says, smiling.

"How bad is my breath?" he replies.

"Pretty bad." She throws back the covers laughing.

"What time is it? Can't we sleep?"

"No. I'll stay with my mom outside the city and drive in. At least for the next few days."

"I don't blame you. Did you get some sleep?"

"Actually yes. And we've got to get up because we've got to attend the conference."

"Conference?"

"There was an email. Saying we should go to it instead of Professional Development."

"An email?" Kierk says, squinting over at her, propped up on one elbow.

"We have to attend the NYU neuroscience conference."

"NYU neuroscience conference?"

"Stop echoing me!" Carmen says, giggling again, hitting him with her pillow. He wrestles the pillow away, throws it across the hotel room. He slumps back with an arm over his face groaning—"Noooo the fucking conference. The fucking conference . . ."

"Oh, does poor Kierk need to go to an adult place?"

Kierk is muttering under his breath—"Officious, meddling, inter-fering . . ."

"You're half acting," Carmen playfully calls back to him as she pads away. Kierk sits back up in the bed, surprised that she knows him that well.

"Half real though!" he calls back, hearing the bathroom door close.

KIERK FOLDS UP THE conference schedule on Promega letterhead, which he had been reading in the dim light of the auditorium, trying to figure out what the hell the speaker's been talking about. Earlier Carmen and he had gotten their complimentary breakfasts together. Since the incident with the mannequin she has seemed sensibly reluctant to be alone. But this morning it became obvious to Kierk that she knows he is aware of her reluctance and fear, and that today she's putting on a brave face and pretending everything is fine, and so is off somewhere networking and doing everything she ordi-narily would, determined to have an absolutely normal day.

Sitting in the back alone Kierk has reached a point of complete indif-ference after four straight hours of listening to undifferentiated drivel. He reads the tattooed writing on his left forearm. *Where Do We Come From? What Are We? Where Are We Going?*

He finds himself staring at an empty seat in the front row. Atif had always sat up front. Maybe that would have been his seat right there . . . He looks around the darkened rows of quiet figures, all still alive, but suddenly so fragile in the context of Atif's empty seat. Morbid from boredom, Kierk wonders what Atif had thought at that last moment. What will all these people think? What will they think in that panic-attack moment where the great unfair equation comes into full view? As the PowerPoints run together Kierk can't help but view everyone around him as mere biological ticking timebombs waiting to go off, some internal imbalance or closure or pressure buildup or asynchrony in their parts, some tiny minuscule mistake in the transcription of an oncogene, to be drunk and woozy in the underground heat while above a storm raged and then to trip or be shoved from behind and land in a drunken and dazed heap as a thing a thousand times bigger than you and made of materials a thousand times harder slams into you with a planetary roar, or for a surgical scar abutting an artery in the back of your throat to aggravate and aggravate until it punctures through and blood spurts out in great arcs in time to your heartbeat.

The lights switch on and everyone perks up, stirring like autotrophs under the glare.

"Time for lunch! We'll reconvene after."

People shuffle out, stretching and yawning, bearing Promega tote bags and Promega name tags. Kierk follows the crowd and finds some lunch laid out. As he's filling up his plate he finds himself across from Max, who nods to him.

"So what do you think of the talks so far?" he says to Kierk, taking a stab at small talk.

"I've been more focused on consciousness, lately. Stuff about the molecular machinery of an individual neuron . . . I don't think it's helpful."

"Why not?"

"Because neurons are neurons."

"That's a tautology."

"Look, nearly all that stuff is already worked out. Neurons are just anything that can integrate across thousands of inputs, funnel the input into a single binary output, and that are plastic in certain ways. That's it. They don't do anything special that makes minds work. They're too simple. But when you get millions of them, billions of them, they start to do really, really interesting things. Have you ever seen flocks of starlings?"

"Yes, Kierk, I know about the starlings analogy."

Kierk continues as if Max hadn't spoken—"When the flock forms different shapes they're all acting at once. There's no hierarchy, no starling leaders. Same with neuronal activity, but it's not thousands of birds, it's hundreds of millions of neurons. Neurons themselves are completely uninteresting."

"I know, Kierk, but there are questions of memory and attention and all these things that—"

Not looking in Max's direction Kierk waves a hand as if shooing away a fly. "Memory, attention? What are these things if not synonyms for selection? Selection of a change to keep. Selection of one stimulus above others. And we already know the physiological correlates of this selection: the literal selection of neural connections, their random growth providing variation and their preferential survival based on their utility, their use. All those neurites growing, pruning, triumphing, dying, forming alliances, and carving out the territory of gray matter. Render a monkey's arm inert by tying it to its side, and in a week the neighboring neurons will have taken over the neural territory that belonged to that arm. Playing out the only game in town. The elegance of our genome is carved out of the violence of selection. Did you think that the elegance of our thoughts was any different? Oh fall to your knees, you lovers of peace, for the brain is a war!"

Kierk shoots his gaze to Max, a wild Celtic look in his eyes. This should annoy Max, but something in the desperate look of Kierk's eyes makes it not. Max has realized that none of this is directed at him anyways, and that Kierk is always talking to himself.

"It's just gotten so much clearer to me lately!" Kierk goes on. "There's only one real question in all of neuroscience: how does the continuous activity of twenty billion cortical neurons generate a stream of consciousness? That's it. Everything else is just chump-change correlations. Or tracking the minute changes in a complex and endless competition that we cannot unravel with all the supercomputers in the world. Neither of these gives us a science of mind. In the end, nothing in the brain makes sense except in the light of consciousness."

Max internally debates arguing but finally just sighs. "You're only interested in revolution, but you don't realize how rare that is. And in the meantime, someone has to get the grants and develop the techniques and teach the students and actually do some neuroscience research. No?"

But Kierk just nods vaguely, already moving away. He's off to find Carmen, drawn to her in this crowded space of Promega tote bags, and although he doesn't know where she is her presence is palpable, an electric charge in a substance beyond perception, like his own personal magnetic north. Like action at a distance. Now he feels the way needles feel, always.

ALEX'S APARTMENT IS, IF it were emptied of everything, identical to Kierk's. The same shape and structure, the same eggshell white paint, the same crisscross of small bars across the windows to suicide-proof them, subsidized by NYU just like his. But Kierk, now being given a mini-tour of it by Alex, is struck by how incredibly different the two apartments are. Here there are art prints on the wall. A black-and-white minimalistic color scheme. The kitchen is well stocked with what looks like a full set of porcelain matching cookware, as well as stainless steel cutlery hanging on magnetic strips and an array of wineglasses and champagne flutes. The living room has a giant liquid television screen hung up on the wall, trailing cords behind it like a peripheral nervous system, with multiple of the latest console gaming systems hooked up at the bottom. In the middle is a large black leather couch that looks like the plastic was just taken off. Kierk doesn't say anything but feels the casual parental wealth of it all, seeing the multiple Apple gadgets and how even this technological plenitude stays a kind of chic minimalism. The whole apartment feels like a user interface.

"How's Carmen?" Alex asks from the kitchen counter. "That whole incident gives me the creeps."

"She's okay. Driving upstate to stay with her mom tonight."

Kierk lingers over the bookshelf, looking at Alex's collection, which is mostly left-wing political stuff and some history.

"I do a lot of my reading on the internet," Alex says preemptively, as Kierk looks it over. He continues to pull out titles as Alex says—"I also have beer."

"Thanks for inviting me over."

"Hey, did I tell you I was switching to take over Atif's old position?"

"You're doing primate research now?"

"Yeah. I always wanted to get away from neurons in dishes. Real intact networks. Lowering the recording needle down into macaque brains is pretty crazy. And Melissa's lab is cool, she's super nice, and there's obviously an opening for a postdoc due to Atif."

"And how is it?"

"Actually I really like it. It's fascinating. As you're lowering down the needle into the brain you hook it up to speakers so you can hear aloud the pop-pop as it passes individual neurons. Like little firecrackers of sound. Sometimes we hear radio signals when we lower down the electrode. Classical music or pop songs. Sometimes I think I can hear phone conversations. Like voices from another room that you can't quite make out. But that can't be right. I mean, that's not even physically possible."

"Mmm," Kierk says, taking a swig from the beer he's just been handed.

"So I was presumptive and packed a bowl, if you'd like some."

Kierk assents and soon the two stand in the kitchen and trade hits, Alex laughing at Kierk's fit of coughing after his first big one.

"You know I was thinking that maybe I could even fill in for Atif in that project you cooked up with Carmen. The brain-to-brain stuff? I mean once I'm trained up enough."

"Are you sure?"

"Definitely." Exhalation.

They quickly exhaust the first bowl as Kierk matches him hit for hit, burning it down to the resin, until Alex has packed a total of four bowls. He doesn't say anything but observes that Kierk's pupils have completely dilated; yet Kierk hasn't mentioned slowing down, and every time Alex has proffered the pipe another hit is taken. Eventually Alex decides to spare him from himself and puts an end to it.

A high Kierk notices a framed photograph on the refrigerator. It's of a young man, short and lithe and with dark hair, wearing only boxers and a white T-shirt, not facing the camera but turned to the side and holding a confident arabesque with one leg far out behind him at a 90-degree angle, his back arched and his hands turned and held up over his head, posed in an apartment cluttered with flora and books, the light from a tall window with drawn-back curtains streaming in and Kierk thought that it must be California light as no other light looked so slow moving, so rich and heavy with itself, so like golden cream.

"Who's this?"

"Oh . . . That's just somebody that I used to know. Jason. His name is Jason."

Kierk opens the refrigerator door, digs out a pair of beers, passes one to Alex, and the two stand together at the counter. Alex looks doubtfully at the beer he's been handed. One eyebrow goes up as Kierk takes a deep swill.

"He was someone you knew in California?"

Alex nods. "Old boyfriend. How'd you know that picture is from—"

"The light," Kierk says, walking over to explore Alex's copious gaming shelf.

"Oh . . . Well, he's actually in the city. He moved here across the country two years ago. That's why we broke up."

"But you were living together?"

"For a while actually."

Kierk looks over from thumbing through titles. "You contacted him?"

"No . . . No, I unfriended him on Facebook. It was a pretty hard breakup."

"Facebook . . ." Kierk mutters angrily under his breath from his crouch, then—"You should get in touch with him again. If the big problem with the relationship was that he moved then the only thing that's stopping you is pride. Besides, you two looked like you were good together."

"Thanks but uh . . . How would you know?"

"Oh, it's obvious from the photo," Kierk says distractedly as he pulls out a game from the shelf. The plastic in his hands makes him feel nostalgic for his fifteen-year-old self and there is a delay before he speaks again. "You were living together. The whole aesthetic is different than here, far livelier, more plants. It's softer, tempered, a good aesthetic alloy. Your intellect, his heart, that kind of thing. And that photo has a lot of love in it. You know? The things with love in them are so vulnerable to criticism, you can always tell."

Alex is staring at him from behind the kitchen counter, paused mid-sip. Kierk holds up the plastic green container, shakes it.

"Hey, so I'm pretty high. Do you want to drink beers and play Halo?"

Alex just laughs—"I knew you did other things than read. You're just like everybody else, you big poser."

"Think what you want," Kierk says, putting in the game, "just be ready to back up your shit talk with action cause I'm 'bout to get my PhD in brutality."

Alex takes a controller as the high-definition intro starts up on the big screen and the music blasts out of his subwoofers but his thoughts have returned to an old problem, which is suddenly being reexamined. That hypothetical that had seemed so tenuous to him had been treated like such an obvious fact, injected into his thoughts by Kierk like dye into a river, spreading everywhere from a single focal point, and he's so shook that he gets blown up by a grenade right away.

"Get it together, Alex!" Kierk yells as he unloads an entire clip of ammunition.

KIERK'S PACING BACK AND forth in the box of his apartment in the early morning hours, pulsing with a tired energy, a feeling of great psychological change building up.

From the frantic work of the weekend there is paper all over the floor. On the pages the Turing machines were in bloom, sending their long tongues of ticker tape in tangled ropes across sheets. Over the white landscapes specimens crawled, like the beasts of mechanical rovers, some had the extending proboscises of limbs, von Neumann machines, looking ready for reproduction, crawling about like low-slinking cats.

The revelation . . .

When he had woken up in Carmen's apartment on Saturday the first thing he had seen had been a framed drawing. A self-portrait by Carmen. Maybe an exercise from a class of hers, and an amateur work, yes, but the shaping of the white space into the elegant form of a standing figure with one leg back, along with the determined nature of the charcoal that filled the rest of the image, gave the central form an undeniable power, carved from the black page like a statue from marble. It had slowly come into focus, and his waking thought, that first fully formed cogent experience, had been—you can draw using only negative space and so cannot I root out a theory of consciousness from where it hides by solely drawing the negative space around it? If he could charter the problems of each approach to consciousness a global outline would emerge, something from nothing. Yes, he had explored many things before. But he hadn't used them to create a web of *commonalities of failure.*

Thus, he had started with computation. After a weekend of work the conclusion was what he had known already. Computation alone could not explain consciousness. Any system of sufficient size and complexity could be interpreted as running any number of programs, all at once, an interpretation that is dependent on an observer. And thus the loop was closed—because how could consciousness depend on some observer, on another consciousness? Proof of impossibility by infinite regress . . .

With computation thrown out he had spent Sunday on its more general cousin, information. He'd examined the exchange of bits, the changing of states, considered the fundamental equations of information theory. But measuring information required specifying both a state-space and probabilities. Yet what state-space? That, he had finally concluded, must be delineated by an observer as well. And what probabilities? In the basement of probability theory there were also observer-based decisions being made about token versus types and reference classes and probability as degree of belief. His reasoning is that if probabilities and state-spaces aren't objective, there's again proof of impossibility by infinite regress.

With these two proofs of impossibility constructed he felt he had filled in some small part of the drawing. But progress had felt slow. So Kierk had grown depressed, anxious in his febrile dreamings of automatons, disgusted by himself, by his egoism and his failure. He had doubted his genius at every turn. He had paced the distance between shadows like Eratosthenes. There was a fermentation taking place within, he knew, but it was stymied. He had felt like a fly flitting from wall to wall, slowly mapping the contours of a bottle it couldn't possibly understand. He wanted to scream so loud and for so long it would travel from earth outward and outward until it became part of the cosmic background radiation and was forever.

All at the same time there was Carmen . . . who is now popping into his head as much as anything about consciousness. Her influence on his thinking is growing. A distraction that had been present all weekend. Every time he goes to work on the issue, in his awareness she becomes more solid, like the development of a haunting, a carmine rose growing up out of equations. Sometimes beautiful thoughts, sometimes bawdy ones, sometimes about protecting her, all were blended together—he wants to fuck her in every position, he wants to lay his head between her breasts, wants to tease her and spank her and kiss her and hold her down and save her. Wants to stay up all night talking. Everything he eats tastes like her. For he himself has been dumbstruck these past few days by the happiness that suddenly seems so graspable. The two of them together made him feel a poet, a teenager. He knows he could circumnavigate the globe and find nothing like what he has found here.

He feels guilty about not responding to her calls and text over the weekend, when she had needed him. Yet in a sense he's also wary of these feelings. There is developing a clear choice, a metaphysical choice, two roads. Because he cannot help but think—FURTHER. I must go further. Something calls to me, tugging at me. Carmen is an exit on the highway, a highway headed to . . . I don't know, but I do know that this age needs me in some way and that I, like the storm petrel heralding a hurricane, must comply.

He has not told her everything. He wonders what she deduced from his journal. Had there been mention of his fatal melancholy? For he knows there is a fundamental flaw deep within him. He could leave, run from her, but if he does he will be forced to love her forever but from a distance, an infinite resignation. There must be some way he could spare her from his melancholy, his torment and ephemeral nature, from his monomania. Sometimes the Egyptians would grow corn out of the mummified bodies of their sacred dead . . . What will grow from me? Such a thanatological crop can only sprout from a gift wrapped with appropriate ceremony and set out upon a sacrificial altar, a body primed and stripped of everything . . .

The other path is to cast everything away, all these strivings, so that he might be light enough to follow her. He knew this was inevitable because it had happened before. A girl he had known in graduate school. Their hookup at some bar which led to a relationship. Seemingly without any demands or expectations, it had all fallen together easily as they had just followed what everyone around them was doing at the time, pairing off, going on the same types of dates, the same restaurants, the same parties. And after a year of that relationship had passed, he had been smoking outside at night on the balcony of their joint apartment, while inside the lit living room she waited with their freshly cooked dinners to start a TV show they had been watching the episodes of each evening, and it was only then Kierk had realized he had not accomplished anything that whole year, produced no writing, no theories, that his journals had no entries, and suddenly going back through that glass sliding balcony door into the light had seemed unbearable. This is the dilemma: if he loves he loses himself and perhaps his genius. He thinks—whatever little creative spark I have left will vanish into Carmen and I will again live a normal life, just a normal life, and the flaw in my constitution is that I can handle anything but a normal life . . . How can we make choices like this? If my consciousness could take both roads in the woods, I wouldn't hesitate. Something is so fundamentally wrong with a universe in which you can only live one life. How many times in history has this choice been made? How many times has it been made wrong?

And how impossible to explain such a decision! What vague metaphysical reasons they will seem! How crushed she will be. Because he feels the same. The deep cut of it, with no way to spare her . . . unless, perhaps, if he dissembles, if he gives some other reason, or acts sardonically and like it was all just raillery, nothing too serious at all . . . A conclusion part of him must have known earlier when he hadn't responded to her calls or texts. He rages at the unfairness of it but this is a paradox he must protect her from, a naked singularity. He must from now on make her believe that he will not, could not, does not, love her. This way forward imposes no burden upon her, makes no demands of her. And years from now if they see each other at a conference or event they can be cordial and she will not know that he still carries his love in him like a secret stone, a hidden altar, an inexpressible heart, the last solid remnant of a body become a sprouting garden.

TUESDAY

KIERK WAKES UP TO his phone ringing. Answering it, all he can muster is a bleary, "Yes?" before a salesperson launches into a robotic spiel. The phone spirals away across the room to a disconcerting crash.

He sits up on the bed with his feet on the floor. He's confused by a strange sensation for a second. Looking down, his bare feet are resting on sheets of white paper filled with his drawings and writings and equations.

Sighing, he stands up naked amid them. They extend outward, an entire carpet, spiraling until his whole bedroom floor is covered with the overlapping sheets. They are slick under his feet as he walks but some adhere and stick. A path is traced through them.

Brushing his teeth in the bathroom he rubs at his bloodshot eyes. He opens up the window and is hunting around for clothes as he smokes inside. The screen on his phone is cracked but it still works.

Outside he crosses Union Square, still bleary and blinking against the light, moving amid a giant crowd of other morning-goers, a brusque human flow. In the thick of the moving mass, Kierk, about to step, glances down and sees lying there on the sidewalk the body of an albino pigeon, its feathers ruffled and claws curled up in death, thick with itself. Shoes step around it. Having stopped so suddenly in the moving crowd he is jostled from behind, hears a muttered exclamation. But Kierk is entranced. Its eyes are clenched shut, its head bowed into its fluffed chest. It is a bright white and surprisingly compact and solid in its physiology. He glances up at the building that towers over the sidewalk, a great glass plane extending up and up. Had the pigeon, only minutes ago, thwacked into the building and plummeted to the crowd? Kierk wonders—Did you become sun-blind from the glare? Or did you think as you sped forward that the other pigeon would swerve away at the last second, only to find it was your reflection all along? Or did you see the glass as a transparent barrier, a thing you could breach if you tried hard enough, but in your velocity you fundamentally mistook its substance and the impact snapped your poor neck . . .

Kierk maneuvers through the crowd and grabs from a nearby crate two newspapers. Returning he again guards the albino pigeon with his feet, people giving him strange stares as they pass. In a forest of legs he crouches down. From on high he is a still, bent dot amid a moving arterial stream of pedestrians.

He uses one of the newspapers, rolled up, to scoot the pigeon onto the other one that he holds flat. Then he carefully maneuvers out of the crowd with it. By the trash bin off to the side of the flow he gives it a tiny burial, wrapping it firmly up in the newspaper, a small package he places softly into the bin, quietly saying a prayer over it, and gives a final plea for its little bird consciousness to have lived a good life expressive of platonic pigeon essence.

Subject line: Urgent! Missing brain
Subject body: Going over inventory after Day in the Lab we are short one of our example human brains. It was stored in ethyl alcohol. These are really difficult to get, guys. We need it returned promptly, so please check your cars, desks, and home for the brain.

Carmen clicks out of the email and at the same time gives a squeeze with her left hand to a tiny squishy foam brain. For stress. She looks over at Kierk, but he's preoccupied reading papers at his desk. She approaches him and he takes out earbuds. In the relative silence of the lab, she can hear the tinny sound of classical music coming from them.

"What's up?"

"Whatcha reading about?" She gestures to the screen.

"Oh, it's just some technical stuff on causation. You'd think this would all be worked out, but actually no one has a damn idea what causation is or how it works."

"So did you get the email about the talk on Saturday?"

"Is it required to attend?"

"No. But I think you'll want to. Antonio Moretti is flying in to give a talk on his theory of consciousness."

"So?"

"So you're going to go see him, right? I mean, he must know you're here. And you haven't seen him since you left after telling him his theory was wrong and this talk means he's still going around peddling his theory, so what—"

"I never thought he would stop."

"Well do you want to come with me because—"

"Alright. That's fine."

Carmen is put off by Kierk's curtness. She says, hesitantly—"Maybe we could do something afterward?"

A very long pause. "Yeah, we'll see what happens."

"Is everything okay?" she leans down to whisper to him.

"Oh, it's fine. I'm just concentrating on this. Sorry."

"Okay," she says, straightening. "Just checking." He doesn't look at her as she makes her way back to her desk.

Sitting, still thinking about Kierk's distance, another email arrives. It takes Carmen a moment to absorb what she is casually reading:

Subject line: something you should know . . .
Subject body: his real name isn't Greg Monroe. It's Greg Alpern. And he's a liar.

Clicking on the embedded link takes her to a site called Retraction Watch, which she'd heard about before but never visited: a tongue-in-cheek listing of the constant stream of retractions from scientific journals. Papers were retracted for sundry reasons, everything from having improperly analyzed data to outright fraud or misrepresentation, and the entire spectrum in between.

Totally regular star dimming: missing data leads to retraction of weird astronomical findings.

Apparently, there was a little mishap involving how bright stars are at the Massachusetts Institute of Technology. The journal Nature *has issued a retraction of "Anomalous star dimming in the Milky Way." The now-unavailable paper claimed that various instances of star dimming could not be explained by comets, solar dust storms, or any other natural cause. Obviously, that only leaves aliens! Apparently the paper advocated that such dimming anomalies might be because of Dyson spheres: structures alien civilizations would build around a sun to extract more and more energy from it. They even said this increased the chances that aliens would have visited earth. But an internal investigation carried out by the funding agency of the study, DARPA, concluded that the authors could produce no lab notebooks nor any electronic copies of the data reported in this article in any form. The authors claimed that the electronically-stored data had been accidentally deleted and that the physical lab notebooks had been lost. Therefore, under suspicion of data fabrication, the paper was withdrawn. The first author on the paper, Greg Alpern, is a 2nd year PhD student at MIT. We've contacted Greg, his principle investigator, and DARPA, and will let you know if we hear back with any updates.*

The entry was dated three years ago. Carmen digs around the internet some more and turns up a host of innocuous information about Greg Alpern confirming that it really was Greg. The email had come from an anonymous address. She fires back a quick email asking, "Who the hell sent this?"

So Greg had faked data. And had previously been funded by DARPA, although that could just be a coincidence. Greg had probably changed his name in order to avoid the exact kind of search result that Carmen was turning up now . . . Everything she knew about him is falling away, every comment he had made didn't seem awkward anymore but creepy. Maybe he had lied his way into the program, maybe Atif had found out, maybe when Greg had left early that night he had gone to make sure Atif didn't tell anyone else . . .

Her mind churning with such thoughts she again approaches Kierk. About to speak, she pauses, thinking—but what if Greg had nothing to do with it and I am about to spread that he faked results . . . It's enough to ruin his career here, and who really knew the whole story? Carmen couldn't let that happen without knowing for sure. Two years ago she had attempted to replicate a famous neuroimaging experiment. But Carmen had failed to find the effect, indeed, her data hinted at the exact opposite hypothesis. The advice from on high had been to drop it. Everyone she had talked to paid due respect to replication of course. "The backbone of science!" they all declared, but at the same time she was told that it would take months to make the replication attempt ironclad, only to submit it to a bottom-tier journal where it would be peer-reviewed for publication by the author of the original study who would tear it apart in revisions anyways. Since then she's watched the original result rack up a string of citations, filling her with more doubt than a case of outright fraud—an example of the huge gray area of statistical analyses and leading questions and unexamined assumptions. Scientific methodology, she was beginning to feel, was not more special and self-correcting than anything else: garbage in, garbage out.

She regrets not publishing her failure to replicate. But she also doesn't want to start a witch hunt without knowing all the facts first.

Before reaching Kierk all this goes through her mind in an instant, a nonverbal conceptual structure activating memories without needing to replay them, a turning of some high-dimensional object faster than language or logic.

Instead she just says to him—"Sorry to bother you again. Can I bum a cigarette?"

Kierk looks up at her, rolls up the paper he's been reading and punctuates each word by slapping the desk with it—"This. Paper. Is. Horrible."

KIERK IS WANDERING THE city after work, his feet a steady rhythm into a thready evening red, a spillage of light bisecting the grid. It is as if heavenly forces were about to trumpet in and charge from the west. Men and women move in outlines from dark to red and back again. He'd left work with his mind spinning, and he's been steering his way by the spire of the Empire State Building against a sky streaked with bleeding cirrus clouds.

Up ahead a small crowd has gathered, staring at something, and it takes a moment for the thing itself, a transparent cephalopod, to lift above their heads into view: a plastic bag, handles trailing behind. For a while he watches it rise, and then fall, and then skyrocket to rise again, drifting up the evening-scaled sides of the skyscraper, then fall, and now it sweeps across the sidewalk twirling and the children in the crowd follow after trying to catch it but with pirouettes it evades them, letting them get close before darting mockingly away. Kierk, standing apart, viewing the scene through several lenses simultaneously, settles finally on the most physical and melancholic, as befits his mood—that this plastic bag dancing in the wind is an illusion of personality. There is a conspiracy of trains of air and in truth it is not coy, nor playful, nor coquettish, and so, further . . . is not all life an illusion of this nature? Are not organisms similarly mere structured materials pumped full of the wilds of outside energy, of cloying storms and coquettish asynchronies, and cut off from their external sources would not all vibrant life fall just as limp as the bag does now, in the energy doldrums as the wind leaves it, each organism revealing, as it collapses into a rubber mask of its former self, what it has been all along: an inanimate object?

He knows such thoughts stem from the papers he's been gobbling up. As usual there's no one to talk to about these things, it's all internal, a hidden layer between input and output sparking off in convolutions as he walks. The wordy but logical sequence of the dialectic is what comes most naturally to Kierk, so that's how he often engages these subjects, like he's having an internal argument with himself, switching to play both parts, as if he were an actor in ancient Rome donning first the crying mask and then ducking backstage to reply with the laughing mask.

Crying Mask: You've been spending an awful lot of time trying to finagle your way around the laws of physics, looking for your precious Theory of Consciousness. But the laws of physics are what they are, and there's no room in there for minds. It's full, causally complete. Seems to me you're on a fool's errand. Stop sticking your nose where it doesn't belong.

Laughing Mask: How can you say there's no room for minds because of causal completeness when causation is just another frame-variant phenomenon? Causation requires observers, interveners. Causation requires consciousness. Besides, the so-called laws of physics are just averages that seem to work rather well at predicting simple, two-body systems.

Crying Mask: Predictable that your objections depend on baseless assumptions. Who cares about causation? I'm talking about the wave function. That's all there is. One big wave function evolving, spinning off many worlds as it does so.

Laughing Mask: Oh really? And how sure are you about that?

Crying Mask: Do you really not know how well we can predict at the microscopic level of physics? It's perfect.

Laughing Mask: But the same laws don't work at other scales. They lead to contradictions and absurdities. Particles with infinite force, that sort of thing. You people pick and choose your laws without thought as to how they all fit together.

Crying Mask: Even if that were true, there will be a theory of everything soon enough.

Laughing Mask: Since the invention of physics it always seems to do everything it's asked until it doesn't.

Crying Mask: I swear, your attitudes are positively medieval. You can't escape the laws, they apply everywhere. Even in your precious wetware brain.

Laughing Mask: When was the last time you opened up the brain and looked? Here's how you actually see if a system follows the laws of physics that we have. You create a model of that system on a supercomputer, a model system. And you build the model system out of your very best descriptions of fundamental physics, whatever you think the lowest level is, say, the wave function. Now, you put both the model system and the real system into exactly the same initial state. If their following state-space trajectories are totally identical, then yes, the real system was totally reducible to the microphysical laws. But if their trajectories differ then you know that you can't model the real system using just the most microscopic laws of physics.

Crying Mask: That's not a feasible test for any complex system! If you didn't get the initial states just right, chaos theory would kick in, and then the state-spaces would diverge. How could you tell if the reason your results are different is really that the laws are different or just that there was some noise that's been amplified?

Laughing Mask: Exactly! See, chaos hides emergence! How would anyone notice? It's all heuristics and coarse-grains with complex systems. Just like how new laws of physics were needed once you started looking at the very small and the very large, new laws might be needed once you start looking at the very complex. You just can't be sure that the physics of two atoms interacting in a void obtains in complex systems. Or conscious systems, for that matter. You have the laws for the microscopic and macroscopic, but where's the mesoscopic?

Crying Mask: An impossible standard. You'd need a supercomputer the size of the galaxy to check that there's no deviations from physics inside the human brain.

Laughing Mask: You can't just wave your hands and say everything is just the wave function with no exceptions when we've only stringently tested it with isolated atoms. Physics isn't complete, it isn't done yet, and yet we act like the current version is the bible. There's going to be a twenty-second-century physics, and a twenty-third, and you're arrogant in your statistically-unlikely assumption that you happen to live at the end of science. It's not over till it's over.

Crying Mask: Absence of evidence isn't evidence of absence. That's not a flaw in physics, not a flaw in materialism. You're just overly skeptical. Nothing wrong with that, but no reason to cast away the edifice. If your demands are so high, the burden of proof is on you.

Laughing Mask: As a stand-alone point, perhaps. But if a consequence of a belief is that you shouldn't believe it, then that belief in invalid. You must not saw off the branch you are sitting on.

Crying Mask: I assume you have another point then, but I've been wrong before.

Laughing Mask: If materialism is true you're more likely to be an alien's dream than yourself. You are more likely to be the random interactions in a gas nebula than yourself. You are more likely to be a simulation running in a simulation running in a simulation than yourself. You're more likely to be a brief improbable atomic configuration achieved by leaving a rock in a warm heat bath for a few quadrillion years. Any system at a state of high entropy generates, automatically and within it, parts that have lower entropy. Order from chaos, given enough time. The simpler that order is, the more likely it is. So if you're just some configuration of physical or functional states of atoms, and the universe, multiverse, whatever, is astronomically large or infinite, then you'll pop up over and over again. And since simpler order is more likely, you won't be on this planet with these people, you'll just be a brief conscious phantom, what's called a Boltzmann brain. And if you are a Boltzmann brain, which in all vast likelihood you are, you have no reason to believe in contemporary physics. Therefore to believe in contemporary physics leads directly to disbelief in contemporary physics!

(This is followed by an extended wave of disembodied clapping from the many hovering masks arrayed in a darkened amphitheater around them. Each mask in the audience is a different emotion.)

Crying Mask: Do not applaud, you fools. There is a flaw. I know that I am not a Boltzmann brain because a Boltzmann brain would only exist for a moment, whereas I can check my own mind, check my own memories, which extend over time, thus proving I am not a Boltzmann brain.

Laughing Mask: Too easy! There's no time for you to make sure you aren't a Boltzmann brain if you are a Boltzmann brain, although there's plenty of Boltzmann brains who think they just completed such a survey!

Crying Mask: The Boltzmann brain paradox may seem to be true, under some interpretations, but—

Laughing Mask: Imagine if every night everyone on Earth dreamed they were you . . .

Crying Mask: . . . What?

Laughing Mask: No nothing, continue your point.

Crying Mask: As I was saying, simple solutions in how we deal with probability and physics might rule Boltzmann brains out.

Laughing Mask: As if it were a stand-alone issue! Consider that most cosmologists agree that there's an infinite multiverse.

Crying Mask: As do I. All things happen.

Laughing Mask: Another way of saying nothing happens.

Crying Mask: That's it? That's your objection?

Laughing Mask: Imagine an infinite checkered quilt with a repeating finite pattern of three black squares and one white square. You randomly throw a dart at the infinite quilt. What is the probability that you hit a white square?

Crying Mask: That's easy. One in four.

Laughing Mask: Now imagine that the quilt is the infinite multiverse, and each square is a possible version of your current conscious experience. The finite pattern of possible worlds, even though astronomically large, eventually repeats, which is why there are multiple copies of you on that quilt. Some will be identical to you in every way, some are different. But it is impossible to tell which square on the quilt you are. Now consider that reason is a highly ordered state of affairs. Coming to a logical conclusion, to a justified belief, is itself a highly ordered, highly organized state. Yet, Boltzmann's insight was that there are always so many more disordered states than ordered ones. Astronomically more. Now you throw the dart, your act of self-identification in the multiverse. How likely are you to hit a version of you that has a reasonable and justified belief in the multiverse? Astronomically small. Justified beliefs can't be supported in your embarrassment of worlds. Disproof via contradiction.

Crying Mask: Another overelaborate argumentative contortion!

Laughing Mask: Don't you see that these problems, these paradoxes, that these are signposts! They all involve observers. In information theory, in causation, in philosophy, and yes, in quantum physics, in cosmology, in thermodynamics, in time and space! Don't you see what all these signs are pointing toward?

Crying Mask: I see that you are suffering from pareidolia! Where you see great signposts I see scattered matchsticks. But I will let you play out your game. Tell me your madness and I'll save my diagnosis for the end.

Laughing Mask: I . . . don't know for sure. No one tries to fit anything together, make sure it's consistent! Everyone is concerned only with local cohesion, not global. Except, perhaps, us consciousness researchers. In the end.

Crying Mask: For all your strivings there is only a slim number of possible ontologies: materialism, dualism, monism. As the princess first pointed out, dualism has fundamental holes in it. Monism is nonsensical. Materialism is all that is possible.

Laughing Mask: It's not the kind of problem you can map out all the solutions beforehand! The prior space of possibilities will look childish in retrospect. Yet you base your life and beliefs off of it?

Crying Mask: Now we see you for what you really are. A science denier. An intelligent mind struggling to get out of iron bars. Sorry the universe didn't turn out the way that you wanted it, but this is about feelings. About what you want to be true.

Laughing Mask: I'm the scientist, not you! I'm the empiricist. You're the metaphysician, talking about deducing the rest of the world through the base axioms of microscopic physics. Believing in theories that contradict their own formulations. Fantasizing an infinite multiverse just to get your equations to make sense.

Crying Mask: Not all consensus is metaphysics. The fact that you can marshal a few rhetorical tricks means nothing against the usefulness of physics. Your intuitions are not justifiable given the evidence.

Laughing Mask: Consciousness is the evidence! We've been pretending that the world is a game for so long! Just mathematics and relations. Just trajectories through a state-space. But mathematics is mere syntax. Consciousness is more! It's the fire in the equations. Our reality isn't just numbers, don't you see! There are feelings, willings, thoughts, all in there as well! It means the world is not definable as a game, as any kind of complex billiards table! It's more than can be defined by those methods!

Crying Mask: Haven't you already wasted enough time on this? I seem to remember just two years ago you went through a six-month phase where you thought you could reformulate the laws of physics in intentional language. Start with the simplest intentional states, show that basic forces can be redescribed as instantiations of these intentions, and build up to larger consciousnesses from there?

Laughing Mask: Well, yes, that was a failure, but—

Crying Mask: So then what do you really have? Are you going to rewrite the laws? Sneak intentionality and consciousness in? Where? Even if you could put in the ten years to get the level of expertise you would need for that, how will you feed yourself? How will you survive, both physically and psychically, for that time? And if you fail? Or if you are one hundred years too early? A thousand? If you need three Einsteins to make their discoveries before you can proceed? What then? You'll waste your life . . . You fool, you'll waste your life . . .

"Can I help you?" An old man is looking at Kierk, who has stopped with one hand out and is leaning on an iron grate outside an unfamiliar park, his lips moving, his gaze on the ground.

"What?" Kierk startles, then sighs. "No. No, you can't help me."

"The movie," the old man says, "is that way."

"Oh, okay. Thank you."

A small sign outside the park reads BEER AND WINE LEGAL DURING MOVIE SHOWINGS. The park is covered in colored blankets, and Kierk traces his way through the crowd without stepping on anyone's blankets like it's a path-optimization problem. Eventually he gets close to the exact geometric center and finds a small square of unclaimed grass in which he can sit cross-legged like the Buddha, facing the waiting giant screen. A breeze is rippling across the blankets and keeping everyone cool. The setting sun is pure red, a spill against the whole western sky, sporting around it the amorphous, lazy thoughts of clouds. The zenith is crossed by the strokes of two contrails forming a perfect giant X. The shadows of the horde around him are elongated, the whole world becoming a piece of art, impossibly real with talk, an extended thing. In the middle of it all he closes his eyes and lets the conversations wash over him—listening to the two white women with a picnic basket and an uncorked bottle of wine, toeing off their sandal wedges; the boisterous group in bright South African colors speaking English so fast and so accented it sounds like another language; the mother and father of a nearby family arguing about politics; some college kids all wearing Ray-Bans and playing cards; the cackling laughter, everything overlapping in a rising and falling surf, even the tinny digital sounds of a smart phone—that mix of conversations making a pastiche, an imbrication being constructed for no one, a dialog merging and breaking. A question is asked from somewhere and then, a few seconds later, Kierk hears it answered from somewhere else entirely. The crowd is having a conversation unknown by its parts. And in that darkening scarlet, in that ocean of sound, there comes through it, in one of the troughs of sound, a very specific voice, Carmen's voice, speaking only for a single sentence that is clear and untouched—"I want to believe there is more to this world than we know."

Kierk's eyes snap open. But looking around he doesn't see the speaker, not even when he stands and shields his eyes from the setting sun and scans the crowd for her. Then everyone stops talking, the entire park falling off in its noise, leaving Kierk standing alone, paused, looking at all the silent faces, until the sound of a lion roaring brings him around to the giant MGM logo on the outdoor screen. Sitting back down, a perplexed expression on his face slowly transforms into a grin; he opens his notebook in the waning colors. There's still light enough to write by.

WEDNESDAY

KIERK WAKES UP, A thing previously untethered made fast, a boat moored to a dock. A dock somehow exactly the same as the one off the Union Terrace, and the lake blazing with summer sunset was Lake Mendota, for the dream was of his past, Madison coming and going, buildings rising and leaving as if through a fog, and there had been old faces he once knew, among them his younger self, four years ago at twenty-three, the two looking at each other in sadness. An old life is woken from.

Standing, he stretches in the harsh morning light coming through the window, blinking in it like an owl.

On the way to work the air is crystalline clear, a prism, and the city glints off itself. There are wild calls—everyone seems energetic in the sunlight. Kierk gets coffee from a food cart, then walks by the drifting snatches of a conversation in French, and then another right after in Spanish. Kierk finds himself at that spot on Broadway where one can see One World Trade Center to the south and the Empire State Building to the north.

Wasn't this city itself also dreaming of its own past? In fact, looking up Kierk can almost see the ghost of Walt Whitman taking one of his carriage rides up and down Broadway, from the height of his swaying passage observing the hustle of horses and stands and merchants, men and women in the latest fashions, the gangs of workers in their overalls clamoring out construction, Whitman trying to identify from all these material signs the hidden consciousness of the city. He was right to seek in the city a consciousness, for it seemed to Kierk not impossible that the city might be pacing out a slow oscillatory phenomenology across the decades, following the organismal rise and fall of neighborhoods, that the universe might just allow for such a thing, a steel and concrete teratoma with an inhuman mind subject to sensations beyond expression. Like an oyster slowly building a pearl over centuries. After all, from where Whitman sat on his carriage swaying he would have nodded hello to the walking and bearded Herman Melville—the two had lived in the same few square miles for most of their lives. They never once met but surely must have passed each other, faces bearing the weight of history, a secret electricity leaping from one to the other, unknown to all but the city. The ghost carriage continues out of sight and for the rest of the walk Kierk wonders what has been lost, or if anything was lost at all, if it was still here in this great grid. New York seems to him to be a sworn promise once made, broken, made again, a thing forever imminent but never arriving, and even now Kierk felt the attraction to it, passing the people dreaming Broadway dreams, everyone seeing not the New York it is but the New York it could be, the island waiting to rise again, the Once and Future City.

THE SEVEN REMAINING CRICK Scholars are all gathered on the fifth floor of the CNS attempting to find a means of entry to a lab there. Carmen is trying to espy one of the researchers who had first collected their skin samples, Todd, through the big window. She'd emailed him to see if the cerebral organoids were finished in their growth. Todd had replied that they were still relatively young but all the mini-brains had been successfully established in their tanks for growth, and were ready for a visit from their progenitors. For Carmen it is a good mask for an ulterior motive, which is to get Greg alone afterward and ask about the retraction. But Todd was late and now all of them have tried their respective keycards in succession, only to have the door beep in denial—all but Kierk, who just said something about induction and didn't bother trying his.

Finally Todd arrives to usher the seven into the cool bright space. Carmen, Kierk, and Alex start barraging him with questions, and he raises his hands for them to desist.

"Okay, so clearly there's a lot of interest here. Very exciting for me. But maybe the best way to do this is to give a general tour. You can ask your questions as they come up. Okay?"

There is a brief chastised silence. Carmen notices in her peripheral vision that Jessica just rolled her eyes at Mike, and also that the two have been standing close together the whole time. Leon interrupts her thoughts by clearing his throat loudly above the humming of fans and equipment—"I think we all agree."

"Alright. Everybody follow."

While Todd talks them through the rows of shelves and open lab spaces, Carmen steals the occasional glance at Greg, who seems less talkative than usual—she wonders if he somehow knew the email to her had been sent.

"On the methodology. First we take the fibroblast samples from your skin. We take those skin cells and reprogram them. Basically we induce pluripotency again. We do this by using retroviruses to insert genes that encode transcription factors into the cells. These genes are then read by the cell's own internal machinery, and then revert back to pluripotency. Effectively, we've transformed an adult cell back into its original embryonic state. Which means that from there it can differentiate into anything."

"What happens if you just let it grow?" Carmen asks.

"It develops into a teratoma—a cancer basically, a big cell mass, but it would still manage to produce the normal germ layers: endoderm, mesoderm, and ectoderm. You might find some hair or teeth or something, some stuff that looks like gut. For the cerebral organoids we removed the part that differentiates into the central nervous system and grow it separately."

They're all grouped outside the door to a Faraday cage, waiting for Todd as he continues describing the process, until finally Carmen yells—"Just let us in!" to general laughter.

As they enter—"The organoids grow in Matrigel, which is just this substance that gives it all the nutrients it needs to develop. Once it's grown enough to attach to the dish we transplant it into a separate bioreactor."

The room is extremely warm. A table is against the far wall of the space, illuminated by a giant red heat lamp strung up above it. On the table are lined up eight tubular vats—they look like modified Erlenmeyer flasks, but at their top is inserted a ridged plastic engine. The beveled edges very gently stir the fluid, which glows pinkish under the red lights. At the bottom of each vat sits a cerebral organoid. They are pale colorless lumps. But not uniform in structure. Some have bumps and ridges others don't have, while one has a deep central groove. Another has a large cataract-white rounded protuberance. They look truly mysterious, alien, and in their whiteness, their colorlessness, they impress upon the observers their protean nature.

"In the bioreactors," Todd continues, "it can grow in 3D so it starts to differentiate into a recognizable cerebral phenotype. Neurons, ganglia, glia, and so on. All in a manner similar to the cortex. There's even the cortical layers."

Mike approaches one of the vats, poking a finger at an organoid—"What's this liquid?"

"That's the Matrigel. The stirring creates currents so the organoid gets this continuous nutrient bath."

"Oh my god, they're so big!" Carmen exclaims, examining the lump nearest to her, as large as a baby's fist. "The last paper had them at, what, ten millimeters? The diameter must be three, maybe even four inches! How did you solve the problem of blood supply?"

Todd blushes at Carmen's words—"Actually it was a rather ingenious idea we had. We provide a structure for them to grow around, like a—"

"A tree?" Carmen asks, glancing at Kierk, struck by a sense of déjà vu. The flash of the great tree Yggdrasil at night. But while Todd is still nodding, she exclaims—"Oh! You mean like a garden trellis for a growing plant!"

"That's, that's exactly—"

"But that doesn't solve the blood supply problem," Carmen continues, "unless . . . wait, unless it was a tree that was both porous and hollow! That way the Matrigel circulates to the inner cell mass that normally gets starved because there's no vascular system!" She looks over to Todd for confirmation, who is flabbergasted.

"Yeah, exactly . . . an artificial vascular system of our making. It really does look like a tree, but small and fine. Like you said, porous and hollow, so the Matrigel can reach the inner cell mass. The organoid grows around it. It took us . . . a really long time to figure out . . ." He's still ogling Carmen.

"Applications?" Alex asks, standing back from the table, unnerved.

"Oh, everything! If you're suffering from a neurological disorder, we can make a few of these from a skin biopsy. We can test drugs on them before we try them on you. Check toxicity levels. Or identify the etiology of the disease. This is the future of personalized medicine."

"So whose is whose?" asks Jessica.

"Oh . . . well I think that we just labeled the samples as they came so whatever order—"

"I was second," Carmen says, sliding up to hers. They quickly sort themselves, and soon each Crick Scholar is contemplatively face-to-face with their own cerebral organoid. Kierk is squatted between Carmen and Alex. Up close his organoid is just as pale and colorless but no longer so lump-like; indeed, it has shallow convolutions on its surfaces. It reminds him of the surface of Europa, with its crags and vents and canyon lines betraying the deep ocean within. Like some Precambrian sea creature it waves slightly in the current but is sessile, anchored to the glass base by a near-invisible stalk that must be the trunk of the tree. If Kierk looks close enough, he can see the incredibly fine tips poking up through the organoid, the tops of the branches barely beyond, granting just a small amount of room left to grow. Little bits of sloughed-off brain matter bob in the slow circulation, swim by the main blob like fish passing around a great coral growth.

"So what are you going to do with our clones?" Kierk asks from his crouch.

"We don't use that word."

"But that's what they are." Kierk is still staring at the blob swaying in the current. "This is the excised neural tube of my clone that is now trying to grow into a brain. But it can't self-organize well. No morphogenic cues."

"Well, I mean, technically . . . yes."

"So what's this white bubble growing off of mine?" Carmen says, pointing. "It looks like a little cup or saucer or . . ."

"Oh," Todd says, stopping to lean over Carmen. "It's trying to grow an eye."

The look on Carmen's face. She backs away, shivering suddenly. "It's trying to *see?*"

"Don't worry! It's not like the eye is going to be functional," Todd says.

"Did you test it?" she asks. "I mean, it might have working photoreceptors. It might be able to distinguish light and dark, that kind of thing. Maybe even simple outlines . . ."

Todd appears disconcerted. Carmen continues—"And what about internal neural signals?"

"Oh, yes! Absolutely. Recordings definitely show neural activity."

"What type of activity. Dreaming?"

"Dreaming of things they've never seen," Kierk says quietly. "Dreams made of ancestral memories. The genetically pre-programmed connectivity of the network. A blueprint left behind by all the humans who ever lived. Ancestral memory. Predators and prey. Mother and father. Comfort and cold. Food. Lovers . . ."

"Well, I mean . . ." Todd starts to respond but no one is listening to him because Jessica has approached the first bioreactor in the line of eight, staring down at it, and soon everyone is silent, realizing. All the gazes of the Crick Scholars are drawn to the first vat and its small gray-white content, the slow stir of it, almost like it was breathing through the thrumming fans of the room.

"Atif was really nice to me," Jessica says quietly. Then she lets out a soft sob and Carmen rushes over, hugging her from the side, stroking her hair and saying—"Oh, honey. Oh, honey."

"It's not like they're conscious," Alex says, somewhat nervously, glancing in the direction of his vat.

Kierk, now down in front of Atif's organoid, so close he is micrometers from pressing his nose up against the glass—"Now how could you *possibly* know that?"

CARMEN LAGS BEHIND AS everyone leaves. She's thinking that it'll be easier to get the truth out of Greg if it's just the two of them—it's not like she's unaware of the effect she has on him, and though sometimes the way she looks slips her mind (or of course when she internally feels underdressed or bloated and gassy or awkward or fat, and so on), she's currently very cognizant of it, expressing it, right now trying to radiate an interested look. So when she tugs on Greg's shirt he pauses, hooked, his worry replaced by consternation combined with hope.

"Could I talk to you a moment?"

"Of course! What's up?"

"Privately."

Carmen beckons him into a nearby break room, closing the door behind them. Greg stands nervously, fidgeting.

"What's, um, what do you need?"

"I didn't know you used to work in astronomy, Greg."

His face drops. "I . . . don't do that anymore. I switched to computer science in graduate school."

"Because the paper on anomalous star dimming was retracted."

Now Greg's face pales to an even purer shade of egg white.

"How'd you find out?"

"The internet."

He lets out a breath. "Does Kierk know?"

Carmen's eyes narrow. "No one else knows. So far."

"Please don't tell anyone. I switched to my mother's maiden name. And it follows you around! Forever! It's impossible to shake, a stain on me, a stain on that name. And now it's followed me here. Fuck. Just . . . Fuck."

"Why'd you do it?"

"I really did lose that data. The files! The files became corrupted. Some sort of virus. I've never seen anything like it."

Carmen shakes her head softly, holding up her hands. "Stop, Greg. That's impossible."

"It actually happened! Someone did it to me on purpose. Framed me."

"You lost all the data. That's just not possible."

Greg moans. "Oh, Carmen, you don't . . . You don't know these people."

"What? What people?"

He looks around like he's checking the room for listening devices, which makes Carmen nearly laugh aloud.

"If someone signs a nondisclosure agreement, they can't even say if they've signed one. Is all I'm saying."

"Wait. DARPA? You're talking about DARPA."

" . . ."

"You're lying."

"Did they make you retract?"

"No!"

"Did something happen? What?"

Greg, his face red, looks like he's about to cry. One of his hands clenches, drawing her attention. Carmen suddenly realizes they are alone in the room and Greg is between her and the door. And that this man is deeply emotionally unstable right now. At the completion of that thought, Carmen splits into three personas: one of whom is scientific and calm and giving a mini-lecture on the physiological fact that men have 50 percent more muscle mass than women, and due to their muscle fibers being larger, their muscles are pound for pound stronger as well, and that even a flabby guy like Greg is probably much faster too, because men's sensory frame shifting and reaction times are quicker, their grips larger, their weight distributed better for fighting and capable of producing far more power per movement, and all that is because beneath the veneer of civilization women like me have been mating with men who are good at killing other men and slowly breeding a weaponized sex to protect us and now here I am paying the price for that sexual selection that all my female ancestors enjoyed . . . while the second part of her is becoming itself violent, a heated demon, a cartilaginous message, a bone spear losing language in its flight and fear and reactivity. The further third, which is being shunted all the emotional intelligence, becomes a flirtatious psychologist, a concerned matron with the whiff of sex, a pretty face with big eyes.

"Hey, Greg," she says, smiling at him, tilting her head, feeling herself adopt a posture with her chest out, entering a standing lordosis, one leg crossing behind the other. "I didn't mean to interrogate you. But I need to know: what exactly happened? That's what I want."

"Why do you even care?" he cries angrily, gesturing. "Who made you a detective? I know what you're doing by the way. Everybody does. Carmen's little crazy project. Or is it just a way to flirt with Kierk? Because both you and Alex seem to be fucking in love with him for some reason. Everyone who isn't in love with him hates him, just so you know. And for the record I didn't have anything to do with Atif's death."

"It's not a secret what I'm doing," Carmen says defensively, even as she surreptitiously thumbs Kierk's number on her phone, stealing a glance at it as Greg turns around as if he's searching for something—words, emotions, it's unclear—but when he turns back he continues as if she hadn't spoken. Carmen's phone is back in her jeans, but still on, hopefully ringing.

"You got the email from his mother too, okay?" Carmen says. "Don't you care at all what happened? Don't you want to know?"

"You're saying because I don't care that I murdered Atif? Why? Why the fuck would I do that, Carmen? Or do you just think that I'm some lesser creature compared to you, that maybe me, the fucking morlock or whatever, that I did it? Why? My morlock ways? Isn't that how you see me? Some kind of freak?"

Some primate survival mechanism in her further clicks on, her appeasement takes a begging tone, and she can't control the words coming out of her mouth—"I don't see you as a freak at all, Greg, that's ridiculous—"

"You can't go around doing this. It has to stop."

It is like gears clicking away in her as one mode is swapped for another. Drawing herself up, haughtily, angrily—"You will leave me alone. This is utterly inappropriate for a work environment, Greg!"

"Do you want to fucking know what I was doing that night?" Greg has tears in his eyes and is shaking, red-faced.

Finally, panicking—"I'll scream."

Greg pauses, unreadable but clearly tormented. She waits as he decides, but she doesn't know over what—her mind is going wild in its search of the possibilities, and its own internal preparations. Then his face transforms from anger to anguish, melting in front of her with a brief sob. At that moment the door bangs open and Kierk enters the room with the phone pressed to his ear.

"What the fuck is going on here?" he says, looking between Carmen and Greg's blotchy face.

After a glance of fear toward Kierk, Greg is looking pleadingly at Carmen as Kierk gets almost nose to nose with him.

"I asked what the fuck is going on here."

"Greg was just leaving," Carmen says.

"He was, huh?"

Greg wipes at his eyes, trying to move past Kierk, but Kierk puts up an arm, blocking him in.

"Got something to say, Greg?" In response Greg tries to duck under his arm but Kierk slams him back into the wall to an indignant yelp.

"You ever raise your voice to her again and your face won't be your fucking face anymore. You get that?"

Head hanging, Greg won't look up but just breathes heavily, giving barely perceptible nods.

Carmen's hands go to Kierk's back, light against the broad tightness. After a moment Kierk lifts his arm and Greg scoots past, trying to hide the tears as he rushes out the door.

Kierk turns to her, his face breaking from an intense scowl into concern. "Hey. Hey. It's okay. What's going on?"

Carmen hugs him tight, getting underneath his arms, feeling his tallness over her, pressing her face against his shirt and inhaling the distinctive scent of him.

"What? What happened? Carmen?"

She says into his shirt—"I don't know. Maybe a misunderstanding. I asked him about Atif and he got upset. He lost it. He just lost it."

Kierk strokes her hair. "So what should we do?"

"I don't know."

"So . . . Everything is alright?"

"Sure," Carmen says, calming down, suppressing a tremble in her leg. "You're busy?"

"I was actually about to head to the gym."

"Oh, no. Yeah, that's fine," Carmen says, pulling away immediately.

"Are you sure everything is okay?"

"Go. Go. I'm fine. I have stuff to do here anyways. I'll see you later, okay?"

"Are you sure?"

Her brave face must have worked because he seems to accept her nodding.

He looks about to say something more but instead says—"Okay. Good."

Leaving, Carmen makes sure she goes the opposite way down the hallway, then immediately rushes to the women's restroom where she sits in a stall and cries and cries.

PANTING, WIPING THE SWEAT from his forehead, Kierk is finishing his post-workout run, stalking through the lobby of his apartment building. Even despite the drama with Greg, and his guilt about trying to remain distant from Carmen, Kierk had spent most of his workout thinking about Antonio Moretti's upcoming talk. In this field he would have to see Antonio again at some point, it was inevitable.

It hadn't always been like this. Indeed, Kierk still misses the intellectual stimulation of working with Antonio in the early years. Sometimes the pair would have four-, five-, six-hour-long discussions. Hours and hours working on the details of the theory. Most people, outside of obsessives, have never experienced the true intellectual exhaustion that comes from thinking about a single complex problem for hours on end—the buzzing, drowsy feeling from your cortex burning piles of calories just to keep up.

When there were others in their conversations Antonio and Kierk would outlast them all, a young marathoner and an older experienced one, still talking after everyone else had rushed out in tears of frustration or lapsed into a drained silence. Once a conversation about consciousness had begun at two in the afternoon and only when the night janitors came in to clean Antonio's office had they realized how late it was. At near midnight the two had walked out together to their cars, the only ones left in the vast empty lot on the outskirts of Madison, a park set aside for research by the university, so the natural night world was all around them as they kept talking under the vastness of the Midwestern stars—the Milky Way a bridge of light above them, the dark grasses on all sides a sleeve running itself off in secrets, and after the headlights of Antonio's car pulled out Kierk had been left alone, just him, the low-hanging moon, and an owl landing like a horned messenger in the trees. Kierk had followed its tufted shadow as it had winged from tree to tree, followed it as it followed the moon, and he himself then became a whipping form, a thing left running, a poet of the secrets kept by the grasses and the trees and the owl, real things casting shadows which were words which were thoughts, the living park a great mystery speaking to itself in the dark, a hued eye cracking, an old Egyptian myth reincarnated again, an irreducible animus, all of it alive, part of some larger structure, and everything had seemed possible to his running form as he sprinted across a field and into the soft bulk of night yelling at the moon, which yelled back in its stone language. He was right where he should be. All was phenomenon.

Now those early experiences under Antonio Moretti seem like another life. He can't believe it's only been weeks since he moved to New York. The city is already familiar to him: its frenetic pace, the clockwork and machina of it, the curbs littered with garbage, the food trucks, the skateboarders, the beautiful women in their summer dresses, the yellow cabs glinting like beetles in the sun, the lances of buildings, the feeling of possibility. Lately every day has seemed voluminous in its contents. Comparatively, the last few months in California had been a trickle, a blur. He can pick out individual events but not days. Kierk knows that this is a common psychological effect. A week of vacation is clear and extended, lingering and rich, while a week of normal routine flies by. An exemplar case: Kierk as a skinny kid, his hair everywhere, his limbs thin around knobby red knees and elbows, up in a tree, his hands sticky with sap. Not sticky enough. The branch in one hand had broken and he had slipped off, a long fall where he somehow had the time to maneuver his body so that he rolled down into pine needles when he hit. Thought he was dying before his breath came back. Time during that fall had been like a big bubble. The current neuroscientific explanation for the effect is that memories are laid down in greater detail and in greater number during novel experiences, so it really just *seems* as if subjective time slows. But to Kierk this can't be the entire explanation; rather, it has to be that each conscious moment is actually deeper, richer—there is a greater *volume* of consciousness. Or in a more Jamesian phrasing, time is the depth of the river of consciousness. And normal language doesn't have that distinction at hand, so people say time slowed down, when really they should have said—"There was more me. I existed more." In which case the amount of time experienced is a function of the richness of the experience. Maybe a bug's life, with its consciousness of tiny volume, rushes by in a subjective blink. Maybe a dog's days are like water, the stream of their entire life rushing by intrinsically at the same speed at which a year passes for humans. In the reduced consciousness of dreams the events are compressed, happening over and over in an impossible time frame. What about for a cerebral organoid? Kierk's deformed clone, its life one contextless dream, its fluttering experience a thin fast-flowing liquid. And for a hypothetical being with an infinitely rich consciousness time would never pass—frozen, it would live forever in its own subjective moment even as the rest of the universe spun the way toward heat death.

Kierk, shuffling out papers with equations scrawled on them, chewing on a pencil, spirals once again, moth to flame.

THURSDAY

KIERK **WAKES UP RAPIDLY** expanding from a smaller trickle. He's leaving a dream filled with only the vaguest outlines, tall creatures lacking all definite form or identity, sensed not by vision but almost as if by vibration. Giant figures that had emitted nonsensical sounds crouched before him. And then some force brought him from the dream and deposited him into sunlight and a fully grown body pleasurably resting under a cool sheet.

The walk to the CNS is so windy it actually slows him down. Above the clouds are streaking and rolling across the sky, furrows and troughs of them, blurring together. He thinks that clouds are all pulling a neat trick on us, fooling us into thinking them separate, when really there is only one cloud . . .

Arriving at the CNS his mind is all maths, the problem of consciousness a great puzzle laid out before him. He feels on the verge of a critical avalanche. There's a momentum behind everything he's doing and he doesn't want to lose it, he wants to keep this cognitive engine running as long as possible, putting in everything to burn, filling it with the buckshot of his meager young life, stuffing it with everything he has left.

BUSTING THROUGH DOORS SUSPENDED an inch from their frame, racing down corridors, bounding off corners. Faces he doesn't recognize jump out of his way. The text from Alex had just read HELP ME ASAP REC

ROOM. Only a brief stop to yell at an undergrad about where the recording rooms for primate research are.

Turning another corner, he sees the door to the recording room just as Carmen skids into him.

"You got the—"

"Go!"

They sprint down the hall together—Kierk body-slamming the last door open so that Carmen can race through—and find Alex standing outside the entrance to a recording chamber in full personal protective gear, his mask pulled down to reveal a wild look on his face.

"Oh, thank god!"

"What's going on?"

"Mars Bars. It's Mars Bars."

Carmen, after a moment where she considers whether she just had a stroke—"Your damn monkey?" She exchanges glances with Kierk.

"We thought—"

Alex makes a face—"What? No. I have a monkey situation. Mars Bars has injured himself."

"Do you have anyone with actual primate experience coming?"

"I sent the research assistant to get the veterinarian on call. But I have no idea how long it will be."

"Can we wait it out?"

"What's the actual problem?"

"Fuck, fuck, okay, you know the recording chamber on the top of the skull, where we lower the needle in? Well, you're supposed to screw the top to a bar above their head so that they can only look in one direction. Otherwise they won't face the screen and you can't show them stimuli. But I guess Mars Bars' chamber got weakened or something. He got so mad. I have no idea why. We're friends normally. But I've been told he can be unpredictable since Double Trouble died. They were cage-mates. Basically he just ripped the entire recording apparatus off."

"Off his skull?!" Carmen says, horrified.

"It took a good chunk of the skull with it," Alex says, wincing.

"That's really not supposed to happen."

"No shit. The bone could've weakened by infection or . . . Anyways, it doesn't matter why now," Alex says. "What matters is that there's an aggravated monkey in there with his brain exposed and literally no top of his skull."

"Christ. What if he shakes?"

"Shakes?" Carmen asks.

Alex—"When they get mad they like to shake in their chairs. Really hard. And with his skull open and in the shape it's in . . ."

Kierk tosses Carmen a mask and a lab coat as he and she begin immediately stacking on protective gear, grabbing the chain-mail bite gloves.

Carmen, her voice muffled by the mask—"What exactly are we supposed to do?"

"Alright, here's the plan," Alex says. "There's a sedative that they taught me how to use. For emergencies."

"Should we wait for the vet?"

"He would just try to do this anyways. And I have no idea how long he'll be."

"Don't they have like a dart gun or something?"

"Oh yeah, Carmen, for taking down all this big game."

She grimaces. "But we're adding new people he doesn't know."

Alex appears torn. "Listen, he's been in there alone because I freaked out. He's gonna start freaking out too if he doesn't see someone soon, 'cause he's just stuck there alone and in his chair. Monkeys want people around when they're in trouble. And Mars Bars is normally just a total fatty who wants food. So the plan is, Carmen, you get the food and the tongs. It's a bowl of grapes on the left. I try to approach him and calm him and you give me the food. Meanwhile, Kierk, you go for the syringes and the bottle marked 'Domitor.' I can't fill a needle while I'm feeding him to keep him calm. Plus, with three of us, if we're near enough we might be able to grab him and restrain his head."

Behind the armor of their personal protective gear both nod.

"Also, when we go in, don't look him in the eyes."

"What?"

"Just stare at his forehead. He will freak the fuck out if you look him in the eyes. Alright, we good?"

"Let's do it."

They file in wearing their gear. When the door closes behind them the exigencies of the situation become fully apparent. Mars Bars is situated in the back of the room in his see-through glass box/chair next to a screen which is still blinking with stimuli, but he's twisted around so that he's facing them, his arms and legs gesticulating from within the box whatever strange emotions are thrumming through him. Above his protruding head is a mechanical strut. The top of the recording chamber is normally screwed into the strut, but now it's just holding the ripped-away recording chamber itself hanging entirely free of the monkey's head, off to the side. The fur has kept his face free of blood, but the top of his head is more than scalped. It almost appears to wobble, and when he dips his head slightly there is a literal hole, a curved, gelatinous gap, red at the edges and a darker shadow within, and it is unclear exactly what they are seeing, but during the dip there is a shifting of something inside his skull which causes Carmen to gasp.

Mars Bars' breathing is a loud wheezing. He's looking over at them, his hands trapped in the glass box clenching and unclenching over and over. But his face is almost quizzical, like he's honestly confused about exactly what's happening, like he's puzzled why they won't entertain him or feed him or cart him back to his cage.

Carmen is the first to move, scooting over to the side and grabbing the bowl of grapes—her vision a tunnel, flitting hurriedly on the grapes, the table, her own gloved hand out grabbing the edge of the bowl, another hand to grab the tongs, not looking over at Mars Bars, moving back to Alex, her feet tracking beneath her.

Alex meanwhile has started cooing at Mars Bars, talking to him quietly, while Kierk is scanning the shelves on the other side of the room for the Domitor.

Carmen hands Alex the grapes and tongs, begins backing away.

"Nope," she says, glancing at the monkey with its exposed scalp, the top part of it all wrong, its eyes darting black marbles, its mouth expressive, but of what?

"Nope," she repeats. "Nope. I'm going to let you boys deal with this. Nope. Nope." The door closes behind her and immediately the portal is filled with her face, her mask is pulled down and she's pointing to the monkey mouthing—Go!

Kierk and Alex look at each other, then back at Mars Bars.

Spotting the Domitor Kierk takes a step toward it but there's a snake-like hiss now coming from Mars Bars, a strange alien spotlight falling on Kierk, a primitive attention now fixed.

"It's not working. We're aggravating him." Kierk backs up. But Mars Bars growls. Kierk stops. They are both careful to avoid its gaze.

Still, Alex asks—"Kierk, are you looking in his eyes?"

"No!"

Kierk takes a step back but Mars Bars gives another growl and shakes his chair, his head bumping into the hanging recording chamber and its partial ring of still-dripping skull.

"Whoa!" Alex says, as Mars Bars continues to eye Kierk angrily.

"Monkey," Kierk says soothingly, "if you keep shaking your head, you are going to lobotomize yourself. Please, don't shake your head."

Mars Bars is looking at Kierk with a fierce intensity, still giving off a harsh hiss from thin lips. Kierk is struck by its frantic grin, its vivid maniacal expression. He feels like he has seen this before. Its lips look like they are whispering, and it seems it is trying to communicate something through its manic graze, like the macaque has just been being seized by something, possessed by a secret it wants to tell, filled with a preacher's mania, a theological energy, a cosmological terror and ecstasy. Mars Bars, with his face stuck in a rictus of this expression, and his eyes locked on Kierk, begins to shake uncontrollably.

To shake and shake and shake.

Alone and outside the CNS, Carmen lights up a cigarette she had taken from Kierk's desk. Her hands give off only the slightest tremor. The night outside is a thick cloud being relieved of heat by the breeze. Groups mingle as they head to local bars. She feels estranged from their laughter over simple things. They are not confronted, pushed against, by things beyond our current conceptions of the world. Normally she didn't envy them, but right now she'd envy anyone who hadn't seen that.

A deep drag. A flash of an image. It's burned onto her visual cortex: the shaking and grinning form of Mars Bars, viewed through the portal window of the door. The short clip of memory has been running in her mind like an internet GIF played over and over—the top of him unhinging, dissolving into a cloud, a whiplash of pieces, a whirlwind of matter. And throughout it all, that grin.

The veterinarian, after arriving in profound shock, was apparently going to list the cause of death as "aggressive self-lobotomization."

Kierk and Alex were still inside getting some kind of emergency immunizations, given their experiences in the room. Quarantine from which Carmen had been spared. Kierk hadn't said much afterward, like he was avoiding her.

The whole thing reminded her of the dummy's head in her apartment, her own fear. Had the monkey done it on purpose? Realized that this was his way out? Mars Bars had been, according to Alex at least, a relatively happy monkey who liked his treats and comforts. More probably, she thinks, he simply hadn't had the ability to understand his situation. Which makes her think that maybe, in a way, everyone is like that. How are we all not just monkeys? Primates playing around with things we don't understand, congratulating ourselves at being able to predict things better and better but irrevocably tainted by our primate-like nature, by the fact that we are evolved beings viewing only that tiny sliver of reality which maximized our fitness values. How was science not just better eyes for seeing more of the spectrum, or smaller fingers for manipulating more accurately, sonic amplifiers for greater hearing, logic an extension of our primitive reasoning abilities, statistics to pick up on correlations in nature better than we naturally could, and so on—just tools to supplement our bodies so we could survive a bit better, a bit longer. How was science not merely a collection of mental prostheses? And that's so problematic, she thinks, because how could this trumped-up ape, aided only by some mechanical devices strapped to its limbs to extend its senses and a few calculating devices to extend its thinking, all modifications built on a limited foundation anyways, discover the real truth about the fundamental nature of reality? Maybe that's horrible, or maybe that's wonderful and beautiful, she thinks. Because to solve this great mystery of consciousness we therefore need something qualitatively different, as if the history of science has actually all been children playing with toys on the floor, and while I don't know what consciousness is, my hope, my unsupportable hypothesis, a beautiful dream worth having, is that it's a phenomenological signal, a qualitative bonfire etching itself onto reality. That people are transmitters and that consciousness is a radio to God. And it's sending up our thoughts, always sending up our thoughts . . . all the feelings of the people passing me, everyone in the city, the entirety of the world, going up now, each conscious moment a kind of prayer, a rain in reverse . . .

.   .   .

THERE HAD BEEN SOME sort of accident. Melissa Goldman had been waiting outside the recording room to greet Karen, her face lined with worry. As Karen approaches she decides to consciously break the normal workplace boundaries and takes Melissa's anxious hands in her own. The two women stand this way as Melissa fills her in on the situation. Throughout, Karen can hear a low murmuring of voices from within, the quiet phonetic downward turns of instructions at an autopsy.

Eventually she and Melissa go inside, where the vets look up grimly from behind their personal protective gear. At the center of the room is slumped the body of Mars Bars. Karen flits away her glance but the image stays with her long after—the strange weight of the body, all of it tilted downward, its placid white-eyed death mask sending a visceral shock through her, the unnatural hang of its open mouth with the red tongue already blackening, all of it obscene in its slouching, all protuberances and parts made unfamiliar by death. The rest of the room isn't much better. Bits of gore and brain are still being scooped up by the vets. One is taking pictures like a crime scene investigator.

"Kierk?" Karen asks.

"Currently being cleaned up."

"Why is it always Kierk?" she says.

"No, he was in the room when it happened, but it wasn't his fault. Mars Bars was in Alex's care. Kierk got called in after, came to help, and was here for the worst of it."

"Mm," Karen replies, watching something unidentifiable be put in a yellow BIOHAZARD bag.

"How are you going to tell the Institutional Review Board?" she finally asks.

Melissa sighs, her mouth pursed. "With everything that's going on this is exactly what I didn't need."

"They're going to know it was an accident," Karen reassures her. But Karen knows that this could spill beyond Melissa's domain . . . There were joint department-wide grants to think about, and possible public blowback could influence whether those grants were renewed. Particularly the Crick Scholarship, which was up for review by DARPA at the beginning of next year. One Crick Scholar was dead, another had let a valuable research animal kill itself, and Kierk was a loose cannon . . . The entire program was beginning to look like a disaster. All those conservative neuroscientists who didn't believe consciousness existed, and who had been extremely critical of the program, would be able to say that the first government-funded research into consciousness unraveled in ignominy.

Something in her field of vision makes her turn and she confronts Max's face in the portal of the door. After a moment of eye contact he disappears. A vanishing that causes a stab in her chest.

Excusing herself from Melissa, Karen finds herself in pursuit of Max, tracking him through the CNS. In an empty stairwell she leans over the railing and calls his name. At the echo of it he stops one flight below her. He ascends slowly, she descends slowly, and they meet in the middle on the platform.

"So now you decide you want to talk to me?" he says furtively, glancing around to make sure they are alone.

"After what I just saw . . . I don't know. Things haven't been so great with me."

She vaguely reaches out a hand, brushes against his thigh, but with no response forthcoming she drops it down to hang at her side. He's staring at her in a defensive posture, his arms crossed. She doesn't know how to articulate everything that's churning inside her. There's no obvious end or beginning, and no conclusion, because she doesn't know anything now except what she wants at this moment.

Finally Max nods his head.

"I shouldn't have booked it like that," he says stiffly. "I won't be so awkward in the future. You'll have your professional atmosphere."

"But what if I don't want . . . things to be so professional," Karen replies, moving forward, although she can't muster any eroticism in her advance. Instead her voice betrays emotional need. And she knows immediately that it was a mistake. If she had said it in a flirtatious or sensual way, had tossed it off like this wasn't the gravest matter in the world to her, then he probably would have smiled and moved closer as well, instead of giving her the pitying look he does now, his expression shifting to the sadly nostalgic, letting go in that instant.

"You're saying you want to start up again?" he says. "Now? It's been weeks. I needed you during that time. And you weren't there."

"I didn't—"

"You did."

Her voice is tremulous as she speaks—"But I need you now."

A penitent nod of the head, trying to project grace like he had suddenly transmuted into a saint, a holy man who was trying to communicate by his body language the impossibility of the situation without breaking her heart. But his words are harsh.

"You need me now. I needed you then. Looks like we're perpetually out of sync."

Someone enters the stairwell below them and just like that he gives her a final glance and descends. The reality of the ending is upon her. Karen says his name twice. The first is loud enough for him to hear but the second is just for her.

Later, there she is utterly losing her shit behind the locked door of her office, losing her research program, losing Max, hell, who knows, maybe losing her own shot at tenure here if the Crick Program goes under, a total dissolution. All her failures beat at her like winged devils, and she realizes that the wolf of time has eaten up the hours of her life and it is too late to correct any of it.

KIERK IS LYING ON the floor of his apartment next to a shrinking To Read pile and a rapidly growing Read pile. It's everything he originally rescued from Atif's desk. When Kierk gets to one of his own papers he lets out a laugh, thumbing through it with nostalgia. Some handwriting in the margin catches his eye.

He's not going far enough. But perhaps there is a way. A real theory of consciousness could begin here.

Kierk pauses. The paper is not one of his better ones, he had thought. But maybe Atif had seen some way forward, or suspected something . . . Kierk couldn't figure it out. Had Atif been secretly working on a theory of consciousness without telling the others? Kierk raked his mind, trying to remember the various conversations . . . Maybe he had been afraid to mention it? Fear of someone, specifically Kierk, stealing the seed of his idea and extrapolating it faster than he could? Had there been some hint that night, some way Atif had acted that showed that he was ripe with an ultimate notion? Had there been a dissertation blooming like a flower bed in his gut, a symphonic thesis playing behind his calm eyes? Honestly Kierk doubted it, but who really knew when it would come, and to whom. And what if it hadn't been just any theory, but the correct theory, that paragraph of perfect language Kierk had been searching for . . . But maybe such a revelation wouldn't have been so lucky. Maybe the thought of it was so intense, so shattering in its weight, its implications spinning out, Atif seeing all of it, drunk and underground in that yellow halving chamber, just him and the greatest scientific theory of all time, not beautiful but horrifying, the cruel joke exposed, turning into an infinite unstoppable laugh track sounding off all throughout the universe, and, unable to bear the jeering weight of its consequences, Atif had dived headfirst into that bright light just to erase from his mind the idea that had colonized it with omnivorous intent.

Kierk knows he is letting his imagination run wild but it feels good to even be proposing an explanation that made sense to him—what if, for instance, Atif had discovered some perfect theory that implied consciousness was entirely useless, epiphenomenal, that it never did anything at all but always occurred after the fact. That our selves really were just meat marionettes jerked about on atomic strings . . . Or that this "I" has never truly felt anything, thought anything, but instead has always just passively watched feelings and thoughts play out . . . Or that each day an entirely new consciousness is birthed into existence, a golem, etched only with inherited memories, and that each night our consciousness goes unknowingly to its death, so that the span of our lives are macabre shows, oblivious massacres, sick jokes . . . Or maybe something even darker, unimaginable to anyone who hadn't made the breakthrough yet. Spiraling out now, Kierk thinks that perhaps this could explain not just Atif's death but also perhaps the Fermi Paradox: that the galaxy, where life has had ten billion years to develop on the billions of planets orbiting in habitable zones, and the entire span of which would take only a few million years to fully colonize from any given starting point . . . was lifeless. And that maybe the mystery of consciousness was the great and final filter, a cosmic pitcher plant eventually winnowing out all the civilizations that figure it out. Implying that every civilization of conscious beings, after solving the mystery of themselves, recoils in total horror and wipes itself out, tearing itself apart in nihilism, reactionary politics, fundamentalism, barbarism, and self-loathing.

Aggressive self-lobotomization.

FRIDAY

KIERK WAKES UP FROM a dream of bodies. Carmen naked before him and then a fast-forwarding to that grinding underneath, the writhing, everything opening and the penetration and envelopment, her legs wrapped around him . . . So that on waking he rolls onto a taut bladder pressing from within and an erection now trapped uncomfortably underneath him.

Eventually he has to hurry down Broadway, late.

Approaching the CNS something catches his eye—a police cruiser and ambulance parked in front of the building, the alternating red and blue lights faded to almost nothing in the glare. Kierk begins to jog up, crossing the street during a break in the traffic, but as he gets close to the blinking ambulance, it, like a beast startled from sleep, pulls away from the curb.

"Hey!" Kierk cries, but it drives unhurriedly away down the cobblestone street toward the park. Despite being only a block off busy Broadway the street is a simmering quiet except for the bouncing and receding ambulance.

He turns to the still cop car but he can't see inside the tinted windows. From a few feet away he stares at it for a while, his face scrunched up in the brightness, the car a dense machine radiating heat—he's expecting it to jump into motion as well, or at least for a window to roll down. Finally, he walks up and knocks with one knuckle on the black driver's-side window. When there's no response he leans over and peers in, cupping his hands around his face, to only a dim and empty interior and the outline of a secured shotgun. The lights continue to blink in silence.

The CNS appears calm enough on the inside, although the security guard isn't there to swipe Kierk's card as usual. When he gets to the lab, he immediately heads over to Carmen's sitting form. Coming up behind her, Kierk realizes that Carmen's monitor is filled with information about how to create a psychological profile of a serial killer. FBI profiles, articles, and Wikipedia pages proliferate. In the mirror of the screen he sees her notice his reflection. Her face morphs to a smile, her eyes dancing to his.

He points. "Why?"

"Did you know that male serial killers generally kill for sex, but female serial killers kill for money?"

"I did not."

"So a tenure-track position is basically a lot of money, and health insurance, and job security, and social standing—"

"Except Jessica is not a serial killer, and also accounted for because Mike took her home," Kierk says sharply.

"I know!" Carmen says defensively. "It's not like I was accusing her. Besides, that's not why I've been reading about this, exactly. Listen, we need to go somewhere private."

"What was that ambulance doing outside? Who got—"

Carmen nods excitedly. "I'll tell you but I need somewhere private."

He eyes her. "Actually, Carmen, I'm sorry I asked. I don't have time for this right now."

"What's the matter with you? What's going on?"

"Nothing. I'm just busy."

"This is important."

"Fine. Alright? Fine."

Carmen, confused, leads him out of the lab and into the side room down the corridor. It's the same room where Atif, Carmen, and he had first talked about their joint project weeks ago.

"What's going on with you?"

"What is it that you wanted to tell me?" he says brusquely.

Hurt, Carmen lowers her voice. "Okay, whatever, I don't know what's wrong with you but this morning outside the CNS this homeless guy was yelling—"

"What was he saying?"

"Listen! He was shouting at everyone entering the CNS. Screaming about how we had taken his friends, that we were kidnapping people. So

I asked him. And it took a little while to get it coherent, but the gist of it was that, last night, a friend of his was taken into this building, in here."

"Into the CNS?"

"Yeah, he was saying that they were taking the homeless. That everyone knew it too. That they took them at night."

"Really."

"Listen, and then he said that afterward they're different." Carmen has gotten incredibly serious. "Kierk, he said that they had been lobotomized."

"He probably just saw the sign 'Center for Neural Science' and remembered something about lobotomies and was out there screaming."

"He said they were doing experiments."

"Oh come on." But at her reaction he quickly says—"Listen, I know you're sensitive about that. Given what happened. It was a sick joke. Maybe even a real death threat. And that's upsetting. And then what happened with Mars Bars . . . It's odd. I agree. But what's the motivation?"

Brushing aside his earlier words Carmen says—"I had the same thought about motivation. And then I realized something. Come with me."

The TMS/EEG lab is empty. The big plush chair sits in the middle of it like an obscene throne with the extended metal arm a mini-crane looming over it. The coil was attached so that the transcranial magnetic stimulation could be maneuvered to any position above a subject's head and a magnetic pulse delivered. The webbed hats of electrodes hung in rows on the walls to dry off like wet scalps after an Indian raid. To the front of the chair was the large monitor where visual stimuli could be presented.

Carmen swipes her finger across the armrest and shows her blackened digit to Kierk.

He gestures. "So the cleanliness of the experimental chair is a tragedy of the commons. And?"

"Kierk, sniff this chair."

He takes a whiff and then pulls back, eyes watering. "And what exactly does this tell us?"

"Not just the chair!" Carmen rushes over to the trash bin. "I found this earlier!" She picks out what looks like an old blanket, frayed and caked to stiffness by dirt and stains. She's holding it pinched between thumb and forefinger.

Carmen sees Kierk's expression and says—"I'm a scientist, it's not my job to be politically correct. It's my job to go where the facts lead. And the facts say that there was a homeless person in this room, or several. Over time."

"It's your job to be skeptical. Extraordinary claims require—"

"There being no simpler explanation for the data," Carmen finishes.

"Hmm . . . But he was saying they were giving them lobotomies. Why would they do it in this room . . ." Kierk drifts off, eyeing the claw-arm of the TMS.

"No . . ."

"Yes!"

"You're saying that someone turned the TMS all the way up and was burning out lesions."

"Yes!"

"As what, the patient, ah, abductee, watched stimuli?"

"Imagine how much you could learn about consciousness by triggering real lesions in real time. In humans."

"Yeah, that's not going to be approved by the Institutional Review Board."

"Obviously. But it's a motive."

"Anything else? Or are you going to draw a straight line between your two data points?"

"As a matter of fact there is. Follow me."

She leads him down a few floors to where the giant tube of the MRI machine rests. Carmen flips the lights in the control room on to a bright hospital-like hum, illuminating the computer terminals. Nearly jumping into the swivel chair, she pulls up a program.

"Look. Here's the activation times of the recent scans. Look!" She points to two tiny numbers that Kierk squints at.

"Last night?"

"Last night at 3:02 a.m."

"So?"

"So who the hell is using the MRI machine in the middle of the night? Unless they were getting anatomical images . . . to use for targeted transcranial magnetic stimulation. With the stimulation turned up so high it burns out lesions. Which you can then check to see exactly where they are using the MRI."

Kierk stares at the little numbers.

"And three makes a trend line," Carmen says smugly.

"That's quite an elaborate secret experiment."

"Don't Scully me!"

"Alright fine," Kierk says. "Do you want to know when it's used?"

"Like when the program is activated? How?"

Kierk pulls up the command terminal and a text doc, fingers flying.

"I'm hiding something, a small function in the code for the fMRI machine. Code that sends you an email whenever the fMRI gets run."

They are silent as Kierk types, Carmen examining him under the pretense of studying the code. He is focused on the screen and doesn't look at her. A realization is building in her, that sickly sense of something being deeply wrong.

On clicking to a finish he says, "Okay that's that. You'll get your email. I gotta go get some work done."

"Fine. Do whatever. I'll see you later."

Carmen watches him retreat. Her hands go up to rub the goose bumps on her shoulders. It's freezing in here.

KIERK IS LEAVING THE CNS after a day spent studiously avoiding Carmen and just focusing on his research. He's so close . . . But there's so much going on and she's the center of all of it. It feels like some otherworldly conspiracy keeps thrusting them together. He's going to have to try harder, make a cleaner break, if he can.

As he steps out of the building into the still-blinding light his name is called and for a second he's unable to locate its source, until he sees a middle-aged man in a Hawaiian shirt and khaki shorts. The man is taking off his sunglasses as he speaks and had obviously been waiting for him.

"Kierk Suren?"

Kierk shades his eyes—"Yes?"

"Hello. It's a pleasure." The man motions Kierk over to the side of the sidewalk and into the minimal shade provided by the CNS. Once there the man, forgettable, suburban, smiles at him.

"I wanted to meet you in the flesh."

"I'm sorry, who are you?"

"I work for DARPA and the Department of Defense. I was responsible for setting up the Francis Crick Scholarship."

"Oh! Well . . . Thank you. It's been interesting."

"Yes, well, it's good to finally get the next generation together." He purses his lips. "Actually, to be honest, we've had our eye on you for some time. We keep track of certain individuals who we suspect might have a chance—"

"Of cracking it?"

"Precisely." He seems to be judging Kierk's reaction. "And you're not bothered by this?"

Kierk shrugs. "I can understand why the DoD would be interested. Solving consciousness would probably lead to next-gen artificial intelligences. Personality uploads. Brain-to-brain communication. Conscious tech."

"Precisely. We are highly interested in its strategic importance. At the national level, I mean."

"So you keep track of those . . . on the edge."

"Of which you are one. There are others. Some in other nations. But given all that, do you mind if I ask your opinion on some things? A freelance consultation, if you will. Based on the research proposal about brain-to-brain communication in primates you were going to do with Carmen and Atif. And now possibly with Alex."

"How do you even know about that?"

The DARPA agent just smiles.

Kierk shrugs again. "Fine, shoot, if you'd like."

"Take some set of independent systems and then continuously couple them. At what level of integration, of coupling, do they become complex enough to give rise to consciousness?"

Kierk laughs aloud at the specificity and peculiarity of the question but the agent doesn't laugh back so Kierk clears his throat and answers—"Actually that's completely unknown. But we do know it's not just how integrated a system is, not just informational bandwidth. It has to be the right kind of coupling. Less information is going across the corpus callosum, that is, the bridge of nerves between the two hemispheres, than across a higher-powered modem. But we do know that some correct form of complex coupling breeds consciousness. How exactly that works, and what degree of coupling you need in order to get a conscious agent from nonconscious parts, is unknown."

"My second question: can you make a larger conscious system out of independent conscious systems?"

"Ah, sure. Some might argue that the ant colony is conscious, not the ants. But for direct evidence look at our own brains and consider the two hemispheres, which are largely independent but coupled via the nerve fibers of the corpus callosum. You can do the Wada test, which I've seen done by the way, where one hemisphere is shut down with anesthesia but the other is not. It's eerie. Spooky . . . I saw one test where the left was shut down and the right hemisphere remained. The right hemisphere couldn't talk to me, only grunt and whistle and sing. The man was a construction worker who they were considering for brain surgery. Epilepsy. Didn't talk much. Stoic, everyone said. But once the right hemisphere was alone and in control he seemed so happy, so alive, rhythmic . . . I played him music and the man, or rather, his right hemisphere, danced in the chair, waving his arms about. So within this man was this incredibly cheerful nymph-like child, humming to itself, inviting me to dance. And I watched as the anesthesia wore off and that childlike musician was subsumed as the other hemisphere gained consciousness and the man became a stoic construction worker once again. I asked him if he could remember it. He said no. See, a consciousness abhors other consciousnesses. It eats them. Subsumes them, I mean. There's some law of the universe, some consequence of the nature of consciousness itself, which entails that a consciousness subsumes those that it is composed of. Like soap bubbles. Press two bubbles together and they merge into one. Pop a big bubble and you'll get a bunch of smaller bubbles—but in what sense did they exist before the big bubble was popped?"

"You planned to do this with a network of monkeys. But let's say then you have a network of humans instead. Or an entire civilization . . . our civilization, if you will. And you couple them more and more. What will happen if you project that into the future? Feel free to speculate wildly."

Kierk's eyebrows shoot up. He can't help but show off in this type of conversation. "Isn't it obvious by now? Human civilization, the biosphere, etcetera, becomes more and more coupled via technological advances and growing population. Like ants or cells learning to cooperate . . . Sure, we're individuals in the early stages. But as the noosphere grows in concentration and integration, a phase transition takes place at some point. The first sign is actually the construction of cities. Eventually as a civilization becomes more concentrated, its tasks and workings more globally distributed, and its energy demands greater, it might later concentrate itself around a sun. Perhaps it builds a Dyson sphere, drawing tighter and tighter, coupling its individuals together more and more through interaction . . . It's all merely the evolution of integration. Or the right kind of integration. Perhaps even its technology itself becomes conscious, integrates with the growing hive mind. Step-by-step it will undergo sub-Omega-Point integration ratchets until . . ." Kierk makes a gesture that indicates he can only guess.

"You've read Pierre Teilhard de Chardin then. I thought as much. A favorite of mine, personally," the agent says, wiping at his forehead.

"Sure."

"And you read a great deal of literature."

"I suppose."

"Do you think that's why you're good at this . . . line of work? I've always suspected that the central requirement for studying consciousness is to possess a radical form of empathy. To be able to understand what it is like to be another person: male, female, or a different orientation or age . . . But also what it is like to be a bat, or a network, or a city. Perhaps, as you indicate, even what it is like to be a post-biological group mind."

The agent grins like he's said something very funny.

"What do you care about any of this? DARPA, I mean."

"Well, such post-biological group minds . . . Such hive-mind entities might be very different from us. With very different reasoning, motivations, and capabilities. Not like dealing with individual rational agents anymore. You have to throw out a lot of game-theoretic reasoning. In any . . . dealings, let's say, with post-biological consciousnesses, we'll need to know something about them, and of course, prepare ourselves, should they exist. We can reason with a civilization made up of individuals, but if we encountered say, artificial group minds the size of entire civilizations, well . . . First we'd need to know whether that's possible, and, if it is possible, how to deal with such an entity. You'd need . . . radical empathy."

"I'm sorry but why are you asking about this? Why now?"

"Oh, just personal curiosity on my part. But at an institutional level . . . Well let's just say that the timescale we're operating on is perhaps a bit longer than you're used to. Maintaining the individuality of consciousness is essential for the continuation of democracy as we know it. And thus America as we know it. Eventually a confrontation may be inevitable in regard to ourselves."

The DARPA agent gestures to the passersby on the street, all unique, brushing past one another in all colors, complexions, genders, classes, clothing; the movement chaotic at the local level but each trajectory perfectly sorting into a pattern absent of collisions, people self-organized into a fluid.

The agent says—"This period of personal and individuated consciousnesses may just be a historical interlude. The next emergent step may be inevitable. Brain-to-brain group minds will be the norm. Maybe even in just a few hundred years they'll think we were primitive barbarians because of the antiquated individuated way we lived. How to communicate to such a future what it was like to be an individual, to have just one body, to wake up alone in your own head every day?"

Kierk doesn't know what to say to this so he just takes out a cigarette and proffers it, but the agent shakes his head.

"Well, sorry this was such a short meeting, Kierk. I wish it had been longer but I've enjoyed our conversation . . . So I will say to you what I came to say. And that is that we'd encourage you, strongly, to stay on. That is, we'd like you to get one of the positions. However, our influence is not infinite. Everything is bureaucracy, in the end."

"Why do you want me to get one of the positions?" Kierk asks, blowing smoke that dissolves in the light.

"There may be, in the near future, certain . . . think tanks, appropriate for you. But you don't even officially have a PhD yet. That's problematic. Please, if you can, keep your head down, and it may be possible to secure you a position. Or even something bigger."

"Bigger like what?"

"DARPA and the DoD view the problem of consciousness as central to maintaining technological sovereignty. Of course, this is also a concern for NASA. Perhaps a sort of Manhattan project will be set up. I'm sorry I can't be more definite. I advocate for the problem's importance within the organization but I am merely one voice. Anyways it's been a pleasure—"

"Wait wait wait. There's something I need to ask you. Concerning Atif."

The DARPA agent frowns. "Yes, we had high hopes for Atif as well. That was very unfortunate."

"Too unfortunate. Some of the Crick Scholars, myself included, suspect . . . how do I say this . . . foul play?"

The DARPA agent looks askance at Kierk. "You believe that Atif was murdered?"

"And you . . . DARPA . . . wouldn't have had anything to do with it," Kierk probes.

"My my, you truly do believe it. Interesting. No. To answer your question. Of course not. DARPA and the DoD have no interest in murdering scientists, just funding them."

"He was Indian. Ethnically and nationally."

"Atif was a citizen of the world. According to his file he was probably more loyal to Britain than India. He had no nationalistic leanings."

"Perhaps you were scared that he had figured it out. You want the secret of consciousnesses to yourself. Like the A-bomb. Think what you could do with it."

The DARPA agent laughs easily. "Like I said, given that Atif was chosen specifically as part of our funded program to work on this problem, what sense would it make to . . . eliminate him?" With no answer forthcoming from Kierk he says—"I'll tell you what. I'll look into it. Although it certainly wasn't DARPA or the DoD. And I can't promise anything. This may just be your imagination."

"We understand that."

"Alright, well, I could make a phone call to some friends in the FBI." He shakes out his sweat-stained Hawaiian shirt, squints up at the sky. "It's been a pleasure, Kierk."

"Wait. I never got your name."

"Well, it's not like I'm some sort of secret agent," he says, and lets out a hollow laugh. "Anyways, keep cool. Get out of this heat. I'm sure we'll see each other again."

Slipping back on his sunglasses the DARPA agent nods promptly to Kierk and then merges into the stream of individual passersby and is quickly enveloped, just one of the crowd, utterly average-looking, until Kierk loses sight of him.

Wandering, smoking, watching, Kierk eventually heads over to Washington Square Park and begins to trace out a continual circle around the fountain as the families and street performers play around him and the arch dusks itself orange before the curtain of dark is drawn down over the city's game of faces. The conversation has left Kierk spun; he's become a revolving galaxy of thoughts, watching a future history bloom on fast-forward as considerations of post-biological group minds run away with him, clash with the normality of the busyness of the park, the comings and goings; he feels like he has just brushed up against something beyond that is straining to get in, a Second Coming hundreds of years hence that could not be described as either beautiful or horrific for it will be just a roar beyond human comprehension, speeding toward them all backward in history, its manifestations echoing in retrograde through time like ripples spreading out in the small pond of space-time. And who will cast that first stone?

His peripatetic wandering, cut with wonderment and fear, has taken him once more to Bleecker Street Station. Entering down the stairs is like descending into a clay oven that is simultaneously an organ breathing away in machine dreams. Even through his dress shoes the ground radiates an organic heat and the metal he touches hums hot. In this aquarium air he swims about, misting, uncertain why he's been driven here again—perhaps by the agent's words, perhaps by the events of the morning, perhaps by thoughts of Carmen. Swiping his MetroCard he enters and is surprised at the ping of sound, a note, as the turnstile revolves. Examining it he sees that it is some kind of art project. A woman clutching numerous shopping bags pushes through after him and another, different note sounds, lingers.

First he paces the track for a while, timing the subway trains coming and going. The mean is every eight minutes, with a standard deviation of about a minute. The music from the turnstiles is haunting but he ignores it, concentrating instead on where the man vanished and where Atif must have died as well (given where he'd seen the toe), right by the liminal space where the subway platform ends and the dark tracks begin. The direction where the train comes from. For that space seems a dark labyrinthine siren, promising an answer. Kierk goes back and forth with himself as he paces—for no argument pro the action he is leaning toward could be summoned, only intuitions, fantastical intuitions; but under the influence of such phantasmagoria he at last makes his decision and waits at the ledge, at that dark lip, for the train to come. And after its departure, Kierk, looking surreptitiously around as the platform empties, makes his move into the black mouth as the train screeches away.

At first he is just groping blindly, one hand out, back pressing against the wall behind him, sidestepping. He eats up little space with his inching, yet somehow the tunnel swallows him whole immediately. Ahead of him lies the curving wall to his right and the tracks following that curve, lit only by distant emergency lights. The wall is an amalgam of rock and metal, grimy, while below him the shelf seems impossibly narrow, not even a foot wide really. He doesn't know if that foot is enough space for the train to not reap him if it comes—if the sucking wind of its passage will pull him in, or unbalance him, or if there's any hitch of metal protruding from the train that might tear him apart easily. After a few feet he's more sure of where the ledge lies under him and so now he can scuffle sideways at faster pace.

Ten feet out and he feels like he has been ontologically separated from the lit world of the platform. That he is violating some deeper order and is now irrevocably apart.

Twenty feet out he has the feeling of being underwater and, looking back, he can see the surface, but physics is working differently here, light bends in odd ways and he feels unnaturally buoyant, like his own nervousness and expectation could lift him up and he might float down the tunnel.

Thirty feet out is a spacewalk, the light from the platform a thin lifeline already curving away out of view. At this point there is the sound of a train coming, which freezes him for a moment, but then his pinna, millions of years in their evolution, pick out that it's coming from the other direction and will arrive safely on the opposite side of the platform.

At forty feet out the platform is gone from view and in front of him is only an emergency light glowing a biological red and the long track of metal is a gut, a lair—he's a mere microbe in an entrail. The train that had come from the other side of the platform thunders past and from his vantage point he sees sparks underneath as it grinds away.

Coming up there is an iron girder in his way, blocking the path. He feels around it, and leaning out sees the ledge continues beyond it on the other side. Pulling back, he notices something right next to him on the wall—an opening, and with a square of light that he can just get his head through and peek into. He sticks his head into a concrete box the size of a studio apartment, lit by a halogen lamp propped up in the corner, unattended and disorderly. The floor is dusty and scraps lay in shadows, but one clear part was illuminated, the wall maybe just ten feet to his right, which he turns his head to face. There, writ large in red spray-painted letters against the far concrete wall is DOUBLE TROUBLE LIVES. TORTURE FOR TOR-TURERS. And beneath it, drawn in the same bloodred, looms large graffiti of a monkey's face. But it is distorted, human-like and showing human teeth. The grin manages to portray in simple lines both malevolence and exultation. Exactly, in fact, the same look Mars Bars had given Kierk right before he had vibrated away the material of himself. The all-too-humanoid

drawing seems a perfect facsimile of Kierk's own memory. There is a shifting. Something huge moves in the corner of the room. Before it moved it
had just been a shadowed scrapheap. Now it towers, unfurling its limbs,
standing bipedal but wrong, too tall, with dangling arms, its enormous
head towering above in the darkness, and Kierk rears back, almost falling
off onto the tracks, then flattening against the subway wall with the small
passage he had been looking through right beside his head. A thrill rushes
through him, right down his spine, and in the mechanics of darkness his
heartbeat is a piston and his skin a sheet of electricity. There is more movement; something is knocked over, a scraping, and then silence. Slowly Kierk
goes to look again, not breathing as he does so. The room is empty of all
but the graffiti.

Stealing a glance behind him in the dark, observing the distance between
himself and the faraway platform—what had he just seen? He needs to
know. Looking around he notices, on the other side of the iron girder, a
larger opening created by another giant steel *X*, which looks big enough
for Kierk to squeeze through into this back room. But to get there he must
cross the iron girder. Pulling his head out of the box, he feels around, leans
out into the air of the track. Groping forward with one arm he maneuvers
his way until he is stretched out, with one foot and arm on each side of the
girder, ready to swing to the opposite end, clinging to it like a fruit bat in
the reddish glow. And it is then that a voice speaks to him from inside his
skull. But it is not in his own lighter-than-air internal voice but rather the
deep and real voice of a man, a stranger, speaking directly to him from a
place inside, but slightly left-of-center and above where the *me* of Kierk is
normally spatially located.

The man says—"*What you are doing is very stupid.*"

A pause in action. The girder digging into his dress shirt. The reddish
glow. A laugh out loud. What the fuck was he doing? Withdrawing his
limbs he swings back to the side where he had come from. Panting, he
withdraws. What is he withdrawing from? He doesn't know. Maybe it had
just been a homeless man whose sleep Kierk had disturbed. And the light
had changed the angles, made him seem . . . enormous. His head spinning,
he begins retracing his steps.

About ten feet away from the girder and thirty feet from the barely visible lit curve of the platform, he hears it . . . another threatening rumble, but
this time from farther down in the tunnel, definitely on his side. Far earlier

than he had calculated it out to be, at least two standard deviations too soon, a statistically unlikely event whose likelihood was irrelevant because *it is happening*, which he verifies by grabbing onto a metal lip with one hand and hanging all the way out, a scarecrow in the dark. There it is, vibrating toward him, a great slug half-tunneled back, a metal worm of the earth coming in a long shriek and with hateful momentum, slowly turning the corner but he knows really it is speeding along, closing even now, in these few seconds of thought. Then he's off, running toward the platform down the ledge he had just crept carefully on, feet pounding on that thin shelf, eyes on where it drops into oblivion. He spares a brief moment to glance back and there it is, a bright monstrous cyclopean eye pursuing him; it captures him in its light, it roars a greeting, it is upon him . . .

His form comes tumbling out onto the subway platform not five feet before the hurricane of steel rushes past him.

A woman gasps from nearby but Kierk, breathing so hard it hurts, silences her with a look. Beyond some glances and movement away from him he's left alone to lean against the wall—he can feel every inch of his skin and his head is spinning, ripping from him in this heat where he can't even catch his breath, so he ends up a staggered figure, just a heavy-breathing delicate chemical balance almost obliterated, a standing negentropy wave that had just escaped from materials harder and faster than it, a standing negentropy wave that is strongly reconsidering this whole investigation, that is reaching certain decisions vis-à-vis the pursuit of this strangeness (like finding that graffiti so far back on precisely the same subway where Atif had been disembodied, dissipated, and then the form itself, the thing towering up in the darkness, it must have been ten feet tall), specifically, he's leaning toward abandoning the pursuit entirely—for left alone the strangeness might be harmless but in these investigations it is a strangeness that always seems to push back.

The minutes pass and he recovers himself. He's watchful of the end of the platform where he had seen it but nothing emerges, everything passes normally. It's Friday night, which he'd forgotten, and the citizens of New York are traversing the underground. Eventually he moves closer to the turnstiles where the art project is installed, sitting down on a nearby bench, his clothes streaked with rust and dirt, completely ruined. In the flow of those entering and exiting there is music. With each passerby a note is sounded, building until the chthonic music is an ambient *étude*, like listening to a great thought accumulating over decades, a pattern spaced out temporally to such an extent that it was only just recognizable as such. But the nature of the song is not threatening—just big and sad, a melancholy witnessing of the short lives passing through, utterly inhuman but not ominous at all, just a city-size organism unassailable by demands of morality or purpose. And now the patterns of the comings and goings seem finally to have given it a voice to slowly sing out its centennial song. And with that voice a peace has descended over the subway, and Kierk, lulled by this entelechy of city to sound, sits monkishly until quite late, his fear fading, his uncertainty growing.

LATER IN BED, AND with barely a coherent mind left, Kierk recognizes something fundamental about his investigations into consciousness, but it also applies to the mystery of Atif's death. He has been using the same strategy as Bobby Fischer—complexifying the chessboard to an insane, absurd degree, building forks and pins into gigantic towers of counterfactuals, and then trusting in his innate ability to see a way through when his opponent couldn't. But Kierk has cluttered the board too much, he knows—everything contradicts everything else . . . which is his last thought before going the way of a shoal breaking into fishes swimming off on their own as he drowses off, not even anxious about the questions that have been haunting him. Rather he has quickly become a sleeping form dissolving into mere ruins. As it happens the pandemonium of demons falls silent and without the tyrant of the self the throne sits empty and Kierk again becomes automata, fully clockwork and puppetry once more. Now the great Cartesian theater is deconstructed, the wands of props and the full houses of sets are hustled into the dark corners of storage, the boom mics unrigged in dark wirings and the stage lights cooled down with a vibrating hum. Backstage the actors are tiredly wiping away makeup with wet washcloths in front of mirrors and removing the pageantry of feathers and elaborate costumes, not prepared to dream themselves because they are the miniature demons of thoughts and thus themselves dreamless; beyond them, past the dressing room of melting and scaling lights the deep-red curtains are winging close, the stage is swept dry by a lone janitor, and then the lights are shut off, leaving only a pregnant darkness, and then not even that . . .

SATURDAY

KIERK WAKES UP AND immediately has the acute awareness that Moretti will be giving a talk later today at the CNS. As he lays on his back looking up, soon the textured ceiling is occupied by the empty screen of his morning mind and a memory plays out of the last day of his PhD . . .

The memory was of the Madison winter skyline receding in his rearview mirror, seen from across a frozen Lake Monona, heading out of town on John Nolen Drive. He was leaving, pretending to know what he was doing. The unreal morning light stroked the smoothed throat of late November. Everything was a.m. poetry, everything was snowy math. Events let themselves off, unmoored and floated up, weightless—two possible worlds hovered before him like spheres. Kierk wanted to throw it all away just to see what would happen, to see if it would free him, allow a movement to greater heights. Some voice whispered: further, further and faster. He was sick of this cold, he could go somewhere warm. Simultaneously he knew that nothing would happen, he would dissolve into himself, his own personality turning self-cannibalistic in the manner of the consumptive. It's too late to make any improvements, Kierk had thought, the universe has been finished for a long time now, it's wrapped up, all that's left to do is the casting. You, you're the cowboy. You, the Roman soldier. You, the geisha. You, the failed scientist. Action.

OUTSIDE THE LECTURE HALL Kierk sits with his knees up to his chest listening to the familiar voice of his mentor echo out from within.

Occasionally Kierk shakes his head, or laughs darkly to himself as he catches the old phrases and terms, some of which he had invented himself. Inside he knows is the entirety of NYU's CNS faculty, a huge number of students, many of them crouched in the aisles and standing along the walls, and of course all the Crick Scholars except himself. Finally, there's the rising of applause that goes on for a long time. Then low murmuring as Antonio responds to a few questions that Kierk can't hear. The audience members come streaming out, discussing in excited voices, gesturing with their arms. Kierk sneaks away to the nearest restroom to wait for the crowds to pass, determined not to be seen. After washing his face and hands he goes back out into the hallway, having avoided most of the foot traffic. He can hear Antonio still packing up inside, the sound of someone saying goodbye to him, the unzipping of a laptop case. Kierk considers—he could just walk away right now. He doesn't have to see Moretti, doesn't have to talk to him. On the other hand, they hadn't spoken since Kierk had left, hadn't corresponded since Kierk had published a paper arguing against their former work. And here was Antonio, nine months later, still giving the same spiel that Kierk had helped develop. Kierk hangs between walking away and confrontation, the two possibilities flipping back and forth, a thing that could only be examined from one side at a time, reality itself, and then Kierk makes his choice and opens the heavy lecture-hall doors.

Antonio, looking just as Kierk remembers him, glances up from closing his bag with huge hands and locks eyes with Kierk. Neither says anything. They are completely alone in the auditorium.

After a silence, Antonio says—"You didn't come to the talk."

"I know it by heart."

"Ah," Antonio hangs his head, grabs a final cord from the podium, puts it into his bag.

"Where is everyone?" Kierk says. "I assumed there'd be a crowd of questioners."

"They've given me a reprieve. There's going to be a gala afterwards. Norman Bennett told everyone to wait until then."

"A gala . . . for you?"

"You're invited, of course."

"Of course."

Antonio is still on the stage by the podium. Kierk takes the two steps up to it slowly. They face each other on the creaky wooden planks and under the bright lights, Antonio tall and looming at center stage.

"Since you stormed out, telling me everything I did was wrong, I had thought to hear—"

"Since *I* stormed out?"

"—because you left with no degree. They want me to sign something here, you know. For you. To grant you it."

"You know I deserve it. And you read the paper, you know my ideas."

"You'd like to have a debate, Kierk," Antonio chuckles, then gestures to the empty rows of seats. "Now that we have such an audience?"

"Did you read it?"

"Yes, of course I read it."

"And your response is what? You haven't issued any. Just going to ignore it, I suppose?"

"I said everything I needed to. Things play out in the literature."

"You mean in the arena where you have the greatest advantage in terms of time, money, connections, a team."

"That is the way science works. It's not perfect, but if you stay in the game, I look forward to many—"

"So you're just going to ignore it."

"There are so many different things that are wrong with your thinking that I wouldn't know where to begin. I wonder if you ever understood me at all."

"Oh really, and what didn't I understand? Your theory rests on information theory. Information is frame-variant. So we can just start there, if you really want to do this." Kierk gestures to the throng of empty seats.

"The theory carves nature at its joint. It finds precisely where consciousness resides in the brain, and reads it out. You know all this. You worked on it. I cannot believe it is you who plays Brutus."

"You're not carving nature at its joints, but at your own. You can't construct a theory of observers that requires there be observers in the first place!"

"You're too much of a philosopher, you always were. Abstract jabberwocky without any rigor."

"No! You're the philosopher! With your calculated metaphysics, with your systems of the world!"

"You claim you are the scientist here?"

"No! I'm not anything anymore."

"You were always like this, Kierk. This is why you did not graduate. You could never complete work. You were a poor excuse for a graduate student."

"You were a tyrant to me! A petty tyrant who tried to crush me at every chance. I didn't do the work because, not only did I see the flaws, but also because of the way you treated me!"

"Dramatic accusations! You always had a flair for drama. You've warped everything through your own biased perception."

"Then what about Daniel?"

"That . . . was unfortunate. He came to the lab just as he was developing schizophrenia."

"I don't think that's what happened. He brought a fucking gun into lab. Remember when his wife called sobbing? And the police took him away? Now he's in some sanatorium. Five months under you was all it took. I did five fucking years."

"Mentally ill people crack under the intellectual pressure of working at the very cutting edge of science. I gave you an opportunity few people in history ever have! A chance to prove you're a genius! And you threw it away!"

"You were afraid of me! Some part of you suspected that I wasn't a convert. So you made my life a hell for years. I was a threat!"

"Will you continue to blame me for all of your failures your whole life, Kierk, or will you ever get tired of it?"

"You fucking son of a—"

"Kierk, what the hell is going on?!"

From where they've moved toward each other on the stage the two men spin to the door, where Karen is standing with a look of total outrage on her face.

THE GALA IS BEING held in a great hall off Washington Square Park. The interior of the building is decked out with long tables, paintings on the walls, elegant chandeliers. Carmen notices that everyone has gotten surprisingly dressed up for an academic setting. She wanders around a bit in the little black dress she had thrown on, looking for Kierk. People are already sitting at tables, especially a lot of the higher-ups, all talking over wine that servers are bringing around. Others, like her, mill about between the tables, sipping glasses and pilfering hors d'oeuvres. Finally, she runs into Alex by the cheese platters.

"What'd you think of the talk?" she asks him.

"I really liked it. Antonio is just so ambitious, I love it. But I've also talked to Kierk a lot so I think I've become corrupted."

"Have you seen him?" Carmen asks.

"Yeah, Dr. Moretti is over there at the table," Alex points to where all the top researchers are sitting, laughing and talking, and Antonio Moretti is at the center.

"No. I meant Kierk. Have you seen Kierk?"

"Oh. No, no I haven't seen him."

"I just thought that, since he wasn't at the talk . . ." Carmen trails off.

"I'm sure he just didn't want to go. I'd love to talk to Dr. Moretti, though. My PhD mentor knew him pretty well. So I heard some stories. Apparently he's from this old, like, noble Italian family, right? His father, Giuseppe Moretti, was a famous politician, the mayor of some big city in Italy for many years. And Giuseppe had three sons, all born in wealth and privilege to their doting mother. Private tutors, the works. There were high expectations for all of them. One son was to go conquer the world of politics, to follow in his father's footsteps. He's now a cabinet member of the Italian government. The second son was to go conquer the world of finance. That son eventually worked his way to becoming a partner and managing director of Goldman Sachs. The third son was to conquer the world of ideas. The world of science. There sits the third son."

Carmen looks over to the big table where Antonio is sampling a bottle of wine that the waiter is holding out. Sitting next to him, looking small and childish in comparison, are Norman Bennett, Karen, and Max, along with another man Carmen doesn't recognize. Antonio is moving his hands about dramatically like he's telling a story, gesturing, shaking his head.

"Who's the other guy next to him?" Carmen asks.

"Oh, he's actually from DARPA, I think."

The man from DARPA is looking on as Karen and Norman are nodding sympathetically to whatever Antonio is saying. Then Karen is talking, looking like she's agreeing with Antonio. The man from DARPA seems unsure but Max is the only one who is openly uncomfortable at what's being said. He stands up, putting down his napkin, walking toward Carmen and Alex.

"Now that Dr. Moretti's surrounded I'm probably going to miss him again," Alex says, disappointed.

"What do you mean 'again'?"

"Didn't you know? He just gave a talk at Columbia University like three weeks ago. Guess he's been in and out of New York. I figured you'd know, it's your alma mater."

"He was here three weeks ago? He was in the city?"

"What? Yeah, he gave a public talk that Saturday morning. And of course, I didn't go. What with Atif and all. What a terrible weekend."

Carmen is shaking her head, backing away, setting down her wineglass as one hand goes to her mouth, looking over at Dr. Moretti. Alex is staring at her quizzically.

"Carmen, what's up?"

"What? Oh, nothing . . . Nothing."

Max is now beside them, letting air out in a great sigh, filling up his plate with cheese. He shakes his head, gestures with his toothpick over at Moretti's table.

"Lot of bloviating over there. I'll be honest, I think Kierk's a dick. Then again, he might be a genius. But the complaints have reached the funders now so tell your boyfriend . . . I did what I could. I'm sorry."

Max moves off into the crowd, grabs at a champagne glass and immediately begins to drain it. Carmen, with one look at the still-animated table, is already heading the other direction toward the exit, leaving Alex glancing around bewildered.

THE TENNIS BALL RICOCHETS angrily off the wall, and Kierk slumps down to a sitting position on his mattress. He's looking at his hands and feeling this space-time world line slip from his grasp, a rope falling away into darkness. He hasn't been able to stop the mental replay of the fight, his words, Moretti's words overlapping—and Kierk's hatred is a sickly tide, a green and red synesthetic torrent; and high above it, from a tight, protected place, a small low voice of logic, telling him that he will remember the moment he made the decision to speak to Antonio, that he will remember it in a month, a year, in ten. That the decision will be one of the defining events of his life. Such a small movement on the tree of possibilities has destroyed everything, and he wishes desperately the world was like the video games he had played as a teenager so that he could reload some previous save—why should this be so irrevocable?

A knock on the door. He jerks up from his slump, his mind focused for the first time since he'd left the CNS. Right before he looks through the peephole he hears a questioning call—"Kierk?"—so he throws the door open to Carmen in a dress clutching her purse to her chest and looking worried.

To her, Kierk looks wild, his eyes emotional, tired and angry. When he sees her he just puzzles his face, waiting for her to act, and Carmen doesn't know what to do.

"I wanted to come by, I heard . . ." she starts, but he just waits, leaning there against the door, so she continues—"Did you eat dinner? 'Cause I was thinking of making something, maybe I could do that here, or if you wanted to get a drink . . ."

"Come in," Kierk finally says, waving her in, and Carmen enters his apartment for the first time. Initially what Carmen notices is the spartan nature of it. She surveys the white walls of the small living room area, a place unfurnished except a worn, standard-issue couch. On the floor there are books forming small towers, bibliocolonies spread out and constructed into parapets and castles, falling into spilled arrays, interspersed with a few tennis balls—she reads titles like *Nonlinear Dynamical Systems Theory* and *An Introduction to Set Theoretic Paradoxes* and *Moby-Dick; or, The Whale* and *Causation: a Mathematical Exploration* and *Introduction to Quantum Physics: Vol 2* and *Connectionist Principles* and *Crime and Punishment* and *The Logical Structure of Reality* and *Conscious Experience* and *Short Biographies of Prominent Intellectuals* and *Timaeus* and *Information Theory Proofs* and *Infinite Jest* and *English Poetry: 16–19th Centuries* and on and on. She notices in a corner there is one of those blocks of printer paper they sell at UPS stores that had been torn open and half emptied, which accounts for the scribbled-on sheets laid out everywhere, so many that she had, she now realizes, originally mistaken the floor for tiling but actually at its edges there's a scruffy carpet. The floor-covering layer of paper forms almost a canvas and on it those harsh scribbles and diagrams, unreadable and hieroglyphic. Kierk is silent behind her leaning against the wall in the hallway as she takes it all in, then she slowly steps over to the kitchen and opens the refrigerator door to find it bright and humming and empty but for a packet of butter, and in the freezer only a plastic ice-cube tray, and after she closes it she gives up on looking like she's examining the apartment by happenstance and now openly catalogs the contents of his kitchen, rummaging through empty drawer after empty drawer, finding only a single salt shaker, one pan, a stack of paper plates in ripped plastic. Sitting drying on the counter is a single plastic fork that Carmen picks up and holds in her hands, looking at the small tines. On cradling it she feels a wave of inconsolable sadness sweep over her—an ache in her heart pulls at her eyes and mouth like there is a string between the pit in her chest and her face. At the same time she feels an anger toward this man who has been so studiously ignoring her, pretending nothing happened.

"Predators run for their supper. Prey run for their lives," he says, then gestures one hand around like what he just said was an explanation for the state of the apartment.

"What is all this? What are you working on?" She already knows the answer. She sees it in the arrows and diagrams and equations in his haphazard scrawl; even the air feels hothouse-hot from thinking, from the growth of invisible things, as if in the small one-bedroom apartment an entire jungle had grown up, died out without a trace, grown up again, on and on, cyclic with Kierk's moods, thoughts, ravings, the boom and bust lifecycle of ideas rushing in to fill the space, failing, detritivores rushing in again to trigger pullulate growth. An ecology of mind. Inhalation wets her lungs.

"In every field I look I find the same thing . . . I fought with Moretti about it today . . ." He rubs at his face violently. "Here, let me give you an example. Neuroscience relies on information theory, but information theory presupposes an observer. A conscious observer. Causation presupposes a . . . a set of counterfactuals, a set of possible world and distance and difference relations. Again provided by an observer. In computation: a readout, or code. Again provided by an observer. In biology there's teleology and function, the notion of some fundamental unit of selection . . . again provided by an observer. In physics it's all over the place. Quantum physics, possibly. But also maybe renormalization group theory. The flow of time. Some other issues. All of science has these . . . classical conscious observer mechanics. Do you remember our conversation at the bar together? That first night? We talked about how the relations of the brain, the relationships between the neurons, the, the damn meaning of it all, where all the consciousness must be hidden, is itself dependent on some consciousness. Dependent on an observer consciousness to carve out those relations. To say what's what. And it's true everywhere I look. In every science I find the same thing: frame-variance. Trace back any field for long enough and you'll find observers standing at the end of a long regression. I thought maybe I could define the phenomenon as a kind of operator that conscious beings apply to systems to give them definitiveness. Then you can apply this hypothesized observer-operator to get semantic contents from mere syntax. You can apply it in the form of interventions to get causal structure. To get borders from chaos. Spatiotemporal scale. Functions. Probability. Difference. That sort of thing. The operator really triggers a form of collapse, in a sense. Ontological collapse brought about by conscious observation. I don't mean in physics, I'm not talking about that, but something resting at the heart of nearly every scientific field. And this can all be formalized mathematically!"

For Carmen, sympathy mixes with awe. Once mixed, they cannot be separated. Careful not to sound accusative, she says—"Kierk . . . When was the last time you ate?"

He looks confused, then shakes his head vaguely.

She continues—"All the easy stuff was figured out first. And here you are. You've chosen what might just be the most difficult problem in all the universe and declared you will throw your life against it like your existence is just some sort of weapon. Is this why you've been . . . you've been . . . ?"

When she looks like she might cry, he shakes more viciously. "No, you don't know. There is a duty to genius." One finger points to the floor, to all of it. He expels the words with force. "There. Is. A. Duty."

"I know. I know. But are *you* okay?"

"Does it look like it?"

"Kierk, he has so much control over you. Don't let him. Just stop. Stop seeking his approval."

His face is tortured. "He's still the smartest person I've ever met."

Carmen starts to cry. She sits down beside him, grabbing at his arm.

"I'm out, Carmen. I'm out of the program. Karen saw Moretti and me in a shouting match. I can already see it coming. Karen is going to get the committee together and we're all going to have a little chat . . . I can't go through this again."

"No," she says, grabbing his arm. "You have to stay and fight. You have to. It's not fair. And we're so close. Listen, listen. Moretti, he was here. He was in town the night that Atif died."

Kierk's face transforms from sadness to confusion, then to something like pity.

"What are you talking about, Carmen?"

"Well, I . . ."

"No. What are you talking about?"

"I just meant . . ."

"That's insane. He's many things, but he's not a murderer. There is no murderer."

". . . What do you mean?"

"How long do you want to do this, Carmen?"

"Do what? Us? The investigation? You staying and fighting for a position here? What?"

"This so-called investigation, Carmen. How long do you want to keep chasing these supposed leads? And why? Why *this*?"

"Longer! We can figure it out. Listen, Atif's death was mysterious. And you can feel it too, that there's something mysterious going on in the CNS. Something is so . . . *wrong* there. I know there is. You know there is."

"Just because two things are mysterious doesn't mean they are related."

"Don't you think that, just perhaps, a mystery in one area might be related to a mystery in another?"

"It's time to let it go. Why is this . . . puzzle that you've constructed so important to you? I know you got an email, and you knew the man. Briefly. But why? Really, why?"

This is something Carmen herself has been thinking a lot about lately, so she's ready with her answer.

"In the end how we orientate ourselves to mystery defines how we live our lives. You're asking me to abandon something that's important to me."

"It shouldn't be. Because one of these mysteries doesn't even exist. It's mere pareidolia. It's seeing faces in the rock structures of Mars. There's only one mystery here, Carmen. And it's mine."

SUNDAY

KIERK WAKES UP ALONE. A dream leaves him . . . a series of strange meta-morphoses, the morphing of his body and consciousness as he had been taken from stag to bat to sparrow to woman to laurel tree . . .

One hand goes out, pats the space next to him, before the night comes back to him in flashes, a great weight. Groaning, he rises. Sitting on the edge of the bed he considers how lucky it is that most of his things are still in boxes. He remembers Carmen leaving angry, her disappointment in him.

"Fuck."

A cigarette is lit as he looks around the apartment, which is itself a failure, an incompletion. If only that infinite-sided die would have landed on just a slightly different number. He can still feel the younger version of himself for whom the future was all promise. Zoom in on Kierk's brain and there it all is, the portrait of an artist as a young neural network, contain-ing a whole world kept in miniature: there's his hometown street, a long wooded cul-de-sac composed of ill-kept lawns that went back into the New Hampshire woods, and it was in those woods, the miles of forested reservation land, where Kierk as a child had tramped about in a paracosmic word of immense complexity, a physical world melded at its joints to an imaginary one, and at the points of contact raccoon prints could morph into human footprints, or brooks swell into impassable rivers, a bouldered hill could become a castle, the decaying skeleton of a fox a necromancer's ritual. It had been a dangerous, wild place, where sharpened denticulated sticks soared through pine glens with a speed and precision lent by a carefully constructed atlatl, Kierk skinny and dirty, sprinting close behind his throws like a hunter, until one day he had speared a crow and struck it dead. He had cried over its body for a long time in that glen, dirty lips trembling, and he had promised and prayed and cried more and then had spent the rest of the day in an elaborate burial ritual, become a shaman laying it solemnly to rest, because back then all things had had an animus, a consciousness, from the trees to the crow to the creek, even the cervine saucer of grass where a doe had made her bed, or the perfect coins of snake holes, the tiny death's-heads of ticks, turtles red amid the pebbles, all had been imbued with alien minds, like there was some great portentous spirit in the woods that whispered to him of his destiny to uncover their secrets—all of this, these landscapes and feelings, still there in that reddish mass of his brain, strung out in the finest bloody filigree, still located somewhere, though perhaps not even Laplace's demon could chart such a map.

Everything is finished. He wonders what to possibly do with himself. He feels hungover, but not from any drug. With movements cycling between angry and sluggish he stuffs things into his old ratty backpack, first his new writing and journals, then a few changes of clothing. There's so little of anything else besides the scattered books. How much would he get for the collection at a used bookstore? And with that thought Kierk knows he needs to leave this sad stripped apartment.

After shrugging on clothes he makes his way out to the bright streets. Unlike usual, the city to him seems ungainly and dirty, bombarded by light. People huddle about like refugees, moving quickly. There's an ugliness to it all he hadn't noticed—beggars on the side of the street, the sweat on people's brows, the towering bland artifices of buildings, the grime on the glass, the wilted leaves of the trees. It doesn't seem threatening or beautiful, just sad and overcomplicated.

Ambulation takes him all the way down to the location of the church where Carmen and he had gone to the Following Brothers of Christ meeting. It looks small and unimposing in the morning light and indeed, seems incredibly normal. In the cold, dim interior, Kierk's steps echo as he descends into the basement, where there is a long hall.

"Hello?"

Finding the room where Carmen and he had snuck into the meeting, Kierk pauses at the doorway. Inside is what looks like a children's playroom.

Blocks and toys are strewn around, with some children's books lying open to pages of illustrations. There are drawings and hand paintings on the wall, even a little cubby for shoes.

Kierk backpedals, checks the room next to it, which is a small storage closet. This had definitely been the room.

There's a clattering as a janitor dragging a bucket and mop descends the stairs.

"Hello, sir," he nods to Kierk.

"Hey . . . What happened to this room?"

The janitor peers in from the hall, as if looking for the source of what Kierk found disturbing.

" 'Scuse me sir?"

"It was a meeting room."

"It's a playroom. For during the service. And for bible study. Parents bring their kids."

"Is it used for anything else?"

"You looking for something?"

"Yes, the Following Brothers of Christ. They had meetings here. Right here."

The janitor shakes his head. "Not anymore they don't. They move, city to city. Stay for a while, preaching. Then they move on."

"What?"

"They're gone. Just a daycare now."

"Where'd they go?"

Janitor looks at him strangely. "I don't know. Why would I know? What're you looking for anyways?"

Kierk lets out a breath. "I have no idea."

"Then stop looking," the janitor says, clattering away into the depths of the church.

The greenery of Washington Square Park is baking into yellow. Kierk doesn't want to go home and face what he has to face, so he's here. At the center of the park, by the fountain, he notices the girl with the dog he'd seen before, the one who'd reminded him of Alice, the PhD student he'd known back in Madison who became homeless.

She is sitting in a spot of shade, wiping at her face with a bandana. Her cardboard sign reads: KICKED OUT OF HOUSE NEED $$$ FOR ME AND ALSO DOG FOOD THNX. Kierk watches her dog struggle to breathe in the heat, a ragged wind ripping through each respiration.

Kierk approaches, kneeling down to hold out one hand to the dog, which sniffs at him tiredly. The girl is looking at him bored like she's had this interaction a thousand times. From his kneeling position Kierk pulls out two cigarettes, lights both, hands one to her. A small hand with cracked nails takes it.

"Hey," she says, her voice rusty. "Thanks, man."

"What's your name?"

"Glia. Nice to meet you."

Kierk's mouth hangs open. "Glia. Your name is 'Glia'?"

"Yah."

" . . . "

"What?"

"Oh, nothing. That's a really beautiful name."

"Thanks."

A student walks by, slipping a dollar into the cup next to the dog.

"It's the dog," Glia says.

"What?"

"See that, it's the dog. Kids at NYU care more about an animal than me. If I died they wouldn't blink an eye. But the dog . . . the NYU students . . . they're getting to me, man. Just yuck. Apple this and Apple that. Skinny jeans and lattes. Rich bitches with parents paying their cell phones. Care about animals more than me."

"Hey listen, I wanted to ask you something."

She shrugs in the heat, wipes her face again with the bandana, takes a drag.

"Yesterday a man was outside that building." Kierk points to the CNS, a hermetic tower rising over the other buildings, not even a full block away. "He was saying that people there were taking street people, the homeless, inside of it and doing things to them."

"Why are you asking?" Glia says, suddenly attentive but also cautious.

"I'm just trying to figure out what happened. Seeing if there's any truth to it. Do you know anything about it?"

Glia gestures. "There's been lots of rumors about the park."

"Rumors about what?"

"Just to avoid it. That it's not safe. Especially at night."

"Why isn't it safe? What's been happening?"

"I don't know, just weird stuff."

"Be specific."

"People who sleep around here, total creeps lately. I did know one nice guy who used be around. Hung out with him. But he got weird. Like the area got to him or something. He just changed overnight. Started getting so angry. Didn't really remember me. It was totally unreal. So I don't sleep here in the park. Not anymore. I head to one of the eastside shelters."

"So the people who normally sleep in the parks, or around here, they're getting strange?"

"Uh-uh. Yeah. And also . . ."

"What?"

"A guy comes around here too. That's the rumor. That he's experimenting on people. You know. Messing with their brain."

"What? Who is he?"

"I don't know. Like I said, I'm trying to stay out of all this stuff. Always drama. All the time it's drama."

"Glia, it is extremely important you describe this man to me."

"Well, let's see. Big. Very big. And they call him 'the Nazi.' Everyone scaring themselves. The Nazi is coming, the Nazi is coming."

"Why the Nazi?"

"I don't know. 'Cause he sounds like a Nazi."

"He has a German accent?"

"Yeah."

Kierk rocks back on his heels. His thoughts are following an anxious beat, his mind racing down the corridors of the CNS, plowing over memories, overturning comments, trying to reconcile this. The dog laps at his hanging hand.

"Hey, you okay mister?"

"What? Oh yeah, yeah thanks. Anything else you can tell me?"

Glia shakes her head, pinching off the cigarette to save it for later.

"Alright. Hey, listen, stay here. I'll be right back with something."

Kierk walks while dialing Carmen. It goes to voicemail. Eventually he finds an ATM. Punching in his PIN to the account containing his stipend he looks at the remaining, still large, amount. He withdraws the maximum, five hundred dollars, then walks back to Glia.

"Hey," he says, as her face wars toward amazement. "Take this."

She's hesitant, like the money comes with some unspoken consequences. But after dumping it into her lap Kierk just pats the dog on the head.

"Stay away from this park, okay?" he says, and then is jogging off through the arch.

She shouts, "THANK YOU" from behind him, scaring the pigeons to flight.

NIGHT FALLS OVER SUNDAY. Kierk has been going back and forth within his apartment, a blur of energy. His impending eviction from the program is mixed with the discoveries of the day, and he's been moving from depressed to frenetic within the same hour. He wonders if it's better if Carmen never calls him back. He's been trying to get through since the afternoon. Sitting in his apartment he broods, throws the tennis ball, stampedes over the books, takes a bath, sobs a few times, punches the wall, screams once or twice, reads, waits, indulges in suicidal ideation, washes his hands under water hot enough to purposefully scald himself. Finally, he grabs his electric shaver and in the bathroom slowly and surely buzzes away all his hair. Blood from where his hand punched the wall mixes with the hairs falling into the sink. When he's done he looks extremely skinny again, his figures sharp, a totally new primate just arrived.

Exhausted by himself he lies on his bed, rubbing at this prickly new sensorial dome. He's nowhere near sleep when his phone rings. It's Carmen on the other end. He scrambles to pick up.

"Hello? I'm sorry."

"That's it? I mean . . . wait, okay, I shouldn't have said—"

"—well no but I also—"

"—because it wasn't right to suggest—"

"—and I'm sorry that—"

"Listen!" Carmen says over him. "It doesn't matter now. Because you were wrong about my mystery being nothing. I just got an email. From the code you wrote. The fMRI machine is running."

"It's like midnight."

"I know."

"Are you heading to the CNS?"

"Right now."

"No, don't do that. I'll meet you outside. I have new information. Where are you?"

"I'm almost there. Like two blocks away."

"I'm on my way. Carmen, don't go in! Just wait outside."

She's already hung up. Swearing, Kierk fights on a shirt and pants and then is out the door still putting on his shoes.

The heat is a syrup that fills the dark streets. Kierk runs down Broadway, which is empty except for some couples walking arm in arm and the odd lone figure that stands to the side to let him pass, and soon he's near the great black steeple at night, sweat already pouring down his back, accompanied only by the pounding rhythm of his shoes echoing off buildings, a Doppler effect left behind. Without a breeze he's his own wind as he turns a corner, dodges another couple, crosses the street to the honk of a cab as he sprints through its headlights, then he's turning the corner to the lightless CNS and just catches the form of Carmen opening the door to enter.

He calls out to her and she holds the door for him as he thunders in. The lobby is dimly lit and empty.

"We've got to hurry." Carmen is jamming the elevator button. The doors ding open and then they're both in the elevator, Kierk bending down to catch his breath.

"We should talk first."

"Kierk . . . What did you do to your hair!"

Her fingers are cool on his prickly skull.

"No time," he says, and then quickly fills her in on what Glia had said. Carmen's eyes get wider and wider as the floors pass.

"Remember that Leon has an MD. In psychiatry," she says.

"There could be a perfectly reasonable explanation," he says, as the elevator opens.

"For Leon to be abducting the homeless from the park at night to perform experiments on?" Carmen replies incredulously.

They both stop just outside the fMRI room. They can hear the prosody of conversation through the door, the moving of something large.

Carmen and he nod to each other, and then the two burst through the door. At the far end is Leon, with a clipboard, and nearer to the door, a brown-haired young woman wearing a lab coat, and, sitting in the chair by the fMRI, eating a bag of chips, a clearly homeless man.

"Ummm, Institutional Review Board!" Kierk yells to the scene, and then, commandingly—"FREEZE."

There's a scream. Everyone looks at one another. The homeless guy smiles.

"Kierk?!" says Leon, putting down his clipboard.

"What are you doing?!" Carmen yells, pointing to the homeless man, who waves at her.

"We're doing a study!" the brown-haired girl says. "What are you doing?! Who are you?!"

"They're Crick Scholars, Sandra. Like me," Leon says, moving toward them.

"Oh, so they're those people."

"What do you mean *those people*?" Carmen says.

"Consciousness researchers," the girl says, making a face.

"Hey!"

"Oh, like regular neuroscientists are going to nearly break down the door at midnight and scare me half to death. Why can't you people be normal?"

"What are you all doing here anyways?"

"A study, geniuses? What are you doing here?"

"We're looking for someone. One of the homeless said one of their friends had been abducted."

"And you believed them?"

"What's going on?"

"They're Crick Scholars."

"So what are they doing here?"

"Shut the fuck up!" Kierk yells. Everyone quiets. "So you're doing a study. You explain it to us, and then we'll tell you why we're here."

Leon puts up his hands. "Alright. I'm assisting Sandra. Sandra is from the NYU School of Social Science. We're doing work on profiling the neurological effects of homelessness. Right now we're looking at the effects on disrupted sleep, so Mickey here is going to sleep in the scanner. Isn't that right?"

Mickey grins over his chips, nodding. Kierk notices blankets piled up in the corner.

"But why are *you* here?"

"I wanted to get fMRI experience. They were kind enough to allow me to, ah, how you say, tag along."

"Did you help recruit?"

Sandra nods at the two of them like they're idiots. "Yes. Leon went out around with me to recruit a few times."

"And . . . and the TMS?" Carmen asks.

"We don't even use the TMS. We have been using the EEG, though. Look, you can see. Check out the IRB on the wall," Sandra says.

There's a big board labeled WALL O'IRBS with Institutional Review Board approval sheets tacked all over it. Carmen browses them, scanning the pages with her finger.

Turning, with a disbelieving look on her face, she nods to Kierk.

That's when the power goes out. Darkness envelops them. Sandra yelps, there's the sound of chips spilling to the floor, and for a moment absolute blackness descends until an emergency power light on the fMRI blinks on and casts them all in red.

"Well, there goes the study for tonight," Sandra says. "Sorry, Mickey. Don't worry, you'll get paid anyways."

Leon and Sandra start checking the machine. Carmen throws up her hands.

"Alright, well," she says, "I need to go check the computers in the lab to make sure my data's okay."

"I can go with you," Kierk says.

They turn to say goodbye but the other two are busy checking on the machine, and only Mickey, his face lit red, waves to them as they go.

The corridor is completely dark and Carmen and Kierk fumble for a moment to turn on the lights of their phones, creating bisecting cones of light that dance over the ceiling and sparsely illuminate the long hallway.

"Oh my god, the organoids!" Carmen exclaims suddenly, "They'll die without power. We have to check on them."

She grabs Kierk's arm and pulls him to the elevator. Its chrome inanimately reflects the light and its digits above are dark.

"Do you really think—" Kierk begins.

"Why plan for a serious power outage in a Manhattan research facility?" she replies.

The two of them head to the stairwell, entering a labyrinthine darkness, their phone lights spearing wildly at it. The inside of the stairwell is pitch-black and on entering it they both pause, Kierk leaning over the railing with his phone; everything reveals itself only for a moment before vanishing and they cannot see the bottom. Once the door clangs shut behind them, sealing them in, it is possible to entertain the idea that the stairwell goes down forever, that there is a mind-bending infinity both below and above and that they have found themselves at some random location in a great unfathomable infinite structure, a thing ignoring all ideas of scale or meaning. Standing on the landing the two look up and down as the echo of the shut door fades into the depths. Carmen's reason tells her that she is only five or six floors up but some other, deeper sense is screaming that she is entirely wrong, that she's nowhere at all. That this goes all the way down and all the way up, forever. Kierk, madly, feels like laughing, or crying, or fucking, or reciting poetry into the abyss. Or letting loose some endless howl. Instead Carmen tugs him upward. Neither can bring themselves to utter a word during the time inside the utter black of the stairwell, both just breathing as quietly as they can, making their way through, and they don't talk until the door slams shut behind them on the ninth floor.

The lock to the organoid lab beeps red to both their cards. Carmen is already calling before Kierk can suggest it. She paces the hall.

"Hey! Hey, it's Carmen, from the CNS."

". . ."

"Look outside. The power is out. All over Manhattan, I think. That's why I'm calling. We're here and the door is locked and the power is out."

". . ."

"Should we break the glass?"

". . ."

"Alright, we'll sit tight."

She hangs up, then leans with Kierk against the glass.

"Why isn't there a backup generator?"

"There is one. The MRI gets juice. This is a big building. Apparently it's limited."

Carmen's phone buzzes and she says—"Alex is on his way."

Kierk realizes something. "God, what do you think is going on with the monkeys in the basement?"

"I don't know. Maybe chaos. Or they're all asleep. Maybe there's emergency power there too?"

They sit illumed by phone screens, both very aware of their touching knees, looking online for the causes of the outage—there were a lot of different claims going around social media, but the most oft-repeated cause was some kind of freak blowout at a power station north of Manhattan, and then like dominoes the overstressed nodes in the network had gone down one by one.

Minutes pass. Carmen keeps standing up and peering through the glass, trying to see if there's any sign of power from inside. She feels energetic despite the late hour, full of nervous excitement at the commotion, but some smaller part of her is getting flashes of tiredness, like she is two reservoirs and one is filling up as the other drains away.

At one point they hear the voices of Leon and someone they don't recognize stomping up the stairwell but the voices pass in echoes and soon ascend into silence. At another point the door opens and stepping halfway through, freezing when he sees them, is the pale face of Greg. On seeing them he's clearly startled, immediately withdraws back into the darkness like a wraith, a ghostly presence slinking away without language.

Finally, they hear a clattering from the stairwell and then through the door comes Todd and Amanda, looking flushed and breathing heavily. Kierk and Carmen immediately ply them with questions about what's going on outside, getting only that the two had just biked here (Carmen didn't remark on what a coincidence it was that they both got here at the same time, unless they left from the same location) and that the city, past midnight on an early Monday morning during a blackout, had been completely empty, and that they hadn't seen a single living soul as they flew through the streets of Manhattan on their bikes.

"It was like one of those children's books where someone casts a spell and the whole kingdom goes to sleep," Amanda says breathlessly as the four head inside, past the stocked shelves and shadows of microscopes, to the inner sanctum, which is opened with a trepidatious intake of breath.

It is completely black inside the room, and to Todd's cry of—"No, no, no!"—Carmen pans her light over the far table where the eight Erlenmeyer flasks sit silently like tombs. With the heat lamps off it's much cooler, and on closer examination the Matrigel inside the flasks has already begun to separate. The organoids are perfectly still at the bottom, strange planetoids out there alone, glinting and fleshy and white.

"They're dying," Carmen says sadly, crouching down to examine hers. When she holds the phone light up to it she swears that the white puckering cup of its eye darkens slightly, as if attempting to dilate.

"We have to do it now," Todd says grimly. "Accelerated timetable. More than a month's work . . . Damn!" He slams his hand down on the table and the Matrigel jiggles slightly. Then he disappears into the larger outside room.

"What are you going to do?" Carmen asks Amanda. "Can't you just restart the heat lamp and the stirring mechanisms, the bioreactors or whatever?"

Amanda shakes her head sadly as she snaps gloves on—"No, they're irrecoverable at this point. And even if they were savable, how can we be sure this didn't affect the results? If we do the slices right now, then we can at least run histology, look at the cytoarchitecture."

"Slices? You're going to cut them up?"

"Yes, and thank god you called us. I mean, we were asleep, we never would have known—" Amanda cuts off, looking at the two of them, shocked at herself. Carmen is already shaking her head, rubbing at Amanda's arm. "Don't worry. We're not going to tell anyone about it. I know how things are now."

"I might never even be back in this building so I wouldn't worry too much about me," Kierk says sardonically.

Amanda looks at him quizzically but then the form of Todd, backlit, comes through the door. He grabs up the first flask, Atif's, and heads back out. Carmen lets out a low moan of protest. With a sympathetic look Kierk grabs up his. Carmen looks extremely torn, and Kierk briefly wonders if Carmen is going to make a break for it with hers, but soon she's joining him in delivering their mini-brains to the outer room.

Todd has set up the brain slicer, a vibratome, on one of the lab benches where he's also got the one lamp up, so bright after so much darkness that Kierk and Carmen shield their eyes with their free hand. Both the lamp and the vibratome are plugged into a big silver battery with TESLA on the side. The vibratome is a long metal malocclusion, a decked-out and sinister deli slicer. On the front is an open jaw area sporting a silver metal pad, immersed in some buffer liquid, while tiny blades like needles wait to be lowered down. Todd has laid the flask down on the table next to it. He reaches down into the ooze of the Matrigel with his gloved hand, a grimace on his face. Amanda passes him surgical scissors and carefully he pulls Atif's cerebral organoid up off the base of the glass, and, cupping its underside, uses the scissors to cut the anchor of its ingrown tree, releasing it from its roots.

"But the branches," Carmen begins, and then her eyes widen as Todd, with a look of intense concentration, begins to steadily pull the trunk of the tree. It slowly emerges from the bottom, slipping from its biological host, until the last of the fine tips clears its rubbery underside and Todd discards the spiky translucent structure onto a paper towel that Amanda laid down. Then Amanda uses a small bottle to squirt a drop of superglue to the base of the organoid and affixes it to the metallic plate of the vibratome. Atif's organoid, nearly four inches in diameter now, white as undifferentiated flesh, sits on the cutting plate like a wet tumor freshly removed. Amanda starts up the vibratome.

"Set it for fifty microns," Todd says, and then the blades are lowered with a hum, just like an electric razor, and it takes the thinnest sliver off the top, almost impossible to see until Amanda, using a thin tweezers-like instrument, scoops it off. The slice hangs in the air, a tiny sheet, translucent tissue without visible structure, like the effluvia of a ghost. She lowers the slice into a small plastic container filled with a clear but viscous liquid. It floats to the bottom and then the vibratome hums and another slice is placed into the container, sinking down to join the first. This continues in silence, both Kierk and Carmen gripping their flasks with white knuckles, and in only a few minutes the organoid has been halved—Kierk, leaning over, can see white-matter tracts running in bands through the center. There had been neural activity. Meanwhile, Todd has scrounged around and come up with another vibratome, which he sets up next to Amanda, filling it with the same fluid. Amanda, finishing the last slice, scratches off the last of Atif's organoid from the metal plate and chucks it into a biohazard bag. The two turn to Kierk and Carmen expectantly, and, after a moment's hesitance, they hand over their flasks. In silence they step back and watch the same process unfold. First the organoids are extracted, their ingrown trees carefully pulled out, and then they are glued to the plate and the hum of the vibratomes start. Carmen's hand searches and clasps Kierk's. At the first slice Carmen gasps and her hand tightens, the two of them standing just inside the circle of light where the other two are carefully slicing, removing and storing the tissue, thin as paper, and there is a meditativeness to it, a silence, both Kierk and Carmen hypnotized by the pair leaning over their tasks Talmudically, like they were two medieval illustrators at their desks in the dim light of a monastery, accompanied by just the hum and the barest sound of liquid as the slices enter their respective containers. As this occurs a strange state has stolen over Kierk, perhaps from the nervousness of the night and the lateness of the hour but he feels almost out of his body, leaving it, hallucinatory. He keeps blinking away strange fantasies that come and go, indescribable, forms beyond language, like he is downloading dreams bit by bit, memories of pure space and pure consideration and attention but all with only the minimal outlines of any content, experiences coming in flashes of awareness which feel like they are from a different time or from a different self, and at the end of it all he feels changed, expanded, like he has discovered some extrasensory dimension closed off to him previously, the shock of another so close entering him slowly. He also knows that he must be imagining this, this bodily sensation, whatever it is, a mere trick of the mind, an influence from the gravitas of the setting and the strangeness of it all and his current suggestible state. But looking over at Carmen, who has tears running in tracks down her face, and whose eyes are wide, he wonders if she felt it too. He squeezes her hand reassuringly.

Todd wipes at his forehead with his wrist, turns to them.

"Listen, I appreciate you calling us, you really did save the whole experiment. But we've got this if you want to bug out. It's going to be a long night of this."

"We've got stuff to do anyways," Carmen says quietly, wiping at her eyes discreetly.

"So what are you going to do with the slices? Will you be able to do a paper with the data?" Kierk asks.

"Probably not. This time around we're just going to be checking the cytoarchitecture of the slices, making sure there really were neurons, that kind of thing."

"What do you mean 'this time around'?" Carmen says.

"Well, we're going to be redoing the experiment of course," Todd says. "And the original samples from your skin have all been reverted to pluripotency. They're effectively stem cells, which we can use to make more if we want to."

"How many more are there going to be?"

"I don't know. People like to use cell lines that get established early on in the field, for replicability. That and you're, well, you're Crick Scholars so there's the novelty aspect. They grew exceptionally well too, so I would imagine your lines will be extremely popular in the future. And the lines are kept around forever. So in theory people in a hundred years might still be using these. Congratulations, you're immortal." Todd laughs thinly.

There is stunned silence, and Carmen's hand slips from Kierk's.

"What? A cell line? A fucking cell line? Are you kidding me?"

Kierk is struck at the thought of all his clone's brains growing, again and again, the same struggling pattern repeating until one day their total mass exceeded not just that of his own body, but exceeded this very building, the gigantic weight of existence of all those future hims grown in dishes all over the world, his own personal Boltzmann brains.

"Come on, Carmen, let's go." He tugs on her arm, backing away, glaring at Todd.

"But . . . You had no right!" Carmen raises her voice. "We didn't know it'd be a cell line! You had no right!"

"What? What's the problem?"

"You had—" Kierk tugs her away into the darkness as she yells "—no fucking right!"

Kierk, hustling Carmen out, takes one last glance back to the bowl of lamplight with the vibratomes set up side by side and Todd and Amanda conferring in fast whispers.

Outside Carmen leans against the wall, her fists clenched.

"It's been a long intense night. Just cool down, maybe you can talk to him in the morning."

"Shit. I lost it," she laughs, brushing away tears. "Maybe they're right about us consciousness researchers. We aren't exactly stable."

"Believe me, the talk tomorrow is going to be about me and about the blackout, not about you."

"Maybe the blackout will obscure everything and they won't even be talking about you. You never know."

Kierk shrugs wearily, rubs at his head. At this point the existential dread over his future has been turned over enough times it feels dulled by repeated handling. Though just the mention of it now still makes him feel vaguely nauseous.

"Do you need to check on anything before you leave?"

Carmen nods tiredly. "Yeah, I could check on stuff in the lab. Unplug the computers and confirm my backup. I should, probably . . ."

The two of them head once again to the stairwell. Again it is pure dark except for the flashlights of their phones, ascending. Carmen walks first, slightly slumped. They're quiet the whole way there.

In the lab she starts booting up her computer from a buffer system. Meanwhile Kierk goes over to his station but doesn't see anything he wants to keep. In the dark it looks abandoned, like he's been gone for weeks already.

Coming back to her, he sees that Carmen has found a working emergency outlet under a blinking light and is dragging over extension cords. Soon she's got her monitor hooked up and is busily clicking about in the blue light.

"Hey. I'm going up to the roof. I want to see the city."

Carmen looks up, drained. "Alright, I gotta stay here for another fifteen or twenty minutes to make sure the backups are okay and secure. Just in case there's a surge or something."

Her phone buzzes.

"Apparently things are insane in the animal rooms. Alex says the monkeys are all freaking out. Throwing themselves against the cages. Fighting one another. No one knows why. He says not to come down though, it's a madhouse and they've got enough vets there."

"Alright . . . well . . . Maybe find me up there when you're done?"

"Okay, see you soon."

THE MOON HANGS ABOVE the roof like pure science fiction. The city before him is dark all the way south but lit up like a beacon to the north by the throbbing egg of light that is Times Square. The power ends there, at a line drawn via the negotiations of electrical companies decades before; it seems a barrier built of light, a spell cast by a wizard. Kierk leans off over the side and can't see ground—it's just a dark abyss populated by meaningless and indiscriminate shapes, objects without names. Wind whips at his face, then dies down to stillness. On the building opposite he can see the rising and landing outlines, maybe bats, as bits of black moving in a bulk of night. The city is a spun sculpture, airless and hot and onyx, the metal a mythology so pressured it had become architecture. From his sleeve he withdraws the transgenic blue rose. He had secretly plucked it from the lab while attempting to save the organoids. Pressing his thumb against one of the thorns, bleeding just one drop, Kierk's thoughts, philosophical from the fantastical cityscape, romantic from the beauty of the night, in tune with the sleeping burrowed giant of the city, wild from the lack of sleep and adrenaline of events, circle yet again around consciousness, drawn to that ever-fleeing attractor, unable to break his own trajectory—and that's when her face flashes yet again, distractor stimuli, but this time he, instead of pushing the thoughts of Carmen away, accepts them, begins with them . . . Carmen laughing, all that beauty, the stunning cheekbones and emotive mouth, the large eyes electric blue—and everyone Carmen would ever meet would agree on the fact of her beauty, and since her beauty was agreed upon, was it truly a subjective issue, like asking whether chocolate ice cream is better than vanilla, or Hemingway a better prose stylist than Joyce? Rather her beauty is real, objective, a fact, having ceased long ago to be merely a matter of opinion—but was it really real? Because the fact of her beauty was, after all, a fact dependent in its existence on human consciousness, without which Carmen's face may as well be a rock structure on Mars, and therefore is not her beauty observer-dependent in its reality? Frame-variant, a relational property really, just as they'd discussed at the bar originally and then again in his room yesterday. And weren't other entities that seem so naively real in the scientific world actually observer-dependent in precisely the same way as Carmen's beauty, even things normally considered so obvious like neurons and livers and circuits and plants and cells and suns and species . . . all observer-dependent . . . not that they were in their properties arbitrary, but just that, without conscious minds to give them relations, to read into them borders and scale and roles and functions and causal structure and information and theoretical relevance, these groupings, without some kind of observer-operator, would all fall away back into the colorless nameless stream of reality, and it's striking him that science as practiced is just the ugly and messy assortment of all the conceptual tools that could possibly allow for the better prediction or manipulation of nature for egocentric purposes, not carving nature at its true joints at all, and thus stands in stark ersatzism to consciousness, which is self-defining and precisely frame-invariant, *given*, true, ultimate, really real, and therefore, following this logic, Kierk reasons that the difficulty of developing a theory of consciousness is so hard precisely because of the mismatch between these frame-variant scientific entities and the frame-invariant reality of consciousness, a thought which causes him to wheel about the rooftop like a bat undone, thinking—I can even go one further—for there exists a formal paradox here, a proof of sorts, with regards to consciousness, something touched by Gödel, but also by someone more ancient, eldritch . . . Euclid! Because the basic structure of formal systems, defined as a set of axioms and subsequent theorems, inherently means that one cannot derive the axioms of a formal system or formal method from *within* the system or method . . . axioms must always stand outside of it . . . And if one wished to ground all of science in a well-founded and formalized manner, that is, to construct hierarchically the great tree of knowledge Yggdrasil itself, one must build it on some implicit, long-unacknowledged set of axioms. And the ultimate of those, the basest, most fundamental, the very root system, would have to be consciousness, holding up the entire tree with its unjustifiable nature. Giving everything else its definitive form. And if the existence of consciousness, of observers, is one of the axioms of science then a science of consciousness would be the ultimate begging of the question, *petitio principii*, a victim of the Münchhausen trilemma, because consciousness can't be justified using consciousness . . . just as if man is the measure of all things, then how to measure man? . . . For even great Yggdrasil cannot hold the weight of its roots upon its boughs—and at that moment Kierk is so overcome with this vision and so sure in his ability to formalize this paradox that he feels powerful enough to break the tree of knowledge over his knee like a mere stick; in doing so he would sunder science itself, show it to rest on untenable foundations and paradox just as Gödel did to mathematics, and he sees all of this theory, the line of argument he's uncovered, laid out before him, a thing of terrible beauty and utter destruction, a completely alien form of wreckage—and then he is human-size again and standing next to the sundered Yggdrasil, science itself, which is smote, a great tree cracked in half, lying on its side riven with breakages, its insides visible now, and it stretches before him like the giant body of a tortured saint, and to this vision Kierk nearly weeps, struck, for if it is true that science is fundamentally paradoxical then the universe is fundamentally alien and unknowable, a great white entity approaching in the ocean, a swimming beast, a grand hooded phantom, a snow hill drifting in the air, a mountain coming on with incomprehensible purpose, all of us Jonah and the universe the whale.

Just like that the vision vanishes. He is alone on the roof, and a mere failed scientist once more. This winding culmination is impossible, far-fetched, and even if it were true he is no longer the man for the job, and he, delusional with lack of sleep and stress, is suddenly sure he is merely indulging a runaway train of thought. He stumbles away from the ledge.

The blue rose is still in his hand. Examining its cosmic shade, a near-blooming star of night, Kierk has his second realization of the night, more significant, faster, simpler, more overbearing, time slowing down when he thinks—really, this has been a love story all along. He hadn't been expecting that, even in all this authoring.

The door to the roof, which has been kept open by a cinderblock Kierk dragged over, opens, and the darkness is pierced by the light from Carmen's phone.

"Don't close the door!" Kierk says. "It locks from the inside. Leave the cinderblock."

Carmen carefully closes the heavy door on the cinderblock, then walks over to join Kierk at the edge.

"What are you doing up here?"

"Just thinking about stuff."

Standing beside him she looks out over the expanse of the lightless city. They are silent for minutes on end, taking it all in. His eyes have adjusted and now he can see the finest details of the barren streets, which are inky and silent up to the wall of light that is Midtown.

After a while Carmen finally says—"Sorry for getting you dragged into all this. I really thought there was something . . . to solve. And I'm sorry if it impacted, you know . . ."

Kierk's hand finds hers and she trails off.

"It may have been inevitable. Which means," he says, both facing out to the dark streets, "that I'm going to be leaving."

Carmen's hand squeezes his as he continues. "There is a choice to be made on your end. Because the Francis Crick Scholarship Program? It's a failure. One Crick Scholar is literally dead. Another, me, is being kicked out. And another's monkey self-lobotomized. Next week is going to be a political circus. Bad press. Bad rumors. They won't get the funding renewed for next year. Certainly there's not going to be those prestigious NYU tenure-track positions for any of us anymore. You can stay here and inevitably have all your funding dropped. Or . . ."

"Or what?"

"Have you ever been to Paris?"

Carmen laughs. "Wait, you're serious?"

"The Sorbonne has a burgeoning consciousness science program. For you, I mean. I'm through. It's over for me. I'll do something else. I'll show up to the after-work parties and make everyone mad but that's it. They'd take you in a heartbeat and no one will blame you for leaving a failing mess of a program."

"But what will you do?"

"I don't know. Something else. And I think I'm finally okay with that."

He hands her the blue rose, which she hadn't noticed in the shadows of the roof, and she, perplexed, takes it from his hand delicately. One hand goes up to her mouth when she sees what it is.

"So you are serious . . . How serious? Because—"

He kisses her and feels the great tremulous activity in him mirrored in her. Faces together, unwilling to part, his cheek is touched by the small wet of a tear.

"Just leave?"

"Just leave."

"Together?"

"Together."

Afterward they spend a while by themselves on the roof in a night dream. The sky caves off and a timeless zone without modern technology is reached, a completion. The Milky Way is a bridge above. At various points in their laughter, their clutching, their kissing, they break to look down off the roof or to lie on their backs. One time Carmen stands and, laughing wildly, screams off the roof to the empty streets below in excitement, and Kierk, following her lead, does so as well, and they listen to their echoes chase and reverberate. Other moments they spend huddled next to the small ledge together, heads touching. Carmen keeps rubbing his shaved head and chuckling, or kissing it.

It is so real at this moment for them, so obvious of a future, a thing completely decided—can't you see them even now? You're crossing the Pont des Arts and you pause in the middle of the bridge to look out over the Seine, the river itself reddened by the setting sun and moving like heart's blood through the beautiful grandeur of the buildings rising around it; from afar Kierk is that lone form dangling his legs off the point of Île de la Cité that juts out into the Seine, bent and writing in a notebook but occasionally looking up and out at the Seine and toward your direction, the fall verdure of the Square du Vert-Galant an impressionist painting of gold and red behind him, and he has just finished jotting something down when a long-legged form comes up behind him, dipping in for a kiss before procuring a bottle of wine, Carmen settling down next to him, and in a break of a great cycle of history the two are just lovers in Paris talking about all the mundane but beautiful and true things they will do together.

Back on the roof, at the point where their lips are bruised from kissing and Carmen's eyes are swollen from crying and her voice hoarse from laughing, they have both reached a state of bone-tiredness. Neither knows what time it is, only that dawn has not yet come. There is a last glance at the stars as they stand, under which Carmen spins out in dance and Kierk spins her back, dips her, and they kiss again, bruising a last time. She has not let go of the rose this entire time. Then finally they make their way, still holding hands, to the door, shove aside the cinderblock, and enter the dark stairwell. There's a clang behind them as the door swings shut on its hinges.

The light from Carmen's phone illuminates the otherwise pitch-black stairwell, going down like an endless maze below them. They are just half a flight down when the knock comes from behind them.

Explosive, loud, and three times. Carmen grabs at Kierk, the light from her phone frenetically bobbing up and down on the door, which is a metal monolith still reverberating. The sound goes all the way down into the depths and echoes back up. Carmen muffles a scream. Kierk's heart jumps tachycardic, a thin beat in the dark, a connection stretching out, racing away.

They are both frozen on the steps, looking at the door, waiting in the hot dark.

"It could just be someone trapped on the roof," Kierk says, unsure, his adrenaline rushing over him like mad already, but Carmen is shaking her head quietly—"How? Who? Behind us? We have to go. We have to go now."

The booming knock comes again, and Carmen shrieks, grabbing at Kierk. Her hands are randomly clutching at him, her legs shaking. Kierk, his eyes wide and fixated on the door, slowly begins to climb back up the stairwell.

At this Carmen moans, whispering harshly, pleading with him, going up with him a step, trying to stop him, but he still reaches it despite her pulling on one of his hands. He no longer thinks this is an illusion. A terrible curiosity has overtaken him, a monomaniacal drive to witness what waits on the other side, the inexplicable source of the noise. What is it? A tunnel to everywhere? A carpet of stars? A minotaur slavering to chase them down and root around their corpses in some shadowed corridor of the building? Perhaps nothing at all, an empty roof just how they left it, or really nothing, a silent void of it like the null set had pushed up against physicality, a bauble of the blackest black pushing out . . . or perhaps a great probing unblinking eye surrounded by a wall of white rubbery flesh that fills the entire doorframe. He must know! He must open the door. Beyond will be a new Babel. A last and perfect language, syllables made from the sound of Bruno's flesh reknitting, unburning. Beyond is Descartes waking from a science-fiction dream of a glittering city in a new world, a new Amsterdam, amid the monoliths of which some rough beast is slouching toward birth . . . Kierk knows that he must not open the door . . . must abort this creature clawing its way out from somewhere unthinkable—yet I am going to open it. For behind it there is the thing itself, the answer, Carmen, I am so sorry for this—the deafening knock comes a fourth time, even louder, and faster, a growing impatience. Carmen jumps at each individual sound which go off like rapid gunshots. The light she's holding is violently shaking as she's still silently tugging at Kierk's shirt as his mind ricochets between possibilities—I am not going to open the door. I cannot open the door. If I do it will eat us up. Consume us. I must not open the door. It will dig open our insides and spread them around the stairwell but before it jellies my eyes I will see its face and I will know. I must open the door. Just so I can know. I am going to open the door, to see what it is behind, I will embrace it even as it eats me even as it blinds me . . .

He wants to open it because he wants to finally wake up, for the first time in history.

"Kierk, we have to go, we have to go now!" Carmen hisses, trying to tug him violently down, but he shrugs her off and takes the last step up and holds one hand out to touch the door. A knock so hard and loud that the metal shrieks like a subway train and Carmen begins to scream and scream in the dark of the stairwell. The door had nearly vibrated off its hinges and Kierk's ears are buzzing. There is a presence beyond, just beneath his palm laid against the metal. Hand against the door he can almost feel it, almost see it. A dark star. A dark star throbbing with the sound of itself. The shape of an iris. A dark star in the sky spreading like liquid over the pond of night. The tide of pure black liquid meets the bloom of blood coming the other way, curling, mixing. A sound so loud and so deep it is a stone vibrating at the center of the universe. The view of an alien desert at night cyclopean with obelisks. His and Carmen's bodies lying contorted in the White Room. Both corpses have been surgically altered. Kierk has been given the lower body of a horse and Carmen's hair has been replaced with snakes. Then mold spreading over their bodies, eating them, turning them into gardens. Foliage sprouting. The unearthly sound of a blue rose growing up out of her eye socket. The outline of him snatched away and inserted, waking, now sent into an entirely new body plan. The disorientating proprioception of having so many newborn limbs waving about weightless. Limbs that are not limbs but people. Not one but many, the many in the one, each a digit or appendage looking out, millions of eyes at once. Nausea rising at the ant-like patterns flashing too fast in a thousand languages. Syllables out of order, backward. Screeching. Pulled in all directions at once. Too stretched, his remaining disembodied bloodless shell of a ghost is ripped apart by the force of it, a husk dissolving fast. The planetary roar cuts off into silence.

A hand on his, pulling it away from the door. In the bobbing lights from their phones he moves slowly at first, Carmen still gripping his hand, and then faster and faster down the stairwell. As they descend it is like he is being woken from a dream into a world beyond this one, realer than this one.

Wake up.

ACKNOWLEDGMENTS

Thanks to the two who believed in this book when it was just loose pages and binary strings: Chelsea Cutchens, my editor, and Adam Schear, my agent.

Thanks to Noreen Tomassi and The Center for Fiction, the missing connection without which this book may never have been published.

Thanks to Blaise Lucey, my oldest and dearest friend and fellow writer, who shared with me worlds when we were young and words when we were old. And to my other first readers: to Peter Watts, for taking a chance; to Allen More, for understanding; to Isabelle Boemeke, for her encouragement and her insight into the world of professional modeling; and to Katrin Redfern, for her writerly eye.

Thanks to my mother, Susan Little, for life and for books and for care and for love. And to the rest of the staff of Jabberwocky Bookshop, for helping raise a writer.

And, of course, thanks to Julia Buntaine Hoel, first of readers, first of women, first, first, first.